NOBODY KNOWS HOW IT GOT THIS GOOD

AMOS JASPER WRIGHT IV

Livingston Press
The University of West Alabama

Copyright © 2018
Amos Jasper Wright IV
All rights reserved, including electronic text

ISBN 13: 978-1-60489-208-6, trade paper
ISBN 13: 978-1-60489-209-3, hardcover
ISBN: 1-60489-208-0, trade paper
ISBN: 1-60489-209-9, hardcover
Library of Congress Control Number 2018936406
Printed on acid-free paper
by Publishers Graphics
Printed in the United States of America

Hardcover binding by: HF Group
Typesetting and page layout: Sarah Coffey
Proofreading: Sarah Coffey, Daniel Butler, Josh Hall,
Shelby Parrish, Tricia Taylor, Joe Taylor, Erin Watt
Cover design: ha-lup-ka.com
Cover photograph: William Widmer (www.widmerphoto.com)

Dedicated to my father and my mother

Livingston Press is part of The University of West Alabama,
and thereby has non-profit status.
Donations are tax-deductible:
brothers and sisters, we need 'em.

first edition
6 5 4 3 3 2 1

NOBODY KNOWS HOW IT GOT THIS GOOD

"And who is really guilty? Each of us. Each citizen who has not consciously attempted to bring about peaceful compliance with the decisions of the Supreme Court of the United States . . . every person in this community who has in any way contributed during the past several years to the popularity of hatred, is at least as guilty, or more so, than the demented fool who threw that bomb . . . What's it like living in Birmingham? No one ever really has known and no one will until this city becomes part of the United States. Birmingham is not a dying city; it is dead."

—Charles Morgan, addressing the Birmingham Young Men's Business Club, on the day subsequent to the Birmingham Church bombing that killed four girls.

TABLE OF CONTENTS

THE JAGUARS OF SOUTHTOWN

Forty days passed without landing a sale. For a while, I felt sorry for myself, and then self-pity shifted gears and boiled into a rage that curdled everything I touched. The Deepwater spill down in the Gulf had put a damper on auto sales. The economy in general was in shambles, but this beat-up town hadn't prospered much since the Red Mountain Cut. Meanwhile, we're dumping good, hard-earned USD into foreign countries, and our Harvard-educated Kenyan president was doing all of jackshit about it. Instead of buying new cars, people just drive them longer. Used to I could sell forty cars in a month. You don't need a Harvard degree to do that.

When DOT took a slice out of Red Mountain for the expressway, and the folks with means moved south to bedroom communities for the schools like college campuses, most of downtown Birmingham self-actualized to antique ruins, reverting to a giant used-car lot, a smooth asphalted prairie where trash and news blew before the winds. I managed a downtown lot on 20th street. My office was in a portable trailer stacked on cinder blocks. Long silver strands of concertina wire outlined the perimeter of the lot like a concentration camp. The warehouse next door had been abandoned since I got my driver's license. Sale banners in conflicting primary colors flapped and whipped in the hot winds and the flat air in that metal can was tight as my collar. We parked cars on the sidewalk. On Saturdays, when the urban prairie land was empty and dead, looking more and more like a southern Detroit, instead of making cold calls and getting hung up on by irate voices, I played lonely games of golf, as blue and red klaxon dopplered by.

I positioned my belly putter, searching for that sweet spot on the face-balanced club head, a custom job where I had detached the putter's iron head and refitted it with a chrome leaping Jaguar hood ornament. Every putter has personality, and you have to learn what they want deep inside like finding a woman's g-spot. With this special Jaguar putter I tapped the ball down a thin green strip of Astroturf toward a red plastic cup. Even though the trailer yawed toward the street, the putt was straight and simple. Then my lot attendant barged into the trailer without knocking and swiped the ball with the edge of the door and it skittered off under my desk.

—Goddamn it, Larry. I was about to sink that son of a bitch.

—Hey Rick.

—This better be important. You see I'm busy.

I brandished the club in the air, twisting it in my hands, admiring my craftsmanship. Kathy always said I was good with my hands.

—Guy out here wants to trade in his car.

—What kind of car?

—One of them banged-up Toyotas.

I looked around the trailer office for the golf ball.

—Let me guess, it's one of the recall models with no brakes.

—You'd be guessing right.

—Tell him to write a check to Birmingham Tow Company, or give us fifty dollars to tow that piece of shit off the lot. This is a used-car dealership, not a junkyard, goddamn it. We don't want people's scrap metal.

I ducked under my desk. Larry's boots were muddied up and dogshitted from where he'd been traipsing through the alleyway. I was about to yell at him for wasting my time and the good, untaxed money I paid him under the table every week, when he slammed the wafer-thin door on his way out. The trailer floor shook beneath my feet and yet the swiped golf ball did not roll out of its hiding place.

I leaned on the window, mummified moths windrowed on the sill, and watched Larry hustle the rice burner off the lot. The Cityville Lofts across the street were almost complete and then the lofties would move in with their two and a half kids and the value of surrounding real estate would appreciate and before long the dealership rent would go up and Larry and I would be valeting the cars we'd just sold for Monopoly money. The Red Mountain Cut was a nasty scar dynamited in the mountainside, but if it could let them out of the city, it could let them back in again.

The best were the cash-in-hand adrenaline junkies who'd come grandstanding into my Madison Avenue trailer, their Viagra-dicks hanging out and wanting the fastest production car on the lot. I'd sell them something that would explode when they banged into a telephone pole or drove through somebody's kitchen wall and into the family dinner because they didn't know the gas from the brake. Ever since I got into a fisticuff with some rube who wanted to haggle over a below-market sticker price, I'd been angling to exit the business. Move somewhere nobody knew me, start fresh, maybe Miami, some place with a lot of golf green and no barbed wire, I don't know. I once threatened to floss a customer's yellowed teeth with that barbed wire and was sent home, because the owner said I was not the type to cross the street to avoid a fight. Right now I just wanted my goddamned golf ball back. I was about to place another ball through the office window overlooking 20th Street, and watch it bounce through traffic, maybe put out a windshield, when the owner of the Jaguar dealership off University waltzed into my trailer condo.

—Nice office, Rick. I love what you've done with the place.

By place, Springs meant a steel tanker desk and a sheetless brown mattress from my picayune marriage, the one thing I got out of the divorce, aside from lawyer fees. I'd been sleeping on it in the trailer mortgage-free since the Sheriff served me an eviction notice a year back. The divorce was made final a month ago; the summer months are the longest. The heartbreak, what there was, slowly drifted away until a man just let himself go. My trailer office was starting to look like a college dorm. An empty beer can rolled across the curling linoleum and stopped at Springs' feet.

—What the hell is it with people can't knock, I said to Mister Springs who was scanning the trailer like an interior decorator looking to queer up the place. Springs' luxury car lot was about a 5-iron distance from my trailer park, no farther than I could drive a ball down the fairway on a calm, windless day. He looked at the custom club I brandished, and I followed his eyes down the length of the putter where it stopped at the leaping Jaguar mounted at the end of the club.

—That's a nice club you got there.

—Thanks. I made it myself.

—Where'd you get the hood ornament?

—Stole it off your lot, where else?

—I knew there was something missing. I can sense it. That's why I come here.

—You need a used but not abused jalopy, Mister Springs? I got just the deal for you.

—See that pen on the desk there.

I looked at the desk, an old Cold War desk built to withstand a nuclear attack. An oak partners desk in a corner office would've been nice.

—Yeah, I see it.

—Sell me that pen for at least twice what you paid for it.

—Pardon?

—The pen. Sell it to me.

—It's my pen.

—Sell me the goddamn pen.

—All right, all right.

The cinch to moving cars off the lot, to the vendition of inventory at a criminal markup was to assume that the customer was no brighter than the light bulb in your beer fridge. Through the artful manipulation of tone and demeanor, just the right edge and quantity of condescension, but not so much that you offend them, just so they know you're sharper than a golf ball, you present yourself as a professor of cars, an academic of the catchpenny auto-industrial complex. You know the car's specs better than you know your own family, and if you don't have a family then you make one up, because car-buying people trust a family man. A man's handshake can seal a deal, or break it, whether firm or flaccid. For the evangelicals with money, you put a little Jesus into the sale and mirific things can happen to you. Follow me, I shall show you how to fish for people, you tell them, and you do not look back to see if they are following you. Most customers will follow you into the showroom like sheep to the slaughter. There's a lot of high-fiving, fist-bumping, tie-pulling, arm-wrestling, soft-soaping and frat-boy monkeyshines. You do handstands or cartwheels if you have to, whatever antic it takes to make them think they're the brightest bulb in the meat locker and take their checkbooks out. And when the checkbook comes out, you act like you've been in the End Zone before.

I picked up the pen, hefted it in my palm and screwed the cap off.

—You know, my wife uses this pen when she writes love letters to me. She says the ink dries as soon as it hits the paper, so she never smears it when she writes words like love and fuck me.

I no longer had a wife, but your buyer doesn't need to know that. I could have rattled on about overhead, bottom line, peak oil, the rising cost of ink, but that's the kind of business talk that will bore the good thrifty folks who buy used cars. I knew that Springs was the type of dealership owner to shoot from the hip, and any highfalutin talk about economics would have put him off.

—And if the ink dries soon as it hits the paper, it'll be dry on your customers' checks when they sign it, before they can think twice about how much they're paying you for the best purchase of their lives. It won't bleed, won't run, writes with the grace and speed of a thing alive.

He snatched the pen from my hand, hefted it in his like a weapon.

—See Rick, that's what I'm talking about. That pitch right there is poetry. Sales ain't nothing but rhetoric. You could convince a man he's got a soul and that he needs to pay the retail price for it, plus tax. Or that a man ain't got a soul, and he needs to buy one, Springs lectured, still cockblocking the doorway, looking me always square in the eye. —I seen what you done selling rattletraps and jalopies before the market got shitdeep in bubbles and riskiness. But that ain't your fault. This morning I had to can my salesman because he couldn't sell pussy to a thirty-year-old virgin.

—What is it you want, Mister Springs? A round of golf? You want your hood ornament back?

His nose minutely twitched like a rabbit sniffing a threat.

—I want the shirt off their backs, their shoes, their credit cards, their wallets, their wives, whatever will make them put down a deposit on one of these cats, you got me? You got too much sales talent to be wasting it in this fucking trailer park. Now, get your ass out of this dump and hustle some real cars for me, Mister Springs said as if pulling the cotton viscera out of a knifed stuffed animal.

He still had the pen in his hand as he opened the trailer door and descended the wooden steps I'd skill-sawed from 2x10's.

—Oh, and keep your damn pen, he said and angled around, under-handing it to me. —Your wife may need it.

The pen sailed by, end over end, and I grabbed only air, the pen lost among golf balls under my desk.

Although I never formally agreed to take the Jaguar job, I drove my shit-kicker Nissan 720 pickup truck the next morning and rattlebanged into a space in the employee lot and cut off the engine. To my right, overlooking the street, was a relucent silver sculpture of a leaping Jaguar, modeled exactly like the hood ornament only big as a real puss and chromed so bright in the sun it burned your retinas to even glance at it. No more sleeping on the floor, or sad, kitschy sales banners. I had never sold new cars before, but I figured I'd give it the old college try, and if that didn't pan out there was always the Army, Miami, prison, other planets. I stayed strapped to my seat and listened to the faucet of oil dripping from the cylinder heads into the oil pan, the metronomic plinking of the engine, and I remembered that Mister Springs built his Jaguar lot on top of a black cemetery. Nothing to do with race or whatnot, he said — the land was cheap. Rumorists said his cars were spooked, the engines starting and stopping themselves, radios anachronistically tuned to old broadcasts from the 60's like Radio Free Dixie or a soul music station. Remember soul music? Neither do I.

Mister Springs swaggered out of his office, a starched white shirt his wife ironed coming out of his khakis, the collar so tight it enhanced his considerable dewlap, ducking under a Jaguar banner, and hustled across the lot toward me and my truck. I cranked the window down, positioning my arm on the door like a long-distance truck driver.

—Look, if you're going to sell cars for me, you're not going to show up to work in that oil burner. This piece of shit truck will downright terrify a Jaguar buyer. Get it out of here.

He handed over the keys to a new Jaguar XF, one of those luxury sports saloons that was worth more than I would ever have. A 5.0-litre supercharged V8 petrol engine under the hood. Chrome glittering everywhere, and the grace and verve of a natural creation that was born, not machined by the same species that invented carpet-bombing, leaded gasoline, the Segway, CFCs, asbestos, New Coke, and plastic grocery bags.

—Product knowledge is essential, Springs said, tapping his forehead. —You got to know these cars inside and out, just like you would your wife if you had one. He was eying my bare ring finger.

—Good morning to you too, Mister Springs.

—And another thing. You got to stop snubbing out cigarettes on plates. I saw those plates in your trailer office. Well, this ain't your trailer, got it, Rick?

—Got it, Mister Springs. I got it.

Mister Springs disappeared into the heat vapors floating over the rolling necropolitan blacktop, and I thought, as I handled the truck door open, it ain't so bad to be buried under a black field of Jaguars.

I spent my first day washing down the cats in the lot, waiting on a buyer Springs had set me up with to keep an appointment. I was getting sunburned from the reflection off the cars and seeing floating white spots, hallucinated blobs and splashes of color, so I pulled aviators out of my shirt pocket and slipped them over my face and buffed every XF until my arms were sore and Springs went home for the day. When he was gone, I walked the lot, checked all the doors to make sure they were locked and pulled the razor-wire gate behind me when I left.

I did not knock at my old trailer office door. Larry was throwing darts at a board he had chalked on the wall.

—I'm gone less than a week, and the whole place falls to shit.

—Rick, you back for more?

—I see you moved up in the world of used cars, Larry. Who's watching the lot?

—Ain't nobody watching the lot. You want your old job back? I can throw darts against the side of the trailer from the lot.

—Larry, this is a very classy office, don't trash it. I want to trade in my Nissan.

—Think we got enough of those, Rick.

Larry disagreeably cleared some phlegm from the back of his throat.

—You got any idea how many Mexicans you can fit into the back of this here thing? Look, I already feel like I'm donating an organ by giving her away. Do you know how it feels to give up an organ, Larry? The heart, say? Your liver? All that bile stored up for years just gone like that. Any idea?

—All right, we'll take it.

Larry had always been a pushover. The place would be crowded with unsellable cars by the end of the month. Buy low, sell high should be the Alabama state motto.

I fumbled through my pants for the keys and then sent them sailing through the air and Larry caught them against his chest like a basket of eggs. I wrote myself a check from the used-car dealership and pocketed it and headed for the door.

—Hey, Larry.

—Hey what, Rick, as he aimed a green dart at the trailer wall.

—You know what the Jaguar motto is?

—Meow?

—Grace, Space, Pace.

—Grace, Larry said. —That's real funny. I used to run around with a bitch named Grace. Good luck, Rick.

Across the street from Springs' showroom was a long low concrete wall that marked the territory of the vintage Southtown housing project, thrown up long before Hope VI. The city had commissioned a local unemployed artist to paint over all the graffiti tags: *The Jaguars* in looping bubble script and the words *Birmingham City Jail* slanted cryptically down the concrete wall in plain view for any potential car buyer to read. Over half the scene was executed before Springs recruited me for his dealership. The mural would be done and signed by the muralist's handprint by the end of the day.

The muralist crouched against his work, moving between buckets of bright paint with many brushes. What must it be like to create a thing like that, and the thing for a time is you, and then you are finished, and it goes on in the world without you. To be interpreted by scalawags and villains according to the critical vogue of the day. The car is the closest thing we will ever create to something that is alive. Without knowing either from what it comes, or toward what end it tends. I think now the mural, though still there, is old and grey, graffiti covering it again, sun-faded and dead as the used cars I once retailed.

I was the only salesman on that lot no bigger than a slave ship. Jaguars sell themselves. You're not going to sell a Jag to anyone who doesn't already dream about one. The crossless Negro dead beneath the black tires of white-collar luxury were silent, and I prospered in the easy coolness of the showroom, behind a sun-sparkled field of glass, sipping weak drip coffee from a Styrofoam cup, and in a plane below the showroom's crystalline quietus I detected the movement of southbound traffic on the Red Mountain Expressway thundering by Southtown — the engineers routed the Expressway within inches of the projects. Mister Springs said that the hot coffee cup warnings everywhere were symptomatic of our pantywaist culture. I blew breath over the surface of the coffee, stirring shallow waves that died against the cup's white walls, anesthetized by the white noise of Jaguar commercials buzzing in the background, and watched the artist erase the graffiti of Southtown's gangs, the urban poetry of dogs marking their territory.

As church bells signaled the hours, the artist elaborated the overpainting — I don't know how long I stood there, entranced behind showroom glass — into a tropical mural painted lengthwise across the concrete wall that separated the housing project from the boulevard down to the Expressway overpass. From his painstaking brushwork emerged banana leaves and floral motifs, pink blooms of exotically extinct species, a different kind of mesmeric graffiti. A tropical paradise like Aruba or Miami — places where a man's reach does not exceed his grasp — overgrowing this concrete jungle, in the gray wastes of which only one thing stood out: the silver Jaguar sculpture scintillated in the sun like the silver bean I saw when I was so desperate for a sale I drove a car to Chicago.

When the mural was almost done, the jungle leaves were layered thick enough to get lost in. The artist's illusion was so complete I felt I could part the verdure of the jungle leaves and walk into some prelapsarian village. At last, he brushed over the Jaguars' tag. I wanted to talk with him, but knew I had nothing to say, and neither would he. I recalled some drunk's bar joke, told around the time of my separation from Kathy, about why the car salesman crossed the road, but couldn't remember the punch line. Remembering how a thing begins is easy, but how a thing ends I never could count on. Just as, after making a sale, you know who drives the car off the lot, but where it goes is a blind spot, because the mirror is all rear view.

I knew that the muralist couldn't see me eclipsed behind the angry white glare flashing across the showroom glass. But he must have sixth-sensed the presence of an invisible omniscience, for he turned around, dripping brush in hand, squinting into the glassy second sun behind which I kept an eye on the lot, picking apart my Styrofoam coffee cup till I had a harvest of snowy foam pieces at my feet.

The muralist had dark eyes that drooped with drink and which the light avoided. The brushes disappeared in his big hands, became an appendage from which the jungle spontaneously burst forth. The artist stood just higher than his mural, about the height of a smallish truck. A hard face sensitively set, a blacker version of myself. I have never been what you might call an introspective man, and I see myself only as a shade of others.

I jaywalked University Boulevard and took the sidewalk jagged by magnolia roots and turned down an alley by a blue metal dumpster, holding my nose, and came out upon an empty, childless playground, swings dangling by rusted chains squeaking in the wind. So this was the punchline. I was searching for the muralist, but he was gone, leaving only his handiwork behind. A plastic sheet flapped over a window. I thought of what I would leave behind when my work was done. Some golf balls in the trailer office, and a dog-eared, fatigued copy of the Kelley Blue Book. Mattresses like the one back in my trailer piled waist-high on the curb, shredded tires and meatless chicken bones whitening in the sun.

I took my jacket off and draped it over my forearm and side-stepped around an overturned, broken-wheeled grocery cart in someone's front yard. A plateless car jacked up on cinder blocks like my old trailer office. A tribe of old men sat silently on dented metal folding chairs and leaned at a Formica table. I thought they might be playing cards, reading the paper, but they didn't appear to be doing anything at all except leaning statuesquely against the table like a taxidermist's work. A man younger than myself was grilling red meat on an open pit and I watched him moribundly chew on a cheeseburger like a zombie as his eyes followed me across the lawn. The whole place skunked up with oniony halitosis. I unbuttoned my collar and loosened the constricting tie knotted about my neck as I stepped over water pooled in the gutters where an unrepaired main had ruptured, my head aching with the pounding purr of new and used cars on the Red Mountain expressway nearby. I find myself in places I do not belong.

But anyplace you can make a sale is the right one at that moment. I've always stood by that. I met my ex-wife when I sold her a used car I knew would fall apart soon as she drove it off the lot. I was counting the cash down payment when she phoned the office, saying the engine failed ten blocks south. I gave her a lift. After we married, she said there was something wrong in the way I looked at people. I didn't look, she said, I assessed people with an emporeutic scrutiny — she'd seen her father, who made a living breeding dogs, look at dogs and women this way — and tried to calculate how much money was in their wallets based on such W-2 form categories as age, sex, race, creed, marital status, hourly wage and salaried income, etc. No one was an equal. I called her a bitch, like Larry's Grace. You have to see people this way if you want to make it in this racket. Because they see you worse. Kathy called me a bigot. Anyplace you make a sale is the right one at that moment, but the sale might be the wrong one.

I was a colonial in the habitat of a people who probably had relatives buried across the street, beneath the hot blacktop where Springs sold Jaguars to trust-fund golfers with popped collars and the alcoholic bachelor doctors, the workaholic lawyers and shrewd, sartorial investment bankers. That's when I saw the stockpile of red gas cans, trophies of the Jaguar gang's graveyard pillaging of the lot, serpentine siphoning hoses coiled up on the ground. The price of gas after the Deepwater spill was worth the taste of siphoning. What the future shall pave or build over my dry bones I am happy not to know.

I blundered down another alley and out of the Southtown projects and, through a momentary hole that opened up between passing cars, stalked back across University Boulevard. How quickly death can overtake one crossing the street in this town — one misstep. I spotted a woman browsing the cars on the sloped lot over the Negro cemetery. The back of her blonde head glinted in the sun glare like the windshields of the cars. She was eying a Jaguar XJ, one of our flagship models, an excellent choice that hinted at good taste and carefree money. She looked dressed for a funeral. I approached from behind, startling her, but before she had time to say anything I introduced myself and she said her name was Ellen.

—What can I do to get you in one of these cats? — as if asking her out on a date, something social I had not done in a long time.

Most women do not buy cars alone, and those who do usually think you're a predator or a felon before you even open your trap, so you start out with one foot in the hole and the idea is that you turn on just the right quantity of charm to get your ass out of it.

—I'd like to test-drive the new XJ, she said.

—This thing's got claws. The exterior design makes a formal and radical break from the previous models. The designer, Ian Callum, started over, went back to the drawing board, so to speak.

—I used to have an XJ-S.

—Did you buy it from us?

—My ex-husband did, yes.

—What happened to it?

—He dumped it in East Lake before we signed the divorce papers. It was an older model. Do you think it's a good idea to let cars idle or turn them off?

—Depends upon how old it is. The carburetor cars, I would say let them run. The fuel injectors weren't designed with fuel economy in mind. They burn off more gas when you start them back up.

—That's what I told my ex-husband.

—Is it still at the bottom of the lake?

—The police divers said to leave it there. He ran it into the lake with a mannequin dressed like me in the passenger seat.

I'd heard enough about this Ellen's conjugal problems. I'm not a marriage counselor, so I angled to get her in one of the Jags and go for a joyride.

—Let me fetch the keys to this one, I said and left her with the pack of cars before she could say no. Never let them say no, especially a woman with a checkbook and legs like a marathon runner.

The keys were in Mister Springs' office. I did not waste time knocking, but barged in and lifted a key off the rack and gave him the thumbs up. Mister Springs was seated at his Resolute Desk, flipping apathetically through an ancient copy of *Playboy* while he made sales calls. I recognized the woman on the cover from my adolescence.

Inhaling the manufactured smell of new leather, that zesty pungency of a dead animal's hide, I inserted the key into the starter, but the engine spluttered and wouldn't roll over. I looked at the gas gauge, wondering if the float switch was busted. I got out and tried another model, and that too was out of gas.

—One more try.

—Look, it's all right. I can come back another time, she said apologetically.

—No, it's not all right. I jumped into the third jag and jammed the key into the ignition. The engine bucked up and I gassed the pedal, thinking back to the red fuel cans I'd seen in Southtown.

—Wait right here, I grumbled and dove through the showroom and bolted into Mister Springs' office. He was still perusing his *Playboy*, brow furrowed studiously like a scholar poring over a lost text in search of meaningful ciphers. Mister Springs could look more pensive over a *Playboy* than if I'd put his own obituary in front of him. I'd seen him this pensive once, when he thought I couldn't see him through the labyrinth of showroom glass, tracing his fingers along the pages of *Where's Waldo?*

—Can you people knock? Springs bellowed at me in the middle of a sales call, not even bothering to cover the receiver.

I bowed out of the office and closed the door behind me and waited a few seconds, then gave the dealer's door a smugly polite knock.

—Come in, his voice muffled behind the door. Voices behind doors are not to be trusted.

He'd hung up the phone. For the first time I noticed a cheap reproduction of a painting exhibited on the eastern wall of his otherwise spartan office. The reproduction made me think of the Southtown artist's tropical mural across the boulevard with its botanical landscape. The painting behind Mister Springs featured yellow-skinned women who dwell in a blue and rambling Tahitian landscape.

—That's better, Rick. Now, what's the problem?

—I just lost a fucking sale because some dipshit can't fuel a car. Every car in the lot is out of gas.

—Yes, that's a problem, now isn't it? But whose problem is it, Rick?

I was not meant to answer this question.

—It's your job to sell the cars, so fix the problem.

—What's that painting, Mister Springs?

He stretched back over the chair and looked behind him at the painting on the paneled wall as if he'd forgotten it hung there behind his head every day.

—Oh, that ugly thing? Springs said, reclining back in his squeaking throne like he was sunning in a deckchair. —My wife liked it.

—What's it called?

—It's called go sell some fuckin' cars, Rick.

—I can't do that until I know what the name of that painting is.

—I write your paycheck, Rick. You do what I say, or you go

back to peddling used cars in the trailer park.

—The painting.

—"Where Do We Come From? What Are We? Where Are We Going?" What's it to you?

—Too many questions.

—It's the name of the painting, dumbass.

—I guess the painting is the answer to the question.

—Get a company fuel card, take those cats to the B.P. Station next door and fill them up.

—Got it, got it.

I still had my hand on the doorknob when the dealer called me back into his office.

—Oh, and Rick.

—Mister Springs.

—My wife said the painter vowed to commit suicide when it was finished. A damn silly and pathetic notion if you ask me.

—Do you know if he ever finished it?

—Looks pretty finished to me, but who gives a shit?

—Have you seen the Southtown mural going up across the street?

—No, what is it? Springs was half-listening, already returning to a spreadsheet of calls to make and the pictures in his *Playboy*. I saw my future columned, rowed and formulated into the thousands of rectangles on a spreadsheet.

—A jungle.

—Suppose a jungle's better for business than all that goddamn graffiti, don't you?

—Maybe he'll off himself when he's finished.

—Maybe.

———————

I returned to the lot with a gas can. Ellen leaned against the razor fence, watching the muralist put the last brush stroke on an extravagant, baroque leaf, her fingers curled through the chain-links like a prisoner looking despondently at the outside, venereal world. I wanted to sneak up behind her and bury my mouth in the nape of her neck. It had been a long time. She pulled her license from her purse for me to photocopy, but I waved her off. After I re-fueled the XJ, it started up without bucking at me, and I knew then what was the problem. I got out and Ellen got behind the wheel, with the engine running quietly. When she didn't pull out of the lot, I realized she was waiting on me. I buckled myself into the passenger seat and she pulled out of the lot and onto University. The muralist was gone by now, though his paints were still on the sidewalk waiting for his return.

She gassed it through a yellow light and took a hard left on 23rd, her funereal black clothes radiating warmth, and I switched on the a/c. The sun was a bomb in the sky. I waved at the old-timers as we toured by Southdown. I saw the man who had been grilling hamburgers walk smilelessly out of a payday loan place across the street. The city had stripped the road surface without bothering to repave and the Jaguar jounced all over the road, swerving around potholes and sewer heads.

—Usually it rides real smooth, I apologized to her. —On a regular surface, that is.

Ellen was silently spurring a round right turn on Magnolia by Brother Bryan Park. Rapes and other metropolitan iniquities were commonplaces in the pastor's park. I recognized a few of the gutter drunks I'd hired to sweep the used lot or wash down a car. When they were finished, boozy breath in my face, they'd always tried to cadge more cash off me than what I told them their time was worth. Ellen flashed through Five Points and around the fountain where there were as many bums as pigeons, and we triangulated our way down 11th Court back to University. I had no idea where she was going. As she shifted gears I thought of her car sitting at the bottom of East Lake, her lookalike mannequin's blonde hair waving like sea grass in the water.

—How many women do you ride with like this?

—I stopped counting, I answered, looking out the window as empty buildings blurred by.

—Do you ever stop for drinks?

—Sometimes.

—Do you intend to sell me this car or not?

—The original XJ was the last to have creative input from Sir Williams Lyons.

—You know a lot about Jaguar.

—I like to think that Jaguar now is a better car than it was back then, those experimental designs, each series better than the one before it, the evolution of an organism. Sort of the Darwinism of the luxury automobile. Takes a long time to squeeze out the quirks, simplify systems, increase shift quality, a real work in progress is what you're driving right now.

—Do you think they'll ever perfect it? Ellen said, running a manicured hand along the hot leather seat, her nails like five long claws in my back.

—If they finished the Jaguar, the automaker would have to kill himself.

—I bet they will finish it one day.

—You know why it's called the XJ, don't you?

—Why is it called the XJ, tell me.

—XJ for experimental Jaguar.

—I just like the shiny hood ornament.

—I've got a dozen back at my place if you want to head that way.

Her shapely knees jutted out below the hem of her skirt, the muscle of her finely toned calves rippling under her tight, tawny skin as she pedaled the clutch like a piano and we crested the hill on 21st Street and coasted over the railroad viaduct and into downtown. At the bottom of the hill she turned into a parking deck and we spiraled up the ramp to the top deck with a masterful panorama view of what passes in this town for a skyline. Vulcan — Birmingham's pagan deity — standing sentinel on Red Mountain, guarding the Cut and the cupcake suburbs from the hordes of Southtown. She keyed the ignition off and we sat together but separate in the experimental car, me thinking about all the important moments in movies that happen behind the wheel of a car. For a long time we didn't say anything. Church bells at St. Paul's tolled the evening hour. Black colonies of bats took to the air from their caves inside abandoned buildings.

She would buy this Jaguar outright in cash, I knew as she leaped the gearshift between us like mounting a horse, legs splayed in a straddle and black skirt hiked up to her waist as I palmed her ass and hefted her body electric on top of me, bumping her head against the ceiling of the car, and I did not turn my mouth away from hers as she leaned my seat back and plunged into me, and I thought of what Mister Springs had said about the shirt off their backs.

———————

After work, Springs and I went for a few rounds at the Highland Golf Course to celebrate the sale of my first cat. The first sale I'd made in over forty days, used or new. We downed Bloody

Marys at the clubhouse, a drink for each hole. Nine holes, nine drinks. The sweltry day was cut with wind, thin pines bent and swayed under the invisible weight of the heat and the nostalgic smell of freshly mowed golf grass tickled my nose. I thought again of the lush, tropical painting on Springs' office wall. The yellowish skin of naked native women, the blue landscape, those three unanswerable questions, or was it four? But then I recalled that the title inscription in the upper left corner of the reprint had no question marks. They were not questions at all, just the date 1897, before even Jaguar.

By the seventh or eighth hole I was pretty cocked and drove the ball wild and high into a low sand bunker where I had to stab at the sand to drive it out. Sands imported from the Florida Panhandle. Springs leaned against his club, soused on Bloody Marys, and laughed at my luck. I holed a few more balls and on the sixth or seventh sent the ball sailing parabolically skyward and then water bound into a clear, blue hazard by Highland Avenue. The wind had picked up and it was blowing our balls all over the green, and we were losing light as the sun lowered behind the pines.

I've always hated golf, but it's a necessary evil if you want to sell anything more than ballpoint pens, like always having on hand the newest edition of the Kelley Blue Book, the Bible of the business. I got so I could recite the Blue Book value of any model from memory, and many nights I fell asleep in bed, my wife's beautiful back turned to me, the architectural curve of her bottom rolling under satin sheets, the Blue Book still propped against my chest. I listened to the ceiling fan turning, thinking I could've stayed in Chicago, pondering my distorted reflection in the silver bean. The Blue Book was shelved now, and in that spreadsheet future I would spend my nights drinking alone in a bar studying specs and performance ratings on Jaguar engines. At least I was no longer playing golf on an Astroturf mat in that trailer park.

—You ever considered owning a dealership, Rick?

Springs was priming me for something, and I wasn't about to fall for it. Yes, I had considered it, but I didn't want to be tied down to anything again the way you get tied to a car note, a mortgage, a woman, a life that you never wanted but come to find out is yours whether you like it or not, love it or leave it. I had an ex-wife with whom I led an unexamined existence for some time. That's all I care to betray about that. Kathy said I had the striated thew in my arms of a man who raced wheelchairs for a living, that was her idea of a compliment, and she said I looked at everything and thought only how to sell it to someone else for more than it was worth, like that pen I told Springs she wrote dirty letters with. And maybe she was right up to a point: I would never sell the custom Jaguar golf club I made though; she didn't know me so deep as she thought in the end.

—You gonna clean out the back of the car before you turn it over to her?

I knew what he was getting at, but sometimes it was smarter to play dumb.

—You were gone a long time on that test drive, he said with a lewd wink.

I knelt by the hazard's edge, saw my own face rippled on the shallow abyss of the golf pond, and fished around where I thought I'd seen the ball splash into the hazard. I sensed another hand fingering my hand, and I thought of Ellen leaning over me in the Jaguar, her eyes shut when I came inside her, the church bells quieted, her mannequin drowned in East Lake. The underwater hand pulled me down, and I sliced the water with my club, and then the blue face of the Southtown muralist merged with the reflection of my face and he let my hand go.

Mister Springs' shadow darkened long over me and the hazard. —Lost your balls? Springs' jowly face then overtook mine in the hazard, displacing it with his pumpkin grin. I didn't tell Mister Springs what I saw in the golf water, I just stood there wondering whether the muralist drowned himself after finishing the jungle or whether the Jaguar gang hunted him out and killed him for erasing their graffiti tags.

That night I crashed on the backseat of Ellen's Jaguar in the graveyard lot. A few late lights winked on and off in the Southtown projects, the jungle mural as though it had never been painted. The showroom was dark, and the lustrous silver Jaguar sculpture gleamed with an obsidian patina. The car's interior was dark as oil, the jet and starless city sky was blotted out by the lot's humming sulfur lights. The smell of new leather mixed with Ellen's perfume. I scanned the lot for trespassers and fuel encroachers. She was coming to pick it up in the morning, she said, and we'd go for another joyride together on my lunch. She wanted me to show her the back seat this time, and the collection of Jaguar hood ornaments I kept caged at my place. I was looking forward to it. The bluish face of the drowned muralist lingered with me still, and they've got used-car lots and concertina wire in Miami too, I thought.

Black shadows flitted across the tinted windows of Ellen's cat like dream panthers prowling in the lot. I had slept many nights in my trailer office like a useless security guard, and I figured I would tell Springs why every car in his lot was out of gas at the Friday morning sales meeting. Jaguar club slung over my shoulder, like Hephaestus with his hammer, I would be in his office to explain everything before the incomplete presence of the tropical blue painting hanging behind his desk. Ellen and I would screw in a parking lot again, the only place I felt anything, and then fall asleep in each other's arms on the backseat.

The jungle mural across the boulevard glowed green in the light of the B.P. I heard the unmistakable guzzle of someone siphoning gas with a drill pump out of the Jag's tank. With one hand I clutched the door handle, the other tightening around the taped grip of the Jaguar golf club, and waited for the moment to spring.

I shot out of the back driver-side door and wielded the Jaguar club like a baseball bat and home run swung at one of the siphoners and missed, the silver hood ornament sailing through the air and cracking the windshield of Ellen's new car. That titillating sound of glass crunching. Jaguar siphoners shadowboxed around me, panthering in the dark, war-whooping and leaping across the lot between cars. These Southtown hoods danced and berserked in the lot's freak light, I couldn't possibly take them all on, but I stood there waving the club as a kid dropped his gas can and broke into a dark run, fuel trickling out onto the blacktop, and he began to scale the chain-link palisade beyond the muralist's wall.

The remaining siphoners huddled close to the cars, thinking I'd never catch them, or that I would not swing at my own cars. Had they come to prey on our gasoline, or as in a mental quarter-moment I believed, to collect their dead who had been asphalted over by Mister Springs, his cars filling the lot like rows of dark headstones? No matter what their color, all his cars appeared wetly black, with a facsimile Ellen ensconced behind the tinted windows of each one. When I saw one of the Jaguar siphoners snap a silver ornament from the hood of an executive S-type, I determined, in a decision that came to me more like drums from the jungle than a conscious choice, to let the Southtown punks scatter back into their jungle — the wild we come from and the wild where we're going.

NOBODY KNOWS HOW IT GOT THIS GOOD

When the Wal-Mart Supercenter bullied into the neighborhood on Aaron Aronov Drive, where the abandoned Western Hills Malls used to be, there was a two-day block party in the newly paved parking lot to celebrate the benefits of one-stop shopping. Barbecue and stump speeches, live soul music and face painting. It was some kind of Mardi Gras meets Donner party. The parking stall stripes were white as a grand wizard's starched bed sheets. Tar fumes smoked up our lungs like unfiltered Pall Malls. Stray ghouls of children, faces painted like skeletons, chased each other with tiny fists balled like black hearts inside the empty carcass of rotisserie chickens.

Ray, the general manager, wore a bright blue Wal-Mart apron and grilled chicken and steaks over a barrel pit. Barbecue smoke ghosted through us like we were nothing, and fireworks flowered in the black sky above our heads and flickered patriotically in the dark windshields of SUV's and minivans. Emergency rooms are going to be busy tomorrow: the wounded, the soulful, the starched, and the barbecued.

Starting a new job always gave me a bad case of the blahs. I leaned against a concrete pillar, watching kids toss a deflated football in a parking lot on the other side of the Drive. At any moment one of them might be struck by a car and there was nothing I could do. Applause and jeers as a shirtless, muscled man nobody knew humped to the top of a streetlight against an artificially blue sky, staying up there all day, crucified to the light, with his view of the Wal-Mart, till we forgot about him. He did not want to come down, even when the cops pointed flashlights on him. The blinking circus lights of the twenty-four-hour payday loan offices — Eazy Money, Loans for Less — lit up the lots importantly, as cars lined up in fast food drive-thrus and the open sign of a thrift store winked off.

Fairfield was once called the model industrial city. After U.S. Steel, where my father worked himself to death, closed the local furnace there was a domino effect: Woolworth, Loveman's, Pizitz, Parisian, J.C. Penney, they all knocked off and ditched

Fairfield and we were left with the empty carcasses of their strip malls whose emptiness never left us. Sinkholes swallowed what was left of the street I grew up on, and the house was burned down by squatters. Mail sent there gets returned. Ray's Wal-Mart pays us a get-by living, and is the only place to spend your paycheck once you cash all three figures of it at Eazy Money. I've never felt closer to the good times than on a Friday with cash in my wallet. Ray should pay us in Wal-Mart dollars with his good arm, and take our money with the other. Before Wal-Mart, we got along at Dollar General or Family Dollar, surviving on the Dollar Tree, supplies for a birthday party on the same aisle as ingredients for a homemade bomb.

After the rockets' red glare fizzled out and the crowd returned to earth, Ray snipped a blue ribbon with a pair of safety scissors held in his good arm, and then raffled off product samples and giveaways. As I watched neighbors I'd grown up with collect their prizes — gift baskets stuffed with BBQ products, sets of golf balls, bug spray, life insurance policies — I couldn't help thinking — from the prosperous shores of the New World I am forever projecting a vampiric dystopia — that one day the spanking-new, state-of-the-art Wal-Mart too would be old and empty and tumble-weeded.

Markus, a buddy of mine from a semester at Miles College, who wears a hat backwards to bed, took the other side of my pillar and together we silently supervised the happy carnival dispersal. Children with faces painted like ghouls and bogeymen turned cartwheels. A preacher seized the mic and praised the largess of Wal-Mart in the name of the prosperity gospel. Wal-Mart had kept us from taking out tabs with the loan sharks. Wal-Mart helped some of us in ways the church with its collection plate and plywood altar could not. Wal-Mart had saved us from becoming a ghost town.

—Nobody knows how it got this good, Markus said, and I hawked up a large quantity of phlegm like a jumbo oyster gleaming onto the blacktop and walked off. I don't know why, but Markus' words about how nobody knows how it got this good stuck with me and they never let me go. It's not for me to judge whether he was right or wrong.

The mayor had been courting Wal-Mart for years, wearily waving the flag of taxes, noisily beating the drum of job creation. In his preachy campaign speeches Wal-Mart was a foreign occupier who'd come in here and civilize the heart of darkness. Who the hell needed the mom and pop stores when there's Wal-Mart to retail every new thing ever made under the sun: hunting supplies and camping equipment, firearms and feminine hygiene products, frozen foods and football fan merch and every kind of citrus out of season, clothes from a hundred Asian countries, a cathedral of electronics, one-hour photo processing, a pharmacy and eye doctor, a lawn and garden center smelling like manure fertilizers and wilting, waterless house plants whose browning leaves descended onto the sparkling white tile floors. Thirty-six merchandise departments in all.

That was before they took the hyphen out of Wal-Mart and then by Black Friday two years after the block party — the Supercenter in the meantime was the site of only two rapes, four fatal shootings, seven non-fatal shootings, one hostage situation, an extraterrestrial visitation, three live births, two apparitional sightings of the Virgin Mary and the face of Christ in the Lawn and Garden Department — it was just plain WalMart, no hyphen. I could buy a gun and ammo in sporting goods right now if I had a mind to. If I had a mind to ever set foot on Wal-Mart property again.

Four thousand applications for one-hundred fifty positions of minimum wage are not good odds, but I look better on paper than I do in person, even though I interview well enough. Me and Markus took the Wal-Mart job after we nearly got caught siphoning gas from the city buses in the bus lot. If you wanted to work, you worked for Wal-Mart. We're not employees at Sam Walton's multinational; we're "associates." You weren't allowed to refer to yourself or anyone else as an employee. Employees go on strike, unionize, cozen their employer, and quit without notice. Associates don't strike, unionize, steal from their employer, and they give sufficient notice before quitting.

My first month I was chronically late to work, which I blamed on the bus. The bus driver blamed it on the cars, and the cars blamed it on the buses, so I saved up some cash and bought me a hot Escalade, spinning chrome rims and windows dark as Sam Walton's soul. I told my little brother Davidson that when he decided to grow up and stop siphoning gas he could drive it. Until such time, he wasn't to think about touching it. His breath stank sweetly of gasoline.

In that Escalade, I could barrel through traffic and never be late for the night shift. Since he learned how to siphon, Davidson had been dreaming of working on an oil rig in the Gulf. I told him he wouldn't last longer than a gnat fart in the wind on a rig. He had a job at a chop shop for a minute until he was fired for pinching gas. He has an addiction to unleaded gasoline. I wised up, stopped siphoning, but Davidson didn't, and was caught siphoning gas from a Jaguar dealership, narrowly escaping being clubbed to death by some maniac security guy with a golf club. I don't miss the taste of unleaded.

No one takes a job at Wal-Mart and expects it to become a career. Except Ray, the general manager. He was career Wal-Mart material, a lifer, born for the job of middle management overseer. We called him Uncle Ray, like Uncle Tom, if he'd been black. Markus and me, in a joking mood, told customers he had a Wal-Mart tattoo above his crotch, so he'd think about Wally World every time he wacked off in the women's room.

If you worked the night shift, you were locked into the store, for "safety" Ray said, and the doors weren't unlocked until he showed up again the next morning. You prayed to the Wal-Mart cave gods in Arkansas he came back in the morning to cut you loose. We didn't know what the hell we'd do if he died in his sleep. Ray was a motherless, pasty, card-carrying Wal-Mart worker bee who couldn't see real good. He was almost translucent and bioluminescent from so much exposure to the store's fluorescent lights. You could stand on the other end of the toy aisle and flick him off and he'd think you were waving. Markus wished god had given him more than two middle fingers.

The first thing you noticed about Ray was what he lacked: he was missing an arm. A freakish accident on the job, and his armless sleeve dangled limp from his shoulder. You got to have a slobbering make-out session with Ray to move up the WalMart hierarchy, no hyphen. I started at the bottom of the totem pole, a night shift stocker. I'm still at the bottom of that pole. The pole is interminable, greased by men like Ray, and even if you make it to the top you lose an arm. When Ray locked the doors at night before hobbling homeward, Markus and I had the store mostly to ourselves, a dangerous situation.

We zipped up and down the aisles on mountain bikes, and target practiced with pellet guns. Markus took the shenanigans too far when he tacked up local union posters on the break room bulletin cork board, right under the sign that said all associates must associate on Black Friday or risk termination. Loss Prevention is as humorless as a judge. They saw the irony alright, but Markus' prank was political enough to make Ray's nub tingle where his invisible arm thrashed at Markus' throat.

—Have a seat, the one-armed general manager said to his associate.

Markus hesitated, then sat down at the only table in the break room, picking at the gum stuck to the table's underside. Ray wasn't one of those chummy general managers who'd invite you to lunch with him out of the low-priced kindness of his general heart. Markus' union posters were still thumb-tacked to the corkboard behind Ray's head, and Markus fought off a shriek of laughter.

—Look, Ray. Sorry about those tire marks in the sporting good aisles. It won't happen again.

—This ain't about no bicycle tire marks.

—What's up, boss?

—You're being terminated, Markus.

—For what?

—Theft.

—I ain't never stoled nothing long as I been here and you going to accuse me of stealing shit from this pukehole. Ain't nothing here worth stealing anyhow.

—You took a nineteen-minute break two weeks ago. We need you to work the Black Friday holiday, but after that you're being dismissed for time theft.

—Fuck y'all.

And this is what Markus did: Markus pushed his chair back, stood up and said good day, overturned the table and glided out of the break room. Markus had flair.

Black Friday was Markus' last shift at Wal-Mart, when customers were corralled into the store with door-buster deals and loss leaders placed in some out of the way region of the store. Making customers walk by made-in-China goods with higher profit margins is how Ray explained the theory. Like catching flies with honey, he said. Ray was a retail theorist, really going places.

Whenever Ray plunged into his general manager ideas about how to make the store more profitable, I nodded, pretending nothing more than a general interest. I thought about all those people who were willing to stand outside the Supercenter, open before even the sun was up for its bright business, blankly staring at each other as if waiting for a late or missed revelation in the damp cold with their cups of gas station coffee and thin wallets primed for Ray's loss leaders, their bloated stomachs still turning turkey from the night before. Our history is full of such crowds and mobs, capable of anything.

On the eve of Black Friday Ray found me breaking in the break room at a folding table, my attention sharply focused on the empty, off-colored square where Markus' union poster had been. Ray hadn't slept in two days, and he looked bad even by his standards. Readying the store for this moment gave the man some meaning. It made up for the arm and so much more. Half-moon bruises like purple pouches sagged under his eyes, crow's feet cracking at the edges. He slouched more than usual, oddly in the direction of his missing arm, as if being pulled by it into the same void his arm had disappeared in. One day his missing arm would pull him totally through the void and all of Ray would vanish but he would be reunited with his missing arm on the other side of the void, which I envisioned as the Wal-Mart parking lot in the wee hours, empty and inhospitable to life. Ray near-about lived in his office, a hermit's quarters littered like a landfill with takeout boxes and men's magazines. He had a dumbbell up there to work out his one good arm.

Riveted by this blank spot on the cork board, I didn't hear Ray jawing about no breaks on Black Friday. The union poster's ghost square was about the size of Ray's head, which was large for a head. I'd never been in a union, but I found that if I focused on empty places — parking lots, the warp of a man's mind while driving, your own self before you had a name, my wallet before I began associating — the life around me seemed less empty, fuller of direction and marked with the high-toned chemical feelings my family found in church. The world is full of many such empty places, and they're gaining ground.

—What are you doing? he asked, standing next to a Christmas tree decorated with holiday-themed photos of the store's associates.

Ray is always asking questions he knows the answer to. He was sporting his fake arm this time, and I was afraid he would make me shake his fake hand. Ray's fake hand tormented me. I wondered if Ray used his real arm or the fake one when he fantasized about Wal-Mart while standing over the women's toilet with a full-color spread from the magazine section.

—Taking a break. What are you doing, Ray?

—Went looking for your ass in the Lawn and Garden Department and what do I see?

—What did you see, Ray?

—I didn't see nobody working.

—You going to fire me too for time theft, that's fine. Just show me where to sign. Me and Markus need all the time we can get.

Ray ignored this empty threat and told me to stop what work I was breaking from and to get those manure pallets off the floor in the Lawn and Garden Department before some shopper tripped on them and we had another lawsuit on our hands. Wal-Mart is apparently shit-deep in lawsuits, a fact which concerns Ray very much.

—This ain't shit season no more. Get them shit bags off the floor before I come back to open the doors at five. This is your first Black Friday, ain't it? Just you wait.

Ray said he was going home to nap before "all hell broke loose," the kickoff of the Christmas shopping season. The ex-felon dressed up as Santa Claus for the Salvation Army outside the store rang a tiny bell that made me pray for deafness.

Markus was assigned to toilet duty for his last shift. Yellow latex gloves and gallons of antiseptics. I heard him whistling tunefully in the bathroom as I walked by the unending cash registers that would soon be beeping with deep discounts and holiday sales.

I was once in the Wal-Mart across town on Lakeshore and became disoriented. The men's clothing department was identical to the men's clothing at the store on Aronov Drive. The line of registers, the bright gym lights above, and the ugly people sadly shopping were all the same. It didn't matter which Wal-Mart you were in, the emptiness was a species of sameness. I almost offered to help a lost old man find the white tube cotton socks he was hunting for, until I realized that I wasn't working.

Forty or more associates were on duty that night before Black Friday, and I knew no more than a dozen faces, maybe six names. Management's strategy is to keep you isolated. Returning to the Lawn and Garden Department to move Ray's bags of shit, I waved politely to an associate organizing hair products. Both hands over-full with shampoos and conditioner, she did not wave back.

I was forklifting a palette of manure onto a high storage shelf when the fork clipped a metal rung and I sat helplessly watching the manure palette tumble and bust open on Ray's immaculate white floor. A more gratifying sound has never been heard in a Wal-Mart.

—What the fuck was that, Markus whooped from within a janitorial closet.

—Shit, Markus. That's what that is. That is the sound of shit falling.

Markus barked with laughter, his white teeth gleaming in his dark mouth. He was still wearing those yellow latex gloves elbow deep. He returned with two shovels from the utility closet and said, —We got to clean this shit up, thrusting a shovel into my hand.

He rolled the yellow gloves forward and popped them off. We started shoveling, and dug into a rhythm, lobbing shovelfuls of shit into a wheelbarrow like gravediggers until Ray's immaculate white floor reappeared beneath the manure. A lifetime could be spent shoveling shit for management.

—I remember what you said when this store opened, I said.

—What'd I say?

—You said, Don't nobody know how it got this good.

—Shit man.

—Have you told your girl yet?

—Told her what?

—That you got canned.

—Naw, I ain't yet. Figured I'd just tell her I quit. We'll be alright for a while. She just got a job at the car wash.

—You ought to steal Ray's fake arm first, I said tucking my own arm up into my sleeve, mocking Ray's invisible arm.

—I never seen it.

—He wears it sometimes up in the office when he doesn't want corporate folks to know he ain't got but one arm.

—If I got ahold of that arm I'd knock his ass into next week with it.

—Cain't beat a man with his own arm. It ain't right.

—Hell you cain't.

We both laughed at that. After almost an hour of shoveling, we were sore and the floor, although not speckless, was ordered as an apple pie. Then we heard a rioting, glassy clamor from the direction of the store's automatic doors like the cheering uproar a home team football crowd makes on a touchdown. I thought the hullabaloo was in my head, but then I saw Markus look up too and then at the clock above the registers. Thirty more eternal minutes until the store opened for Black Friday.

—What's that racket? I asked.

Markus leaned his shovel against a shelf and went to investigate. He came back looking like he'd seen his own corpse. I'd never seen him like that before.

—We got a whole 'nother kind of shit on our hands, Markus said.

—What the hell is going on out there?

—It's them crazy ass customers. They want in. They want the holiday deals man and they want them bad.

—It's not five o'clock yet. They'll have to wait. And Ray ain't here yet to let them in.

Markus and I dumped our shovels on the floor and split off down separate aisles. I charged by associates mopping, stocking and shelving, and toward the front doors, passing the shopping carts arrayed in long silver rows and the gumball machines and arcade games blinking dumbly. I thought of fireflies, but I haven't seen those in years. I stopped between the security towers before the mob crushing against the front doors, their hands and faces pressed against the glass of the automatic doors. Markus was gone.

I fished two quarters out of my back pocket that I'd found on the floor underneath a register and coined them into the slot on the face of an arcade game machine. We're supposed to put lost change back in the registers, but I'd been collecting lost quarters since I started here and no one said anything. I had me maybe ten dollars and twenty-five cents in lost quarters.

The swarming sea of people behind the glass doors looked on as I craned the game machine's metal claw over a furry, stuffed smiling dinosaur, a tyrannosaurus, its plastic button eyes fixated on me. I thought about my dad angling on the Black Warrior River after he got laid off from U.S. Steel and the otherworldly by-catch he'd dredged up from those poisoned waters, and I wondered what fish-thoughts the sturgeon and darters and the few freckle-belly madtoms had as they dodged dad's wormed hook sinking from the world above. The stuffed tyrannosaurus, as I clawed him up, thought of Ray's missing arm and all the humans he would eat.

Someone tapped on my shoulder and I lost the stuffed dinosaur. —Goddamn it, I spun around, the empty metal claw craning up into the game sky above that soft sea of stuffed creatures. Markus had Ray's prosthetic arm, and was tapping my shoulder with it. He pulled his real arm inside his shirt and fitted Ray's fake arm into the hole and faced the parking lot of faceless, milling and desperate Wal-Mart fans. Still sunless, I couldn't see my Escalade for all the people pressing against the sliding doors garlanded and wreathed in red and green, wired white lights blinking like distant stars. The Salvation Army's bell drowned out by the din of consumers. BLITZ LINE STARTS HERE a crayon sign cautioned, the wobbly script written with Ray's good arm.

When armless Ray didn't show up to open the doors at five, I began to wonder if he'd done it on purpose, leaving Markus to scrub urine rings off the men's toilets all night, and me to meaninglessly forklift shit off the floor of the aisle where the Virgin and Jesus were seen.

More customers were crowding around the doors now, wordlessly demanding that we open the store. I couldn't make out the individual words, but I knew what they wanted. The Salvation Army bell rang in my ears now. Squished faces of the cahooting horde bottlenecked against the doors. I thought of the tumultuous multitudes that stormed bastilles, and the charges of ignorant armies on green fields that are today's parking lots. I thought of traffic jams, the depleted masses of honking cars unconfederated in purpose, and I thought of the black flies swarming to the rotten deli meats the store threw out once a week at the expiration date.

Markus was brazenly taunting the rabid legion in a pantomime with the general manager's fake arm, beating it against the glass, egging them on to greater crowding, and then he ripped the fake arm out of his socket and feigned agony. His stagecraft had them right where he wanted them. In this telling, I saw fake blood spewing from Markus' shoulder. Bodies were hammering down the doors now like wild animals, foaming at the mouth to get inside the store, as if they and not we were locked in, as if some abnormal, imminent horror pursued them in the parking lot. A single white hand pressed against the glass of the door. I thought I picked out my little brother Davidson in the throng, and maybe one of the self-appointed non-denominational preachers who counted the quarters you tithed, but I couldn't be sure, it happened so swiftly, the apoplectic society tiding in upon us, the muscled streetlight climber still hanging fast to his post for dear life — I never got a good look at his face, would not be able to spot him in a police lineup, and whatever he was trying to escape down below was now upon us all, though the streetlight must be out — and Markus brandishing that third arm, now a slapstick gag routine where the fake manager's arm appeared from nowhere, grasped him by the neck and dragged him kicking out of sight.

But I did recognize one face, that of Ray the one-armed, life-time store manager quelled among the press of crazed customers, and then Markus' words returned to me, —Nobody knows how it got this good, my last thought as I heard the doors shatter before I felt the glass flying. I threw my hands up in defense and searched through the rushing welter for my associate, and the last thing Markus saw as he went down beneath the shopper's stampede were the black linoleum tiles he fell into like a grave, then only scattering feet blurring facelessly store-ward across the blitz line before he closed his eyes, the air wrung from his lungs like popped balloons, and shrapnel of Wal-Mart door glass was buried in my face to this race-to-the-bottom day.

SETTLING DOWN IN PECKERWOOD

Every house in Alabama is on Peckerwood Road. Where, if you hold the door for one person at the Wal-Mart or the gun store, you end up holding it for the next fifty faces. People take advantage. I tried to assimilate. I really did. I even started to like S.E.C. football. After too many gunshots disturbed our dreams at night, and the County started digging a landfill next door — all those refrigerators, couches, TV's, stoves, the rotting appliances of our lives piling up till it blocked our view of the sunset; I could hear the metal rusting in the subtropical night, the roaches breeding in the offal — my wife and I deserted Norwood and, like so many who escaped through the Red Mountain Cut, moved upward on the *nouveau riche* ladder to the cheap magic of Mountain Brook — a ritzy, overbaked, plutocratic suburb of Birmingham, but not just any suburb: the most affluent in Alabama.

I am here as witness that the grass ain't greener on the other side. There ain't even grass on this side. The neighbor's kids have booby-trapped the neighborhood, and I threatened to call animal control. We are surrounded on both sides by stay-at-home moms — former Miss Alabamas — who are vocal members of the local chapter of Housewives for Trump. Mountain Brook's most distinguished resident is someone with no grave: Natalie Holloway, the white girl who went missing in Aruba. You'd recognize her if you saw her picture. Blond, expensive smile, average yet pretty. People pay oodles for garbage collection. This is not a starter house. It's a rambling palatial ender house to end all houses. The omega of houses. The ladder's rungs greasy from chrematistic climbers before us.

I've recolored the cosmology of everyone on Peckerwood Road, where everyone is a peckerwood. Even my own son, side effect of a one-night stand that turned into a marriage, even this little brat is a peckerwood. Everything y'all say starts with, "Have you seen the ESPN commercial..." If only Home Depot sold beer I'd get a Home Depot credit card and play with power tools. Using goats to graze-cut the lawn. Tan daughters who go to Africa on missionary trips to work on their tan or ride hippopotamuses with the Peace Corps. Sons who watch Sportscenter every night. Wives made of peanut brittle who spend their days testing expired foods from the family refrigerator. I am prone to generalize, it is a fun sickness. But everyone is so genial, so Christlike, so white — Jennifer sugarcoats it. Yeah, they're such goddamn Good Samaritans they'd show you how to load a gun if you were trying to blow your head off.

A hard, short day at the County Annex and I spend almost half as much time going nowhere in commuter traffic as I do at my desk, covered in so much paper I no longer see the point of life. Another workday ends when I hold my own front door open and let myself in. I've waited hours at the front door for someone to open it for me, but eventually I got tired of waiting — I don't like to be out after dark. Every room is jammed floor to ceiling with cardboard boxes. The volume of stuff is staggering. I angle down a hallway narrowed by boxes on both sides, the boxes stacked up to my shoulders.

Jennifer is at the kitchen table, looking younger in the evening than she did this morning, flipping listlessly through the decadent pages of a Paula Deen cooking magazine, a geological casserole on the cover — reminds me too much of the landfill. I don't know why she picks up such tripe at the checkout counter. Buttery, lardaceous recipes for fat people and how to get fatter. Paula Deen — a fat boiled dumpling of a woman — has been dead, or living in a crypt beneath the Wal-Mart ever since it came to light that she planned an antebellum Southern plantation-style theme wedding with black male servers. Jennifer is in a gossamer nightgown, though the sun is still unset. Her dark saucer nipples poke out of the thin gown translucent as a curtain of rain penetrated by falling light. She wants it bad. I can smell it. She hasn't changed clothes since she got up on the wrong side of the bed this morning. Jennifer's sable hair is flowing and curly like a white woman's. The hairdresser says it looks good and I have to agree. Looks real good. Jennifer turns to the next page, rips out a full-page smorgasbord of fried fixins and hands it to me, —Here's your dinner.

So I crumpled the magazine dinner and shoved it into my mouth, trying to chew it seven times, like my momma taught me, before swallowing.

—How is it?

—Needs salt, I said, moving on to the chessboard on the kitchen table. We've been working on the same game of chess since moving here. I lean over the board, my tie brushing the side of Jennifer's face, and move a black pawn up one white square.

—Honey, she says musically.

—Honey means you want something.

—It smells in here.

—Open the window.

—Will you take the trash out? It's something *in* there, she says pointing a long, painted fingernail at the kitchen trash, accusing it of olfactory wrongdoing.

—You're home all day and you can't take the trash to the curb?

—I'm afraid of that dog next door. My daddy was attacked by police dogs. You know I don't like dogs. And the creepy neighbor guy is home all day.

—Cut you a deal. I'll take the trash out, if you take that nightgown off.

—Take my queen or get me in checkmate and the gown comes off.

Jennifer's people hail from Storyville. When that quarter was torn down, they came to Birmingham and stayed because it was safe from hurricanes and the alligators on Basin Street. She talks nostalgically of the tribes of cannibals in New Orleans, a soggy wet sock of a city. In her slumming days, Jennifer starred in local commercials for used car dealerships, ambulance chasers and barbecue restaurants. She has a toothpaste commercial smile and she can talk chocolate into your ear. I thought she had no problems, so I went to the BBQ restaurant advertised on channel six and asked for the girl in the commercial. I got a BBQ sandwich, six beers, and the girl in the commercial. Hoover got himself born without his consent approximately nine months later, give or take, but who is keeping count?

I pull the prime trash out of the can by the draw-string, the white bag about the size and weight of our son Hoover when I carry him on my shoulder up the stairs to bed, and dump the trash by the curb out front. Through the front window — she hasn't hung the curtains yet — I can see Jennifer brooding over the chessboard, determined not to let me win. Power. The bagged trash slumps at the curb like a dying man. I pat him on the head and go back into the house before I am locked out.

Jennifer will not look up from the black and white squares. I pull two beers from the fridge and twist the caps off the bottles and toss them like quarters into the new black trash bag lining the can like a female condom. She picks up a rook, hesitates, and leaves a bishop on a black square.

I'm an aficionado of games of logic and strategy such as Mastermind, Battleship and chess, but Jennifer prefers language games like crosswords or Scrabble. She is a sore winner. Losing doesn't rankle, I'm used to it. I've introduced some new spicy rules to the Victorian game of chess. For every piece one of us loses we have to remove an article of clothing. Most nights before checkmate, we're down on the kitchen floor like dogs in heat. Whatever virgin said that marriage sex goes downhill after the first year has never been with my lioness.

—Baby, you need some white pearls on your beautiful neck.

—Sweetheart, you should get your head out of my ass once in a while. Go outside, or go fix something in the garage.

—Not the worst place to be.

—Not the best either.

I move my knight in an L-shaped formation towards Jennifer's King and Queen. That gown is mine.

—Don't make plans for Saturday night, she says sacrificing a rook for a bishop.

—Is it the New Year already?

—Funny. The O'Neills next door invited us to their cookout.

—Do we have to go?

—They live twenty feet away. They'll know we skipped out.

—I knew we should've gotten a bigger yard. Is this so they can show off how liberal they are with their token black friends?

The chessboard makes sense in a fitful flash of inspiration like a cotton field illuminated quickly by lightning before returning to its original darkness. I move my knight and corner Jennifer's king on a white square. —Checkmate. Game over.

—Only took you all week.

—I'll need your gown, please. Where's Hoover?

—He's upstairs watching *Sesame Street.*

—Why is he watching that?

—He likes it, okay?

I wasn't watching all the superhero movies with my kid: Superman is a premature idea that presupposes man.

—Shouldn't he be in bed?

—It's six o'clock.

—He sleeps at school and then he's not tired when it's time for bed.

Jennifer shuts me up by pulling her gown over her head and she drags me down onto the floor by the refrigerator, and it ain't over till the skinny lady sings. I can't talk about it with my kid in the house. Jennifer's back is winged with cold sweat beneath her shoulder blades. I think of the grotesque whip-lacerations on the scarred back of a former slave, a man named Whipped Peter, I'd once seen in a history text Hoover was wiping boogers in. I told Hoover to close the book and go to bed. Why do they subject kids to the ulterior outrages of history at that age? Hoover's youth is being eroded by schoolmarms obsessed with pogroms and the banality of evil. Women just love being loved, that's what I learned from history class.

Didn't stop me apparently, as I lay sweating under Jennifer, my back cooling against the checkerboard linoleum. I can see in Jennifer's face that I look at her as if she is not my wife. From the kitchen floor, I reach up to the table and swill down the last of Jennifer's beer. —Don't waste beer, I inform her departing backside, —All the children in Africa are sober.

Every dewy morning I slipper to the end of the circular drive to fetch my copy of *The Birmingham News,* squinting to read the headlines in the dark. Mostly padded with ads, yes, but in this morning's edition there is a front-page exposé on the County's five most wanted fugitives and my mug shot is grinning at me like I won the lottery. The scoop is this: as one of five County Commissioners, I've worked sixty hours a week for a year cleaning up after the previous administration's nepotism and graft, getting the County of Jefferson's inflationary bankruptcy under control and uncooking the books so that zero equals zero again. During my next job interview, when they ask me why I left this one, I will lean forward, look them squarely, fearlessly in the eye, pause for a full five seconds, and say with irresistible and doomed certitude, — I guess you don't read the papers.

After a sky-is-the-limit sewer debt incurred through toxic bond swap deals and interest rate swaps, the County is so bankrupt, monetarily and morally, the receivership won't even be able to buy a fan for the shit to hit. Peckerwood Road is in the County of Jefferson. I'll be the first to admit that the four other commissioners are crooks with online degrees from for-profit diploma machines like Trump University.

A black Lexus with its headlights off slows in front of my house as if I'm up to no good in my own front yard. —What the hell are you looking at, asshole? These peckerwoods see a black man out after dark and they get skittish and lock their doors. Sometimes the red dot of a laser pointer dances over my chest. I stay out of the neighbors' booby-trapped yards.

A garbage truck muscles up the hill and I watch the crew scatter in the streetlight, swarming on our curbside trash and one of the crewmen throws the white plastic bag of trash I put out the night before into the rear of the truck. Ripe with symbolism. Your garbage disappears overnight, but no one but me knows where it's trucked. I used to leave all the lights on in the house in Norwood and talk to the landfill, feeding it leftovers and tormenting it with my enormous qualms and regrets about the future.

I wave to a goggled trash collector wrestling with the O'Neill's trashcan, which is about to out-man him and dump him in the garbage truck. Surely, there will come a day, probably not too long from now, timed with the technological singularity, when our own sentient trash will stuff us into garbage trucks.

—You need a hand?

Trash man stops what he's doing and looks at me like no one in their right or left mind would ever ask him if he needed help, the very thought a crime that would produce lawlessness and disorder, anarchy and bankruptcy. A private citizen on Peckerwood Road help the trash man lift his own litter into the truck? Mob rule! —Yeah, sure. Sure, I could use a hand, I guess.

I must've looked a commiserable sight in my bathrobe and slippers, pathetically unfit for the advent of daylight. How do you tell a man like that, "No, you cannot help me with the trash?" I shuffle over the grass and help him strong-arm the Rubbermaid up onto the truck. The O'Neills can make some trash!

—What do these people put in their trash to make it that heavy?

—Don't know, man. You'd know better'n I would.

—You know what. I think I know what they put in those trash-cans once every week.

—What?

—A bad conscience.

For once, the house doesn't reek of trash. Jennifer has been letting Hoover make simple breakfasts like eggs and toasts, rec-ipes that are hard to botch, and even when botched, not costly. He'll microwave a jumbo bag of marshmallows for breakfast if you let him. Hoover is stabbing at a plate of eggs with a fork that has a bent tine.

—Daddy, do you know what color your pee is supposed to be?

Not now, Hoover. Not now. Think of something to shut him down.

—White wine. Your tinkle is supposed to be the color of white wine.

—No, Daddy. Ick. I was going to say green. It's supposed to be green. Like money.

—Like money? Why not like trees or grass? Son, some things are meant to be one color and only one color. Your pee is one of them. The grass, for example, is supposed to be green. Money is green. If anything comes out of your peck-er that's green you run straight to the hospital, don't even ask Mommy, just run and scream for help. Call 911, ask to speak to the adult in charge. You'll change your mind about the wine one day, although I agree with you that white is pretty icky.

Having an autistic ten-year-old is just like having a pet. You have to plug all the outlets, hide the knives, kid-proof everything. Ex-plain with a straight face that Daddy is not hurting Mommy when they spend Saturday night together in the dark behind a closed door. Jennifer descends the stairs, curlers in her hair, and begins pouring cereal into a cold bowl without a good morning. Hoover spears the last of his eggs, and his mom pats him on the behind, his signal that it's time to give Mom and Dad some peace and quiet and ready up for eight hours of schooling and brainwashing that is required by law. They're learning about Indians and Andrew Jack-son right now. I don't expect it to go well: for the teacher, Hoover, or the Indians. He gets a good de-education when he gets home.

My son, Hoover, is not afraid of moving vehicles. Instead of running away from an oncoming vehicle, he will play chicken and win. I have yet to see the SUV he can't make yield to him. Hoover is also a species of albinism, a condition we explained to him with the aid of an albino ladybug I found hanging around the trash. Let me just say it. He is the offspring of two very handsome, African-American parents, but he's white. Snow white. Second reason to leave Norwood. Make no mistake, his physiognomy would make Malcolm X proud: kinky hair, protuberant bottom lip, gleaming opalescent white teeth, bulbously squashed nose that I am to blame for. Indeed, he resembles the younger frog-eyed James Baldwin. Is this description of my own son making you uncomfortable yet? It gets better: he glows in the dark. His peers maintain a disrespectful distance from him, never trespassing Hoover's private circle. He labored like a sharecropper over a two-page essay about science for his literature class and the teacher calls me up at work accusing him of plagiarizing from the Internet. I didn't think kids his age were even smart enough to plagiarize.

—We should hire bodyguards, Jennifer. My face is on the front page of the morning news. The neighborhood is booby-trapped. There are laser pointers on my chest. They'll have a lynch mob with Tiki torches and pitchforks at the house by noon.

—You don't need torches at noon.

—Imagine there's a total solar eclipse.

—We haven't been here long enough for this kind of paranoia, she says pushing dry cereal around in her bowl with a big silver spoon. —And we're out of milk, she says squinting into the wan light of the open refrigerator.

My best chance of survival is to divert her away from me and to incite her state-of-the-art motherly talents to focus on Hoover. His friendlessness is an easy target.

—Hoover needs friends his own age.

—His own color, you mean.

—Let me guess. You think his pee should be green too.

I hear the toilet upstairs flush.

—Frederick, what are you talking about?

—Do you know what he told me?

—He knows how babies are made? That Santa Claus was invented by corporations to sell wrapping paper? That the Underground Railroad was not an actual railroad?

—He told me the Cookie Monster is a Bolshevik.

—The Cookie Monster does have those googly eyes. Why

would Hoover think that?

Jennifer is now crunching on dry, brightly colored cereal marketed at moms and kids. I asked her to please stop buying the cereal with marshmallow ghosts. The old house in Norwood was haunted enough, and exorcising the evil spirits of Birmingham was the reason we moved to a place where neighbors judge you by the species of grass you choose to sod the yard with. I don't need ghosts in my morning cereal too.

—Who cares why he thinks that. More importantly, where did he learn the word Bolshevik? Is he lurking the Internet on your iPhone? He says the Cookie Monster is a Bolshevik because he lives in a trashcan.

—That's Oscar the Grouch, she corrects me.

—Oh.

—The Cookie Monster wants nothing but cookies and more cookies. He's the proto-capitalist on the show.

—Oscar doesn't have a nose because he lives in the trash. That makes sense. I don't live in a trashcan, and I don't want a nose sometimes.

—There's more inside that trashcan than you think.

—Do you think I should have my nose reduced? I ask, a trick question, touching my nose.

—Only if I can get my boobs reduced.

—Okay, no deal. That's my favorite part about you.

—The only part. Want to poke around under the hood?

—Maybe tonight, babes. Got to go say goodbye to Hoover and then put a paper bag with a smiley face cutout over my head before I go into the office.

—Don't, you'll scare Hoover. You know he hates clowns.

—I am very seriously considering a career as a mall clown.

—He needs a better role model than that.

—What do you want Hoover to be when he grows up? Wheel-chair racer? Mall clown?

—Why don't we let him decide? Also, dear, please stop making Hoover get the TV remote for you. You're setting a bad precedent. If the folks who backed you in the Commission knew that your son fetched the remote for you, what would they think? And can you pick up some milk on the way home? Make sure it's one percent.

Jennifer sure is getting uppity with all that milk.

—And can you take the trash out again? It stinks already.

How is it already full? Didn't you empty it last night? Do we really produce that much trash?

—I need to tell you something. Prepare yourself. It's like if you caught your kid humping the family dog. You have to get him to stop, but even then the door is open.

—Oh god.

—It's about the trash. Hoover has been refilling it. He sneaks out of the house after he thinks we're in bed, collects the trash at the curb, and brings it back in the house and fills up the trash can. We've been doing this little charade ever since we moved here.

—Why on earth?

—Something about Oscar the Grouch. He's worried that if Oscar doesn't have any trash in the can that he will be unhappy and leave. I just go along with it. Obviously, it would be catastrophic if Oscar the Grouch left our house.

—Oscar isn't real, she says with the same flat realism she deployed when disillusioning Hoover that Batman isn't black.

—No less than that landfill we used to live next to.

The roof of a five-bedroom house on Peckerwood Road, climbed on a weekday, will put things in perspective. The asphalt shingles abrade my arse. Occasionally, an acorn will plunge from the green world above me and thump me on the head. The vista is about what you'd expect: power lines and a water tower, residential streets perpendicular with main arterials, some leafy nonentity trees, a CVS, a Walgreen's, couple of cars burning gas, some condos slap-dashed together and still unsold in this bear market, more peckerwoods. Yes, it is a beautiful world; even more so, I imagine, when viewed from Mars. I spot Jennifer coming down the driveway. She looks even better in aerial. Why don't more homeowners capitalize on their views like this? These Peckerwood houses should be built with aeries and lighthouses, minarets and watchtowers like old medieval castles.

Without taking off her sunglasses she looks up, —Should I even ask? Did Oscar leave? Is this about your spirituality, Frederick? Because if it is, there's a Baptist church the size of the Pentagon down the road. You'd be the first black member. You can integrate them.

I hate it when she talks to me with her sunglasses on. I need to be able to see how much she's rolling her eyes at me.

—The view up here is spec-tac-u-lar. Come see.

—The view's just fine from right here.

—You're looking at the ground, my love.

—What do you see?

—I see a bunch of children born with silver spoons in their mouths. Only they never took the silver spoons out. They're still crammed in there. They're choking on silver spoons, Jennifer. They are goddamn choking on them. Hoover was eating eggs with a bent fork this morning.

—Okay, Oscar the Grouch. What are you doing home early?

—I didn't go in. I just circled the block a few times and came back.

—How long have you been up there? Jennifer demands, looking over her shoulder at all the curtained windows, making sure no nosy neighbor is witnessing this connubial comedy, the husband trapped on the roof like a flood victim, the long-suffering wife trying to talk him down.

—I've been waiting all day for the lynch mob and the torches. They're a no show. No solar eclipse either.

—Maybe they're busy.

—I'm also trying to escape the Jehovah's Witnesses. And the Mormons. The Mormons come door to door with their brochures and those perfect white teeth in their creamy white faces like Paula Deen's kids. It creeps me out. Like those little marshmallow ghosts you used to get in the cereal. I can't stand it.

—You're afraid of little white boys on bicycles?

—They won't stop.

—Don't let Hoover see you up there.

—I was going to put on the clown costume, but whatever you think is best.

—I think it's best for me to go inside. I don't want to watch you fall.

To fit in, to assimilate into Peckerwood, I tried to create as many white people problems for myself as I could without rocking myself out of the boat altogether. As soon as I brushed my teeth, I was hungry again. No matter how much dirt you sweep into the dustpan there's always that thin line of dirt left at the edge, waiting to be sniffed up my nose. If I refer to myself in the first person, it is because I learned how to discuss investments and stocks, even invested in what amounted to forty acres and a mule in a mutual fund, which make me a realer person on bank ledgers.

Everyone wants to rob the banks, but no one will while their deposits are safe. I pick up a book I never finished reading in college and cannot recall any relevant biographies of the minor characters. How am I supposed to talk about *The Great Gatsby* at the O'Neills? I learned to make the sign of the cross when in the presence of someone mentioning Bear Bryant's name, and that the Republican Party was the party of Lincoln. I studied the copyrighted solecisms and shibboleths of my neighbors and made them my own. I threw out all of my baggy clothes and only shop at Whole Foods on Saturdays and Sundays after church, when it's busiest, and I can best maximize the exposure of my shopping habits to public scrutiny. Sitting on your roof in broad daylight waiting for a solar eclipse, counting cars, cowering from Mormon boys on bicycles is no way to assimilate among peckerwoods.

Jennifer returns, looking pleased with herself. I know what she keeps in that box under the bed.

—Just couldn't get away from me.

—That shouldn't be difficult now that you're living on the roof. There's a news crew here.

—A news crew? Where? Why?

—Are you going to finish with the five W's? Parked out front. They want to know if the County is declaring bankruptcy. They couldn't find you at work, so they came here.

—How did they find out where I live?

—Where *we* live, Frederick. You're a public official. They probably found your address on Facebook.

—Tell them I am incommoded.

—I don't think that kind of double entendre is appropriate under the circumstances, do you?

—My agent says I am not to do interviews without her prior approval. Damage control.

An anchorwoman appears in the drive in a Hilary Clinton pants suit and made four inches taller by heels escaped from an avant-garde zoo. She wags her ass down my drive like she's strutting across a carpeted modeling runway. Her business blouse is open and from my elevation I could swan dive and plunge straight down her shirt and never come back. Flesh-colored brassiere. She is pursued behind by a lackey cameraman and an intern with a boom mic. Wait until my neighbors get their peepers on this spectacle. Already the curtains are parting.

—Do you mind coming down, Mister Yessick?

For you, anchorwoman, I would live in the trash with Oscar the Grouch. I recognize her face from the ten o'clock news. The cameraman and intern pointed their equipment at me.

—I'm not coming down. If you want to interview me, fine. But I'm staying on the roof. If anybody needs me I'll be up here working on the rocket ship to get me off this effed-up planet.

How do they find you? These reporters would still find me if I was encased in lead in an underground bunker on one of Saturn's moons, or inhumed in Paula Deen's crypt beneath the baked goods aisle of the Wal-Mart.

—What can you tell us about the County sewer crisis? How will this impact homeowners and ratepayers?

—Best-case scenario, y'all end up paying more to flush the john for the next forty years.

—And the worst-case?

—I'm not authorized to speak about that.

—But the County already has the highest sewer rates in the nation. How will you get that by your constituents?

—I was elected by popular vote to clean up after the previous administration, which my electorate also put into office by popular vote. If they're looking to do some good old-fashioned finger pointing, my wife has a collection of silver spoons, given to us as a wedding present, they can use as mirrors. I'm not coming down from this roof till they find Peking Man.

Carl O'Neill is on his back porch, wide as the deck of a ship, standing over a leviathan grill that could cook a rhinoceros. The first time we met he was asking his dog how he felt about black people. Carl is a lifelike facsimile of what white people believe Hannibal looked like. I resisted thoughts of the O'Neills' overweight trash can I assisted the garbage man in heaving into the garbage truck. I tried to care as Carl whined their house was too big. Days passed without seeing his wife. As long as I can avoid talk about the election. A ladder leans against his house; buckets of white paint where the ladder meets the earth. Carl and Jane have two older daughters, varsity cheerleaders, and you feel dirty just looking at them. Jane is regularly confused with her daughters, and does little to discourage this. There is some marital spat,

Carl says, about Jane forbidding her daughters to travel to Aruba for Spring Break, citing the Natalie Holloway case. As if Aruba is some *terra pericolosa* that ravages only young white girls. Missing white woman syndrome is epidemic on Peckerwood Road. Jennifer could disappear and no one would notice for weeks.

Carl squirts lighter fluid over the coals, a flame burping in his face, and makes half-assed conversation. —So Frederick, what made you and Jennifer want to adopt?

—He's not. He's albino. It's a skin thing.

And no, he doesn't have beady red eyes like a white rabbit.

—Oh, he says inanely, flipping a burger onto its pink side. —Sorry.

—It's fine. People ask all the time.

No, they don't ask all the time. It's rude to ask questions like that, you rube. What was that commandment in the Good Book about loving thy neighbor as thyself? Assuming you're self-intoxicated enough to love thyself. How am I to love Carl and Carl's wife as myself, haunting my own roof in a clown costume? —Let me ask you something in confidence, Carl. Carl coughs into his fist, sorry his homemaker invited us over now.

—Do you think Oscar the Grouch is a Bolshevik?

I'm having fun with him now.

—Katy Perry can't show her cleavage on *Sesame Street*, that's all I know.

—Because I think Hoover learned the word Bolshevik on the show.

—How old's Hoover?

—He's ten.

—Little old for that, don't you think?

—He might be eight. Or nine. I'm not sure. He has Asperger's.

—Ass burgers.

—Autism. He's...

—Different.

Carl got an A+ in school for subtlety.

—Yeah, you know, he runs towards cars instead of away from them. No sense of danger. Struggles to make lasting emotional connections. Plays in traffic all the time. Jennifer and I were thinking about putting up a big fence in the front yard.

—Like a dog.

—Yeah, like a dog, except he's a kid.

—I don't think the neighborhood covenant would be on board with that.

—With my kid?

—No, with the fence thing. The covenant restrictions are really against certain fences. Because they look cheap and trailer parkish.

I'll build the fucking Berlin Wall Part Two around my house if it so pleases me. I did not climb the ladder to Mountain Brook to be told by a peckerwood flipping burgers that I cannot build a fence. Carl tries to change the subject, —What was that news crew out front all about? as he transfers burgers from the grill to a side plate.

—Just some attractive anchorwoman asking about the new folks in the neighborhood. Some sort of welcoming committee. We used to live next to a landfill.

The new black folks in a lily-white neighborhood.

—That's a nice welcome you got. When Jane and I moved in we just got our house rolled like the trees at Toomer's Corner. The trees at Toomer's Corner. Some sort of code or reference, an insider's bromide. Were those trees on Tuscaloosa's or Auburn's campus? Did it matter a lick? Toomer's trees were the only non-human plants Carl had ever thought about in his life.

—We used to roll those trees until they were snow white after Auburn won a home game, he brags. It looked like it had snowed toilet paper, the white paper flapping in the breeze. Made a tremendous mess if it rained.

Rolling the trees at Toomer's was Carl's greatest feat of athleticism. Ever considered wiping that shit-eating grin off your face with that toilet paper? Maybe wiping your wife's cute butt she talks out of? I eyed the height, pitch and texture of Carl's roof. Maybe the roof is where I belong.

—Of course, my two girls won't be rolling any trees at Toomer's Corner when they start next fall.

I thought Carl was about to cry. These Irish are always weeping. Carl's little sorority isn't even admitted to Auburn yet, and he's already bemoaning their college lackluster. He wanted boys to throw the pigskin around with. Blames it on Jane.

—Since that maniac from Tuscaloosa poisoned the trees, he gasses on in this wistful vein about the tragedy of Toomer's trees while I blanked out building that fence around myself.

The world's dichotomies are clearing up, really taking shape for me now. The roof's vista and the fence put things in perspective, delimiting the garbage and the chaos like the black and white squares on the chessboard. I watch a squirrel jump agilely between the high branches of the thin pines that block Carl's view of an interstate. It occurred to me, I am not ashamed of it, to poison Carl's pines, so he can enjoy his view of the five o'clock traffic piling up on the interstate like a clogged artery.

—They should really throw the book at him for that lark, I agree. —A crime like that, poisoning trees, ought to be punished to the fullest extent. Well, I should see what trouble Jennifer and Jane are getting into.

I leave Carl with his meat and grill and walk into my own advancing self reflected in the sliding glass door. It hurts longer than it should.

—You're supposed to slide the glass open first, Carl suggests helpfully.

I place my palm on the glass and slide it into the wall, and walk rapidly, as if across the roof of a burning house, to Jennifer. Isn't that a nice, inoffensive white girl name?

Jennifer is elbowing her way to the box wine, plundering a spread of cheese and crackers. Jane must have a Paula Deen magazine around Jennifer can feed to me. If I were hosting this meet-and-greet neighborhood soirée for the dads to check out their friends' daughters, I'd have fifteen buckets of fried chicken and Milo's sweet tea on the menu. Maybe some slaw. Beans, lots of beans sweetened in maple syrup. Everything would end up in the landfill or the sewer. I can't remember the last time I took communion. Boxes of wine creep me out, that depleted, baggy bladder of bloodshot juice inside like a collapsed internal organ.

—Did you hear what Carl asked me?

—How could I? You were outside. Let me guess. He wanted to know what it's like being with a black woman.

—Jesus, no. It's worse than that.

—I didn't know sleeping with a black woman was so awful.

—He thought we adopted Hoover!

—You afraid Hoover's going to have an identity crisis, or that you will?

—Always some sort of crisis. Identity crisis. Debt crisis. What about Carl's wife? You talk to her?

—She spends her time haggling over the price of a kiwi in the grocery checkout line. Then she comes home, puts on makeup, an expensive dress and high heels and just sits on the couch until Carl gets home. I found a hat box in the fridge.

—What was in the hat box?

—You don't want to know.

—And his kid?

—Which one? They have three. I thought it was just the daughters, but they have a chip off the old block as well.

—I just know that Jane won't let them go to Aruba, but they can go to school dressed like Hooters girls.

—Whatever happened to that Holloway girl is horrible. Every woman of every color will tell you that.

—But what about the chip off the old block?

—He practices soccer tricks for six hours and then you ask him to do the trick, he can't do it. I can't believe we moved here.

—You wanted to. Can we leave? I feel like a hostage here that they might actually shoot.

—Wouldn't that be rude?

—To shoot the hostage, or leave?

Jennifer laughs into her drink, —To leave, dummy.

—They're three sheets to the wind. Never notice.

—Okay, but let me fill up with wine one more time. We'll owe the babysitter a fortune.

—I asked Carl for some Sprite but all they have is Coke and cans of Diet Racism. Since when did you start drinking wine?

—About the last hour or so, she says refilling her cup —I think I want to start drinking it more. Maybe take Communion on Sundays. Jane says it's healthy and she looks great for a mother of three.

—She ought to. She's a former Miss Alabama.

—Stop picturing her in a swimsuit.

—I wasn't, I lied. —I was picturing her demonstrating some stupid talent like reciting all the state capitals or performing "The Star-Spangled Banner" with armpit farts.

The cup overflows with red wine onto the O'Neill's luxurious white carpet. Blood on snow. I think of the Holloway girl, those years ago in that tropical island paradise, and how delightful it would be to disappear into nobody, a crumb thrown down the hellmouth of the void, to vanish like the white of the carpet in the blood of the Lamb.

Later, I can hear the phone ringing like a five-alarm fire inside the house before I get the front door keyed. I know who it is and what she will say before Jennifer hands the phone over to me, holding it away from her body like a dead rodent.

—Frederick, you're not happy.

No hello. When Mom cries, you'd think the president, who used to be black, had just been shot.

—Mom, you named your black son Frederick. How am I ever going to find happiness in this world with a name like that? You should've just named me Quentin Compson or somebody.

—It was your father's idea. He was a big fan of Douglass.

—Mother, I'm happy. I'm so happy I crap happiness. It clogs the toilets. I've got a plumber out here the toilets are so shitty with happiness. The toilets are overflowing with shitty happiness. I can't even see the happiness is so thick in this house, it's like Jennifer burnt dinner and filled up the place with happiness smoke. It's great, mom. It's really great.

—You sound great, she mumbled, eating something.—You don't belong there. You belong with your own people.

—My own people? We're not in the Jewish diaspora, Mom.

—Think about Hoover.

I did think about Hoover. I thought about him finding his father's mangled body on the ground after a fall from the roof.

I hold the phone out to Jennifer and as far away from me as possible as if it might claw me. Her lips and teeth are stained red from the O'Neill's box wine. A vampiress' crimson simper on her luscious lips.

—You deal with her.

—She's your mother, Jennifer retorts.

—I can't deal with her like this.

I holler upstairs for Hoover. He's in the room, an achromatic and neutralized presence buzzing around blurry edges, before I'm even finished forming the words into sounds, as if the utterance of his name automatically materializes him like a magic watchword. How does he do that? Poof.

—Hoover, your grandmother wants to talk to you. She's concerned about your wellbeing.

Hoover takes the phone and peers into the mouthpiece, looking for his grandmother inside the phone. Unable to find her, defeated again by an inanimate object, he drops the phone on the floor. Maybe Hoover was right to look for her inside the phone: my mother's voice shrills as if she were standing right here in the room.

—Hoover, put the thing up to your ear, and talk into the other end, I instruct him again in the ways of simple routines. Potty-training this kid was more gauntlet than anything endured by peckerwoods. He said the pure whiteness of the porcelain bowl scared him, and I conceded his point.

This kid is never going to make it. But once he figures out how to use the phone, he is an unstoppable force of stuttering pleonasm and mumbled digression. He can *ad lib* for hours about the measliest bagatelles, the color of a shadow, the angle of a corner, the texture of a scab, and my mother humors him laudably. I hear footsteps overhead even though all three of us are on the first floor. The marshmallow cereal ghosts are haunting our house!

—I told you to stop buying those marshmallow ghost cereals.

Jennifer is painting her fingers nails, indifferent to the room around her, like a cat bathing itself, unspooked by the marshmallow ghosts walking around upstairs. Maybe it's the light, but I think her skin is getting lighter, like Michael Jackson's. Is she chemically treating it? Her skin is almost the powdery white of winter frost on the car windshield, the stuff you have to scrape off with the sharp edge of a credit card. Jennifer breaks the ice finally, —Jane and I are going out.

—You're going out with Carl's wife? I thought she was a creep. Hat boxes in the fridge and weird stuff.

—You sit on the roof like some latter-day prophet waiting for the sky to rip open. We're going to see *Harry Potter,* she declares.

What would mom say? Black people don't watch *Harry Potter.* They watch black romantic comedies and fast cars with explosions and black booty taking up two-thirds of the screen. Soon Jennifer will be wearing track shorts and yoga pants to Whole Foods.

—Remember that time at the Chinese place—

—What Chinese place? You can't just say Chinese place. It's offensive and unspecific.

—Who cares what Chinese place? They're all the same, with golden dragon wallpaper, an overweight golden Buddha statue, maybe some fish tanks and a buffet, and secondly can I finish before you butt in?

—Finish.

—I was saying, do you remember that time at China Garden when I got a fortune cookie and there was no fortune in it?

—Nope. Don't remember that.

—What do you think that meant?

—Probably that the underpaid Chinaman in the fortune cookie factory forget to insert one in the cookie.

I never should've handed the phone to Hoover who is honest to a fault. He's telling his grandmother how he hasn't made friends with any of the boys in the neighborhood. He is persecuted at school. He's worried about what the Indians are up against with this Andrew Jackson character. Daddy is in trouble and Mommy found him on the roof of house.

One day, when he's older, and has to think about taking care of himself, and doesn't have his parents around to lie for his own mortal safety, he'll learn the value of prevarication. You don't always have to blast your neighbor with the inconvenient onus of your own foulmouthed truth. Wearing such obscene honesty over his head like a halo he's going to grow up to be a narcotics agent or worse. Thank Muhammad there is no family business to hand down to him, because he'd surely drive it into the red with his incorrigible Boy Scout goodness. Now he's jabbering into his grandmother's ear about his ant collection. I expect Hoover to take up weird hobbies, but insects? As if the human zoo out there wasn't fascinating enough.

—Shouldn't he be interested in girls and cars by now, Jennifer?

—My gosh, he's ten. Before long you'll be asking him how the girls are between the sheets. What were you interested in when you were ten?

—Oh, I don't know. Probably the same things I'm interested in now.

—So, shit. You were interested in how to financially and effectively move shit from Point A to Point B.

A young woman, college age, maybe younger, you never can tell these days, appears in the kitchen doorway, leaning on the jamb. She yawns and rubs sleep from her eyes. The marshmallow cereal ghost has come down for revenge.

—Who the hell are you? I want to know before I call the cops or animal protection.

—I'm your babysitter, Mister Yessick. I saw you on the roof the other day.

—That was someone else. Jennifer, do you know this person?

—It's the babysitter, dear.

—Oh, why are you still here?

—You never paid me.

—How much do we owe you?

—Six hours at ten bucks an hour.

—That's more than I made per hour for my first job, I said patting my back pocket for my wallet. —Where is my wallet?

—I think it's in Hoover's room, Jennifer says looking up at the spot in the ceiling where Hoover's room is.

—What is it doing there?

—He needed some money for Oscar the Grouch he said.

—What is he paying Oscar for?

—He wouldn't say.

—That little capitalist.

The babysitter retrieved my wallet, the marshmallow cereal ghost's footsteps thudding in Hoover's room. I open the wallet and inspect its contents, counting the bills, and note that two dollars had been given to Oscar the Grouch. I peel six tens from a green cache of bills and follow the babysitter down the narrowed hallway of unpacked boxes.

—Where are you going, Frederick? Hoover is handing the phone back to me. Your mother wants to speak with you about Hoover's wellbeing, Jennifer says.

—I'm going outside to thank the front yard for being so damn green. And why doesn't someone unpack these boxes? Are we moving in or moving out?

In slippers I slink like a noctambulous trespasser to the terminus of the circular driveway to read what libelous smears *The Birmingham News* is printing about me this morning. A tightly rolled newspaper stuffed in a plastic bag in every drive on Peckerwood Road whose inhabitants' newspaper subscriptions were an act of protest against the 21st century. My family threatened in letters to the editor. Jennifer will be sleeping on her side, taking up more than fifty-percent of the bed. We have a big couch.

Another magazine breakfast torn out of the Paula Deen magazine will be waiting for me on the table. After I stormed out to give thanksgiving to the grass, Jennifer set up a new game of chess, stared discontentedly at the board, and then went immediately to sleep. I put the phone in the trash. I hung around under the oak tree and watched the bedroom light until it winked off and then, on the couch, dreamt about Whipped Peter climbing an endlessly long greased ladder reaching into the azure firmament over Peckerwood Road.

I can smell the foul moving atmosphere of the garbage first, and then hear the garbage truck announcing itself in mechanical chundering as it struggles to gear up the hill on Peckerwood Road. The truck slows in front of each house and the men dismount like shadows in the dark and disgruntledly toss bags of weekly rubble into the open back of the truck where it is compressed by a hellmouth trash compactor. The three man crew is working furiously this morning, their reflective safety vests flashing in the streetlight, a sinister triangle of yellow light oozing from the street lamps in which thick curtains of humidity hang glistening and moths zigzag on an aleatoric, kamikaze course. Some houses generate three, four bags of trash per week. Messy adults, or they have lots of kids. Bags of silver spoons. I haven't shaved since the County sewer crisis debacle began.

The truck is circling in the cul-de-sac on its way back to the landfill. I can play chicken with the garbage truck, and get squashed like road kill, the armadillos you only see dead, or I can stop pretending to be walking on water.

I jog alongside the truck, its yellow caution lights blinking. I hope Carl can see me now, and the anchorwoman's crew is getting this all on film. What can you tell us, Mister Commissioner? Fuck Peckerwood. Under every residential street wide as a flowing river is a sleeping network of pipes ferrying our shit to the sea. I should put that couch on the curb, a broken sink and toilet, an old hooptie on cinder blocks, class up the neighborhood.

My goggled trash man looks back at me and waves to the driver. I see myself reflected running towards myself in his goggles. He thinks I am running after the bad conscience I threw away the night before, something in the trash I must save. I flag the truck down like a taxi. The garbage man extends me his gloved hand and I grab it like a man about to drown and he hoists me up onto the truck's platform, my feet leaving Peckerwood Road behind. I helped him loft the O'Neill's waste into this truck, and now he's helping me — the truck picks up speed. Dawn glows reluctantly over Peckerwood Road. The succorous breeze in my face and the heinous perfume of ripe trash and sweet shit piquing in my nostrils, we're going for a ride, we're riding this garbage truck like a golden chariot out of Peckerwood Road.

MISCREANT POPULATIONS AND THEIR EFFECTS ON JIM CROW METHODOLOGIES OF STREET PAVING IN THE INDUSTRIAL SOUTH

Picture me now, my name is Jim Crow, as set down in this here report, in an orange yellow safety vest reflective of all lights, dim ones and bright ones, and baggy blue jeans falling loose up around my waist, rake in hand. Our fair yellowhammer state is run by frat boys who become four-star generals and dentists in their bass pro lodges and weaseling quarterback clubs. My shirt-less black back ought to be a familiar view for those with soft hands. I am repaving your roads and streets, your Appian Ways, the highways and byways you career upon murderously.

The paving crew calls me Crow because another paver's named Jim and that's one too many Jims per crew, Chief said. Chief said Chief's word is law. Jim and Crow do not question Chief. I took the crew job because there was no other. I didn't have the grades or the right attitude to work at the Wal-Mart. Then the job became my life. Head to toe to head I am a dark road to a dead end. Your dear Lord and Savior spent but forty days and nights boogieing with the devil in the desert, but I have eaten the stones all my life and the devil's hands are soft as mink.

Jim alone is a plain enough name. Crow by its crowself is a fine name, but sandwich the two together on one man and you might as well have yourself a bank account fulled up with worth-less Confederate dollars. I was near licked within a centimeter of my life and kicked out of Alabama for a name like that. Even with all these stone statues of dead white men, no one likes a walking reminder. The statues of Lee and Johnny Reb don't talk. Pa was the blackest jackwagon in Ensley, though I had an uncle wore Union blue every day of his life, which was long and ended in a gully.

Asphalt is a slow crawling liquid, like a lava flow, a nation of black bodies and emperors of pygmy empires down on their knees crawling through the broken glass of the doors to the house of many rooms spoken of in John 14:2. The roads we pave from an Alabama nowhere to the middle of nowhere are not a solid or law abiding substance you can count on not to move while your back is turned. If the road was a man, I don't doubt that it would knife me soon as he had the opportunity. But I've watched the asphalt for hours at a time, attuned to the black clock of its flux, measuring the master tick of its loitering flow against the tock of slave clocks on Peckerwood Road.

Every Monday morn Sett, a grisly freak from Prichard, comes to work, for torment looking hangdog like he been stood up or out-womaned both Friday and Saturday nights and got real extra drunk under it. Most of them probably plug ugly, barely women at all that men returning from a hundred apocalyptic tours of Iraq wouldn't take a hand job from, just gibbering mouths and cash money legs wide enough to park a double-wide.

I am curator of a collection of female store mannequins in a weedy lot behind the house. Not what you and your family might call a house, but four upright walls and a low ceiling that keep nature out of my doings, otherwise kudzu and rain will come and go as they please. The house is a shotgun, but I do not like to call my home by the name of a firearm — I have been on the barrel-end of too many white men's shotguns. Mostly a parts supply yard — an arm, a magnificent pale torso, entangled heaps of legs and a mountain of heads — the full plastic bodies are fashioned with women's skimpy underthings salvaged from dumpsters and the whorehouse sidewalks in East Lake. On Saturday, maybe Sett comes by, stinking of asphalt, and we split a suitcase of cold ones and fire off some rounds at a female torso. Crudely arranged in carnal positions, our harem of mannequins polaroided in blue jean cut-offs and skirts only a hardened whore would wear. My house is not a shotgun.

I reproduce these particulars of my privacy for the reading public so that they will know what kind of man lives among them. I am a product of your dropout factories, your prison pipelines, I've heard them called, but your lives ruined in comfort and air-conditioning will not amount to even a lesser paragraph of this paper opinion piece.

God have mercy upon the fool who ever tried to separate Sett from his bottle of Wild Irish. It was a task for Sett to work through the week without murdering a crewman. Chief, who had the perpetual expression of a man adjusting himself in public, and had a drunk driving record longer than the State's longest-in-the-world constitution, didn't care if Sett paved the streets with gold drunk as a casino Indian as long as he could lay down some asphalt, Chief's black gold.

Paving season is in full swing. We just put down blacktop on Peckerwood Road — the houses are big enough to fight a war in. I saw a brother shadowboxing on the roof of a lordly mansion. This morning I seen Sett frying his breakfast egg on the balls-hot blacktop. Three for him, two for me. I think Sett learned English in the adult cinemas on First Avenue East, and his cooking skills at a correctional facility in West Jefferson. Climax was impossible for Sett without Dueling Banjos picking and twanging from a stolen stereo in a cockroach motel. I think me and Sett's moms was spermed in one of them motels you drive by on First Avenue East — a road I have paved twice myself. You haven't seen it all till you've seen your own mother walk out of a whorehouse.

If a summer storm kicks up, we shelter under a walloping dusty magnolia or in the cab of the dump truck where we have stashed Bud Light, Coors Light and Miller Lite in a Styrofoam cooler. Sett and I make big plans: we are going to climb the Coors Light mountain and see the world from its summit. We are going to walk naked on the beaches in the Bud Light commercials. We are going to party with the girls in the Miller Lite commercials. We are going to get the hell out of Alabama.

Day before the day of which I speak we were on the milling crew grinding down the old roads, moon grey and alligator cracked with sun. The road undulant and rutted, a wrinkly epidermis like an old woman's. At night, I feel still the jackhammer vibrating my skeleton. The downtown streets at least are straight and gridded. When we got the road good and chewed up, the ancient streetcar lines in the Ensley and Oxford brick remind me of my name. Peckerwood Road is a serpentine road going nowhere.

Average road lasts about, I don't know, six, seven years, depending on such influences as climate and weather, lunar phases, stock prices, subgrade soil and truck axle loads. Seven years is not a long time if you're hitching to outer space. I am a methodist, not the religious kind, but a believer in methods to get the job done right before the second time. There's no other way, and I am the evangelist of that way.

Sett is a veteran paver, and has worked jobs repaving the banked racing surface out at Talladega and the runway tarmac at Fred Shuttlesworth International where planes from fancier cities like Atlanta and Charlotte put down. Sett liked to haw much about horsepower and machinery. I heard it from Sett that the future's got machines can do our work cheaper and faster than a crew of twenty. For a man with a horrible past, Sett talks much of the future. The driving public complains — on their way to church, on their way to funerals, on their way to work — in angry calls to the traffic department and letters to the editor that we're too slow and take too many breaks. Lunch breaks, smoke breaks, piss breaks, beer breaks, self-abuse breaks, jail breaks. Nothing else for the news to report on except a five-year round table on potholes.

But road making is tortoise work, not the running of the hare. You're up against every kind of cold-blooded wind and the weeping August humidity of Alabama's gluey air. You pick up on things. A little bit of geology here, some politics there. I like rocks more than people.

In this Egyptian heat we had well over an hour to work the asphalt, day of the day of which I speak. We worked waterlessly. The road is the only space left to the public. The public buys himself a car to put on the road, to assure himself of his existence, his right to run you over. I've obviously been blowharding through life, but behind your perceptions is a me and Sett you cannot make out anymore than you can make out the driver of the vehicle who T-bones you into the next life.

Now, I was fine with all this — the mummifying heat, the barking, shrill letters to the editor, the asphalt crawling like a snake — until you asked me to pave over my ancestors.

This I could not abide.

—You sissy boys ready to serve your country, the Chief rallied the troops as Sett and I were dining on the last of the eggs, finishing off our morning beers.

We were always pussies, sissies, or pansies to the Chief, who would've been a great little league coach if he could be trusted around small children, or perhaps a warden in one of our county's many fine prisons, where most of my dropout buddies ended up without even a G.E.D.

Chief said we'd been contracted to asphalt a parking lot for a car dealer while we waited for the milling crew to catch up. The dealer was a Peckerwood Road type and he wanted a flawless black impervious surface to park his Jaguars right across the street from Southtown, tempting all them brothers to come and kidnap or strip his cars. This car lot was to be paved on top of the cemetery where my uncle, whose life ended in a gully, was inearthed. Drunk before noon the day of the funeral, my family of fourteen and still growing shouldered the weightless coffin into a dark rectangle in the earth. But not me. I was sober as seven judges, knowing the coffin was empty. The tombstones were hilled up against a fence, grass mowed down to an asshole crew-cut.

—This ain't a right thing to do, Sett said.

I didn't know Sett felt respect for the dead, or felt anything at all except for our mannequin girls or the beer commercial girls, but he had a speck of egg white on his chin.

—Sett, Chief said, —You got any idea how asphalt is spelled?

Sett considered the spelling of this black ooze. I saw muscles contorting in his forehead, light bulbs exploding, cobwebs swept aside. Sett was in the superhuman throes of spelling a word.

—A.s.s.f.a.u.l.t. Ass fault, he said.

Any sensible member of our century could see that Jim Crow wasn't about to pave over his beloved forbears. One fine day I'm going to build something like The Great Wall of Japan around me and there ain't no way I'm coming out dead or dead. Why not just bring back the ill forgotten name of Scratch Ankle for the nigger business district? See how many peckerwoods get hard over that. Separate drinking fountains, separate restrooms, separate cemeteries, the whole nine yards.

We had about two miles of road behind us rolled and cooling when Sett stopped cold and said, —Crow, come looky here. Sett was critical of the odd roadway leavings, the miscellaneous detritus we swept up in the layby and the road's narrow shoulders. Sett's walls were trophied with Botts' dots and bollards, smashed guardrails, bumpers and fenders and stuffed road kill. He had a warm romantic attachment to a decapitated armadillo we found at a railroad crossing. In the carport was a smashed bicycle built for two, wheels bent, the dual saddles splashed in cruor.

I caught Sett hoarding shattered accident glass in his pockets. He was fond of circling the crew around a front bumper, a game in which we guessed manufacturer and model. I thought

Sett might've found another roadside object of interest to add to his museum when he waved me over. If Sett had been white, he'd have been white trash, positively. I never get too close. Sett stank of sun and tar mixed with locker room. We all did. Though I'm no longer a paver, I still smell that ripe stink even after three-hundred and sixty-five showers. When the water runs. Then it mingles with strange deodorant whiffs of highway honeysuckle, and I'm good and bad happy.

Before us was no highway artifact, but a sinkhole deep as a man's thoughts before he dies and big a round as an oil depot tank. I'd heard Birmingham was hometown to many homegrown abysses, but I'd never seen an abyss for myself. Sett edged up to the sinkhole's lip and looked down and down some more. The sinkhole bottomless as the wants of our mannequins.

My uncle committed his soul to the powers that be when he was swallowed up by a sinkhole in the West End just fourteen years to the day after I was popped out of Momma by Daddy's sister. Long after the Tuskegee syphilis experimentations, our family didn't trust no doctors. I'll go to Tuskegee one day, make the crew proud, a graduate of Syphilis University. I got nothing against doctors, and nothing against syphilitics neither.

Pavement makes us commute, work, commute, sleep. Follow the white and yellow dashed lines. I refused to be whorehoused into that life, coat-and-tied, diplomaed, licensed, napoleoned, shanghaied, inventoried or high-rised. The roads I pave are flatter than piss on a plate.

—Sett, you come away from that thing, I hollered at his big shirtless back gleaming black in the sun. I'd seen a sinkhole or three in the valley before, but not a one like this one, itty-bitty and microcosmic craters in lots and yards, nothing abyssal or downright Biblical. This hole had intelligence. Sett's sinkhole was perfectly circular and pitch dark down round the bottom. It looked almost painted on. Sett unzipped his fly and handled his member out to take a long sighing beer leak in the sinkhole mouth. We never heard his beer pee hit any bottom.

The sun brightened and stroked me. The sticky weather seemed in agreement with all that I felt inside my head: light above, dark below. Sett might jump into the hole, he had proclivities. I hadn't drunk water since the beginning of the shift and I was feeling woozy. Then I felt a silver spoon in my eyes as if one of my plastic gals had bucketed Lysol in my face, blinded like old dirty Saul by a refulgent inner light without source as in those angelic lights you see in cheesy church paintings, or the blue velvet painting of a black Elvis my uncle loved for the masterpiece it was.

Indited in the scripture of that calenture I saw the roads of Birmingham paved with a black skin of flailed human flesh, keloid scarred. You start Saul and end up Paul, my uncle said to me. A blue school bus with the back end sawed off, the city streets chewed up and spat out, our paving work undid. Sett's and my mannequin ladies on bicycles, headless, their skirts breezing up their thighs. A blue tank rolled by and an old crony in a Klan getup turned circles in a wheelchair on streets paved with a pure white tar. A dark shadow like the soul of oil blackening a great ocean. A mountain exploding, and a church bombing. I saw the city devoured by a starved, omnivorous sinkhole. The earth hankering for all that is man-made: roads, shotguns, mannequins, cars, cemeteries.

When I woke and saw Sett hovering above me I knew I wasn't dead. They wouldn't want Sett in hell. The sinkhole had closed up like an eye. Sett slapped my face harder than he should've, enjoyment rippling across his face. No one on the crew knew CPR. I got up woozily, looked around me, and turned to Sett.

—Where's the crew? Where's Chief? I asked him.

Chief was weighted with marriage fat and despite his constant sweating never dropped a pound. You couldn't miss him in an angry mob of lookalikes.

—They done felled into the hole and the hole…

—The hole what, Sett?

—It done closed up on 'em.

Sett looked shook.

—Horse shit, Sett.

—I never seen anything like it. That sinkhole just swallowed them up like a whale eating fishes. If you hadn't stroked out you could've seen it.

Before climbing Coors Light Mountain, I suggested to Sett we dig up every Negro in the cemetery and publicly display them so all could watch them spinning and spinning, rolling in their graves. A pure white tar I saw behind my lids.

I thought about my mannequin girls and what would come of

them if Sett and I climbed Coors Light Mountain. They required names, their population tripling every few weeks, my lovely plastic candy girlies. Veronica, Juliet, Mary. We had in our sorority an entire race of black mannequins, but Sett and I favored the white ones. I was partial to miss Mary. My gentle squaw. And to Lucy, so named after the *Australopithecus*. I come home to her after a hard day's paving. Sett, who had an extra sixth digit, never touched her. I thought about her milky skin, cold in the evenings before I warmed her up, and about how she would never die.

I've seen some terrible things. My cousin who lived by some philosophy of muscle gunned by the police. A dropout amigo who died in the doors of Wal-Mart, another victim of high rise prosperity. I was phoned to identify the body, which I didn't mind. He'd have done the same. A simple yes or no. Markus would've done the same for me. That's him, I confirmed, in that basement morgue, glass stuck in his jellied face. Had there been a window, I might've looked out it. The morgue was cold and I covered Markus with a white sheet. A cockroach scuttled across his face, which was bruised and battered as if he'd been stepped on by elephants. They buried Markus with the glass still in his face. So, you might think, because of all that, I wouldn't have done what I done, but I never claimed membership among the sensible of our century, cited above. But as a Dixie deathman mine is an ultramodern thinking.

This coal and iron valley is wrought all over with sinkholes and assholes. They're common as fleas. There must be a sinkhole pocked beneath the streets with my name on it: Jimmy Crow, waiting to swallow up your Father's plantation mansions of many rooms on Peckerwood Road. Yummy!

—We have to pave that cemetery parking lot, I said to Sett whose safety vest flashed at me like an orange shot from a flare gun.

—But what about your dead uncle? What about Markus who got stampeded in that Black Friday blitz?

—He'd want me to do this, I said.

The amount of asphalt will be staggering, new numbers will be invented for it. When this cemetery lot's paved under with your tax dollars at work, I'm not paving no more. But that don't mean I'm a quitter. I'm going to Syphilis University. Gentleman and a scholar. Remember my uncle, his name was Tom, may he rest in peace under your ass fault. This is my letter to the editor, a letter of resignation, and the things I saw are written herein so that those who follow after may not lose heart.

Miscreant Populations

BIRMINGHAM GODDAMN

More than thirty years may have arisen and befallen us since I was dreamily watering mom's imperishable vegetable garden that supplied our table with voluptuous summer tomatoes and autumnal squash, splashing municipal water everywhere, wondering such daft counter-factual things as what the world would be like if humans weren't humans, if water boiled at 300 degrees Celsius, or whether birds realized they were higher up than we are, what language they chirped or warbled their birdy thoughts in, and stamping out colonies of fire ants, when Dad swept out of the back of the house like a fire truck.

—Spray me with the hose, Dad barked, demon-eyed and shirtless.

—What, Dad?

Addled by his insane demand, I balked, the hose drowning an early tomato vine creeping up a wire cage.

—I said spray me with the goddamn hose, son.

His furry caterpillar eyebrows wiggled above his eyes narrow as the hole that leads to heaven, his neck stacked thick as a fire hydrant on his Apollonian torso. He would be an easy target.

I feared he might come after me, as he had before over pettier infractions.

—But Mom said to water the garden.

And before I knew what was happening I was spraying my own father with mom's garden hose, my thumb pinched over the nozzle to jettison the blue white spray onto Dad's pale back. Legs spread and hands planted against the house like a malefactor being frisked by the cops, he seemed relieved after a protracted wait.

—Use the pistol attachment, as if he was ordering the execution of a prisoner within himself.

I screwed the attachment onto the threaded nozzle and aimed the hose pistol at the back of his head and, locking it into firing position so that even if I quailed the hose would not, squeezed the trigger, the pressure powerful enough to take a baby's head off. I have since fired off many guns, not just water pistols, at the backs of unarmed fathers.

I irrigated my father, forcing something to grow out of him.

My father had recently moved us — to say we moved would be revisionist, a charge I wish to avoid; one morning we were dislodged, dispossessed like the many tribes that inhabited this land even before us — from Hoover, a hollow snowflake suburb of livid parking lots and tattered strip malls hugging the highway as if they too might be ousted, into Norwood, an all-black neighborhood on the north side of town. When we drove the moving truck through the Red Mountain Expressway I thought the mountain — a worn ridge fossilized with trilobites and opulent with a blessing of iron ore at the nethermost of the Appalachians — might fall down upon us. A three-story mansion grotesquely done up in the plantation style, an obscene and bombastic white house that loomed darkly over the street corner with its busted fire hydrant that leaked water lavishly. The white of this house was so white it made me look tanned. For the entirety of the short period while she lived there, my mother fought with her mild but lionhearted sense of adventure and pluck against the timeless and deathless dust that settled like the powdery aftermath of an explosion on the dark mahogany in her seasonal campaign to keep each room spotless as an examination room, the commodious rooms swallowing up her time even as the days elongated, dimming down towards dusk, just as she fought the weeds' coup in her garden. She was a great grower of things and her green thumb could revivify a leafless tree struck down by lightning or restore the élan vital of the drooping, dying flowers of a *vanitas*.

The other structures unbulldozed or otherwise halfway tenanted on the block were not mansions, but proper houses, Craftsman bungalows and cottages. We inhabited the big house.

It was in the back of this mansion, built for an executive of Sloss Furnaces — the pig-iron company responsible for that surreal, hellish infrastructure downtown that every Halloween was a satanic cathedral — where Dad was caterwauling a rebel hollering, his back purpling and bruising up. A concerned neighbor woman appeared crosshatched behind the wire screen of her porch and bawled at me across the privacy fence.

—I said hey what's going on over there?

—You stay out of this, meddling old cunt.

Such street language as heard at the school bus stop was my father's native parlance. Mostly he tamed his tongue around my acute ears, but when he was worked up he could really invent some ugly phrases.

—Ed, you stop spraying your Pa right now, the neighbor countermanded.

—I gone too far to go back now, Dad said. —There's nothing the boy can do. This is between me and that garden hose.

Dad's back was bleeding where the skin was chafed off, his blood marbling in rivulets on the ground, seeping into the tomatoes and fire ant kingdoms below-ground.

—Dad, your back's real bad.

—Fine. Turn it off.

I froze, the horror, unable to follow his command.

—I said turn it off!

I dropped the garden hose on the ground, cold water pooling at our feet. I do not know who turned the water off, because I never did and I never bothered again about what birds thought or what the world might be like if humans weren't humans. I watched the water gush from the hose, sunlight dappling in spreading limpid rivulets that thinned against my feet and by nightfall's accession the water was nowhere to be seen, evaporated and guzzled by the ground's many tiny mouths. The water that day nurtured the garden that burst from the ground later that season announcing the rhythmic completion of another age.

—Don't leak a word of this to your mother. Finish watering the garden, and leave the ants alone.

Dad was angry with me, though I didn't know why when I was doing as told. I felt I had just killed my first man, a patricide. From this man, sprayed with a garden hose, I honed the art of rolling with the punches and punching back when you can.

And years later I would recall my mother having to spoon feed my father, who was so stricken by the grief of his own misdeeds that food seemed an earthly indulgence. Whenever the man stepped into a room of that monstrous white house, the air thinned until it whistled out through crack and fissure and the room became a vacuum tight as a fist in which you suffocated, the very light snuffed out like a candle. He felt gusts of cold in the summer no one else could feel.

My mother, he said, looked like a zaftig bucket of ice cream and melted and puddled in his hands. He spoke about Mother in this way, as if she was a character in a D.H. Lawrence bodice ripper. My young adult notions about women were skewed until further corrected. He was mortified by fire, and many winters came and went coldly in which we near froze up, our toes curled under like dead shrimp and feet encased in blocks of ice like those high-altitude frozen mummies, the fireplace dark as the inside of a closed oven.

He took his pisses with the bathroom door not cracked, but wide open as the road to hell. He was known to be dangerous in a car. Only sometimes did he stop at stop signs, and yield signs were altogether out of the question. He downed barrels of coffee like battery acid, yet his teeth shone white as fake snow. He once passed a kidney stone without a peep or holler. I keep it to this day in a Mason jar on the mantle. Shaped like a small ostrich egg, he said if you stared into it long enough you'd see the eleven Confederate states of the South in outline, his body constipated with a bad conscience. I later caught him at his desk drafting a euphuistic manifesto that he said he intended to write in macrological microscript on the surface of the kidney stone. I tell myself now that I should've known then what was to come.

I grew up, without realizing I was growing up, without ever knowing Dad's vocation like the other dads I knew: doctors, lawyers, engineers, tradesmen, drinkers, deadbeats; what profession enabled him to acquire all the things, items and stuffs that surrounded us and made up the home environment through which we obliviously swam, slithered, crawled and walked. I knew only that he received a vigorous pension from the Birmingham Fire Department, the exact sum of which was unknown to me, and probably also to my mother who had nothing to do with the accounts at banks like Wells Fargo.

I have heard it said that we experience the world but once, in the mists and boughs of childhoods rosy or dark, and all that follows thereafter is but a memory retrieved, called up out of the dark. It wasn't until decades later that I understood the purpose of my father's wish to be excoriated by my mother's garden hose. It was a test, so simple and pure I failed it. A lesson in our unhappy condition, that man has a mean streak, and the world's worst was right here in Birmingham.

On that day, after being waterhosed, he entered his study as

Dr. Jekyll and exited as Mr. Hyde. When he reemerged, he looked like a man who'd gazed into a mirror for the first time and perhaps did not like what he saw. Then mother hid all the kitchen knives and I had to cut my sandwiches with plastic utensils that snapped in half.

Until I got older, and he could no longer stop me, I was not allowed in his office where he wallowed in his extra hours. Mother left plates of food outside his door, the way you would for a sick dog or particularly intractable asylum inmate. I wondered if my father had experienced youth, and if it had been at all like mine.

The boy I was never took my father for a reading man, until the surfeit of books overflowed in the mail. And then the manila packages turned into boxes of books and my mother stood in the shadow of the breezeway porch, arms perched akimbo on her double-wide hallelujah hips, as my father whistled through the gap in his teeth, and she said where is all this stuff gonna go? And it was stuff plain and uncomplicated to her woman's reductionism of her husband's hobby, but the very ether and quintessence itself to my father, who even then, before I could ride a bike without falling over, showed uncivil signs of being crack-brained and cratered out by his past I knew nothing of. The big white house stayed clean and the fire ants incorporated my father's blood into their subterranean kingdom.

—You hungry, son? Want a knuckle sandwich? he kidded as he knuckled my head, and the air around him crackled with faradic laughter and rustle. Not once did he open these packages in front of me.

My father was a scholar after all. He was bigoted to some Frankenstein methodology, slap-dashing and macaronic, utterly inscrutable to logic or hairsplitting. A hoarder he had been all his life, but the erudition and the catechistic earful of facts and statistics came at a time in his life when most men retired to golden days on the green sloping hills of the golf course in pastel IZOD sport shirts with tacky Hawaiian patterns, or watched spaghetti westerns and dozed off over a cold can of totally average, lite American lager.

The end started with newspaper clippings: yellowed and foxed articles and faded photos he'd scissor out and thumbtack to the wall of his study, then lean back creaking in his captain's chair to admire his artistic handiwork. An article in bold, **I SAW**

A CITY DIE, by a man named Charles Morgan Jr., was tacked, every page of it, over the windows, so the neighbors could read it, stymieing the natural light my mother's garden synthesized to push up out of the dark ground. Dad's mural of articles and clippings were his wordless way of spelling everything out for me.

The Dirty South is a disenchanted land of guilt and black milk and terror, white bed sheets and burning crosses in the front yard, the charred wood — cut from the same ugly pines used to frame your house and church — never quite cool to the touch. I've taken communion, and been a cannibal. I've listened to a lachrymose grown man preach of afterlife and angels with a straight face and not be institutionalized. This the land, that the sky. And on the third day. Set out silverware properly and orderly, and skin electrical wires for their copper clean as snakes. Never eat before a meal is blessed. Always panic when a white powder falls from the sky by buying loaves of bread and gallons of milk. College football is the second largest religion. Think in dichotomies: good versus evil, black versus white, Auburn versus Alabama, suburban versus non-suburban, evil versus good. The only thing faster than the fast food is the speed at which the future repeats the past, and the plodding tardiness with which the mumpsimus comes to this epiphany by way of ipsedixitism and recusal. Anyone who looks like they might be older than you are is yes mam or no sir. Thus I survived the disenchanted land.

After the newspaper articles were the FBI reports and declassified dossiers, Black Panther memorabilia, a life-size poster of Malcolm X brandishing an AK like a jihadist. The poster of Malcolm X had to be taken down whenever my mother had guests, and the one or two times I remember wary social workers making surprise visits to the white family in the hood. How do you know this is the hood? one social worker asked me. You know you're in the hood because we have to play basketball without a basketball goal, I whitesplained to her.

He fed tin cans of old newsreels into a film projector and sat in the dark watching grainy films flicker against the living room wall like an old movie house: Bull Connor screaming like a red-faced, goose-stepping, fist-pumping fascist, "You gots to keep yer blacks and yer whites separate!" As if blacks and whites were two highly volatile chemicals that would explode when mixed. Connor was a psychotic madman and I did not wish to meet him, but *non compos mentis* is another of the yellowhammer state's mottos. Dad screamed ineffectually back at the screen, as if challenging Bull Connor, driving my poor mother more and more out in the back yard where she enjoyed the green quietude of her vegetable garden. She stopped poisoning the ant colonies altogether.

He sat on in the dark long after the film ended. Inside, he took a vow of silence. Mother and I couldn't get him talking for a long week. He sat in his recliner with a copy of John Cash's *The Mind of the South* and King's manifesto "Why We Cannot Wait" in his lap, reading until he collapsed into sleep disturbed by black and white dreams in which slavering and rabid unchained police dogs snarled at his legs and the city was hemmed in by vast chthonian fires he could not extinguish.

Recall that these events occur some forty, fifty years after the Civil Rights Movement. Peculiar, because we're a white family. Pale, in fact. Pale as a ghost's ashes. A pale people from pale places, thinking only the palest cast of thoughts. Even today the sun will cook me in minutes. Skin cancer — the austral sun's avengement on pale people — will be my demise.

While other dads might read Shelby Foote or James McPherson's tomes on the War of Northern Aggression and history far outside of memory, my dad was steeped in history we were still reeling riven and sore from. I set off fireworks on July 4th in the lush, jungly lots where proud homes once stood, the body parts of rodents strewn around. The trauma these patriotic detonations caused my father initiated a permanent ban on fireworks as long as I lived in the big white house. While other kids were flushing weird objects down their parent's toilets (dolls, toy trucks, dad's wallet, keys, etc.) and boys were sneaking peeks at their older nubile sisters with pancake breasts — no incest taboo here in the land of Compson — and shooting pellet guns at passing cars and cats, or having pissing contests, or generally being yard-apes, I endured the Q&A inquests the gentleman scholar thought were necessary for my de-education.

—How many pounds of water per square inch can a Birmingham fire hose deliver upon the epidermis of a Negro youth? he fired away before bedtime.

So, instead of learning something useful like how many quarts are in a gallon, or the capitols of the fifty states, or how to add and subtract fractions, he wanted to know, —What was the name of the hotel in which MLK was assassinated?

—Lorraine Motel, room 306, I answered.

—And what were King's alleged last words?

—"Ben, make sure you play 'Take My Hand, Precious Lord' in the meeting tonight. Play it real pretty."

—And what is the address of the Lorraine Motel?

—450 Mulberry Street.

—What were the names, in alphabetical order and then by age, of the four little girls murdered at the 16th Street Baptist Church?

—Dad, I don't know.

His claim — never refuted — that the Birmingham Fire Department wielded hoses that could peel bark off a magnolia tree, or separate brick from mortar. I thought this was one of his geezer myths, the whoppers and tall tales told to children to put fear in them, like the warnings against having a good time in the Old Testament. I learned the biographies of men such as Eugene "Bull" Connor and George Wallace, the hagiographies of Fred Shuttlesworth (who my father argued was the real brains and brawn behind the Movement) and Spider Martin whose photographs of Selma's marches hung in his study. These men and their deeds populated his dreams and waking mind.

But I never let Dad's obsession become mine. It was common for me to tell my schoolmates my father was dead. If they asked how, I made something up. The tragedies changed, became more tragic. Brain cancer, he fell down a well, kicked in the head by a horse, hit by a meteorite, abducted by Mexican drug cartels, buried alive, ate a poisoned apple, any outlandish way a man can make his exit stage right or left. Kids will believe anything.

The more my life changed, the more his seemed to suffer from an awful backwardation, a museumification among the dust motes in the big white house. I thought my going to college at Birmingham's campus of the University of Alabama would change him, if not me, but he persisted. —You know what U.A.B. stands for, don't you?

—What, dad?

—Your Ass is Back. U.A.B. The University that Ate Birmingham.

After getting myself diplomaed, as my generation is expected to, I self-exiled up to snowy Boston, as far away from the big white house and the everlasting summers and sweet tea and the syrupy, cloying accents as possible; from the pellucidity of this Yankee distance, huddled in the gelid dusk before the rimy bronze memorial to the 54th Massachusetts Infantry Regiment on the Boston Common, I began to see my father not as a sacrificial casualty of Birmingham's regime, but as a rational actor with agency, a man on the wrong end of the hose. I too heard the breathing of bronze Negroes. The fact was, as I discovered that first spring when the last snow melted on Commonwealth Avenue, there was a wide and wholesome world out there totally undisturbed by the Birmingham Campaign and my father's feverish, sweaty nightmares exploded by homemade bombs and the broken shards of stained-glass church windows that fell from the thunderstorms that darkened the rooms in the big white house. My father did not want to be a part of that world which did not acknowledge the unplumbed depths of his suffering. I would not submit to the usual literary litany of Southern vices: whiskey, adultery, violence, bigotry, self-hatred, and noisy nostalgia. Dad was glad to hear that I was living in Roxbury, not far from where Malcolm X lived and his eponymous boulevard. In Dad's sporadic emails, words like "carpetbagger" and "Uncle Tom" appeared with alarming regularity. He claimed that the government knew beforehand about King and Malcolm X's assassinations and did nothing to stop them, like Pearl Harbor and 9/11. But my father was uninterested in large-scale national catastrophes — planes flying into buildings — the future epics of western civilization.

Any letter from my mother was worrisome; she was not a letter writer, and in these pleas for help, dashed off on an unlined piece of paper between bouts with the weeds, which always began with pulling and ended with poison, she divulged how he was reenacting the marches in Selma and Montgomery, some of the sit-ins and boycotts in Birmingham. A solo marcher promenading with lofted picket sign, Dad would prefer it that way — alone, vulnerable to attack, vanguard and rearguard, his sense of normalcy attended by what existed at the fringes. He made a weekend road trip to Memphis, a pilgrimage to the Lorraine Motel, now a museum, and tried to book a room where King had been Brutused. Turned away, he wandered like a lost, heartbroken dog the streets of Memphis, howled in harmony with harmonicas on Beale

Street while I looked for the spot, marked with a plaque I never did find, on Anderson Memorial Bridge where Quentin Compson jumped into the Charles River. I was truly fearful that my father's historical reenactments would regress beyond Jim Crow and back into sharecropping and slavery, the Civil War itself, through the nightmare of history and all the way back to Abraham and Isaac.

Near ghost himself, insubstantial and apparitional the deeper he went, he became a ghostwriter and ghosteditor of Wikipedia entries about the Movement, Project C and the events of May, 1963. Keeping track of his fluctuating obsession through Google searches, I sensed his cantankerous voice behind the editorial slants and bowdlerizations, the belligerence enabled by the Internet's anonymity. Even his shibboleth syntax and grammar were palpable in the word static. On eBay, he bid recklessly for a splinter of colored glass alleged to be from a window depicting the life of Christ at the 16th Street Baptist Church, a relic he cherished as some are said to wander deserts and ruined abbeys in search of the foreskins of martyred saints. The splinter — a red fragment — turned up among his few valuables left to me in a safety deposit box.

I saw him bent and devout over his studies, stopping blacks on the sidewalks downtown to question them, and hang around outside the 16th street Civil Rights Museum to waylay anyone who appeared old enough to have been involved in the protests of early summer 1963. He made much of the fact that I was born in the same month: May.

I realized what this was all for when in Boston — this was a few months before another bombing at the Boston Marathon would continue the family tradition of being nearby tragedy and bombings — I received a crinkled manila envelope in which I would find out what my father did for a living before I was around to shoot him at pointblank range with the garden hose, and the provenance of the pension that housed us in a big spooky white house in the black part of town. The great family secret, hushed and gagged, proclaimed in the daylight. The Oedipus Complex runs deep in Southern archetypal male psychology.

I opened the envelope and dumped out its contents: Xerox copies of black and white photos of firemen throttling young black protesters with hoses designed to put out the great fires of the 19th and 20th centuries, the conflagrations of besieged Jerusalem. The crew-cut cops raising batons, leashed police dogs straining to brunch on Negro guts. Between white official and black protester there was always a mediating object — a hose, a baton, a dog, rocks and bats — scared to get too close. I pictured my old man, back in his executive's mansion, Norwood crumbling around him, his sleep riddled by real gunshots off Norwood Boulevard, and packing this envelope with photographs that captured forever the ineffable torment of his conscience.

You've seen these photos before. They were on every newsstand in the country in 1963, and they've been a public relations crisis for the yellowhammer circus management ever since. Most of the photos were taken from behind the firemen, making it hard to identify them, but the protester's faces are clear as mug shots. I turned to a photo of a familiar-looking stranger: there was my father in fireman's uniform. We had the same jaw line. It might've been a younger iteration of myself in the photo, wielding a fire hose on young, unarmed blacks, many of them my age when I lifted mom's garden's hose against Dad. My mother would be the type to go for a man in uniform.

The last photo was of a young Negro, his back to the cameraman, in cowboy hat and a blue jean jacket with "Birmingham Goddamn" stitched over a rebel flag, a flag of a failed state I've seen on cars, trailers, shirts, swimsuits, flagpoles, and bumpers more times than I have seen the American flag. On the back of the photo I read his name — Worcy Crawford — in the same handwriting as Dad's letters. My entire childhood was instantly demystified for me. My father had done what he was told — the Nuremberg defense of superior orders — by Bull Connor, a baleful, boorish man and the cartoon villain of the era, and sprayed Worcy Crawford with the city's weaponized apartheid water until his Whipped Peter skin bled off. Included with the black-and-whites was a short note in Dad's benighted, damaged scrawl. My father was a fireman until the day he died. Norwood had house fires aplenty.

There's a man over in Ensley ran a bus company in town. He was a teen when I knew him. Took me all these years to track him down. I need you to go fetch him. Go to the address provided. I've done some things I shouldn't have done. Your mother's gone. She left the garden hose running in the yard, and I will not shut it off. Though I know how she hates wasting water. You probably

already knew that. The spoon feeding killed the romance, I ad-
mit. She stuck it out long as she could take it, any other woman
would've quit the day I closed on this boondoggle house in Nor-
wood. There are rooms I haven't been in in years. It gives me the
willies. Alone here one begins to feel like an astronaut stranded on
the International Space Station. This preoccupation of mine drove
her away. It's time to finish all that, though I have no hope of her
return. I have taken the proper precautions, arrangements made.
The house's fire alarms and smoke detectors are in working order.
I test them every morning when I burn the toast. Now I can at last
gratify a few small predilections: running the a/c at a temperature
low enough to kill the houseplants, haunting this house in a cash-
mere sweater. Your mother hated to be cold. That's why she never
came to see you in Boston. There were many multitudes of lepers
in Birmingham, but only one was ever cleansed.

Half a decade had passed since I'd last seen him: at the top of
the hackberry tree, yelling at the traffic on Norwood Boulevard
that he would not come down till my mother turned off the garden
hose. My parents had separated, sundering what they had both
agreed would be a single body until parted by death. Irreconcil-
able differences and several indifferences. My mother had it easy
in the big white house; the hardest thing she ever did was give up
three glasses of wine every night when she was gestating me, con-
tinuing to read Br'er Rabbit and Uncle Remus' tales to an empty
cradle long after it was empty. In matters of the heart, women are
braver than men in uniform. I am told by a reliable source that the
last he saw of mother were her breasts roundly pressed against the
window of her station wagon, her final valediction in a world in
which most of us never get to say goodbye. You're together until
you're not: my father's pithy explanation of the divorce. By this
time my father was old but no wiser than I was, just a fellow trav-
eler who happened to get here before I did, to have completed the
circuit of swim, slither, crawl, walk before me.

I took the first available flight out of Logan airport with a
connection in Atlanta, where I boarded a shaky biplane to Fred
Shuttlesworth International, creeped out by never seeing the pilot
of the aircraft. Hoses, aircraft, and attack dogs — I like to know
who is operating these machines. The distinction between passengers and bums at Birmingham's airport is a fine one and I felt

right at home again. I was sweating before I deplaned. Somewhere above Sherman's March, between Atlanta and Birmingham, I sat next to an interracial couple and felt less worse about what I was doing for Dad. And I think we can all agree, at this juncture of our nation's self-sabotage, when ontogeny no longer recapitulates phylogeny, that is better to be momentarily exhilarated and then disappointed for a lifetime, than it is to feel nothing at all.

Outside baggage claim, I debated stealing a bicycle leaning against the wall. I hadn't been in a car in years. I hailed a taxi and gave him the Ensley address. Ensley is another of Birmingham's hoods, a war zone with no clear victor. Ensley is the fulfillment of the prophecy in **I SAW A CITY DIE.** Whose author was run out of the state for his prognostications and philippics against The Man — "What's it like living in Birmingham? No one ever really has known and no one will until this city becomes part of the United States. Birmingham is not a dying city; it is dead" — dying himself in a tussive, chain-smoking, amnesiac stupor on the Florida Panhandle from Alzheimer's, unable to remember the first thing about fire hoses or police dogs. Dad's incriminating photos in my luggage, we booked it straight to the west side of town in search of the only black man who owned a bus, passing one house fire after another.

—What's a honky like you doing out here? the cabbie asked. Bob Marley sang about one love and Buffalo Soldiers over the radio.

—It's not my business.

I paid the cabbie and entered Worcy's property through a junkyard of buses, chrome coaches and rusting single-decker Greyhounds. One bus had *Plessy V. Ferguson* spray painted down the side. Jurassic weeds and small trash trees growing crazily out of retired, spavined buses. In the middle of this tetanus waste-yard was a small tumbledown cottage on cinder blocks. One entered by a door that might've once been a coffin lid.

A black man, a very black man, answered my knock.

—I'm here looking for a Mr. Crawford, I said.

—You looking for who, son?

—Mr. Worcy Crawford.

—What's this all about?

—It's about what happened to you in 1963. The fire hoses.

Worcy's eyes narrowed suspiciously at me. I didn't expect him to trust me.

—Just a minute.

Worcy led me through his bus graveyard and to an old Greyhound that, with some work and engineering luck, might get us to Birmingham City Jail, though not much further. I boarded the bus after him.

—I'm not a talker, but we going to talk, we going to talk in here or not at all, Worcy said. —I do all my talking in the bus, not in that house. I can't talk in houses.

I sat across the aisle from Worcy and swatted at mosquitoes. The buses in Boston were practically a different species of public transportation. This bus had a bad roof leak, and water pooled in a low spot on the aisle floor.

—These buses yours, Mr. Crawford?

—Every one of 'em. Used to bus folks round town before, during and after Jim Crow, back when it was near impossible to charter a bus with a white company. I rode folks all over, even down to Montgomery and Selma, and on up to Florence and Memphis. Rode a party up to D.C. for King's big dream speech too. Just driving beyond the city limits with a bus full up with blacks was dangerous.

—An underground bus route.

—Some called it that. I just loved busing.

—My dad wants to see you.

—What's he want with me?

—He wants you to come to the house. He lives in Norwood.

—Norwood? Thought all the whites done up and left Norwood long time ago.

—We moved in when I was a kid. Reverse white flight I think is how my Dad thought of it. He was a fireman. He might've been in touch with you.

Trembling, I handed one of Dad's photos across the aisle to Worcy.

—Your dad was on the front end of the hose, Worcy's voice filled the empty bus like water rising in a church basement. — This would've been by the church at Kelly Ingram Park. We was warned we was going to get wet. I said alright, I could use a shower. Them hoses rolled some of us cross the sidewalk and into the streets. I seen teenage girls flipped over cars. Take your shirt and shoes clean off. We bruised and scraped up real bad. When the hoses was turned on the bystanders stoned the police and threw bottles. I tell you there ain't nothing feel better than throwing a rock at one of them angry white cops. And that's when the German shepherds come gnashing at us like a pack of hunting dogs. I remember your old man there behind the water pounding our skin. He didn't look scared.

I was stunned into troubled silence by Worcy's first-person report. I wondered who would spoon feed me when I am stricken low by my own iniquities called up out of the dark.

—We need to go, Mr. Crawford. My Dad needs your help. I'll call a cab.

—No, sir. We take one of these coaches, he said, patting the dusty seat next to him.

Worcy disappeared in a bus barn and came out with a fuel can and gassed up a battered old coach with diesel, a bus that looked like it had survived an assault. The fumes were hot and rankly sweet. We piled into the coach, me right behind the driver's seat, Worcy in complete control of the bus. We herded northeast. I thought Worcy's bus would do significant, annihilative damage to anything it encountered untoward in its path: other cars, bovines, trucks, leviathans, trees, utility poles, horse and rider, houses, fire trucks.

We turned off the main boulevard curving like a serpent and onto a narrower street treed with tall aged oaks and shady magnolias that dappled the street in perpetual glittering shadow. Dad's ridiculous white mansion emerged fleetingly like a white elephant between the trees and empty lots. There were fewer houses on the boulevard now than when I first turned the hose on Dad's back.

—Which house is it? Worcy asked.

I pointed to the end of the street. —The white one on the corner.

—Got himself a plantation, not a house.

Worcy parked his coach on the street in front of the house, a senescent and derelict memory since my mother's departure for Arizona or California, some dry place with conservation restrictions on garden water, white paint flaking off the house in snowy drifts, the fire ant mounds big as wild tumors, the weeds turned to dense thickets of trees and the verduous ferocity of an untended garden making a statement against the big white house.

The front door was unlocked. Pushing it open — the old iron hinges filigreed with arabesques and curling kudzu patterns — was like entering a tomb for the first time. I called out. Only a high and empty echo. I knew he must be home, as he had nowhere else to go. We moved into the house and down the long dim hall, Worcy tracking behind me, my double, and we stopped in the kitchen.

On the kitchen table were the originals of the photos Dad mailed me. I left Worcy to ponder them, and checked on Dad's office, my first time in there in years. The office was relieved now of all the documents and newspapers, an empty white wall where the Malcolm X poster once hung.

Worcy and I came out the back kitchen door and I spotted Dad watering the garden alone, just as he must've seen me all those years ago on the day he ordered me to blast him with the hose. He was wilted, smaller and diminished, his eyes milky and clouded over, like glaucous eggs powdered in dust. The day was hot and he was shirtless, his thick chest villous, carpeted in squirrely silver hair. With Mom gone, he was picking up the watering and gardening at last, a fact of which, as I later read in the letters he wrote to her but never sent after she was gone, he was inordinately proud.

Dad recognized the young man in Worcy Crawford, the marching protester stripped of his shirt and blown sideways across the black tar pavement by his fire hose, and his Birmingham Goddamn blue jean jacket wetted a darker shade of denim. There's not another jacket like it.

—Hello Worcy, Dad said, handing the watering hose to him like it was some gift the refusal of which was more insulting than Elisha's *I will receive none* in the face of Naaman's munificence.

Worcy waffled, some esoteric scruple balanced in his mind on the fine edge of a bombed fragment of stained glass. Dad held the hose in midair, waiting for Worcy to take it and hose him down, take the skin off his back in an exorcistic and ecstatic excoriation, water bluely arcing and splashing uselessly on garden rocks and unseeded earth.

—Take the hose, Worcy.

Worcy didn't comply with my father's orders, but wordlessly followed the garden hose from where it ended, spewing water in my father's hand, snaking greenly through the vegetable garden to its source in the side of the big white house, a nightmarish creature crawling out of the house, and turning the faucet's red handle like he once turned the wheel of his coach bus, like he was going somewhere, after all the intervening years — between 1963's fire hoses and our long, hot summer — the big white house's water was finally turned off.

DEEPWATER HORIZON

It's the East India Company all over again. Stakeholders will be suing shareholders for the next twenty or thirty pollyannas around a medium-sized star. Counter-suits will make fortunes and gilded inheritances. I'll never breast-stroke or snorkel in the Gulf again. Right now, I wouldn't piss on a B.P. oilman after drinking a large glass of cold iced tea if I saw one in flames. Back at Bama's School of Law, before final exams, we used to pull the fire alarm when there wasn't even smoke.

One must have a mind of summer and yet think like a billionaire to regard the sand and palms' tarantula shadows, the Gulf sky's dividing and indifferent blue. Driving towards the spill down Hank Williams Memorial "Lost Highway," I can smell Mobile up around Creole, long before I ever see the Battle House Tower smeared across the windshield like an insect. The vomitus sticky on Dauphin Street, and salty dead fish, the olfactory hangover leftovers of Mardi Gras that will never be scrubbed off the streets, lingering still like a literal presence in a bad dream, a daymare shaped like the Louisiana Purchase.

Finally, to be rid of Birmingham, to put some miles between myself and that city that looks like a crumpled piece of paper — a death certificate, a suicide letter, a ransom note, illiterate scribblings of the moonstruck — fell out of the sky and somehow missed the trash bin. Though I have a vicious allergy to sunshine, Alice and I are early summering in our summerhouse at Seaside, an unctuous master-planned community island with but one entrance and one exit manufactured for the sake of making a point. I'm not sure where the zookeeper is. Even though it is technically the cruelest of months, Alice and I can stay until they kick us out.

I listen to Alice raconteur about a man who left the priesthood and fell in like with a woman who then became a nun.

—That's quite a story for our honeymoon, I said eying her coruscant wedding ring like an antique door knob.

—I was thinking of getting myself to a nunnery before you came along.

—Don't count your blessings so soon. Men have a lower

life-expectancy than women. When I keel over at thirty-seven from a heart attack you can take all my money and open up your own convent in Seaside. Brew wine.

—A nunnery seems like it would be a debaucherous place. All those women confined to their cells.

—They're married to Christ, who was a eunuch.

I hold my breath over the Jubilee Parkway spanning Mobile Bay. Grave of battleships. The sulfuric light intensifies. A watery, Jurassic landscape. A few nights at Seaside to get rid of this farmer's tan. Alice is not bloodlessly pale, but bleached lustrously undark, her skin thin as rice paper, a palatial skin the dreamy pallor of winter glass breathed on after killing a bottle of wine drunk in the dark.

After graduating the good old boy system at Alabama I passed the Bar Exam, on the first try with a concussion of a hangover, and became a practitioner of the fulsome law. Alabama's School of Law has graduated some nasty practitioners over the years. George Wallace. Shorty Price. Jeff Sessions. I think Harper Lee took classes there. You don't really *practice* law. The law practices you like a stringed instrument, or like a contact sport. Perfection is achieved with practice, the shopworn truism, but the law perfects only itself, transcendently leaden and ephemerally fat above you.

I cannot recall a time when I didn't loathe Florida, but the panhandle is enough like Alabama to make me feel at home. The natural habitat of Florida Man — the world's worst superhero, committing bizarre and unspeakable crimes. "Florida man run over by hearse after dog pushes accelerator." "Broward County Sheriff's Department arrests Florida man for drunken joyride on motorized scooter in Wal-Mart after eating his mother-in-law's face off." Such headlines are not fabricated and are not for the faint of heart. Aside from the kitschy pastel surf shops and tawdry palm trees, local economies built solely on a surplus of putt-putt golf and ailing package stores, there's enough bawdy blinking neon and sprawled out tacky strip malls to promote a continuum in my experience of the transitioning landscape. The only thing Florida has going for it is that the liquor is cheaper than clean water. Pick up another drink and then another drink. I imagine the feeling is mutual: Florida loathes me too.

I'd won some uncivil suits against Alabama Power, in defense of the Black Warrior River, which cannot defend itself and glows green with toxicity and radioactive goo. But I'm honeymooning right now, and not back with those talking pencil-sharpeners and apple-polishers in gray cubicles. Office towers give me altitude sickness. I should be able to put these things behind me by now.

Seaside is a theater set for a play written by Thomas Kinkade starring mollycoddled jellyfish and the anatomical spine of *homo economicus*. Where going off the grid is an expression for going to the bathroom. Sure, the naked games of golf and cyclists on rented Huffy mountain bikes are so many tokens that paradise has not been banned, and over in Panama City you can see a building — the Wonderworks — upside down. Most places look better from the air. Dress code is panhandle resort casual (floriferous Jazzfest Hawaiian print shirt and the cheapest flip-flops money can buy). Pseudo-Caribbean blues which unlike us can occur in so many different places at the same time. The panhandle's boiled peanut shacks and hinterland house trailers, the necrophiliacs in the longleaf cemeteries, Florida Man on a stolen bicycle — all are verboten by covenant here. By the time Alice and I turn onto County Highway 30A the stench of Axe body spray and Bath & Body Works is a palpable and malignant smog. I've been coming to this same beach as a child since Jimmy Carter was president, before the whale beachings stopped. A rotting whale carcass will draw humans rubbernecking long after the flies have gone home. The highest point in Florida is a landfill.

I'm sure Seaside is a great place to live if you have one eyebrow and you don't take the handicapped parking space. There's an Olympic swimming pool where you can study women's underwear. Everyone drives a golf cart. An American flag is flogged in the panhandle breeze outside the post office that deals mostly in mortgage payments and postcard scenes of daiquiri sunsets purpling over blue water like it was done in Microsoft Paint. Every sundown there is a Jimmy Buffet sunset, and half of America is inside watching Lifetime movies or flushing the toilet while weight loss commercials play. We are at our terrible best, until tar balls wash up on the white shore scintillant with ultraviolet catastrophe and honeymooners escaping a life of escapism back home.

By appearances, everyone in Seaside knows with quantum precision what happiness is and everyone possesses it in tweet-size abundance. Who am I but a dingleberry's mouthpiece to tell them that they are not? No contraindications here. Practice your backhand or unsportsmanlike conduct on the professionally staffed tennis courts. In the spring, run the Seaside half marathon. At the Seaside Chapel you can sign up for spiritualist self-esteem and team-building seminars. How to make your new condo look like a Pinterest wet dream in the Age of Aquarius. When a family from out of town prays over a meal they bless it swiftly as if half expecting God in the form of their waiter to take the meal away while their eyes are closed. The only nonwhites you see are those who by sun-tanning have broken world records for the world's darkest white person. Packed are a pair of military binoculars to watch the sunbathing mothers of the kids who attend The Neighborhood School, where they learn the names of dead white men in schoolrooms styled after Walker Evans shacks designed by Andrés Duany. They're nice shacks, the color of ice cream flavors.

Seaside's out-of-state license plates: no one belongs here, but in the way of excursionists and rubberneckers everywhere they appertain or correspond to Seaside and its agreeable glitz and its Martha Stewart color palette, so that the town looks like a photograph before any tourist pictures are taken with the obligatory Asians' peace signs, but the colors work voodoo on Alice's complexion. No house trailers here with African-titted mammies suckling a pickaninny at each inflamed breast. See Article VIX of the Seaside Covenant. Someone has to tell it like it nitty-gritty goddamn fucking is. McMansions in orthodontic pastels and creams, weltered in an architectural student's sketchbook of conflicting styles: Victorian Neoclassical Baroque Modern Postmodern Deconstruction Traditional Southern Gothic Plantation Revival. It takes a lot of money to look that cheap.

Ours is a Victorian duplex at the end of a palm shaded eco-gravel street. The lawn green as a golf course; do not disturb tiny grass dreaming. I watch Alice attack the stairs of our rental with a jaunty bounce in her ascending step, the tone of her calves and hamstrings rippling like water under her flowery skirt. Alice keys open the door and slips inside. A high, echoey room, potted palms in the corners. Multi-toned walls in vintage avocado and Space Needle orange. A ceiling fan gently stirs the air. Countertops of glittering granite and everywhere shiny new steel, modern curves and sharp angles that will cut you in the night. I don't even know enough people to fill all the furniture. Two kitchens. A boudoir the size of a three-car garage. God in heaven, we have arrived; where, I don't know, but we've arrived somewhere, the Rubicon has been crossed. I search the room for seams, a painter's brush hair dried in the wall paint, stitching in the granite, any blemish or defect that might be a symptom that I'm okay.

The bedroom is like a Catholic sanctuary, perfumed and heavily curtained. Alice wastes no time undressing, pushes me onto the bed and unknots my tie. I know she's been fantasizing about this moment since I fingered her in the car on the way down. One hand hard on the wheel at twelve o'clock, one hand working Alice to kingdom come as we pass another car wreck.

—Have you ever seen a white elephant? she asks while undoing the knotted geometry of my Windsor tie. Her breasts are level with my face, her nipples staring at me like two dark eyes met in a mirror. A glass cutter couldn't penetrate the carnelian encrustation of makeup on her face. I tell her she doesn't need it, but she applies it anyway. She really doesn't need it. She really doesn't.

Alice passes the time with her latex-gloved fingers crammed in the mouths of paying and indemnified strangers. I don't know how she does it. The dental arts are a haven for sadists. I came to her in need of a filling.

—I don't know how I got it. I never touch sweets, I lied to her.

—Doesn't matter. Maybe you pissed off the tooth fairy. Now just you lay back and let me do my thing.

She leaned me back in the dentist's chair and scraped her dental explorer against my molars, which feels the way rusted metal dragging behind a truck sounds. By the time she began drilling I couldn't feel a thing. My face was anesthetized, numb as bloated ice. I drooled understatements of silver spittle onto my chin that she helpfully wiped up with a square of gauze padding, and I foresaw her taking care of me as a demented, wizened octogenarian who cannot remember what planet he's on. This has not come to pass yet, but there's still time. I spat blood into a small paper Dixie cup. There's not much better than being hypnotized under the anodyne spell of a pretty oral surgeon. The drilling was so titillating I came back for another and then another and her phone number. After winning that lucrative case against the moguls at Alabama Power I threw her a surprise wedding and we got married in Biloxi, and I became the lame duck husband. We have smiles white as the sand at Seaside.

The bedroom window frames a panorama of undulant ocean

and blocky horizon, a suggestion of clouds scudding the sea surface, brightly colored catamarans in the Gulf where the deepwater drillers glow in the night like floating cities. Mama's boys on beach towels are working on their skin cancers, reading throwaway paperback thriller spy romance zombie novels or "How to get flat abs, have amazing sex and rule the world in 8 easy steps." Eight seems like a lot of steps for such little issuance. Hummingbirds fight over hibiscus. A young girl, perhaps eight or nine, tears bites off a slice of brown bread to feed the gangling seagulls, and I involve myself in a reverie in which I am pantsing the little girl and the seagulls' laughter is tall as an oil platform. Alice leans me back against the king-size bed, wide and soft as a dream. The bedsprings didn't make a squeak. Now I can hear the Blackhawk helicopters chopping the blue air into pieces, the stroboscopic blades reversed by the wagon wheel effect, worrying the shit-talking waves — where is King Canute now? — throwing sand in the eyes of the sun.

After dinner — fresh produce and catch from the farmer's market concocted by Alice into a meal like something on the cover of *Southern Living* — we attend a performance of *Happy Days*, a play in two acts, at the Seaside Repertory Theater. Only now do I see that we should've sauntered the beaches, popped open a bottle of champagne like good champagne socialists and rutted in the sandy lap of wind-sculpted dunes soft as shaving cream. But I was trying to impress Alice with a sophistication that was placeless in Seaside. Nothing good has ever come of a man trying to impress a woman.

Alice and I take our seats in the middle of the theater, so there's an approximately equal number of spectators before and behind us. I hate sitting in the front of a theater. All those eyes on the back of my head. She hates sitting in the back of the theater. All those eyeless backs of heads. Compromise.

The play is styled in a laughably unsuccessful realism, a risibly earnest high school musical or pantomime deliberately designed like a seaside postcard, one of those props used by carnival photographers, two holes cut out of a tableau and you stick your head in and squint into a flashbulb. In the program I read that it is a one act, one scene play with two characters, a wife and husband, Winnie and Willie. This should've been easier than it was.

If I dwell long on this play it is because it affects everything that is to come. At least everything that is to come between me and the menagerie that sustains me. I am one to usually forget a movie as soon as I exit a theater. I never dream about actresses or movie scenes. Waiting for the house lights to go down I overhear a woman ask her husband why the ocean is salty. He responds by asking her, without his face ever turning away from the sea, why there aren't more men who are flight attendants.

The curtain slides open and Winnie is plighted up to her bosom in sand. An acidic and violent light burns down the set. Winnie opens a parasol, to protect her lily-white epidermis from the violence of our middling star, but it spontaneously combusts. She is embellished with a pearl necklace that is more thread than pearls. An old present from her husband? Winnie wears a black slip and performs very mundane tasks upon herself, with which we are all familiar, like brushing her teeth. The number of times Alice has brushed the teeth of grimacing strangers would outnumber the grains of sand Winnie is sepultured in.

Two bells ring, one for waking and one for sleeping, like my banshee alarm clock Alice always sleeps through. Winnie is a loquacious female Hamlet, who might've been female anyway, or at least homosexual. She begins each morning with a misplaced prayer and then begins her routinized day buried in sand. Her material possessions, pulled one by one from a handbag, are a comb, toothbrush, toothpaste, lipstick, a music box and a revolver, which she reminds Willie he asked her to take away from him. Peer, take and place. Peer, take and place. A ritualized movement like eat, shit, sleep, in, out, in, out, drill, fill, drill, fill.

A borborygmus in my stomach upsets the theater's dignified and churchy quietude. Alice squeezes my hand. Alice would look kind in that black slip. I could bury her to her tits in sand, and I wonder — not aloud, thank God — whether I left my revolver in the glove box of the car.

Winnie's husband Willie is henpecked by Winnie, a bird with oil on her feathers. Willie is a monosyllabic man who inhabits a cave behind her, gifted with a marvelous capacity for deep and endless sleep. As all men inhabit caves, whether actual or metaphorical. Prayers perhaps not for naught. Daily before and after meals. Instantaneous improvement. A sexless, loveless consortium they have together. Willie is an auditor of Winnie's monologic thwartations; she strikes him to get his attention. Alice has never hit me. Yet, that I know of. Though I am not so proud in my virility that I would be opposed to it, under the right conditions. I try to listen to her words, even when I do not think there is meaning. Willie defines the word 'hog' for her. Castrated swine satisfied, wallowing in mire. I can see only the back of Willie's head, just as the audience behind me sees only the back of my head. I think Willie is reading an old newspaper, yesterday's news today like those skirmishing Confederates who fought on without receiving word of the surrender. He rubs Vaseline on his crotch and buries himself in headlines and erotic postcards while Winnie quotes the classics, referring to some imagined golden age when cities were worth burning and she wasn't ostriched in sand.

At the end of Winnie's days, she returns her aides-mémoire and accouterments to the black bag, leaving the gun out. *Happy day* is her mantra, her bedtime prayer. Winnie is sinking into the sand and only her head is visible now. Another happy day! The echolalia of the futilitarian. As Winnie nears the end, she sinks more slowly, and there is no release from the pain of her predicament. The more slowly she sinks, the farther away the end retreats, a histrionic allegory of Zeno's paradoxical heap: if Willie repeatedly removes a single grain of sand at a time from the heap in which hapless Winnie finds herself buried, at what time does it become a non-heap of sand? This playwright knew what he was doing, setting his play at Seaside.

The end of the play at least is finally in sight. I hope Alice isn't getting bored. I am not prepared for the repercussions of a bored woman on her honeymoon. Winnie will not cease talking, a demonic logorrhea possesses her. Winnie knows that Willie must be looking at her, but the cave husband ignores the fishwife's calls. Dapperly dressed for some unnamed event, as on their wedding night, Willie crawls on all fours out of his cave tunnel, buffoonishly grinning under a Battle of Britain moustache. A few hoots and cheers from the audience. Finally! Willie does something, but is he reaching for Winnie or her revolver? If Roy Raymond — a man who made a killing designing underwear for women who adore Popsicles — jumped off the Golden Gate Bridge, then how are the rest of us to drill our way out of Zeno's heap?

When the curtain closes, there is no applause, except for maybe one drunk thespian in the back row, just a thick stunned silence. Alice and I wait for the audience to disperse into the lobby before getting up. Arms locked together, we struggle through the crowd and into the night breeze whipped with salty air.

I pull a penny from my pocket and present it to Alice.

—A penny for your thoughts? It's all I have.

—How'd Winnie get stuck in the sand?

—That is not for us to know. I never told you, Alice.

—Is this something I should've known before we got married?

—That first filling you did. I felt it, a slight prick of pain in the tooth when you were drilling. The anesthetic didn't do the trick.

At home, our rented home, thinking how easy Willie's role must've been, since he spoke fewer lines than a haiku, I settle down on the bed and pull my shoes off while Alice clashes with something in the kitchen. I wield the shoe by the toe and from the heel I pour out deposits of sand that accumulate in a rising pyramid on the floor, like at the bottom of an hourglass. The sands are running low for all and yet we are never without sand, its store diminishing by the hour but never depleted. I have traveled through this far with sand in my shoes, though the beach has not come to me yet.

Alice is in the bathtub, like a Bonnard woman, but there's no water in it. She is pressing a tenderloin to her eye. Many more such days through which to travel.

—Is it me you're after, John? Or is it something else?

—Why not both?

—Because I didn't give you that option.

—What happened to your eye?

I recall photographically what her breasts look like, but her exact corvine features are a blur now as if she was facedown underwater. I sometimes think Alice's looks are pathological and defamiliarized. She really doesn't need it. From the neck down she is Mother Earth.

—I was opening a champagne bottle and the cork popped me in the eye. Oops.

—That's why you married me. Can I pour you a glass?

—No, thank you.

—You find sand everywhere here, I complained. —In your crotch, your eyes, teeth, your dreams. This sabulous omnipresence seeks you out, invading your most intimate places.

—Maybe you can build us a castle with it.

The bathroom — one of three — is completely Alice's. Her accouterments on the countertop: comb, toothbrush and toothpaste. Alice has written on the mirror with lipstick: *water water everywhere.*

I turn the bathwater on and let it fill up just below the bottom cusps of her breasts, burying her in water.

In the next room, I am gladdened by voices when I click the television on and scroll through the channels: an Animal Planet special purporting evidence for the existence of mermaids, or aquatic apes, some boobless movies to the local news. The anchor, a petite blond with a lisp, narrates an accident on a Gulf exploratory oil rig like she's covering a high school football game. The footage is like a video artist's splicing of *Die Hard* and *Waterworld.* Fire on water; the sea aflame. Black smoke menacing shoreward. I want to set a B.P. oilman on fire and then piss beside him. I'd change the channel but the remote is too far away. Our kids will be fascinated by all this, if kids still exist, and we don't use the jump-up-and-down-on-the-bed abortion method. Only in the Gulf of Mexico is this possible. I picked the wrong week to stop sniffing glue.

My ear pressed to the bathroom door like a doctor's stethoscope, I listen for Alice's breathing or splashing, a moaning, a groaning. Any sign of life.

—Hey Alice, I say to the door.

Out of some perverse suspense, Alice hesitates to reply, but when she does her voice comes as asphyxiated and sandy,

—What is it, John? She somehow sounds closer through a door.

—There's been an accident in the Gulf.

—The Gulf *is* an accident, John.

—We don't want to throw the baby out with the seawater, do we?

—Unless the baby is dead.

—*Quod erat demonstrandum.*

—What happened?

—An oil rig exploded.

There is always one sober party to worry about events going badly. Over the Gulf an electrical storm pulses angry strobes of evanescent light; the power blips down and I hear Alice splash in the dark. The bathroom door remains closed between us. She didn't play with dolls enough when she was a child; a gabled Victorian doll house, gingerbread scrollwork, tediously built over many by her father, but no dolls in the house, she once cried to me. By the time her father finished the doll house Alice was too old for it.

I ghost through the sliding glass door, left open, down a set of stairs to the beach's cold sands. A bonfire burns up the beach. Midnight in this place sighs soughing like the slow migrations of sand dunes blown before the promissory wind. The waves' syntax is unintelligible, disintegrating in doubtful patterns onshore. Baptized by the night, the constellations of my youth are now nameless to me and my feet disappear in the sands' quickening suck, each night's myth's hero dissolved into one continuous scattering of starlight. Orion and Hercules and Perseus who slayed monsters are all dead. Watching Venus set is like watching a beautiful woman tortured to death night after night. If only all the lights of Panama City and Destin could be turned off. Already the waves are pushing the oil shoreward; not even Hercules or knowledge of Laplace's tidal equations can stop it. King Canute the Great, ruler of Seaside. Lightning strikes an offshore rig. Only Seaside is powerless, it seems. I turn to the dark beachside condos and the red eye of a laser pointer dances over my chest and is gone over water. Behind the bathroom door Alice is curled up in the dark in the fetal position, swimming with dolphins, mermaids and seahorses.

The next morning my dreamless sleep ends the moment of sunrise. Alice is still in bed after a somniloquent night in which Willie's name was invoked. She's an eloquent girl in her sleep, psychobabbling at night about what is too bright to be seen in the day. I check my shoes for sand, and drop in at the post office to check for any mail forwarded from the firm. The postal flag should be flying at half-mast, for the oil rig workers killed in the accident, but it's as unashamed and priapic as the flag raised over Iwo Jima.

After tanning all day Alice's skin is smooth and dark as new asphalt. Broken ceramics cobbled into a woman. The tanning lotions sparkle like a tin roof flashing in photons. She suns in a beach chair set in the low-tide shoals, her feet stabbing into the flesh-colored sand burying her only as high as her svelte ankles. Ogled by flatfooted fat men waddling in speedos. Curlicue hair on muffin top porcine bellies like black barbarous squiggles marked on with a Sharpie. Every day she comes home a little darker than the day before, a little more doleful she can't go in the water.

I scrutinize the mute, accusatory objects that fill the living room of our condo. The couch, the talking head of a TV, wall-to-wall carpets, the bed, the bathtub Alice prunes in. Alice herself, an inscrutable object. These are the possessions I take out of the black bag in the morning. I sit on the sofa, catching some indirect sunlight reflecting off glass and mirrors, and harken to the chorus of the cacophonous objects about me.

There's oil in all of it: couch, television, carpet, bed, tub. Our skins are thick with it. Alice and I curl up together on the oil-covered couch and watch the spill on television like it was a romantic comedy with an ending that might not be funny. Black oil drips from the ceiling, oozes down the wall. The tub fills with a blackness like liquefied night. The kitchen faucet runs oil. Out there in the Gulf, out of our shore-bound sight, are black columns of future energy billowing an exit off the seafloor, never warmed by our resplendent days in the sun. The blond news anchor calls it a blowout on the news channel. Engineer's doublespeak for a well wild with a malicious need to sheen on the watery surface. The atramentous spill is burned off in patches of firewall that smoke and roil under a bluescreen sky. It all seems scripted for a Frontline documentary. They write the script, create the disaster and then produce the documentary.

—They'll have it capped soon, right? she asks, running another bath to wash the sun tanning lotion off her skin.

—They'll have it capped soon, I white-lie to us both.

—Willie.

—Who's Willie?

—Isn't that a Britishism for penis?

—Yeah, I guess it is. How much has Alice been thinking about that damn play?

—You're getting some sun, I say to change the subject.

—Do you like it? She holds her bronzed arms out in front of her. Two long golden snakes around my neck.

—I like that ring on your finger. Where'd you get it?

—Just some loudmouth lawyer.

—You better stop the tap before the tub overflows.

I came back later to find Alice asleep in the tub, the floor inundated with water.

Alice and I have been summering at Seaside for over a month

now. Still they have not shut off the well. We play contact Scrabble to pass the time. I buy more tenderloin for her black eyes. Yesterday, I spent a half hour telling a blind woman on the beach how good looking I am — for fun. I watch a dog defecate on an immaculate croquet lawn. The dog crap is gone the next day. Tourists take a guided tour of nature with binoculars and Audubon guidebooks. The car was missing from its spot in front of the beach condo. I had to get out of there. I look up at the sky and the sky isn't there. The sand in my shoes abrades my feet. I'm a good ways outside of Seaside when a flatulent retiree stops a golf cart next to me and beeps the sheepish horn. Of course, I would be picked up by a mossback with a fake tan, not some hot housewife out looking for a good time.

—Need a lift? he asks.

He's wearing argyle socks with sandals. Not the two-toned spiked shoes the golfers shod around in. Reminds me of my father, not in a good way. A soft yellow Brooks Brothers sweater and a watch that could be a down payment on a house here. He's an antique, but not too moth-eaten, and he could probably outrun most guys my age. Sinewy liver-spotted arms. The sky is still that bluescreen color in a studio, and we could be anywhere.

—I was raised not to take rides from strangers.

—Where's your car?

—Parked somewhere, I return to him, looking around as if lost.

—I once hotwired a car.

Please, tell me about the time you stole your uncle's car when you were fifteen.

—Yeah? How'd that work out for you?

—Made it only five blocks before the engine died on me. Couldn't have picked a worse one to hotwire.

—Couldn't have picked a worse time to vacation at the beach.

—Ain't that the goddamn truth. You going to hop in or stand there and bake like a cake?

I slide in next to the veteran.

—Where you going? I'm on my way to Hooters. Want to come?

—Hooters is a titty bar for Baptists. Guess you can drop me off at my car.

—You can pretend to be Catholic then.

—It's parked at that wine bar by the post office.

—Leave it there last night?

The golfer swerves around an ice-cream cone melting on the pavement. What old man swerves to miss an ice-cream?

—My wife Sharon and I shared a bottle there last night.

The old golfer wipes sweat from his forehead with a plaid kerchief. Sharon is an ex, but I have a thing about telling my wife's real name to a Florida Man who picks you up in a golf cart on a state highway. Florida Man takes joyride on golf cart in Seaside Wal-Mart after clubbing Alabama attorney to death with a flip-flop.

—You had a bottle each you mean, he corrects me.

—Your intuition is good for an old man.

—Men should pay, ladies should lay. Is your girlfriend single?

—If yours is.

—What are you doing here, anyway? In Seaside?

—Honeymooning.

—My wife's parked around here somewhere. She still sent me happy anniversary cards after we were legally kaput. We tried to get divorced. Just didn't work out. I tell everyone that I have a failed divorce.

He laughs at his own unlucky joke. Vultures descend on the ice-cream cone.

—She must be a lucky woman, I suggest.

The golf cart pokes along the lane at a calm fifteen miles per, maybe less. We cruise by a set of six tennis courts where you can look up short tennis skirts when the girls put their weight into the ball. The old man whistles and toots his horn.

—Give 'em hell, girls.

—What do you do? I ask my driver.

—What does anyone around here do? Used to be in radio. NPR. I kamikazied my career when I played gospel over the airwaves for three straight days after locking myself in the studio. A great joke on the producers, rabid liberal atheist types, but I really had to fall on my sword after that one. After that got into oil futures. I'm a shareholder in British Petroleum.

I tried to recall whether I'd ever heard three days of gospel music on the local NPR station.

—Aren't you worried about that?

—Exxon got a slap on the wrist after Valdez and came back stronger than ever. Spills happen all the time. Cost of doing business. Cheaper to clean up a spill now and then than to prevent them in the first place. That rig was made in Korea, you know. One more reason to bring manufacturing back home. Right before the rig exploded, maybe even that night, I had a dream I was on Mount Sinai. I bet Moses had one hell of a view up there. Then I woke up to tarry beaches at Seaside.

Same view down here. Some people mistake the dog collars that choke them for angelic halos.

—Unless it was cloudy that day on Mount Sinai.

—You're a glass half empty kind of guy.

—You're assuming there is a glass.

—Could be worse, fellow. You could be black.

So it was that kind of conversation — an old man corners you in his golf cart at 15 miles per hour to enlighten you with his views on the world.

—I could be that glass. Or that melted ice-cream cone back there. Or one of the dead rig workers.

—If I was black I'd move to Belgium. Of course, if you're American black, you probably don't know where Belgium is.

—Didn't Belgium have colonies in Africa?

Thumping along a sandy road in a golf cart with a geezer more garrulous than Winnie was not my idea of a vacation. I can get this back at the office.

—We should just evacuate the continent and turn it into a landfill. Everywhere has been or will be a colony. The seafloor is a colony. My wife is a colony.

—We'd fill it up with trash pretty fast, I think. But American fascism makes the Germans look like choir boys. We all want to be told what to do.

—Watch yourself. I fought against the Nazis. It's never too soon for comparisons like that. And no one will believe you anyway.

—Because the Nazis have more cultural capital than the Museum of Modern Art.

—You're a PhD man. I can tell.

—What do you mean?

—Pretty Huge Dick.

The man chortles, but I try to suppress my disgust and move over on the golf cart's seat before he starts patting my thigh. As if I hadn't made ribald jokes like that in fraternity houses. We once locked a live cougar in the room of a pledge who had an online thing for older women.

I listen to the ancient golfer tell a bar joke about a black woman who locks her door when she sees a white man in a business suit idling in the car next to hers. He's probably told this hundreds of times to people he barely knows.

—Where'd you go to school? I ask him just to change the direction of things. He could say West Harvard State Community College for all I care.

—Doesn't matter. We've educated ourselves into imbecility. Don't get me wrong, friend. I love it here. I love that I can walk into a Dunkin Donuts and get any one of like fifty donut flavors. If that ain't the American Dream I don't know what is.

—I thought all you needed were chocolate and glazed.

—Where would we be without options?

We motor by some million-dollar houses the color of that melted ice-cream cone back there. Everything here the color of melting, Florida is a tropical color hallucination. Turquoise and salmon. The Home Depot back in Bama only sells red, white and blue paint. Driveways paved with shucked oyster shells. Then the wine bar Alice and I closed down the night before. The bar was doing steady business because of the closed beaches, and everyone talked about the oil rig explosion. Some claimed to predict it in the auguring flight of seagulls and the oracles of sand. The play about the woman, if it was about anything, buried to her neck in sand all but forgotten, overshadowed by an awesome spectacle of foundering infernal infrastructure. I didn't even look at the tab. Now I remember losing her in the dark as she took her heels off and walked barefoot in her impossible skirt on the side of the road, a statue of Venus, born from the sea, floating in moonlight, the Gulf transforming into a lubricated black lagoon. She fell asleep on the lawn of one of these melting pastel houses, and I carried her the rest of the way home. Alice was lighter than a seabird's bones.

—The houses here make me think of sherbet and gingerbread. Like you could eat them, he fantasizes aloud. He pulls the golf cart up next to the only car in the lot, my paid-for Mercedes SUV glistening in the sun like the skin of a woman sunbathing.

—There she is.

—That's a nice car, my chauffeur says admiringly.

I don't know whence the caprice originated, but before I can stop myself, —I'll sell it to you.

—How much you asking?

I knew my price.

—That watch.

The old man looks at his watch as if I've asked for his wrist; he considers, then unclasps the watch.

—I was wondering when you'd ask. You been eying it ever since I picked you up. Did you see the sign? he asks, handing the watch to me.

—What sign?

—The sign in the wine bar.

—Must've missed it.

—It says, 'Money has no enemies.'

—Cute. Is that in Proverbs? I'll buy up some billboard space in the Panhandle with your slogan on it. So folks driving into Seaside will know they have no enemies.

The watch feels meaningful and corporeal in my hand, like a baby bird. I fish my car keys out and toss them to the old man. He tosses them up and down, testing them, the keys jingling like coins in his palm. He extends a hand and we shake good on the deal, offering to drive me home in the SUV Alice and I made whoopee in at a gas station on the way to Seaside. In the firm, we say that handshake agreements are worth less than Confederate dollars.

At the rental condo, lady's underthings are draped over a lampshade. The place has either been ransacked or Alice is unsubtly sending erotic messages. I click on the TV. The well still isn't capped. It's going to be a long summer indoors. I hate it here, but I never want to leave. I pour a drink and then another drink. I don't really need it. The news makes me drink.

Oil containment booms have been thrown up around the perimeters of sensitive islands. With fisheries closed the beach towns are spilling over with irascible fishermen and drunken fights break out. I should start a rogue nation, maybe right here in the panhandle, and declare war against the United States, so I can be roundly defeated and then be the recipient of USAID, foreign investments, letting others completely rebuild me, the Sand Mouse that Roared. I am waiting for Google to acquire a country or establish a lunar colony. Buy real estate there and bunker down: no botched honeymoons, no weird minimalist high school plays, no geezers in golf carts telling you how it is. Just a pair of Google Glass that can edit the oil off the beach.

Alice breasts into the kitchen in a picturesque two-piece. I reel her in by the waist and pinion her against the granite countertop. She still doesn't know I sold the car for a wristwatch. Through the window over her shoulder the sea seems calm and ambrosial with colors like in Matisse's *The Open Window*, hanging on the bedroom wall, and *Seated Woman, Back Turned to the Open Window*, hanging in the bathroom, which could be Alice if she had shorter hair, and no matter where I look the Gulf of Mexico confronts me. The sea's black omnipresence can be felt in windowless rooms, but the sky when I look up is still not there.

—I want to go swimming with you, John.

—We can't go in the water.

—Surely there's something they can do to turn it off. They could have surveillance technology implanted in our colons and fallopian tubes and they can't turn off a well? We turn lights on and off all day.

—I don't think it's as easy as flipping a switch.

—You should at least stop watching that dreadful news. It makes it worse. I can't stand to see that black smoke everywhere.

I reach around Alice, and I think she guesses I am going to push my mouth into hers and penetrate her while she's seated on the countertop, but I plunge through her for the tap handle below the sea-view window and turn the water on. It trickles like a leak at first and then spurts forth in a foaming blue column from the spout and gushes babbling down the drain and to the sea as I leave Alice alone with the raving spill slickening on the TV because no one turned it off.

The world is not merely dark when I wear my aviator sunglasses to the beach. No one in Seaside ever gave a hoot about wetlands until now. I've seen Seaside t-shirts all over the country. On a portly old man in a Michigan airport. On the subway in Boston. Hanging on the rack at a thrift store in Scottsboro. Men have been buried in Seaside t-shirts all over the world. Women have been brutalized wearing only a Seaside shirt. They've been cut with medical scissors off the torso of an identified body. Seaside shirts found floating on oily black water.

Alice is laying out on a lawn chair, her feet towards the sea like everyone else. Miles of beach and thousands of pairs of feet, some ugly, some fetishes, pointed at the Gulf. As if, at a precipitant notice, they could leap from beach towels and beach chairs and run headlong into the sea. Temporary emerald waters lap white sands foot-printed and then discreated by the effacing ocean. When the tide swings out to sea like a hypnotist's watch on a chain I can never tell if the sand is rising up or the water disappearing down a drain. Sea oats bend in the wind toward the water in which dogs splash and will soon be blackly anointed with amassments of dark energy.

Children are throwing tar balls at each other like a new sport, and shouting songs, making the best of things. A man buries his son up to the neck in sand. Some angry old man's yellow *Don't Tread On Me* Gadsden flag flies abreast of the red surf warning flags ignored by the swimmers. The snake on the flag is coiled about nothing. Some football fan has carved LSU in outsized letters in the sand. Are you sure that's the message you want to send to whatever intelligence there is above? Dead fish, glazed eyes reflecting a yellow sun, wash ashore in oleaginous droves. A Coast Guard helicopter chops over the beach and low in over the water. Not guarding the coast, but leering at bikini sunbathers, hovering low enough to blow your beach umbrella away. What would happen if I sunbathed supine, head towards the sea, feet aimed at the hinterland, in flagrant violation of an unspoken Seaside code of beach conduct? What if Alice wore mismatched bikini pieces? What if the well were capped today? The more it leaks, the more money I stand to make litigating on behalf of the Gulf, an innocent bystander of the Enlightenment.

We are all alumni of some Utopian experiment that failed in the past, leaving us buried up to our necks in tar balls without knowing how we got here. I felt my cavity smart with pain, the one Alice had drilled and filled. Is the silver crown coming off? What dark gas would billow out of my carious netherworlds?

Alice is so sun-dark she seems to be another Alice. The strange light above us has darkened and doppelgängered her. Having shed the pallor she arrived with as I grow paler. I should have brought a tighter shirt.

Back at the office, on the twenty-seventh floor of the Wells Fargo tower, a deluge of memos and while-you-were-outs. My Microsoft Outlook account maxing out its storage capacity as the in-box fills up. Nature is suing for peace, and I'll be there to help them clean up this mess. We'll have enough blowback business to sustain us into retirement, deep in the black, when we will return to Seaside, perhaps forever. No longer to plough on Sunday. If there is any retirement, if we are not still cleaning up after ourselves. Everywhere the future isn't still climbing out of the cystic rubble of the past.

I look down at the fine crystal watch ticking on my wrist, muffled like a watch ticking inside a corpse. Traded locomotion for time. And then at my fine new wife, her brown cinnamon jacuzzi body and the lighter ghost of the golden band encircling her ring finger. The door knob wedding band on the granite countertops beneath a fan pointlessly turning air in a cold, empty room. Alice has brought a pitcher of iced tea in a cooler and I imbibe a glass and then another. Things will be different for us and just as they ever were in a dapple of uncertainty. The well's gash is still gushing, and may gush for many pollyannas to come. We will coexist peacefully with our contradictions and each other, the bettering demons of our chameleon supernature. Will all Halliburton's ocean wash this oil from my hands? Rather my hand will the deep blue sea incarnadine. Verily, he who has no arms to wave down the ancient mariner has the cleanest hands.

—Can you toss me that suntan oil, darling? Alice asks, her face shadowed beneath her wide sun hat. —It's just out of reach and the sun is something fierce today. When did you want to go home, John? I never want to leave. The water is beautiful today, sheets of waved glass overlaid into a moiré pattern. The seagulls are a nice touch, don't you think? Our neighbors hate them, but I don't mind them. I want to be at Seaside forever. I don't even notice the helicopters and the tar anymore. But maybe we should leave before a hurricane comes whirring through the Gulf and splashes all of us in oil. Wouldn't that be a disaster? This beautiful little town blackened like that. Did you say when you wanted to go home? John?

She still doesn't know I traded the car in for a bigot's watch. Against my better half, I look a final time in the direction of the blackening water. No green light shines beacon bright over the Gulf. An unparented child has been shoveling sand onto Alice, and she is buried ankle-deep, with enough sand left to finish the job.

—We're not, we're walking, I say as I crawl from my cave towards her over the hot sands, palms and knees burned on all fours to dig her out of the third person she has become, before she sinks into the serotinal sandy happy days which we solemnly believe are hallelujah bound just ahead of us.

Deepwater Horizon

TILTING AT WINDMILLS

The days windier than ever before, the discordant white pines and magnolias brushed with breeze, restful and pacific no longer. I steadied myself inertly against a wall, succumbing to another bout of vertigo. The trees thrashed now at all hours. The late air balmed and autumnally crisp, I listened to the windowpanes vibrating in their frames, the pressurized ringing in my ears. The wind consternated the trees until the leaves browned and made their final floating susurrus earthward.

I needed two sleepless nights to connect the state-of-the-art premonitory winds with what I saw earlier that week: the convoy trucking the long white turbine blades through the streets like an army mobilizing for war. When assembled, those towering, three-armed fans whirred like locusts inside my brain. The wind turbines, blowing west, had an altitudinous effect on me. I could never get enough air, nor did my feet seem to touch the ground. A zephyr of nausea followed me like an abused dog wherever I went. Shadow flicker and strobing crept up the walls at the same hour each day. I could *feel* sound. The only description of it: pure sound. The sound of the wind right through me. Time slowed to a torpid drip.

It may have been Columbus Day. I decided to celebrate by walking into someone else's house and telling them I live there now. I picked the house in the Tudor style across the street, where I'd seen lights on inside before. Maybe the power company, for whom I punched a clock on the nightly grind at the Powell Avenue steam plant, kept the Tudor's lights glowing as an act of charity. As a tax write-off we kept the lights on at the Alabama Theater, Colonial Bank and a few area hospitals like Cooper Green where they treated the wounded and casualties of some protracted, unwinnable belligerence and sanguinolency that has been raging since the city's beginning. One of these nights, I told myself, I was going to really punch that clock and see if time gets back up off the floor.

I crossed the street, looking both ways before crossing, not that there was any traffic, but pedestrians had been killed on our

100

street before, the wind at my back. Hit-and-runs go unsolved here all the time. I knocked, waited. No one answered. I reached for the knob and the front door was open, so I let myself into a windless flagstoned foyer darkly lit.

A single abstract oil painting hung on the wall. I read the artist's name: Robert Motherwell. Some simian with a brush I'd never heard of. A somber and moody painting, graywash turpentine-thinned background, pensive splashes of black in the upper left corner. The gray color field was centered by a rectangular construction open at the top, the bottom line dripping black. I wondered how much money the owner had paid for this color philosophy on canvas.

I parked my carcass on an antique empire couch, framed in gleaming golden oak with a diamond pleated back upholstered in academy fabric, a rococo object crafted for looking at, not sitting. At least it looked antique. Not everyone with money has taste. A woman, rococo as the couch, emerged from a room, bath towel wrapped around her like a short skirt and her hair darkened by water. The mirror on the wall steamed from her hot shower.

—Who the fuck are you? she blurted when she saw me sitting on her precious couch.

—I'm Columbus. I live here now.

—I'm calling the police, she said with deadpan, even deadly sangfroid.

She seemed more agitated than alarmed or threatened by my intrusion, almost bored as she covered a yawn with a delicate white hand. I could see the curving fold of flesh where her breasts bunched up beneath her hands.

She did not seem to feel the self-consciousness that the toweled experience before the wholly dressed.

—You aren't even going to ask how I got in? I asked, crossing my legs.

—I left the front door open. You walked in, dummy.

—Why do you leave the doors open for strangers to walk in while you're showering?

—I thought the neighborhood was empty. Most people moved out, or the power company bought them out.

—How do you stand the turbines?

She stopped in the doorway to the next room, leaning against the jamb in roomy darkness. Framed like that, in the dark doorway, she might have been a modern odalisque in a painting, neither exiting nor entering the room.

—The what?

—The blades. The wind.

—Oh, those things, she said diminishingly, as if they were mosquitoes or household pests. —I keep the blinds drawn. What did you say your name was?

—I said it was Columbus and I live here now.

—That's funny.

—Why is that funny?

—Don't you know what today is?

—I guess it's the first Monday of the month. I heard them testing the tornado sirens this morning. Or maybe it's Wednesday, I can't tell anymore, I confessed more to myself than her, looking at my tenebrous, wavy reflection in the window across the room.

—Columbus Day.

—That's right. We're celebrating. I came here to celebrate. Did I tell you I live here now? Get the hell out of my house.

She laughed through her nose.

—Excuse me?

—I said get the fuck out of my house before I call the cops.

—Look…Columbus. I don't know who you are, but the news said there's a serial rapist on the loose in this part of town and I haven't seen the police sketch, but you need to leave. If you go quietly, I won't call the cops, even if you already raped some other woman in a bath towel.

Then I heard the turbines whipping the air softly, which seemed to remind her of something.

—Wait. I know you. You're the guy who killed that couple with steam, she said with a deer in headlights look.

I thought perhaps she recognized me from the local news station, unless *The Birmingham News* had already done me the favor of printing my obituary.

—I didn't kill anyone, I defended myself.

But their death was partially my fault. I'm the safety engineer for the steam plant and the steam I regulated was the steam that killed the couple, boiling them in their car. Call it dereliction of duty, call it the wrong place at the wrong time, call it a cascading failure, call it For Want of a Nail, but I couldn't shirk accountability.

—Yes, it's you. I thought so. Your photo was in the paper.

—They're saying I killed those people?

—They're saying you had something to do with it. Negligence. Oversight.

—Why don't you just pour cold water on me and ruin the celebration for everyone.

She shifted her weight against the doorjamb and her movement, a subtle shift in pressure, evoked my situation in all its vivid dimensions. I had waltzed into this woman's house, a neighbor who I had never seen up close before; a serial rapist was on the loose, these winds were harrowing my faculties, and I was culpable for a ghastly accident.

—Didn't there used to be a woman living with you? What happened to her? A wife?

—My wife? No. Girlfriend.

—Sure. Your girlfriend.

—She left.

—Because of you? she said knowingly.

—Because of because, because of her, because of me, because of the turbines. I have trouble distinguishing between the turbines and myself these days. What was your name again?

—I never gave you my name, and don't try to change the subject.

—What should I call you then? Isabella of Castile?

—Ellen. It's Ellen, Columbus.

—Thanks for visiting.

—You're in my house, she said to convince herself.

—You seem less perturbed by this than you ought to be.

—How do we celebrate?

—I take whatever I want.

—Let me put some clothes on before you pillage.

Ellen crossed the room on the balls of her feet, and I watched her ass wag beneath the white cotton towel and disappear through a door and I adjusted my crotch. Happy Columbus Day.

I got up from the couch and browsed the room. Crockery and sterling tableware and Wedgewood in a glass display case, family heirlooms. A parlor grand piano I hadn't noticed before in a corner, under a sheet like a car under a tarp. I doubted she could play it. I used to play myself. Dirges and funeral marches. I looked at my fisted right hand, opened and closed the fingers. Punch a clock.

I sensed the wind pick up outside as it blasted the side of the house and rattled the fenestella glass that was set high up in the wall. I fetched some earplugs from my shirt pocket and crammed them into my ears, softening the vertigo.

I wandered easily into the kitchen, opened the fridge. The light was dim, but I made out a menu of recherché wines, olive and cheese. Why is it that the rich always seem to live on wine, cheeses and olives? The kitchen was flooded with light reflecting off an island glass-top stove, high windows overlooking a ravine running precipitously through the back. There was a copy of *Don Quixote* open on the kitchen table. I read aloud, hearing my own muffled voice as if the mumbled words were argued through a fan:

> *'Though you flourish more arms than the giant Briareus,' I will make you pay for it. So saying, and commending himself with all his heart to his lady Dulcinea, begging her to succor him in his plight, well protected by his little round infantryman's shield, and with his lance couched, he advanced at Rocinante's top speed and charged at the windmill nearest him. As he thrust his lance into its sail the wind turned it with such violence that it smashed the lance into pieces and dragged the horse and his rider with it, and Don Quixote went rolling over the plain in a very sore predicament.*

I closed the pages on the bookmark — a photo of Ellen and another man I didn't recognize — and put the book down on the stove while spinning shadows flickered across the wall as though a helicopter was landing on the lawn. The oscillations, shadow to light, light to shadow, such that the two became indistinguishable, produced a buzzing vibration in my head. The long white blades I saw lorried through the gridded streets weeks before: Alabama Power was maneuvering to corner the wind market. Their engineers had installed a wind farm on the ridge of Red Mountain to catch the wind, just a thousand feet above my turf, now that the mountain's iron ore was depleted and the mines closed. The steam plant where I punched the face of the clock was being phased out for safer, greener forms of energy. Safer, greener, windier. Perhaps a world operated by technocrats and muckworms will find room for us after all.

Ellen re-emerged, sweeping into the kitchen like a tempest, her footfalls like two stones clicking, having exchanged the white towel for a backless dress. I wondered why she bothered to get dressed at all, but women have more complex ideas on the subject of foreplay.

She stalked up behind me and pulled the orange earplugs out of my ears and said she was happy to have me as a guest. The wind loudened. She seemed not to walk, but to mortally whirl, opening cabinets, banging around in cupboards, then decanting red wine into two long-stemmed glasses — all in one continuous zephyrous motion.

—Cheers, she said, holding up her glass.

—Cheers, I returned. —To Columbus Day.

—Columbus Day.

She had polished off the second glass and was pouring a third behind my back as she wrapped her arms around me.

—You're a very handsome rapist, aren't you, Lee?

Ellen rested her pretty head over my heart that rhythmically beat with the darkled pulse of the shadows dancing like Shiva across the walls.

We sent a man and his wife to the burn unit after an underground steam pipe burst and boiled them alive like lobsters. Horrific accidents happen; you can't plan for everything. Freak accidents occur maybe once or twice a lifetime. Birmingham is a city of freak accidents. The idea, what I'm paid for, was to plan for the accidents so that you can control them. Whether its designing a guardrail around a hairpin turn so a motorist doesn't go throttling over a cliffside and into the treed darkness below, or drafting a comprehensive safety plan that anticipates all known hazards based on real-time experiences, the industry's stock of accepted facts.

Everyone secretly hates a safety engineer, because he is always the harbinger of bad news, the way the solitary survivor of a crash is secretly loathed by the family members of the departed. This doesn't work, that design has to be modified to comply with codes. Sometimes I think they want people to get hurt on the job so they can justify cutting you a check. If someone breaks a leg, that means you're not doing your job, but they need to keep you on anyway so no one else breaks a leg. Software, toxicology, mechanical problems, statics, fluid dynamics, redundant systems, federal and state safety requirements, social statistics, all in one day. Safety engineers have a certain level of professional immunity from disaster. Freak accidents happen, you explain to attorneys and family members; progress has a social cost; they didn't read the hazard signs, the Globally Harmonized System of Classification and Labelling of Chemicals, whatever excuse gets the job done.

In the engineering investigation — there's always an "investigation" — an overlong, overweight and overwrought document that is dilatory to develop a final sequitur, I blamed the superheated steam escaping to street level on a series of faulty relief valves, a half-truth and therefore only a half-lie in this city of half-light, where everything remains unfinished or underground. If you frame the steam in scientific terms it seems more innocuous, controllable. Superheated water phases into steam. The steam spins a turbine driving an electric generator.

It was an open secret that the relief valves were older than anyone who worked at the plant, and it was only a matter of time before that subterranean steam sought relief and made its explosive way to the street under somebody's parked car like a geyser. I never used the words "boiled" or "lobster" in the report. In a landlocked city, I hate seafood. And the Gulf oil spill has decimated the seafood industry — big deal. Ducking the wind nausea and the tossing days spent sleepless and agog before the accident, I cited budget cuts, explained that it's costly to retrofit safety improvements into an inherently unsafe, antiquated system. I blamed everyone and everything, but I did not blame the turbines, nor name the true author of the disaster.

Bill, the plant's foreman, complained that his game of golf had not been the same since the horizontal-axis wind turbines completed their first revolution in September and were blowing his balls all over the green. The guys laughed heartily at that. I expected the foreman's white balls to disappear into the skies, galed westward into the upper atmosphere and splashing down in some rich bitch's martini.

—Why don't you go around the corner and get everyone hot dogs for lunch, he said just days after the steam accident.

At least they still trusted me to buy their lunch safely. I thought this might be Bill's idea of a sick joke, making me stand at the lunch counter to watch an overweight man in a butcher's apron boil hot dogs behind the counter. I loped down Powell Avenue, stepping around a toilet that had been dumped on the sidewalk. Caterpillar earthmovers rowed along the graveled street. Birmingham is an incomplete city, never finished with its self-sabotage.

A rental fence had been thrown up around the lot. Men in yellow hardhats stomped the earth. The construction site stretched for blocks in flat ruination. A surveyor squinted into the sun-shaded lens of a dumpy level mounted on a tripod that made me think of a three-legged dog. I see everything as maimed or injured, unfinished or incomplete. Above the surveyor, I spotted a young man I might have mistaken for myself at a younger age, toeing the bottomless air below the viaduct, a police officer half-heartedly trying to talk him down from the ledge. Just far enough to break a leg. All men are in the South are secretly Quentin Compsons. I looked closer. The kid on the viaduct ledge was holding a college diploma and a cardboard *will work for food* sign around his neck. I'd have bought the graduate a hot dog if the restaurant hadn't been eaten by a bulldozer.

As always, I was the harbinger of ill news to the plant. I found the foreman sweating and cursing in the engine room, loitering over a generator, pipe wrench in hand.

—Bill, they're out of hot dogs.

Bill was built like a smokestack. Schooled by the knee-jerk and the bottom-shelf, although he didn't earn anything more advanced than an associate degree at a tech school, Bill possessed the junkyard genius' robotic intuition of all things mechanical. I cannot believe he ever passed a day sleeplessly staring at the ceiling, watching the fan turn.

—What do you mean they're out of hot dogs? Bill said bearishly. —It's a hot dog place, how can they be out of hot dogs? That's like us being out of steam, we're a steam and power place.

—The building is gone. Only a dent in the ground where it stood.

—Are you sure you didn't get lost? You've been out of sorts

lately.

—No, like it's gone. They bulldozed it. Go see for yourself. They've been knocking buildings down all over town lately.

—Christ, I'm hungry. Where the hell are we gonna get hot dogs now?

—I think the wind knocked it over.

—That's rich, Lee. Real rich.

I followed Bill into the boiler room, the bowels of the power plant. Power is the same thing as energy per unit of time. Because of power, because of energy, because of time. The boiler room was like a steampunk space capsule, a nightmare of the more lugubrious industrial shots of *Eraserhead.* Cogitation or rational thought were all but drowned out by the monotonous, emotionless din of machinery down there.

—Listen, Lee.

I turned around to face Bill in the technical light of the boiler room, pipes clanging around us. I worried that he'd noticed the contused sleepless half-moons that had set in under my eyes.

—Maybe it's none of my business, but shouldn't you take some time off? You're our number one man here. Everything good with you?

I paused, disconcerted by the prescience of Bill's questionings. Bill wasn't a man I had pegged for being discerning or even caring about the private lives of his second-string subalterns.

—Yeah, everything's fine. Everything will be fine, I howled over the pipes, convincing no one.

It was time to go underground with the steam. After Bill left me in the boiler room, I went to his office and found the work schedule on a clipboard. I put my name down for the graveyard shifts. I couldn't sleep anyway, and I needed to escape the turbines, and the turbines needed to escape me.

———

The wind wanted blood. Njord's hecatomb lamb came in the form of a Jaguar XF waiting at a red light over a manhole cover. The fancy couple in the Jag should've run the red light. Why, for god's sake, didn't they run the light? But a traffic engineer would say that red lights are made for traffic safety. One safety negating another. If you run the red light you might get t-boned by a hearse.

I wasn't even supposed to be there that morning, but had taken over the other safety's shift.

Hot steam misted up from the underworld, the new day suggestively summery for October, and the uppermost tips of deciduous trees yellowed as their photoperiods changed. Invisible songbirds chirped melodious nonsense in the trees. The pleasanter details of this memory as vivid as the gray steam.

My wind sickness was especially exquisite that morning and just around cockcrow I had stepped outside the plant to get some fresh air instead of monitoring the pressure gauges on the relief valves. The foreday air was windless and hushful, the turbine blades stalled and stable on the summit of Red Mountain. Soon the advent sun would bud up behind the smokestacks and the strange day's light would spill like oil upon the streets of Birmingham and shadows would dim behind the western faces of the downtown banking towers where lights burned on the upper floors all night long.

The traffic light was painfully slow to change, the result of poor signalization. I had just plugged up my ears when the steam started whistling up to a boil and I heard the manhole cover impact the underbelly of the Jaguar. Ireful steam plumed and billowed out of the ground beneath the Jaguar and clouded its interior, the way steam from a hot shower will flood a bathroom. The passenger door opened. A woman emerged from the steam. How did I know it was a woman? A parboiled woman carrying a man in her arms. At first, I did not process what I was seeing; they didn't look human. Or rather, they still had the form of human, without the content. The Jaguar was invisible now beneath the steam. At temperatures like that steam will liquefy anything organic, evaporating soft tissue in an effervescent foam. Her steamed skin dripped off the bone like egg yolk, the whites of her eyes pleading with me to do more than I could, her muscles and sinews visible for the whole street to see, although I was the lone witness. The birds in the trees silent now, the turbine wind dropped strongly calm as sea breeze.

I have seen parts of a woman's anatomy in ways no man is supposed to see, the muscular darkness of her internal organs exposed to the searing, surgical light of an autumn day like the anatomy lessons painted by the Dutch or the allegorically posed woodcuts in *De humani corporis fabrica.* Probably, she had been beautiful moments before the steam. I leaned against the wall of the steam plant, and I felt the steam plant lean away from me as I heaved onto the sidewalk. Like the college kid on the viaduct, there was nothing I could do for them. I am an expert in industrial safety, and there was nothing I could do. Steam plants produce power for your devices, and to keep the bugaboos and bogeymen in the night away, that we may never see the light of dying stars, and I was powerless before the wind.

Before the steam, my performance was at an all-time low, and it just snowballed downhill until the steam accident. —What's the matter with you? You look like hell, Bill said.

—I can't sleep.

—Drink more. Take sleeping pills. You shouldn't beat your-self up so much over this, Lee, these things happen, Bill said disconsolately.

—These things happen, I repeated, trying to convince myself of its lame truth.

—Why don't you go home, Lee. Get some rest.

Bill had told me to go home the day of the accident, my symptoms worse than ever before. I should have listened to Bill. I should have gone home that day, never borne witness to the steam's sacrifice of this couple whom, I later read in the papers, had just returned from their honeymoon at Seaside. But home was only a black box through which the wind grunted, coming and going as it pleased. I burned that paper in the fireplace, watching the orange and gray ashes coil and dance like a living organism; then the wind blew that out too.

Most of my neighbors had already abandoned their homes, taken the quota of ransom the power company had offered them in exchange. FOR SALE signs staked into the uncut grass of every front lawn. They couldn't take the wind, the shadow flicker across their bedroom walls, the rattled windows. I think a few couples, stable and happy before the turbines, divorced. A small neighbor-hood, its inhabitants made the business of other inhabitants their business. The power company wanted to buy me out, but I let their letters pile up unopened on the coffee table.

I started a shower, turning on only the hot water, and pulled my shirt over my head. Cold water burned too much. I hadn't used the plumbing at my own home in a while and the water creaked through the pipes and then flushed out through the shower head and swirled down the drain in a ferrous bloom of rust.

Though the wind's buffeting of the house was softly drowned out by the watery babel of the shower, I forefelt the disequilibrium portending another episode of vertigo. I lowered the toilet seat and sat down. Even in the bathroom I couldn't escape it. I thought of the grisly bad luck and human costs sanitized by the media. The gory infelicities portrayed as the cost of doing business. A parachutist who drifted into the blades of a mill in Iowa. Towers toppling onto a work crew. Entire herds of cattle mysteriously chopped up. A suicide in Oregon who sprinted into the blades. What drives a man to that? To run full sprint into the spinning blades of a wind turbine, to be liquefied like a carrot in a blender?

And what was energy? I could recite the textbook definition: the ability of a physical system to perform work upon another physical system. But that seemed like defining ice by saying it was cold. Energy masquerades in many forms: kinetic, potential, radiant, numinous. And scales, from metabolism and photosynthesis on up to continental drift and gamma ray bursts, the universe was one vast, bitter big bang of corybantic energy most often experienced as ennui. We were producing energy and using it up faster than the wind turbine blades were spinning round and round.

I revived childhood memories long displaced or withheld: mother boiling water in a kettle on the stove. The phone rang shrill and strident above the steam hissing. She caught the phone between ear and shoulder, pouring roiling water over black tea, and then scalding herself when the voice with no body reported Dad had perished in some strangely monstrous and sublime industrial accident at McWane Pipe. There's only one way to enter the world, Dad once told me, but there's a thousand ways to leave it. I never got the lurid details, and the casket was closed. The service wasn't even paid off when mom convented herself in a lesbian or sexless gloom of poison and privation. She may yet live somewhere, or safe in heaven dead.

With so much time to myself, I planned hurricane evacuation routes and sketched diagrams of underground bunkers in crayon and colored pencil, just in case. These were in the days before The Wall fell. I padded the walls of my room with phone books, mattresses, cardboard and bubble wrap. The outside world terrified me. After watching *The Wizard of Oz*, I devised an ingenious scheme to anchor the house to the ground in case a tornado picked us up from the foundation. Ships, I wouldn't even get on them. I got older and I always applied the emergency parking brake, even on flat land, and enlisted surge protectors against the haywire and psychotic quirks of electricity. But these turbines — there existed no refuge from their bane, the windy affliction they wrought.

I got up from the toilet and peered into the mirror above the sink and scrutinized my unidentical face while the silver steamed over. I hadn't shaved since the boiling. The bristled face of a man whose features had been sketched in sand with a stick, then blurred over by the incoming tidal eddies burbling in from the blue beyond Columbus crossed, aided by the manifest destiny of the trade winds. My shallow face was long as a windsock. I felt hollowed through, a hole cut out of a rock by wind, only proximally existent, a decrescent sandstone. A wind-cut hole that through the ages becomes a cave in which cavemen play with fire. The turbines had blown out an extra circle in hell, the cognitive distortions and slippery slopes, misleading vividness. It took an effort now to detect the locusts of the turbine blades, I carried them with me.

The bathroom was addled with the hot shower's brume and my mirrored face softly smeared and then eclipsed altogether in the obscure steam that settled in doldrums all around me like smoke from hellfire.

I had to see Ellen. Since my accident, as she referred to it, we squandered days bedded together and at night when the winds were forte and my head racked with miasmatic migraines I watched her dreaming, twitching like a cat. In the day, I never asked where she went. The doors were never locked.

I blew by the abstract expressionist painting lit up like a highway billboard in the foyer. Ellen's Jaguar was parked in the garage. How many did she have? Anyone who nets six figures every six months can own one. I returned exasperated and defeated to the high living room, where I saw the note pinned like a butterfly to a cushion of the oversexed empire couch.

I found her alone in a bar downtown, stirring a Bloody Mary

with a celery stick.

—I got your note. Said you'd be at the Aeolian Bar. There's only one bar in town that serves Blood Marys you'll drink. What are you doing down here?

She tipped her head in the direction of the TV mounted on the wall, indicating I should look at the TV, not her. Everywhere there are screens, all of them showing acts of God.

—The resurrection of the dead, she pronounced calmly.

These Chilean miners had been stuck under a half mile of rock for more than two months. I'd forgotten about them, assumed they were doomed, but now they were back in the news. Another drunk in the bar cheered, —Hooray for the miners!

A pale, possibly deranged miner emerged from the Phoenix capsule and hugged the president three times and salsa-ed and skipped in a sort of salutatory rejoicing until a medic pinned him down to a stretcher and the miner gave a cameraman the thumbs up, universal symbol of escape. I still fail to fathom why these miners were so exultant to be back on this planet's surface.

—The president was just desperate to get re-elected, I commented cynically.

—What an awful thing to say, Lee.

—It's politics in Latin America.

—They were just saying that one of the miners ran six miles per day through the mine shafts to stay in shape. At first, they didn't even know the miners were alive, but they sent a note up. You know what the note said?

—What?

—"We are well in the refuge the 33." Notes from underground, Lee.

—Your note said I'm at the bar. I had to guess which one it was.

—I knew you'd just walk into the house.

—I knew you'd leave the door open for me.

—It's like they were brought back from the underworld. It's really great, Lee. Right now, people are sitting in bars all over the world cheering for the Chileans. They're sitting in bars in New York, in Los Angeles, in Miami, in Paris, London, Rome, Shanghai, Johannesburg. Even right here in Birmingham. The global community coming together in one big Kumbaya. I want to hug someone too. Dance salsa.

—And when it's all over we'll go back to fighting each other.

—I understand. You have your lobster people, your steam, your wind.

—Is it wind, or winds? Singular, or plural? I never know.

—Steam. Steams.

—The steam dissolved their skin. I looked into her eyes, steam still filling the Jaguar, and I saw death walking. This wasn't your miners come back from the atramental netherworld of coal, this was death walking 18th Street in broad daylight.

—It happened at night, Lee. Just before dawn. And then your girl left you. Because you survived and should not have. The train derailed and you walked away. She hated you for surviving. You saw another woman beneath her skin. But these miners, everyone survived, Lee. It's making my head spin. Everybody down there must be delirious with joy right now.

—The miners were dead for two months.

—Lazarus wasn't really dead, I don't think.

—After the accident, I couldn't touch another woman without thinking of that flayed woman, all muscle and bone beneath, her hair gone, I confessed to Ellen as if I was the victim.

—Do you know the allegory of Plato's cave, Lee?

—What's an allegory? I said mocking her.

—Prisoners chained up since childhood, arms, legs and neck fixed so they are coerced into gazing only at the cave wall in front of them.

—I'm with you so far, and I let my hand wander under the table on the hem of her skirt.

—Now, behind these fettered prisoners there's a big bonfire, and between the prisoners and the bonfire there's a walkway on which you have men passing back and forth, casting shadows onto the wall in front of the prisoners who can't turn around to see the bonfire or the walkway. All they can see are shadows, but they don't know they're shadows. Then Socrates wonders if it wouldn't be reasonable for the prisoners to take the shadows on the wall for the real thing, and not just shadows of the real? That's your mistake, Lee. You think shadows are actually cast by real things.

Ellen was finished with her Bloody Mary now and was poking at an olive with a plastic cocktail sword. I needed something to say. Too much morbid talk. I was losing her.

—Let's go to Vegas. We'll get a room and wake up wealthy.

Ellen raised her empty glass and the bartender went about mixing up another Bloody Mary. Ever since that day in Ellen's kitchen where I'd read about *Don Quixote* fatuously lancing a windmill he mistook for a three-armed giant, I had stayed at her place, avoiding the windy disaster of my own home.

I was old enough and had been through enough women by now to know that I was one of those men who would never be satisfied with oneness, union, sameness. Nor empire couches and abstract paintings. Willingly, I counted myself among those helpless men who want a new car soon as the old one smelled like cigarettes and the next model rolled off the production line. A consumerist of the fair sex, sure. I get just close enough not to be a danger to myself and then flee dastardly from the scene of the accident. I could still walk like a memory palace the dimensions of my childhood bedroom, defended from catastrophe and cascading failure as it was by bubble wrap, phone books, pillows, and mattresses. Ellen had her Bloody Mary now and seemed satisfied, ready to talk. Our knees bumped under the table.

—When I was a kid, Ellen shattered the bar's subdued silence with her birdsong voice, —I used to watch cockroaches mating. It was fascinating, even titillating in that insect way.

I pushed my hand up her thigh just below the hem of her skirt.

—Weird kid. I bet you doused fire ants with gasoline and lit them on fire too.

The news station cut to a story about the recovery of the Gulf fishing industry after the spill and Ellen lost interest in the miners now that she knew they were safe. I saw the wind beating the trees outside the bar. The strongest winds in the solar system are Saturnian and Neptunian, saturnine and oceanic. Winds that would atomize me, insubstantial already I would be less than a vapor trail. I longed for it. I could not engineer the world safer than it already was.

I envied the miners, trapped below the busy surface of this life in the quiet and windless dark, all mind. Bodies invisible, but of extension in the cave's dripping dark filling them like a substance. I met Ellen on Columbus Day. I live here now. The precise moment she leaned into me like the wind and her red mouth met mine. Her Bloody Mary on my lips tasted like corroded pipe water.

Why do I always focus upon the past, when she's sitting right here with me, open-skirted, our legs pressed together like leaves between the pages of a book? Sailing west with the baffling wind, Columbus was wrong about the longitudinal degrees that separated Europe from the Far East, as I had been wrong about the steam's safety valves, as I had been wrong about so many things. I could predict a lunar eclipse, like Columbus did for the Indians, saving himself and his crew from starvation, but now I could do little more than heed the rumors of the westing wind, judging the survivors of a mining accident in another hemisphere.

—Come back to my place, Ellen pleaded like the whites of the steamed woman's eyes.

—I have to be at work soon. Graveyard shift.

—I could see you as a gravedigger.

—That's the first compliment I've heard from you.

—That's not true. I said you were a very handsome rapist. These turbines are discombobulating your memory.

I thought I heard turbines chopping the air, but it was only her hands running through my windblown hair, mistaken vividness. Really, I wanted nothing more than to descend helplessly into her muliebrous oblivion and never return from the cave. To take her shadow for the real thing. I witnessed a V-shaped flock of migrating geese fly into the turbine, annihilated in an instant, Don Quixotes of the kamikaze sky. She bit my ear and lilted goodbye and I paid the tab, signing the receipt, *Columbus.*

Behind the wheel of my truck is the only place I feel in control. I aimed the wide hood at the two red-brick cooling towers of the steam plant in the distance and gunned it. Like the wind turbines, you can see them from almost any vantage in the city: darkened lighthouses that I followed through to the night shift. The Railroad Park had just opened up across the street and during the day there was a flurry of peopled activity in midtown I'd never seen before. Twenty-five million dollar patch of grass for dogs to crap on, an outdoor living room they called it, missing only the empire couches curated in Ellen's estate room. Millennials doing sunset yoga, and wandering the park like zombies catching Pokémon creatures on smartphones. I stayed away from the park. Picnickers and family reunions, sunbathers in bikinis, toddlers on tricycles. Oblivious, happy families, all alike. But the park was dark and empty now.

I parked my truck on the street and headed for the plant. A cop pulled up on Powell Avenue and questioned me.

I was standing by the roll door on Powell Avenue and I knew we were being videotaped. I could feel it like a pair of yellow-green eyes in the dark, the same camera that had caught the steam accident on tape, and which I watched dozens of times in a darkroom, an experience like watching Hitchcock's *Psycho* slowed down frame by frame so that it takes twenty-four hours to watch it once.

—Hey buddy, the copper greeted me. —What're you doing out here?

—I work at the plant. About to start my shift.

—Alright.

—Used to back in the day this plant powered the streetcars. Been steaming since 1895.

I thought my knowledge of the plant would ease him off me.

—My old man used to ride them streetcars. But that was before Kennedy and the National Guard. You know, the dogs and hoses.

—Yes. I guess it was.

—There's no guessing about it. That's how it was.

—I guess not, I said, laughing.

—You be safe down here now. There's a rapist on the loose, and the cop handed me a police artist sketch that looked a lot like myself if I had been black.

—Is this rapist interested in men or women, officer?

—Just take it easy, the cop said, disappearing behind his tinted window and rolling over the steam floating like angry wraiths above the street.

I ducked inside and went down to the engine room to get a first reading on the boiler's temperature gauges. Most freak industrial accidents happen at night — the voice of safety statistics whispering in my ear. Maybe they're not so freakish if they always happen at night in the caves. After a series of overhauls and retrofits I gave the go ahead on the steam turbines and we were pumping out over two million kilowatts of power. That's a good feeling, steam power. Cleaner than coal, but deadlier in other ways. With hours left to go on my shift, I made the mistake again of stepping outside for fresher air. I searched the street for the cop again, turned north onto 18th, no destination in mind, glancing up at the viaduct's golden eagles dated 1931, just after the economy collapsed and suits on Madison Avenue were jumping out of windows.

The viaduct underpass, just around the corner from the steam plant, luminescent with stark light sheering off the dingy walls, is a hole of mortal description. A drunk slumped within the elbow of an arch. Strange abstract stains splattered like a crime scene against the wall. Dry leaves seasons old windrowed versus as a tallboy rattled hollowly in the anxious wind. My spine fluttered, feet disappearing into the ground, the beery skunk smell of urea as I held my breath and crossed into the darkness outside the viaduct. Trains freighting coal rumble-grinding on the tracks above. A rattletrap Max Bus smoked by pulling out of Central Station, a Wells Fargo stage coach advertisement peeling off the side. The bus was empty at this hour, and the driver looked at me without waving.

No matter where I went, still the wind dogged me, my forehead throbbing and the earth quaking beneath feet that felt no longer mine. Even here, in an Amtrak parking lot where boozy bums snoozed in sleeping bags, the wind afflicted me with its shadow syndrome and squally chatter. Its howling shrill decibels. I expected to seize at any moment, my tongue cut from my own mouth by my teeth. That heart raced in my breast, I hadn't slept since that first night at Ellen's, sedated by her wine. Please, wind gods, spare a mortal who has seen death walk these city streets.

On Morris Avenue, where I saw a Wells Fargo stage coach rattle by over the cobblestones, I stood transfixed before a crumbling brick building covered by a blue tarp that snapped in the wind. I watched back-lit shades come and go from Central Station. A second-floor light in the Young and Vann Building winked off. Insomniacs and haunted workaholics like myself. I scavenged a brown bag of roasted peanuts dropped in front of the Peanut Depot and felt better. A newly married couple were posing happily for wedding photographs against a brick wall floodlit by halogens. I was a menacing presence, as I listened to them gush about their upcoming honeymoon and I watched pigeons peck at the peanut shells I tossed onto the cobblestones. I thought of what my own wedding day might be like, a country courthouse and a sober, twanging judge. We ate at a bed and breakfast, made radiant love in moonlight, and then the thirty-three wind turbines came.

The posing bride, pileated hair piled on top of her head like cake icing, in front of the red caboose now, turned to me and I did not look away, and I saw her squeeze her husband's hand. Other people's happiness leaves me winded. I turned away when her skin dripped from the bone. I emerged from the sullen steam of my despond and came out into the shadowy wind tunnel of

21st street by the John Hand Building, the moneyless safety deposit vaults, crisp leaves newly fallen tumbleweeding through the so-called Heaviest Corner on Earth. I might have been the last shadowy man on the cave's walkway, so bereft and scarce were the windswept streets. I leaned into the wind, and the wind leaned into me.

I held my breath again watching a car pass over an ominous column of steam misting from the piped netherworld beneath the city streets. *We are well in the refuge the 33.* My chest burned, I felt adrift like a carrack without wind in its sails, bobbing aimlessly west on the winedark waves. So I did something I had never done before in this city. I jogged up to the bus at the next stop and boarded without paying and the driver didn't stop me. The only white man on the bus, I felt out of place, a colonial among natives. But I had no ships, no smallpox blankets or royal charter, not even rapine of gold, only the wind in my sails blowing me westward, following the sun that had set hours ago. The driver seemed in a hurry to make up for lost time and the bus galloped at top speed through the empty, windwhipped streets of Birmingham and clopped over cobblestones and the scraped blacktop chewed up for repaving, jostling passengers — mostly black maids and nannies, some Wal-Mart and fast food workers — out of their unbuckled seats. The night beyond the windows acheronian and sooted as I felt.

I didn't even know where the bus was routed, or where I'd be able to get off when my time came. A young man in a basketball uniform bobbed his head to music and when he exited through the back door at the stop I took his seat. Through the back window, I could see the new Wells Fargo sign on the bank tower diminish; downtown and the two red cooling towers of the steam plant slipped away as the bus went on tilting towards the mountain. Several times the bus driver turned around in his seat and yelled at somebody. When an old woman who walked with a cane boarded at the next stop, tapping wearily down the rolling aisle, I stood up and offered her my seat and she took it shrewdly without a word. Some poor man's fishwife. We barreled by a park where I knew slatterns with battle-ax faces prowled the streets and when we bussed under the interstate and ascended the hill up Arlington Avenue I knew where we were going. The bus rounded a sharp uphill turn and I pulled the yellow cord behind my head and a bell rang and I felt the bus pitching forward as it slowly braked. I fished some change out of my back pocket and coined them into the turn-stile and got off the bus feeling that I had been spared some blacker fate.

I stood carless and stranded on the side of the road where Aberdeen and Cahaba converged on a grassy roundabout and watched the bus splutter and puff on up the mountain into Mountain Brook where Birmingham's executive class imprisons itself from the rabble below. Nowhere else to go, I took a goat path through flattened grass and walked a mile or so to Ellen's house. Without knocking, I let myself into the flagstoned foyer and the wind slammed the door behind me. I stood by the melancholy, abstract Robert Motherwell painting on the wall and called out Ellen's echoing name. My hollow voice of Ellen's name bounced back to me, unanswered among her objects: the empire couch upon which wine-drunk I had softly called her name and she had answered in antiphon with my name; wineglasses in the sink; the tarped piano and a deer's head I had not noticed before mounted above the fireplace. The deer's glassy eyes seemed to follow me about the room like video surveillance cameras.

I stepped deeper into the house, went from room to room, hoping to find her in a steaming shower, strangely thinking of the miner who ran marathons underground. The guillotine windows open, papers strewn about the floor, the house ransacked by the wind. I wondered who had opened the windows. Ellen? Had the house been burglarized? I had the sense that someone else, some other keyless interloper besides myself had been in the house, the animal musk of a man's toilet water cologne commingled with Ellen's rosewatered muscadine.

I peeked into the garage. Her Jaguar was gone. Maybe she was at the bar still, sword fighting an olive at the empty bottom of her Bloody Mary, rapturously watching the Chilean miners restored to the diurnal routine of light and dark taking turns in passing dominion over the earth, to politics and business as usual, earth and sky, wind finally, no more running marathons in the dark. Ecstatic in the alienation of her global community. Or maybe it was she who had left me reeling in the steam of my own accident, a *will work for food* sign draped around my neck and a bogus college diploma. It turned out that Ellen did not have a key, and she did not have a key because it wasn't her house. Because of because, because of her, because of me, because the turbines. She was squatting in her ex-husband's house until he threw her out, and then her fascination with the mystery of the miners made sense, trapped as she was in her own bright underground I had walked right through and never known it. How often must we blunder on like this through one another's darknesses without knowing it, even when the canary dies? I suffered sweetly from the delusion that I could make the world safer by eliminating mechanical failure, but through no design or modification could I stop us from being everlastingly trapped in the cave.

It was time to confront the wind.

I left the door to Ellen's house agape and plunged through the ownerless neighborhood's wracked streets, the darkened windows darker than the city below, plywood appearing now where lost boys had thrown brick and stone through tall glass. Three-hundred foot turbine towers, stationed on a remote ridge, spired alienly above the treetops and I tracked up a dirt path aiming for them, and crosscut through an aisle of young pines. The wind was picking up.

I scaled the ridge through autumn trees yielding their resplendent leaves. The gloaming was lifting and pure and violent color scintillated in the early harvest sunlight as I topped the ridge of Red Mountain. Strongly I felt the blades chop the air faster like aircraft propellers, mortified yellow and orange leaves cycloning around me.

If I stood in the wind long enough, would it weather and sculpt me like sandstone? The Aeolian process applied to a man, a shadow fire-thrown upon a wall. I knew that if the blades spun fast enough the turbine would fail without the safety brake that decelerates the blades in tempestuous winds, pitching the blades in a feathered position, minimizing the rotor's torque. The wind tower would buckle, and its blades would carve and cleave me. I would be sundered from myself. An oil spill oozes its tarry black sheen across the ocean like a shadow bubbling up from the earth, a steam plant boils lovers alive, and an ash pond breached blights the land my feet no longer touched with slurry of toxic fly ash. The wind turbine only self-destructs, as the blades yaw and mill out of control, snapping a quixotic lance in half like a matchstick; the grid goes down and the city lights wink out block by block, and a terminal darkness crowns upon Birmingham like a twilit ultimatum. —Spin baby, I prayed to the spinning metal gods of the wind. — Spin, baby, spin.

WELLS FARGO

Before the morning's baleful yellow fog crawled on all fours back into the earth I reverse parked my Jaguar in the parking deck and dragged my briefcase like a bad conscience behind me. These were the last days of October, when the winds were wild and wanton, and the late hunter's moon beetled still over the graveyard streets. The fiscal year had recently ended. I marched east along the deep-cracked sidewalk and around orange construction barrels, hardly enough light to cast a building shadow. If the bars hadn't been closed I might have stopped in for a sunrise drink. Every morning this was my Bataan Death March, only a few blocks, but dress shoes can make sore feet fast, stepping over the sallow, coughing drunks rallying from last night's debauch, pricking me with their switchblade eyes. Sometimes I tossed coins like chicken feed into a velvet violin case.

Crossing the block by the Federal Courthouse, a man descending the marble steps under the Ionic colonnade brushed shoulders with me. —Hey, I turned around. —Watch where you're going. The shoulder-brusher disacknowledged me and tacked on east towards the Greyhound station. Early workers prepped breakfast inside the Chick-Fil-A, which sells bats, not fried chicken, and anthropomorphized cows mooed for passersby to eat more chicken. At the wall fountain, I plodded by candle-glowing jack-o-lanterns grinning toothily in window bays: ghoulish countenances, self-portraits of my inner state; a lumpy, cankerous pumpkin carved into a dollar sign; a tumbledown adjudicated house that might be the House of Usher; vesper bats dispersing in moonlight. I expected the garden variety witches and hobgoblins, standard nightmares one can take as a matter of course, but I got only orangely lambent private messages ciphered and carved in vegetable hollowness. Cottony spider webs draped across locked doors and leering widow's peaked vampires suction-cupped to storefront windows of the few marginal shops that were not plywooded.

In one of those disembodied episodes, where I viewed myself as a third-person observer, a frequent distortion of perspective, I saw myself reincarnated as a scarecrow lofting one of those orange squashes and smashing it against the sidewalk, pumpkin guts and seeds splattered in the roadway. But if I was a straw-stuffed scarecrow, then it would be my own hollow pumpkin head squashed on the sidewalk. Stranger thoughts than these accompanied me on the walk to work each morning.

I sharply turned the corner onto 20th Street and walked into a crowd of Bronze Agers in suits forgathered on the sidewalk, usually peopleless at this hour. I elbowed my way through the craning crowd, bumping into a woman's enceinte belly, apologizing stupidly. I had not looked up yet, afraid of what I might see: a banker such as myself jumping from his office window, history repeating itself on this day of all days, the reeling Black Tuesday anniversary of the stock market crash.

I spotted Byron's mustache in the crowd. Byron had been in the business back when banks were running Ponzi schemes on every gullible investor with an itch to hand his money over to anyone wearing a suit and tie. His suit was too small for him.

—Who is it? I queried him.

—It's Wells Fargo, Byron said. Practically a wordless man, no good morning, Happy Halloween, just a sidelong glance through me and then an entranced, thousand-yard stare back up at the crisp blue empyrean.

—I've always wanted to meet the man in the moon. Is he finally vouchsafing us mortals a supreme visit?

I looked down at a dead bird on the sidewalk and toed it with my shoe. The bird didn't fly away, but lifelessly rolled under my dress shoe.

—I thought somebody was jumping.

—They might yet, Byron prophesied hopefully.

—It's a bad day for banking. We ought to be closed on a day like this, or at least flying the flag at half-mast over City Hall.

I felt an unseen presence chopping the air and then the WELLS FARGO sign hove into view, suspended precariously above the street from steel cables. I gaped upwards at the helicopter hovering in the blue space between the former Wachovia Tower and my as yet unnamed office tower, nameless as an unsigned check, where I loaned other people's money for a morally hazardous living. The helicopter lowered the new sign into position, stirring the trees around us into a welter of autumn golds and titians, leaves ocherous and brass waving goodbye. A flocculent cloud, distant and serene as a ship slipping over the horizon, floated behind the helicopter and was eclipsed by the dark Bank Tower.

As the WELLS FARGO sign was settled into place atop the tower the crowd began clapping and cheering as if they had toppled the equestrian statue of a communist dictator in a public square. *Annuit Coeptis*, some smart-ass banker said. Champagne bottles uncorked and popped, the bubbly wassails of the early drunk, Prosecco effervescing into plastic solo cups. Everyone seemed happy that the building had a name now. *Novus Ordo Seclorum*, another banker felicitously said. One day I worked for Wachovia Bank, and the next it was Wells Fargo.

Bankers are a back-slapping bunch. Any excuse to celebrate. A funeral celebrated the same as a birth. They'd celebrate the assassination of a president who too tightly regulated the banks if they could get away with it. Sobriety among morning drunks is a kind of intoxication itself.

—Here's to Wells Fargo, I toasted. —No longer King Cotton, but King Capital.

Wells Fargo was pieced together like a Frankenstein from wads of mergers, the spare parts of acquisitions, offering an array of financial products to maximize your net worth: personal loans, credit cards, home loans, project finance, hedge fund management, revolving credit, and wealth management services to high net worth individuals like myself. I clocked seventy, even eighty hours a week, and never missed home. No one was there. Not even a WELCOME mat at the door.

I have an eye for money: loose change in gutters, a quarter on the floor of an airport terminal. I can look at the billfold bulge of a man's back pocket and guess to the dollar how much cash is in it. I can look at a woman's credit card and tell how much money she spends by the card swipes rubbed over the dove security hologram. Through the bodies in the crowd I saw a one dollar bill crumpled on a sad, sagging bench in front of the Wells Fargo tower. I scanned the crowd to make sure no one was watching. The dollar piece had been ripped into halves and I tried to surgically piece it back together but Washington's face wouldn't line up. His nose was missing, like the nose of the Sphinx cannonaded by Napoleon's troops. General Washington looked smugly back at me walleyed and glowering from the 18th century with his apple-tree rectitude. If he came riding up to me — I pictured these complacent, superior men of the country's early years going everywhere on horseback — on the sidewalk, I'd have clocked the one-dollar general.

Washington's portrait is ubiquitous: almost half of the currency printed these days is one dollar bills. I don't know if that means we're getting poorer, or if strippers are flattening the Lorenz curve. I wondered how many ones met this fate, torn asunder, abandoned on a bench in depressed downtowns by bums too sauced to care, or the carelessly rich for whom a dollar torn is something to brag about, stuffing for a brassiere. I held the two halves of the sundered dollar up again, like trying to line up the highways on a ripped road map, the unblinking Eye of Providence eying me with contempt. In God we trust my ass. That mantra was added to the bill in 1955, when the collective consciousness feared most that we might be a godless country like the Communists. I pocketed the two halves, wondering if I could use them as fifty-cent pieces now.

I blew by the empty retail and revolved through the glass doors and into the glittering lobby outfitted with green marble and futuristic lights hanging from the ceiling like the office of the Wizard of Oz. Just as I stepped inside and shook off the early chill, a Max Bus with our stagecoach logo stopped across the street. The placement of this advertisement on a city bus was too good to be true. Our red and yellow branding appeared as if overnight on all the city's ATMs and billboards, my pseudonym on fake checks. I watched the bus disappear up 20th street, lost in its own black smoke. Inside the bank lobby, the porcine security guard, Dale, nodded off over a newspaper of yesterday's news. —Gimme all your money, I yelled at the guard like a tommy-gun public enemy.

Dale gradually stood up from his desk, as if pulled out of his chair by invisible wires, trigger-happy hand on his gun holster. He looked me over.

—Are you bleeding, Mister Watt?

—Am I what?

—I asked were you bleeding, Mister Watt.

—Why would I be bleeding? I asked, patting myself over for scrapes, a bullet or stab wounds I hadn't noticed. Stray gunfire in this town is like rainfall. Then I turned around and saw the red shoe prints that tracked a sanguinary progress from the revolving glass doors to where I stood in the lobby before the security desk.

I took off my shoes and deposited them with my briefcase at the security desk.

—Keep both two eyes on these, I said, and trundled sock-foot through the revolving doors, backtracking my steps onto the sidewalk again where I had stepped in a surgeon's pint of plasma. Thousands of Chick-Fil-A ketchup packets strewn deranged across the pavement. Cars had wheeled over them and squirted a jet stream of fast-food hemoglobin all over the sidewalk and onto the bank windows, streaked now in claret gore, an apropos cruor for the orange holiday. I observed one of Birmingham's transcendental homeless lumbering up the sidewalk, dragging a mattress behind him like a snail in his shell. I stepped out of his way and let him pass, considering the torn dollar deposited in my pocket. Thus discalced I stand, present tense, and singular, rocks and glass in my feet, twisted in the tunneling wind, among sidewalk trees that shake their green fists at this hemic mess.

I headed back inside, grabbed my suitcase at the front desk and stabbed my way on tiptoe to the double elevator below the WELLS FARGO in yellow lettering on a ketchup background like an *Arbeit Macht Frei* above the camp gates. I pressed the up button, thinking of how I might reverse them so when a colleague pressed the up button he would go down. There are bankers in this building who will take the elevator one story to their windowless office every morning so that for the best fifteen seconds of the day as they are lifted in a metal box on wires they can feel like genius millionaires. Before I even saw the woman, I smelled the rank perfume that cloyed like fruit-flavored vodka and a J.C. Penney's from 1999. I stepped in next to the odoriferous woman and held my breath like a plunge underwater.

—Which floor? she asked.

—Twenty first, thanks, bubbled out of my mouth.

I watched the elevator doors close on the ketchup tracked through the lobby. She mashed two buttons at the same time, the twentieth and the twenty-first, and the ground lifted beneath our feet. Anything might have happened. At such moments, being mechanically elevated into the sky like the new sign on the building, I felt that I could fleece anyone. I scrutinized her out of the corner of my eye. She was pretty enough that we could pass the time together if the elevators got stuck.

—What happened in the lobby? she asked.

—I think a murderer walked in off the street.

—It's almost Halloween.

—Yes, I said, without seeing the connection.

Before she could ask about my shoeless feet I exited the elevator at the first stop and sprang straight to my office. There was a man in a suit, much like myself, sitting in my chair, except that it wasn't me. He wore a broad floral tie that was too long on his stocky frame, and his neck fat spilled out of his starched collar that garroted his size nineteen neck.

—What the hell are you doing in my office again, Watt? the man in my chair asked indignantly.

—This is my office, Burr. What are you doing in my chair?

—We have the exact same chair. Everyone in this tower has the same damn chair. When we die, they just change us out and everything else stays the same. Same desk, same walls, same carpet, same lights, same artificial plants, and the same chair. You're not special. Watt, your office is on the twenty-first floor, like the century we're in.

Burr pointed up at the ceiling.

—It's hard to tell. All these floors look perfectly alike. I think the night janitors rearrange the offices at night. A cabal among the Masons.

—Are you sure it's not garden gnomes, Watt?

—Look in that bottom desk drawer. Is there a bottle of bourbon and a copy of *Das Kapital*?

Burr opened the drawer, humoring me, and frowned.

—No bourbon, and no Marx, he confirmed.

I poked my head out off Burr's office and saw the brass nameplate on the door: Burr & Forman. Who was Forman anyway?

—You damn lawyers, I said to Burr.

—And why aren't you wearing any shoes?

—See, it's a long story involving ketchup and an axe murderer down in the lobby. You know what I found outside on a bench?

—Puke? Trash? A fetus? Your soul?

—A one dollar bill torn right down the middle. George Washington is noseless.

—Good for you, Watt. Now you got two fifty cent pieces. Buy yourself an ice cream.

—Do you have any idea what today is? The significance of this torn dollar bill on a day like this?

—We're not superstitious in law. Now, Watt, as much as I'd love to sit here and shoot the shit with you, I've got work to do. I guess you bankers wouldn't know what that is when all you do is cadge other people's money.

—That's funny coming from a lawyer. You know what Shakespeare said?

—He said to be or not to be. I say not to be in my office.

—Kill all the lawyers.

—Good for him.

—The lawyers and sophists of this bassackwards world shall inherit the earth, I saluted and strode again onto the elevator and got off this time at the twenty-first floor, same as the century.

Whenever the elevator doors slide open at the beginning of another day at the office, I always expect to see something different: a tropical white sand beach lined with palms and tilted coconut trees bending seaward, a woman sunbathing in a bikini, a narrow café street in Paris, the rolling downs and chalk cliffs of the Isle of Wight and a bosomy woman of raven hair in a blowing gown approaching me out of the mists. But again and then again, each day I am a Birmingham banker in a simulacrum of an office, and when the elevator doors slide open I see that the raven-haired woman in the gloom-dimmed mists was walking away from me all along, her shallow footprints pressed in sand.

On the twenty-first floor now I edged by Janet, my secretary, long platinum hair shading her face, a moonlighter at a gentleman's club where after the first of many separations from Rachel I had gone with banking buddies to drink desperately as if the world was about to end, and then to neck and then to fuck next to a dumpster in the alley behind the club. Honor amongst thieves, we never spoke about it at work. There are no gentlemen in places such as that. Sad old lechers pawing chubbily at the girls, throwing crumpled, sweaty one dollar bills onto the stage like the torn one I had pocketed. Janet was young and attractive without all that dancer's makeup, soft skin and green eyes that always seemed on the verge of squeezing out a tear, with a matronly quality, the kind of woman who wants to take care of an unreformable satyr with deep pockets, one preferably near death and with no heirs, but I wouldn't have married her for all the gold in heaven, for the same reason that if I was a hunter, as my father was, I wouldn't use a gun.

The best thing about working in an office is that all the women wear heels and skirts. Even the bottom-heavy look good enough to eat. I stopped in front of the office with my name on the door: Copeland Watt. I keyed the office door open and surveyed the damage: dry cleaning bagged and draped across the back of a chair. Every morning two rascally faces greeted me: a portrait of J.P. Morgan and a mugshot of Charles Ponzi given to me on a lark by a colleague. He said it was a reminder to keep me honest. Otherwise the office was a replica of Burr's office on the floor below.

Next to the photo-portraits, one dour, the other a Ponzi picaresque that always reminded me of the errant childishness of finance, hung a diploma from the Harvard Kennedy School, Department of Economics, where I'd authored a dusty dissertation on Kondratiev Cycles and the Elyton Land Company's role in settling Jones Valley and developing the Birmingham district that became the principal scene of all this drama. Perhaps all of five people living had read it. Tucked into an addendum, I predicted the second housing bubble bursting, as market indicators and housing price indices all pointed in one direction: recession. No one heeded the warnings, because no one read it. The writing was on the wall like graffiti obscenities and we just whitewashed over it with platitudes about the strength of the bull market. Then I decided that academia was full of virgins, and I wanted to make money out of other people's money.

I put my briefcase down next to the bronzed Hamlet skull I used as a paperweight or a doorstop, and opened a small dressing closet in the wall opposite my desk. I sat down in the chair in front of my desk, the one where clients and debtors sat looking out the window over my shoulder, and slipped my feet into a fresh pair of dress shoes and my secretary, the moonlighting dancer, appeared in the doorway with a mug of coffee, one of those office mugs with inspirational quotes.

—Thanks, Janet. Just set it on the desk.

—You're welcome, Mister Watt. Anything else?

—Just answer all my calls please. Tell them I'm dead. They can send flowers here if they want.

I poured Janet's black coffee into another mug — the quote on the mug vexed me; something feel-good about happiness and dreams — and carried it to the south window to god's-eye the city Wells Fargo had usurped from the bankrupts at Wachovia. Two brick cooling towers, one slightly taller than the other. I recalled reading about a steam accident in the papers. A couple burned alive on 18th street, below the watch of Vulcan on Red Mountain, where the wind turbines I helped Alabama Power finance spun wildly, self-destructively out of control. A pack of wild dogs was savaging a dumpster on the empty street below.

These days it is dark when I arrive at the office in the early hours and it is dark when I leave, shuttled from darkness to darkness. The only natural light I get is mediated through this wall of tinted windows. I see the sun only behind curtains of tinted glass like a creature in a terrarium. A fanged Halloween vampire suction-cupped to a window. At the beginning of September, I watched the turbine blades trucked through the streets. I moved the money that moved the blades that moved the wind. I kept the lights on. I felt elevated above it all, as my feet soared twenty-one stories off the ground, lofted above the quotidian, cozily ensconced in the office of Mammon, where once was air. I could stand at this window and fiddle as it all burned and never blink an eye. The wind blows where I will it.

Today, the polis is nothing without the bank, and Birmingham was now nothing without Wells Fargo. Money makes men move. It gets them up in the morning. Why else even bother? Keeps them virile and potent. Decisive, historic things are supposed to happen before self-important windows like this, but I could stand here until the sun blipped out and turned to ice and the scene would be the same as it ever was, I thought watching a flock of pigeons circle the Leer Tower in widening spirals. At five o'clock, the white collars released from their cubicle cells, the streets empty out, the avenues breathless with moonglow slipping between office towers. Then there was the men's Athletic Club on the top floor of the John Hancock building, where I could steam myself to death in the wood-heated sauna like the victims of the safety engineer's wind sickness. Or play doubles on the tennis courts with wheezing old men, racquet ball and squash until I exhausted myself angrily and broke my racket against a wall. Maybe I would go alone to Bottega for drinks, daydream about the cocktail waitress and then report home alone, which meant back to the office. Sometimes a bird flew into the sky reflected in the window, and fell meteorically to the sidewalk below. Sometimes I feel like that bird. Sick of looking at the blackened flatland of parking lots, watching commuters park, I put the fiddle down in the velvet case and turned away from the window just as Rachel abrupted into my office and I prepared myself to duck and dodge bullets. I headed her off before she could ask me for money.

—How did you get by my secretary? That woman is supposed to be my first line of defense. I need peace up here. This is my ivory tower. I told her to tell everyone I was dead.

—That would simplify a lot of things. And she prefers being called an executive assistant, not a secretary. I need to talk to you.

Rachel deposited her turgid purse among the disorder of my desk and dropped a large plastic bag onto the floor.

—Whatever it is, I'm sure it's not so important it can't wait until after business hours, am I right? The only way you got by the security guard downstairs is because Dale's too fat to run and you wore that obscenely short skirt thinking you could get what you want.

—Copeland, you don't keep non-business hours. You're always at work. And what happened in the lobby downstairs? There's ketchup or blood everywhere.

—They still haven't cleaned that up?

—I made sure not to step in it.

—I thought we agreed that you wouldn't drop in on me at work?

—The house, Watt. They're foreclosing on the house you set me up in.

I put on my best poker face. A face she had seen many times. I knew this was coming, but did nothing to stop it, perhaps because I knew it was the only way to bring her back to me, although when I had her I'd send her packing again. How frustrated Rachel would be in that great house alone, a crazy cat lady with no cats: she needed an antagonist to dramatize the possibilities for conflict she saw in every room, and a room hung with several doors so she could pick a different one to slam each time before she could have a proper row.

—How was Houston? I said, rather artlessly changing the subject.

—I spent six hours in the Rothko Chapel. Best six hours of my life. It was a transcendent experience. Those deep black purples closing in on you like an octagonal bruise.

—You went all the way to Houston to go to church? Babe,

Birmingham has more churches per square mile than any city of its size in the country.

—Do you keep up with anything that goes on outside this office? I had a very spiritual experience. People of all faiths coming together. Muslims, Jews, Zoroastrians, even Christians. It reminded me of Malcolm X's conversion experience right before he was shot.

This is why we never worked out.

—So, what I'm hearing is that you suspect you're about to be assassinated. Is that right?

—I did notice a strange man follow me into the elevators, she said turning around to look at my office door that creaked closed like a casket lid. Sometimes the wind blows through office corridors, winnowing paper and printouts like sere leaves. The building's maintenance team hasn't figured out how the wind is getting inside.

—What'd he look like?

—Sort of fat, a face like oatmeal.

—Sounds like the security guard. You're in good hands.

—Did you know Muslims don't believe in charging interest?

—Muslims also mutilate women who try to leave their husbands.

—I left you, and I still have my nose, she said and I tried to picture what her lovely face might look like with a skull's noseless pumpkin leer, her perfumed skin fresh as newly printed money. I thought of a Muslim woman I'd seen on the cover of *TIME* magazine I flipped through earlier that summer in a doctor's office waiting room, the beautiful young bride's nose missing because she'd fled an abusive husband. The same magazine cover was in the bank's lobby, on a modern gray side table, and because the photo — the noseless stare, the void opening in a human face — so terrified Janet, I turned the magazine over to the back cover's Wells Fargo stagecoach ad.

—A lot of good it's done you. You have to charge interest. Economic growth depends upon it. Why do you think the Muslim countries are still in the Middle Ages?

—I don't want to argue politics with you, Watt.

—Not politics. It's just money.

Rachel rifled through the large plastic museum gift-shop bag on the floor. —I bought you a framed print in the chapel gift shop, she said holding it up for me to see, —Isn't it pretty?

The print she held up was brushed expressively in morbid reds and yellows, like the Wells Fargo branding above the elevator doors in the lobby, the banking colors that appeared all over town. The work of a melancholic. The expressionist seemed underwhelmingly fond of floating rectangles, a study in two colors of two colors, the dilettantish aftermath of time, and therefore money, diverted in a Saturday afternoon finger painting class.

—In his later paintings, just before he died, the darkness is always on top. I wanted to get you one of those, the dark gray and black paintings, but they didn't have any. Too gloomy for sales, I suppose. So I had to get you a colorful one instead.

—You came here to talk to me about art? I thought this was serious, Rachel.

—I got a letter in the mail, she said putting the Rothko print down like it was a gun she had decided not to use, —It's from your bank, whatever it's called now.

She pulled a long white envelope from her handbag and tossed it flippantly onto my desk. I looked at the envelope: she hadn't even broken the licked seal to read it.

—This is from Wachovia. Did you not see the new sign on the building this morning? This is Wells Fargo as of this morning.

—Wave your magic wand, Mister Fix It. Isn't that what you do? Fix things that don't need fixing?

Rachel could never forgive me for trying to fix our marriage. I tried to fix the unbroken, and in the process broke the unfixable. Seeing her again, I thought of the last night we had been together. Valentine's Day, the flowers mixed up and she received a tall vase of the finest white roses with another woman's name on the card. Leave the thorns on, I told the florist over the phone. She'll understand.

Our first date she stood me up. She volunteered weekly at a suicide hotline, and she canceled our dinner plans because she had a call. I didn't talk to her for months after that. There's nothing like a cold dinner while your future wife listens to some boor threaten to slash his wrist with a plastic knife stolen from the cafeteria and then ask her for phone sex. On our second date, we played this game I made up: you stare into each other's eyes while pretending to milk virtual cows.

Together, we had shared bills and bank accounts, the best

parts of our bodies, but she never scrubbed that bachelor smell out of my belongings. We had smoked each other's cigarettes and nightly shared our loneliness with one another in the blue and silent glow of a wall-mounted television set. She could only share her loneliness with me if the TV was on. Afterwards, I would pour a stiff drink and read *The Wall Street Journal.* Really read it, pouring over it like a Biblical exegesis. She would sit up in bed, leaning on an elbow, her lovely face chiaroscuroed in the television shadows of the bedroom.

—You're hiding something, Copeland.

If I had something to hide, I told her, I'd hide it. My own impoverished, exquisite loneliness the most I could give of myself, scarecrow crucified on his own debts. The city is an ugly place and its saddest people are in banks, the moneychangers and the moneylenders, we sharks of the loan and blackball. Underwriters of the underworld's meal ticket. A bank account for every ex-wife. I check in on them from time to time, like estranged children, but the balance is always the same. Not a single withdrawal. They don't want my blood money. Shinplasters used to wallpaper the HGTV homes the divorce attorneys fix them up in. I wouldn't be surprised if the lawyers moved in after them. Rachel was probably the one woman who loved me despite my liabilities. I say *liabilities,* and not shortcomings or peccadilloes, if I had a torn dollar for every one of them.

She had a half-brother who took a census job in the Black Belt and hadn't been heard from since. A tweedy, indulgently intellectual sob who cries over the poems of Shelley into his pint of poison, the type that romanticizes poverty and blue collar work, probably has a *Starry Night* magnet on his fridge with nothing but PBR inside and daydreams about cutting his ear off and giving it to some homely girl who lives under the interstate. But Rachel, like her half-brother, lived half the year underground and the other half in some paradisaical apple orchard, and I was General Washington, axe slung over my epauletted shoulder and the axe blade at the base of her apple tree.

—You're talking to the wrong guy here. What kind of plutocrat do you think I am? I'm not a mortgage broker. I do project finance. Those wind turbines you see spinning on the mountain.

—I've seen them, and felt the new winds. They're almost like an art installation. They reminded me of this Kiefer piece I saw in

France. But still, I don't see what that has to do with you moving some numbers around, flashing a smile at the ghost-machines that run this place.

—You hold right of possession, not right of ownership. The bank has right of ownership as the lien holder. It's a business disagreement, nothing personal. That's the problem with people, they take it personally. They act like the banks are out to get them, but the banks aren't out to get anything but your dough, honey. The banks want people to stay in their houses, because then they're paying their mortgages like good, upright citizens of the Republic.

While working as a bank teller in Harvard Square a shabby old crook tried to open a savings account with a counterfeit one-million-dollar bill. The only difference between that million dollar note and the torn one dollar bill I found on the bench that morning was the zeros after the one. Amazing how zeros — signifying nothing, all sound and fury — can make all the difference in the world. The void opens up out of a Muslim woman's face and spills into territory we thought we owned, blackening everything like oil. Even then I knew the largest bill ever printed was a $100,000 note and that went out of circulation before the oil embargo.

I considered opening the account, becoming a co-conspirator with this slipshod and tattered counterfeiter, maybe get a cut. If I had known then that the counterfeiter was a pre-image of my own future, would I still have done what I did? The million dollar note looked like it had been through a million spin-dry cycles and found between the plush cushions of someone's antique couch. I balked, turned the million dollar counterfeit over to the bank manager, and minutes later the old palooka — my doppelganger — was escorted away in handcuffs. I worked real estate for a time. The first house I closed a deal on still had the previous owner's dead body inside. I should have quit then, a bodement of things to come.

—You want me to goldbrick my own company? I asked Rachel.

—How many times has your company evicted people?

—I am not the company.

The phone rang. What the fuck was my secretary doing that she couldn't answer the phone while I fenced with my gold-digging ex-wife?

I held up a finger to Rachel to let her know I'd have to take this call. She was used to it by now, and even in her surlier moments she could still play the part of the banker's deferential ex-wife.

—Copeland Watt speaking.

I switched the phone to my good ear and listened to one of our mortgage loan officers blather on about the need to make a splash now that Birmingham was nearly a one bank town.

—Stop filibustering, you're holding up progress. Time is money in this business. Now what's the problem? I told the loan officer, a man I encountered only in the elevator.

—They also say money is the root of all evil, Watt.

Rachel just had to interject her two cents into this. —No, not having money is the root of all evil, I snapped at her, my hand cupped over the receiver.

—Sorry, I had someone in my office here. What were you saying about the wind? The wind farm debacle is a non-issue. We can recover our losses from that and Alabama Power will get its wind farms. Yes, I realize that...I'll call up Holland and Don Quixote right now and have them ship us some windmills and tulips, the Cro-Magnons at Alabama Power won't even know the difference, maybe the little blond Dutch boy with his finger in the dyke too while we're at it...who cares if we're supposed to buy American, the Americans don't sell windmills...How many times was Columbus denied financing to cross the ocean blue? And if Isabella hadn't bankrolled his little adventure to the New World, then where would we be? Think of us as the monarch. We hold the purse strings.

When I hung up, Rachel was in a huff, as if I had interfered with her business and not her with mine, unable as she was to distinguish between business and the rest of life.

—I should leave. I never should've come here.

—I have to go to Norwood anyway to assess some of the real estate kingdom we inherited from Wachovia. Why don't you come along?

—Norwood? Really? Since when did you take an interest in affirmative action?

—Since affirmative action became lucrative, I said with a wink and a chrematistic, shit-eating grin. —Come on, get your things, and that means that Rothko of yours too.

My ketchup prints tracked still from the revolving door to a spot halfway to the elevators, as if the ketchup murderer had disappeared midstride. I turned to the security desk, the guard's glabrescent domed head shining like a beacon. I could make out my Jaguar on the surveillance cameras monitoring the parking deck.

—Why are these prints still here? I demanded, pointing behind me. —Get someone down here to clean this mess up, it looks like the invisible man just walked through a homicide scene.

—The janitor called in sick, the guard extenuated.

—Frankly, I find that just a bit incredible, don't you?

—Do you want your shoes now, Mister Watt? I cleaned them off.

—Yes, I'll have my shoes now. Thank you for guarding them, Dale. A real service to the company.

Rachel and I revolved through the lobby doors and gathered ourselves on the street. She trailed behind me, sniffing at invisible essences, stopping before a storefront window display.

I collected as many of the ketchup packets off the ground as I could.

—Watt, what are you doing? she demanded.

—Give me a second, I said.

On the way to the parking deck I stopped in at the Chick-Fil-A around the corner and waited in line ten minutes — and ten minutes of my time is worth a whole day of anybody in that line's time — even though they tout themselves in advertisements as having the shortest and fastest fast food lines in the business. I killed the time listening to a kid lisping about a global hecatomb that would be waged between cows and chickens. I was next; an acned and awkward hobbledehoy in a Chick-Fil-A visor whispered if he could take my order.

—Actually, I'd like to return these, I said, holding up the ketchup packets that had exploded under my shoes that morning. —These ketchup packets bloodied up the lobby of my building.

—What are we supposed to do about it? the cashier asked.

—These ketchup packets. They belong to Chick-Fil-A. They were in the lobby of my office building. They do not belong to Wells Fargo. You ever heard of render unto Caesar? I'm returning them.

I dropped the packets on the counter and the cashier looked at me as if I had just plopped a dead chicken in front of him. Rachel was waiting for me outside, throwing pennies into a fountain.

—You just can't stop wasting my money, can you?

—I'm making wishes, she said.

—Expensive wishes. What did you wish for?

—I'm not telling. What was that about? she asked, under-handing a penny into the silver water, wishing for things I could never give her.

—Just some business. We've been working with Chick-Fil-A on opening up more franchises in the area.

—You talk to the cashier about official business?

My attention was snagged on Day of the Dead decorations in the window of a Mexican restaurant. I pressed my face against the glass and spotted a sepia toned portrait of Emiliano Zapata slouched under a rakish sombrero and brandishing a rifle. I wondered who had been posing for the photo: Zapata himself or his Mexican handlebar mustache. The restaurant's lunch clientele would have no idea who the man in the photo by the register was, just some wetback with a gun, as they masticated burritos and got sloshed on lunchtime margaritas before stumbling back to their simulacrum of an office to stare fixedly at blinking cursors and spreadsheets on blue computer screens.

I couldn't remember where I parked. The security guard could see us on the monitors as we spiraled up and then down again the ramps between each floor of the deck. I had somehow mistaken the 3 for an 8.

—You never used to forget where you parked, Rachel editorialized. —Where's your head been lately, Watt?

I knew this was a double entendre question of hers, and therefore open to interpretation. She often asked equivocally lewd questions without realizing it, then acted offended when I answered in kind. Then I saw the Jaguar sandwiched between a Chevy Suburban and an Escalade. I punched the unlock icon on the remote key fob and threw myself behind the wheel. I loved to see the chrome hood ornament leaping out in front of me, something godlike about machining such a sleek and fast animal, the Jaguar poached and taxidermied mid-leap, silver as a freshly minted dime. I would kill anyone who came near that hood ornament.

We nosed out of the parking deck's concrete dark onto the one-way street, the day's aurous light crashing like falling bricks all around us as I steered the Jaguar smoothly north through a preview of the warfare between cows and chickens: blocks of bombed out, rachitic houses, collapsed roofs, walls leaning at skewed angles, and I swerved around a broken-down Max Bus with our red and yellow ad branding on the side. I always felt like a fish in a barrel driving that car through Birmingham's Bosnian neighborhoods.

—Did you ever find your brother? I asked to steer the conversation away from me and the business at hand, someone more inept than myself.

—Oh, I didn't tell you, did I? He's been living in a plantation house, fixing it up with a meth chemist descended from slaves who worked the plantation.

—I don't have a job to give him, so don't ask.

—I wasn't going to ask.

—What the hell is he doing that for?

—He doesn't like it here.

—Well, I can't blame him on that account. Maybe I can get him a gig washing windows for Wells Fargo. Doesn't he have a PhD?

—Two PhDs.

—And he can't even get a job rubber-stamping at the unemployment office.

Rachel sat silently for a while, staring grimly out the window at the empty houses blurring by and then she started to sing a tune I didn't recognize, as she had in the shower when we were married. Every morning I woke to the dulcet *a cappella* of her showering arias, and I knew by tone and lyric which side of the bed she had woken on that morning. I imagined her standing under the blue curtain of a waterfall, singing until the end of time, the end of money and myself. She sewed curtains to cover our bedroom windows, and always there was a colorful riot of freshly cut flowers dying slowly in a wine bottle. Curtains to block the light, to live in perpetual dark, to hide ourselves from each other, to plumb the shadowy cave where hobgoblins and the Cyclops dwelled. Those wilting flowers snipped from the back garden reminded me somehow of the nuptial nosegays Rachel had thrown blindfolded over her bare white shoulder to the bevy of clucking women at the bottom of the church stairs. Even then, in my tuxedo, owned not rented, I realized that the woman, appearing in the elevator doors, walking away from me through the brume and mists was Rachel, and I had only been following her sand prints all along, even if they led me over the precipice, through a twenty-first century tinted window and tumbling onto the sidewalk like the dead bird I saw that morning.

If you stare too long into the abyss, as I often stared out of my office window at the city valley below, the abyss will gaze also into you — one of the inspirational quotes on the black coffee mug of a banker with long hair who used to study philosophy. Janet gave me the same mug as a gag gift that winter. Oftentimes my own strange reflection stared witlessly back at me, a pumpkin face carved in the window. Why did I keep ex-wives around at all? To have someone catch me when the abyss chews me up and spits me out? In the car, my hand was resting on Rachel's knee, an aberration of the laissez-faire policy we had agreed upon, no ficky-fick after the movers had taken her things out of the house that felt bigger, grander now with only her apparitional absence to fill it.

—My grandparents lived in that house, I said pulling my right hand away from her knee to point to a white plantation style house that reminded me of the carved pumpkin I saw that morning.

We passed by a house with a fake Halloween cemetery in the front yard, gothic winged skulls on black stone, stylized death's heads, laughing and dancing skeletons, a Potemkin cemetery modeled on those in sleepy, haunted New England Puritan towns like Salem.

—A trip down memory lane, Rachel suggested.

—It is home to rats and druggies now.

—Just say what you mean, Watt. You mean it's home to black people now?

—If I wanted to say it was home to black people, I'd say it was home to black people, I said. That rat-catchers have already done their work on this town.

Norwood was an old streetcar suburb on the city's northside where I was looking to site a prison or another wind farm. Private prisons are big money. We curved down the central boulevard under low trees brushing the top of the car and by the weedy, trash-blown parks, a deflated basketball on the courts, the goal's rusted chain hoop swaying in the wind. I braked at a stop sign perforated with bullet holes. Norwood was constructed for mid-level executives and businessmen, their families and domesticated animals, and when the factory smoke from the north wafted through like an airborne plague and then the blockbusting began, the families cleared out in wave upon white wave of flight, many to villainous Mountain Brook, where I had thousands of square feet to myself, a King Lear who had no daughters among whom to divide the estate. If I died, it would all go to the bank. The final solution for neighborhoods like Norwood was to flood it and make some waterfront property for the city.

—This is the address, I said, stopping in front of a row of shotgun houses by the interstate.

I got out of the car and locked the doors with Rachel still inside.

—Sorry, I said and unlocked the doors and waited to relock them until she was out of the car. Rachel had accompanied me before on similar trips; implicitly, she knew her role and stayed back, poking around at trash in a lot across the street. I ascended the unpainted steps that sagged under my weight, their nails creaking against rotten wood. A cat curled up inside a tire. Empty hornet's nest invested in the roof overhang. I took the screen off the eye-screw latch and rapped firmly on the door with my knuckles. The old harridan in the shotgun shack next door came out onto the porch looked me and the car over. —We ain't seen nobody home, she said. I felt like an exhibition in a flannel suit grey as I felt, neck tie tucked into a vest, shoes buffed to a blinding black shine in the reflection of which the abyss stared back at me.

—I'm from the bank. Mrs. Freeman's grace period is up.

—That don't sound like no grace of god I ever caught wind of.

I thought of the torn one dollar bill burning in my pocket and felt that she knew I possessed this worthless talisman.

—You know, Miss, it says in God we trust on the dollar bill.

The old woman's bottom lip bulged with tobacco chew and she projected a dark brown fluid cud out into the grassless yard and said, —God ain't no businessman.

—Yes mam, I agreed. —I guess that's true.

From the porch I tossed the car keys down to Rachel and took the steps two at a time and cut around the back and to the rear door, which I easily kicked open. The house was almost the bank's now. If a sheriff had caught me doing this, I would have palmed him a few fifties so he'd go sheriff somewhere else, and the whole thing never would have happened.

Inside, nothing at Harvard prepared me for what I saw. The habitat of a pathological hoarder. The kitchen was a wrecked mess hall of ancient meals taken alone. I padded through the dark room among mason jars and tin cans, mildewed and rotting newspapers. I looked at the dates that stretched back to the Fifties. Articles of Civil Rights protests in Kelly Ingram Park. Police dogs and fire hoses wielded on children. The 16th Street Baptist Church blown to smithereens. Tanks rolling through the streets below the Wells Fargo tower. I opened a paper to a full page faded photo of Bull Connor and tore the photo out and put it with the two halves of a dollar in my pocket. I searched for a bathroom, but there was none, tripping over items of spoiled furniture lifted from neighboring abandoned houses and a stack of red bricks waist high in a corner. I noted the ceiling medallions and scrolled antiqued woodwork. Someone had put some time into this shotgun.

I entered a small bedroom with a ceiling so low and dark it felt limitlessly high, and the feculent stench of death rolled over me like a black wave. I had smelled it once before. A soft rain dinned on the shotgun's tin roof and then hardened into a crystalline downpour and I thought of Rachel out there in the empty lot, but she would have gotten back into the Jaguar by now, waiting for me with the doors locked and the evening radio tuned to the local NPR station.

On that day I found what became of the misty woman in my elevator vision, whose sand prints I had been following unwittingly up to this point, a terminus after which all things would never be the same, as money is all things all at once because it is nothing at all, exchangeable for house and car, even the wind, but never the things you want, leading me here like bread crumbs through the green-eyed forest, a washer spun down the unraveling length of a rope.

The mortgagee had been dead some time, bone blanched sepulchral and incruent, lightless eyes hollowed from the socket like the bronze Hamlet skull on my desk, and I thought of the pumpkin I had seen that morning, my own soft head atrophying, then smashed against the sidewalk by vandals. I felt light-headed. I sat down in a stick chair with a thatched seat in the corner and listened to the rain drumming down on the steep pitch of the rotting roof.

Thinking of what had happened on this day almost a century ago. The bankers who invested more than just money on the stock market, who bet everything and lost, and gambled again on the existence of God, a dispensation that would stop them before they smacked the concrete below and burst open like ketchup packets, the leap of faith not across the abyss, but from one abyss and zeroing into the next. Would I have done the same? As bankers, they should've known better about what comes after that interminable series of zeros.

Behind the rain there persisted the steady drone of evening traffic on the ribbon roads. The shotgun was within the interstate right-of-way. If it wasn't the banks, the highway department would send in the dozers and in the end the end would be the same as it ever was. I had spent every night of the last week familiarizing myself with Wachovia's portfolio of fixed assets in the area. The Jaguar dealer car lot across the street from the Southtown projects, part of Wells Fargo's extensive parking portfolio, built on top of a black cemetery, where I had bought my own Jaguar. Someone will build a Chuck E. Cheese's or a Rally's over my own resting place. This town's race problems have nothing to do with me. We held a number of downtown properties in vague stages of foreclosure or receivership that would probably be demolished one morning while you sit down to breakfast. Then there were small, delinquent houses like this one that had already been demolished by nature and neglect, still standing only by a technicality.

I got up from my thinking stone, from how the word dolorous sounds so much like dollar, and went to the bedside. I pulled the shreds of a faded quilt up over the dead woman's face. Had I known a prayer, I still would not have said one.

I was projected like a warm shell from the shotgun in a fit of fugue. Rachel must have thought something was wrong when she saw me, because she stepped out of the car, her hair darkening in the rain, waiting on me to say something meaningful or terrible.

—She's not there, I lied. Perhaps the first lie I told Rachel in a long time, sparing her from scenes I thought she couldn't handle.

—You were in there a long time Watt, as if I had taken too long in the bathroom and Rachel had been standing outside the door, counting the minutes with her gorgeous bladder brimful of winepiss.

I learned never to believe a woman who could only say I love you while her mouth was forced open in orgasm. Too, I learned that women came and went in cyclical patterns, like money markets and seasons, Kondratiev Cycles, migrations, and I fit my life into the chaptered myth of Odysseus bouncing from one island woman to the next, an island each with its welcoming and calypso snares, its shipwrecked heartbreaks and venereal vicissitudes. Islands I could possess, but never own. The island will erase the castaway. But whereas Odysseus had Penelope spinning night after night for him in suburban Ithaca, sure of his commuter's return, an allegory of fidelity if ever there was one, there was nothing for me but a collection of untouched bank accounts, ketchup packets splattered murderously on the lobby floor, a Jaguar waiting for me in the parking garage every night the way Rachel used to wait up for me in bed, a dollar bill torn perfectly down the middle across the General's face without explanation. Defacing currency is a crime, but what does it matter? In the end, the ink not yet dry on the divorce papers, we were liaising in hotel rooms, a new name in the registry each night, even though we had a house full of rooms. The last night I signed my name Wells Fargo. The ink from that signature will never dry.

I pensively circled the arc of the steering wheel with my forefinger and watched rain slide down the windshield fogging up with our breath, and I thought again of the couple steamed to death in their Jaguar on 18th Street, a hideous accident without meaning or redemption.

I switched the wipers on and the rain was swept off in two strokes. I wasn't sure how much time had passed in the shotgun. I drove back downtown in silence, running several stop lights at empty intersections, and Rachel asked me some questions about the shotgun house I gave her grunting answers to.

—Why're they called shotguns?

—Because you could stand at the front door and fire a shotgun clean through the house and out the back door and never hit anything.

—They say too that ghosts and spirits are fond of the shotguns. They pass straight through them. Have you heard that before, Watt?

—I'll believe anything right now, I said. —Tell me anything you want, I'll believe it.

—What happened in there?

—I saw a ghost pass through the house, from the front door to the back like a shotgun shell, just like you said.

The ghost was myself. Except that I had ghosted in reverse from the back to the front door. She turned toward me in her seat, her marvelous breasts bursting at the seams beneath her seatbelt that cut across her chest, her eyes seeing something in me I had never seen before, saying that indeed paradise is lost. She put her hand on my arm.

—Come have a drink with me.

—Rachel.

—Just one drink.

—One drink turns into two and two turns into four and then eight. Before you know it, we're married again. Things are better this way, for now.

I dropped her off at the Highland Avenue condo I underwrote for her after the divorce. She reached for the door, paused, resting her hand on the handle. —You can come in if you want, she said without looking at me, a last ploy to ply me with drink and bed.

—I shouldn't, Rach. Work to do at the office, with the merger and everything.

Lately, I had been parturient with ideas on how to innovate new financial products. The driving force of a bank is that you want everyone to be in debt to you. I had contacts at Alabama Power I used to startup the utility-scale wind project to harvest the wind. After dozens of conferences with stakeholders and shareholders, I was still without wind in my sails, quarreling with Rachel in the autumn rain.

—Watt, one day you will regret this moment. Telling me no, you'd rather go back to your office and count change. Henry VIII, even though he had all those wives, was a lonely man.

—Maybe I will regret it. But that day is not today.

Rachel handled open the passenger door, got out and slammed it behind her without saying a word. I felt the slam like a slap on the face. I knew if I ever saw her again it would be a long time. Months might pass before she again barged into the sanctity of my office, guns blazing. I would take care of her letter from Wachovia, of course. That much was understood between us. My foot had been on the brake all this time, and I geared the Jaguar into reverse and pulled out of the drive, squealing tires down the street.

Back at the bank, darkness full upon the street now and the WELLS FARGO neon aglow like a star on a Christmas tree, the end-of-the-workweek Halloween gala was in full swing. I wasn't in the mood. The only thing missing was an apple bobbing contest and a hayride. Adults turn into children on Halloween. Bankers and accountants, their faces unrecognizable beneath the gore and paint, androgynous zombies, women as witches burned at the stake, someone in an Obama mask wearing a red t-shirt with *communist* printed across the chest in Soviet bloc script. A man I didn't recognize dressed in Army fatigues like Castro was grab-assing a young office girl as Alice in Wonderland and drunkenly intoning, *I got married to the widow next door. She's been married seven times before.* Through this masque of the red death I hoped to pass unnoticed. I shadowed myself to the elevator.

—Hey Watt. What're you supposed to be for Halloween? A banker?

Everyone laughed. The party quieted as if they were waiting for me to make a speech. In the elevator, I turned around to face the revelers, peasants frolicking in a Brueghel's, and I held the door open and said, —I'm a ghost, I pronounced. —I was never here.

I mashed the twenty-first button for the twenty-first floor, like the century only barely started, and the elevator doors slid silently and slowly closed, and in the inch or so left before they met in the middle I saw either the real janitor pushing a bucket of mop water across the floor, or else a banker costumed as a janitor.

On the ascent, I thought of my deposits with the bank. I wanted to see them, the Lear daughters, heirs to my divided ashes. I negotiated the dual-control combo dial like a pick-lock, I could do it in my sleep. Normally, the vault requires two people to open, but you can't plan for everything. They build the vault first, a custom job, and the bank around it and stock the bank with bankers who are little more than the fungible shadows of their résumés. The way fishing ponds are stocked with catch. Men in suits, fish in barrels. The vault door swung open ponderously. You expect them to creak like an old barn door on unoiled hinges, but it floats open soundlessly as a ship cuts through calm waters. I could not see that the cave had any end. In the gold light of the bank vault, I was transfigured, elevated beyond the elevator's highest floor, submerged in venal ether. I moved the money that spun the blades that blew the wind. The world is your oyster, Rachel once told me, the moribund flowers in the wine bottle between us on the table. I don't even like oysters. Then I had shattered the glass ceiling and rocketed straight for the stratosphere of finance, a fake science.

At night I sneak into the vault to see the flickering substance behind the electronic shadows and digital zeros that send us scratching at the walls every time the stock market hiccups. But the vault is empty, an artifact of the days when banking was a physical science, and money moves quietly, sleeplessly through wires after hours, yet still I return to the vault expecting to find some token: a torn dollar, a dead bird, a ketchup packet, a smashed pumpkin, anything corporeal at all. In the strongroom, money had become metaphysics. Wachovia was Wells Fargo, and I was not the same banker as I was yesterday.

When I reached my office, Rachel's Rothko print was leaning against my desk. I knew she had done that purposely so it would be the first thing I saw upon entering, as once she left her ample brassiere draped across the back of my chair in the office at home, her way of making me think about her, shaded in the rustling green light of a banker's lamp. Alone with the painting now, I noticed something I had not seen before: a thin strip of fuzzy white stretching like a horizon between the top and bottom rectangles of autumnal color.

Deftly I unknotted my neck tie and threw myself back in my squeaking office chair, slipped my bloodless dress shoes off and stared at the ceiling the color of sky on a grey day. What was Rothko trying to say with these orange and yellow rectangles, with that white horizon dividing the two color planes, if color said anything at all, and what was I hiding? I never told Rachel anything about my childhood, and she never asked. I am not a man to dwell upon the past, in this city choked on the past and history brighter than its future, for money is the language of the future, a language I am still learning to speak. I remembered a tumbledown barn where farm tools rusted and owls hooted, the side gardens blackened even in daylight. I squandered hours in that barn puzzling out what obscure purposes for which those tools were wrought in iron and wood. How if the sun died, like the old woman in the shotgun, it would take six or eight minutes before the last light reached us for the final time. Then the world would be as colorless as this office and my gray suit which blends in with the walls and the people.

I went to the office window and looked down from the twenty-first floor, like the century. I peeled the heather argyle socks off my hooves and thought morosely of the falling man photo and the pinstripes of the World Trade Tower, a photo that stuck with me through the decade only because it could have been of myself on this day. But this is not New York, this is Birmingham. Vulcan's torch burned like a beacon over the city below. I wondered pleasantly what the new fiscal year would hold. The years no longer seasonal, reckoned by summers and falls, but monetary, the years of my life in this city measured in quarters. All this time I had been unconsciously fingering the torn one dollar bill in my pocket. I turned my pocket inside out, and came up with only half of the Washington dollar, the other half missing, and I took the ugly newspaper photo of Bull Connor out, balled it up and tossed it into the nihilist coffee mug on my desk by the bronze Hamlet skull.

A pair of eerie eyes regarded me humorlessly from the wall, with such intensity of focus they seemed to listen. I took down the dark and grey portrait of J.P. Morgan — gold is money, he once said; all else is credit — and trashed it in the wastebasket — Janet would find it the following morning and put it back — and hung the red and yellow and orange autumn Rothko in its place and the banker's office became a chapel and when I came back barefoot through the lobby at the end of the night, the party over, my crimson shoe-prints had been mopped away.

TWENTY-SIX PEOPLE PER SQUARE MILE

I am one of twenty-six people per square mile. Only thing here poorer than the paupers is the earth they will be buried in. The arid, futile dirt which the starving anthropophagous cram into their mouths, gums bleeding. The rainless, vacuous sky shunning promises of manna. Ruined whistle-stop towns faded like old tintypes where even the church is abandoned and the highway signs are drilled with bullet holes. One of twenty-six, and fewer by the day.

Following a long night wasted crossing out the names of authors on the title pages of novels and penning my own name underneath I decided to do something, anything with myself. I had been using bloody band-aids as bookmarks. It was time for a change. Another decade was upon us and the Fed needed temp workers to poll the nation's citizens and non-citizens. I took a census job in the ruralest county of a rural state and never came back. The pay was lumpen-proletarian, but I had hoarded academic degrees, and no notions about how to put them to use. The degrees were just another way of passing the time. Some people play tennis, or watch TV or drink, take out credit. I cached degrees.

Experts say in tiny, spell-checked voices that world population is swelling out of control. Hale County has been shrinking, flinching from modernity ever since the last bale of cotton was sold, the last bipedal property manumitted. There's only one condom in the whole state. We need birth control you can shoot through a dart gun.

I submit Hale County and all therein as a cheerful refutation of the Dismal Theorem.

When my sister Rachel came to Hale looking for me, she made twenty-seven people in our square mile of bankrupt earth. She had married rashly young to get out of the house, an opulent Catholic wedding in which I incanted some erotic verses from the Book of Psalms. An Irish priest officiated in his strong brogue, one hand on the Good Book and the other on an IRA gun. The after-party is a prodigal blur, but there was shrimp and grits, footloose booze and white people trying to dance in ways our ancestors would not have thought possible. They were not soulmates, but I liked my broth-

149

er-in-law, Watt, more than my sister, who is about as interesting as an office filing cabinet. An investment banker at Wells Fargo, he'd make a karmic fortune — enough for them to live like latter-day planter plutocracy — turning people out of their homes. He could knot a necktie like a surgeon sewing an incision. He was the guy who planned his flight itineraries with layovers long enough for a corporate shoeshine from the servile black guy whistling Billie Holiday's version of *Stars Fell on Alabama* at the Birmingham airport. Of course, I knew better: it depends on what's in the office filing cabinet.

I was squatting in one of the chattel quarters attached to a crumbling Greek Revival plantation — white supremacist architecture. This plantation stretched for thousands of acres between horizons, its planter in the top percentile of all landowners before Harper's Ferry. The white leviathan had been chilled for a while as a museum in a state of suspended animation, like a cryogenically frozen slave owner — and not some noble iambic pentameter demagogue before the invention of the French Revolution's trichotomy of values, like Julius Caesar or other Roman Emperors — but the antebellum forerunners of your neighbors like Bubba and Boon, and then the State decided the past was perhaps not worth keeping on ice for some dubious purpose in the future when the country might try slavery again, and so the mansion was thawed out, shuttered and plywooded. Wild fowl and squatters moved in, the plantation ransacked for its chandeliers and rich rain-forest mahogany. The westwork front door, before it was unhinged as a casket lid in a kid's funeral, perforated with bullet holes that lit up like constellations when the sun set behind the plantation. Each evening the last of the sun was split into rails by the bullet holes in the front door. I was starting to like Hale County.

You like to think that abiding and eternal iron laws — the same as governed the plantation in its heyday, and governs it in its aristocratic decay now — oversee every minor detail of our lives, from the fluttering of a thought down to the very movement of our bowels, mentation and materiality alike, but I fear it is not so, only as a group do necessary laws become a factor, but as individuals we are desperately, dyingly free to choose, like Buridan's donkey, between a stack of hay and a pail of water.

I knew it was Rachel in the grassless plantation yard by the plinking drip as the engine cooled, like the sound of cave water slipping off a stalactite into a subterranean pool. Sunglare flashed across the windshield, obscuring the driver. She sat in the cab of the truck, deciding whether or not she wanted to follow through with this. She swung the truck door open and stepped out into the sodium light of an austral afternoon, ridiculously overdressed in a summery business suit. She had recently quit her job as an insurance saleswoman, in the middle of the Great Recession.

—Welcome to Hale County, home of Hale County, I greeted her for the first time in many months, as she sidled up the dirt drive to the great house — my father would have critiqued the renovations. I acted unsurprised — do not confuse my experience in the forgery of emotion with learning the enigmatic rules of the society from whose skeleton architecture I deserted — as though I'd been expecting her any day and she had been late. It was only a matter of time before someone from the old world came back to haunt me.

—Hey little brother, Rachel said.

I was sitting on an overturned milk crate on the porch reading a newspaper I'd found inside the plantation from the 1960's. It was the first newspaper I'd picked up since the Millennium.

—What're you doing, Thomas?

—Sitting, reading.

—What else is there to do in Hale County?

—I could buy up half this county with a single paycheck.

—I didn't see a bank on the way in.

—You know, spec houses, New Urbanist stuff. A rural Seaside, a fortress mall. Lots of glass and steel. Bring in some avant-garde architects like Zaha Hadid or Rem Koolhaas to afflict some kind of vision on the place. Running water, if you can imagine such a thing, I said picturesquely.

—Gentrify, she agreed.

—That's right.

—Not much to work with, and you might have trouble growing palm trees here, but if you talk like that to the county tourism board you might find yourself a job.

I don't know where my sister learned the word "gentrify." I had always pegged her among that odiously bland camp of people who perfectly embody the Webster's dictionary definition of a philistine without having any notion what the word meant. She wore a perfume called "urban decay" without any sense of irony.

She liked carpet and small dogs. Perhaps I had been rash in my assessments. I hadn't seen my sister since the wedding, dressed in irreproachable white, and suddenly there she was in one of the remotest nooks of the state, desolate as a crater. She did that a lot when we were kids — appearing when you least wanted her to — and as adults too.

—This your place? she asked, meaning the antebellum plantation.

I led her round back of my collapsing castle.

—Home sweet home, I said, indicating the glorious one-room shack on bricks behind the plantation.

—What a sad-ass sight to see, she said. —Of course you'd be sleeping in the slave quarters.

I wanted to stonewall her, but retorted, —I'm moving to the big house next week. It's a very and extremely roomy house.

—I am very and extremely happy for you.

—Why are you very and extremely here?

—I thought I'd come put in some quality time with my brother and the local yokels in the sticks.

—That's very and extremely unlike you.

—No, dumbass, I came to drag you back to Birmingham, she plied on.

—That's a very tempting prospect, which I am sure others weaker and less full of bile for that place than myself would be unable to resist, but you should leave now and save yourself the trouble. The chiggers will love a fresh piece of meat like yourself. How did you find me anyway?

—I knew you were answering mail, so I just went to the truck stop meth lab that passes for a post office and asked where the only white guy might be. They told me you'd be at this dump, just turn off the paved road, Bubba said.

—It's not a dump. Letch and I've been fixing the place up, I said stoutly in defense of my crumbling, papery mansion that would wither away in the softest gust of wind or the driest rain.

As I said that a blackbird flew out of an upper window, circled in the wet blue air above us and alighted in a magnolia.

—Nice house.

—Don't mind him. He's a paying tenant now. Just signed the lease.

—So you're a landlord of birds now. I see you found your calling.

—Would you like it more if it had palm trees, a chlorine pool, some kitschy paintings of beach scenes on a condo wall?

—That's a good start. You always were an insufferable ass. No wonder Ellen left you.

—I'd rather not talk about that.

Ellen was of the old world, you see.

—Is Letch one of your buddies? You been making friends, Tom?

—Letch is the local chemist. His house exploded and he needed a place to live so we've been muscling this place into shape.

She stepped into the rear parlor and around a pair of A-frame sawhorses and over a stack of lumber Letch and I had filched from a lumberyard close to Greensboro. Some of the creaking floorboards were warped and contoured from rain leaking through the ceiling — the boards talked to you as you trespassed them.

—I just love what you've done with the place, Tom, my sister said roundly with that brassy flip of hers that always irked me. I told her to be careful, to stay away from the windows, there were sharpshooters and snipers posted in the bushes. She emitted a hollow, cemetery laugh and breasted — yes, that's exactly what she did, like a swan — her way into the next room. A brightly russet box of light slid up the wall as the sun went slowly down behind a line of windbreaks on the western end of the plantation property. That paling hour when all things grow pensive and turn inward or away, like a black bloom closing in upon itself. I noticed these things more after I had settled into the slave quarters of my empty mansion, no longer within the mephitic sphere of influence of the big white house disquieted by the bedeviling presence of my father terrorizing the local NPR station with his routine calls. Once Worcy Crawford refused to spray him with the garden hose — that was all he wanted, a reckoning or expiation of our race's debts — he went crackbrained, a member of the Southern Death Cult proselytizing to the Birmingham Fire Department.

She looked up at a hole in the ceiling where a chandelier once illumined the doings of a family whose money began with human chattel. The room was close and airless, like being inside of a body bag, old leaves from autumns ago windrowed against the wainscoting. Droppings from the resident barn owls littered the floor. Through the glassless window the sky dimmed to some painter's shade of lilac or heliotrope and then bruised a deep color of blackberry jam. Had only Monet lived in Hale County, and not

Giverny, France. No street lights winked on out of doors. The stars came out like splatters of white paint on a black ceiling. The din of the cicadas was overwhelming. You get used to it after a time, and it becomes a white noise only the silent absence of which would be noticed. My sister had apparently noticed my absence. She stopped at the foot of the cantilevered mahogany staircase.

—I'm not going up there, she said to the dark at the top of the staircase.

A swan-neck pediment had fallen off a doorway. She picked the wooden swan up and scrutinized it.

—They mate for life, you know.

—Both black and white swans.

We walked the long crepuscular hall toward the missing front door, I thinking of the tubes of bullet hole light that erstwhile illumined the wall.

We stood on the porch leaning against the Ionic or Doric columns, they're all the same, supporting the rotting tympanum above our heads. I was waiting on her to ask what had happened to the plantation's carpet. A draft of wind sighed rattling through the house like the last breath exiting the lungs of a warm corpse, and the wood of the cantilevered balcony creaked in a dead language close above our heads.

—You see stars out here you never thought existed, I offered.

—Perhaps we city folk are better off not knowing they exist. It seems inhuman to dwell on the stars too long. You'll go insane, Tom.

For a time, we stopped talking and listened to the hoots and lusty calls of the wild animals that skulked green-eyed in the wooded dark, the wind rasping in the groaning branches of the trees, magnolia of star and spiring pine. Then the bullfrogs ratcheted up their primordial throaty chorus and the outer dark clamored high with the rows and shouts of Hale County's species that survived King Cotton's reign. Some reported herds of elephants or mastodons in the woods, the Pleistocene megafauna of Hale County's time warp.

—What's the date? I asked.

—September 15th.

—Ah, I said, as though my worst suspicions had been confirmed, —Birmingham's Guernica.

Rachel moved to another of the house's white columns, one further away from me.

—You want a drink?

—You have a wet bar out here, Tom? And I thought you were roughing it.

I edged inside and returned with two doubles of Johnny Walker.

—It strikes me that you support the census but don't pay any taxes here, Tom.

—There's no one here to do the taxing or be taxed. There are more people in Birmingham City Jail than in this whole county.

—Am I supposed to be impressed with your rustic loneliness? With your bucolic alienation?

—Never said anything about loneliness or not. Just numbers. Census data. Can't argue with the Bureau of the Census.

—The job is over, Thomas. It's time to come back.

—Tom. Call me Tom. We're siblings, after all.

Calling people by their full name was a habit she picked up at the insurance office.

—I never filled those damn census things out anyway. I think I left it in the mailbox.

—It's your constitutional duty to take the census. You can be held in contempt of the constitution if you don't.

—You didactic little shit.

—And then you wonder why Alabama doesn't get any money.

—I don't like the idea of some nosy bureaucrat knowing so much about me.

—The census is harmless compared to other forms of intelligence.

—Still.

—Takes seventy-two years before certain census statistics are in the public domain. Seventy-two. We'll be dead by then.

—When was the last time you talked to someone, Tom?

—I talked to the ghost of a Civil War Colonel just this morning over breakfast. We had grits and eggs and discussed strategy. Over lunch, I spoke with Martin Luther King about the philosophy of non-violent civil disobedience.

—I mean really talked to someone.

—New York cabs have televisions in them. Think about it.

Avoiding a steady vocation devolved into a vocation in and of itself. I took the census job because I knew it would be temporary. I didn't want to be stuck like my sister was stuck. As kids, I once mutilated her dolls, coupled the androgynous looking male dolls with the androgynous looking female dolls. They had androgynous babies. I don't know what came over me. There was simply nothing else to do in the big white house. Although the episode was probably no longer in her conscious mind, I imagined it floated around like a corpse in the general shallows of her unconscious, where she harbored a rankling memory of the happy time I grated a clove of garlic on her braces, which were hideously silver and sharply metallic like a mouthful of shrapnel. It was probably all this brotherly abuse that drove her to a low life of selling insurance.

I cottoned quickly to the job. We're called enumerators. Counting people as ciphers for more general trends, gathering the micro-data which are later aggregated into migration patterns and population shifts. Although we no longer migrated seasonally, I began to see people like the birds, shoving off in search of resources or better employment opportunities, the pursuit of happiness quantified at last.

The only thing more interesting than the people you counted were the dwellings in which they went on living much as they had when Walker Evans was here with his camera. From the road, these jerry-built hovels looked uninhabited. The tin trabeated farmhouses and ramshackle double-wides. Chickens pecked noisily at the dirt. A guard dog chained to a tree. You can't always tell though. Dumps that appear to be unoccupied and condemned turn out to house a family of six or eight people. NO TRESPASSING. I would not be foxed by such things.

You never knew who was going to answer the door. If they were hostile or, at best, only skeptical. I hoped a ravishing country beauty in a negligee would come to the door and invite me in, her husband off rolling in the hay with the farm girl next door, but that was a bodice-ripper delusion. The grim old women who had just stepped out of a Walker Evans silver gelatin. On more than one occasion I talked down the anti-government types waving a gun in my face.

In the local lore these are salt of the earth folks who brought us the Book of Revelations with a country twang and a toothless

Twenty-Six People

smile. I gently explain that census workers have the same impunities as postal workers, we just make less and can't unionize. Never should've used the word *unionize* in front of a man who still thought every state should have a standing militia. If you kill me, judge and jury will not be kind.

I was commissioned to follow up with those who didn't mail in their questionnaires, which was most of Hale County, if not the whole state of Alabama. Authorities need to know the whereabouts of the state's single condom. Census workers in New York's Chinatown had it the worst. You've got to poll people who don't speak a syllable of English and if they do they pretend not to. Fear of deportation, fear of being called *alien.* I read in a newspaper I picked up in Greensboro that a census worker in Montana had been held hostage. Enumerators mauled by guard dogs. Rapings, muggings, stabbings, the sacrilegious and the all-too human. A Kentucky census worker was found hanging naked from a tree, the word "FED" written on his chest in his own blood. Fed. Fed up.

What a lot of these Jeffersonian corn-fed clodhoppers with their georgic politics failed to understand was that the numbers collected were used to distribute federal aid to places in dire need and to allocate seats in the House of Representatives, not to implement the foreign policy of a "United States of Europe," I heard one yahoo say.

—Look, I appealed, trying to affect my best deep-fried southern accent, because they trust you more if you talk like them. I'd hate to see what they'd do to you if you showed up on their rotten, sagging porches with an accent from above the Mason-Dixon. — Whatever you got cooking in there ain't none of my business. I'm here to do a job just like you got your own work to worry about it. Now you ain't gonna keep a man from earning a living now are you?

That was how I met Letch, the meth maven of Hale. He offered me a mason jar brimming with quicksilver moonshine and told me to step inside. You're not supposed to drink on the federal dime, but if you refuse an offer of libation from these people they'll think there's something wrong with you. The inside of Letch's residence was like walking into a deranged man's skull. Letch was blotto as a baboon and his tumbledown house of leaning sticks smelled like a skunk. I held my breath and began the inquisition.

—Do you own or rent, Mister Letch?

—Never done nothing but been on my own property long as I recall. Have a drink? the cipher offered companionably. Letch's bald dome of a head glinted in the sunlight as though it had recently been buffed to mirror-like perfection.

—Does anyone else live here temporarily or permanently?

—Just me and the roaches. Might be a possum round here.

I thanked him for his time and headed for the door.

—You got a plan when the census is done? Letch said to my back.

I was unprepared for this. Sensing my plight, Letch passed the moonshine to me. It tasted like floor stripper, the stuff used to sanitize the halls of prisons, mental asylums and the bathroom floors of brothels. Drink made him chummy. He later gave me the story of his family tree, straight from the beginning. Kidnapped in the Heart of Darkness, his forbears crossed the Atlantic on one of many slave routes and were sold to the southern gentleman who built the plantation I squatted in. I could tell Letch enjoyed this. After the War of Northern Aggression they became sharecroppers, which was worse than being a slave, he said.

—No. There is no plan, I answered uncertainly.

In the first census of 1790, census takers rode horseback through countryside and city. They must have seemed like the horsemen of the apocalypse, harbingers of big government doom to the backwoodsmen of the hinterland where many had never even seen a three-story building or the seagulls that wheeled above the ocean. Slaves were counted as three-fifths of a person. These horsemen enumerators collected data on literacy, insanity, idiocy, blindness, native language. God forbid the state's lone condom should ever go missing.

Next day Letch's meth lab burnt the family two-room to the ground and he — son of quondam slaves — began shacking with me in the chattel quarters of the plantation while we fixed it up. Letch taught me to how to make a floor level, to float fresh plaster, and hang a door so that it would float closed behind you as if automatically. He taught me how to hold and swing a hammer, and for hours at a time we worked sweating alongside each other without speaking, thinking of dad bricking up the windows in the big white house to keep the sunlight out, and Letch told me the life story of an uncle who was one of the nine Scottsboro Boys. Anyone native to the dirt of Alabama knows how that story ended.

Rachel wanted to go to Greensboro, into town, as she said, but I prevailed upon her instead to go hiking through the scrappy, homogeneous woods that environed the plantation. All about the monotonous pine prevailed like a single, archetypal tree had been cut-and-paste. The battery in my wristwatch died, and we just walked and said nothing. I like to feel the planet's resistance beneath my heels. The pines gave way to oak-hickory. Underbrush attacks you. A green sun followed our trek below the leafy canopy. We crossed a shortgrass prairie and scrubby lowbrush where a cotton field picked by Letch's family had once been and then the white pines tall as office towers again.

—Fear the boll weevil, I said to break the silence.

—Yes, I fear it. Whatever it is, I fear it.

—When was the last time you were in nature, Rachel? Really in it? Deep down in its guts, your mouth full of dirt?

—Helped Watt cut the grass a few weeks back. I think I swallowed a bug.

—Alright, alright. We'll start with that. Swallowed a bug.

We stopped to lunch in a stony clearing in the pines.

—What are these stones, Tom?

—Those aren't stones. Those are graves in a Negro cemetery.

She sat down on a headstone, crossing her legs like she was on a park bench in Kelly Ingram Park.

—Turn around, I said.

—Turn around?

—I have to take a leak.

—God, Tom.

As if I'd never seen her hike her skirt up before and squat against a wall. It took me a few minutes to find a tree far enough outside the cemetery worthy of being pissed on — you don't just water any old tree, it has to be the right tree, and you do not water a tree in a Negro cemetery in Hale County unless you want to end up in the next installment of *13 Alabama Ghosts and Jeffrey* — but when I'd marked my territory I went back to the cemetery, zipping up my fly, she was kneeling before a canted tombstone to decipher an illegible name. —How do you know it's a Negro cemetery? she asked the stone.

—A white cemetery wouldn't have been left to pot like this, and most of the markers are crude. You ought to see the cemeteries in New Orleans. The tombstones are so dense they look like a city skyline.

—Dad lost the house.

I was having trouble following Rachel's trainwrecked thoughts. She must have been discombobulated by the heat, not knowing where she was, no traffic lights to tell her when to go, when to stop. Some people need technological comforts to get on, a screen to tell them what to do.

—Tell him to come out here.

—Come back to us, Tom. We're losing you.

—I'd rather stay out here with the hicks.

—And the mosquitoes, as she slapped her forearm.

—You get used to them. I've already started naming some of them. Like the creatures in the garden.

—Mosquitoes for pets. Wait till Watt hears about this.

—Nobody asked you to come out here just because I lost my job.

—It was a temp job, shitstick.

—What's Watt going to do anyway? Use some of his banking voodoo on me?

—We haven't seen a single person since I came here.

—They're all so far apart, it can take you all day to track just one or two people. More wild dogs than people. A lot of these people are really suspicious of the government. You have to explain to them what you're doing and how it will benefit them. Almost everyone here is unemployed and Southern Baptist. I fit in.

—I quit my job, Rachel said abruptly.

—You can't stay here.

—Don't you worry about that.

—You'd fit right in though. Hale County's unemployment rate hasn't changed since the Grapes of Wrath. Just need to get you out of those business clothes and into overalls, knock out some teeth.

—Pity.

—There's a guy on the next square mile who can fix you up with a gig cooking meth.

—I'd rather shovel shit.

—Is that city speak for "sell insurance?"

—Dad's dead, Tom.

Bemused, my first thought was: If dad is dead, then the data from his census tract will be skewed before it's ever aggregated! And then: —You've been here — what? Three days now and you couldn't tell me sooner? You wait till now?

—I didn't know what kind of state you'd be in when I got here. I hadn't heard from you in months.

—What kind of state? I'm not in any kind of state, I said shrilly.

—Listen to yourself, Tom.

—Just because a man prefers Walden Pond to your fucking insipid suburbialand doesn't mean he's in a state. What a fucking self-righteous cunt you can be.

—Tom, I didn't know. I hadn't heard from you.

—Then how did you know I was answering mail?

—Ellen told me.

—Jesus, Rachel. You're rifling through my mail and my past now? I didn't come back to Stinktown for a reason, and you're pumping Ellen for information.

I should mention now that Rachel was only a half-sister. If Dad was dead the filial bond between us was finally broken, the old world's last venomous umbilical purchase on me. A relief of duty which she had come to discharge. I may have stopped breathing. I confess to strange family thoughts about her in negligee. There would be a safety deposit box at the Wells Fargo — I didn't know what was in it, but my father's larksome wit was such that it could be empty. But the bottom line of his death would be delayed till I opened that black box. With dad gone that was one less person per square mile. He kept two addresses: one in Norwood and one that moved around the State. The census probably counted him twice. I remember, as a child, the enumerators coming to the door, and my father telling them not to count him, to zero him out. They could count the household if they wanted, but not the householder.

I told Rachel there was nothing in Birmingham worth returning to — the big white house could sit devoid of his minatory presence on its shady boulevard till the termites ate it and the wind knocked it over — and I think she agreed, as we marched back from the Negro cemetery in the sultry silence, mosquitoes eating us alive. I searched about the wood for elephants or mastodons, and Rachel complained that her phone didn't get reception out here.

From afar I heard Letch's hammering before the plantation emerged out of the magnolias and pines, its columns whitely agleam in searing light. The columns were Doric, and the porch wasn't a porch, it was a portico. The plantation's future was bright and sunny, a new coat of white paint and good glass in the windows, the gaping hole in the front plugged with a door and the roof patched up — Letch and I its plantermen.

Like the galloping, apocalyptic census horsemen of 1790, my sister drove out here while the old man's body was still warm in the morgue, harbinger of an omen to the backwoodsman, but I will not be moved from my forty-acres and a mule. This new plantation house Letch and I are restoring together: no bricks darkening the windows, and I tied a knot in the garden hose.

A dead man counted as two living people. I'll wait around for the next decennial census. By then this plantation house — Letch and I's bastille against the century's horsemen — will be the centerpiece of some tract housing development, paved roads terminating like cancerous outgrowths in cul-de-sacs and street lights whiting out the starry night. FED will send out another temporary enumerator to count me and I will answer the door Letch and I hung, without armament, but I will be but three-fifths of a slave.

AVE MARIA GROTTO

Try pulling a Mississippi lane change like only a white man in deepest Christendom can. The state troopers patrolling Jesusland are the most lethal drivers on the road like they'd just learned to drive yesterday. A scream of choleric car horns jolts Clare from a shallow catnap snuck behind dark sunglasses, ripped from a dream of a normative land of milk and honey, the disenchantment settling in as she finds herself again in the passenger seat of my truck. The unvarnished, adamantine reality of Alabama cannot be wished away. She's about to tell me to get out and walk. To maniac down the freeway like I'm a black ex-athlete in a white Bronco runs against my principles — the principles of stone and mineral are leisurely and glacial, sometimes drowsing into stern inactivity and vernacular mountainous apathy — but it's the survival of the fastest on the blacktop named for dead Lost Cause Generals or Hank Williams. Clare is looking out the back window, as if someone in a dark cruiser is tailing us. She looks like a valedictorian who's settled for being a career airline stewardess. All the cities look the same to her. Campanella's City of the Sun the same to her as Sodom and Gomorrah; the simulacral Las Vegas Eiffel Tower no less charming than the Champ de Mars' Eiffel Tower in Paris. I can live with that, if she can. Pray for us in this welter.

I ceased smoking back when Bush was in office, but I still favor the caliginous, secondhand aroma of a burning cigarette, so I fire one up and let it smolder and blacken down. Clare rolls down her window, ahems a croup at a passing poultry truck, feathers flailing wildly like a pillow fight in its wake. I see myself reflected back to me in Clare's sunglasses, as she must see me, like a prehistoric fly resined in honey-colored amber.

I tally the families of handmade crosses — three crosses on the right, a grouping of five crosses after the next exit — between the road and tree line, commemorating the scenes of gruesome accidents, finally losing count. Decapitations, impalements, defenestrations, disembodiments, transhumanizations. A big rig spirits brusquely by us in the middle lane, in a hell of a hurry to stick to his schedule. Drivers pedal faster these days to get their rocks off, titillated by the transcendental terror of supernatural speed and black curtains, burning pyres, and a hootenanny afterlife. The highways in this state are overnight becoming a metaphor for the midgeted souls operating mammoth machinery that could extinct us all faster than I can shift down to second from fifth gear. The earth may not last long enough for the Second Coming.

Command line: End human experiment. Reboot dinosaurs. Run.

Clare takes my eyes off the road. I am razed by Clare's saintly good looks, hot as jalapeños. She could stare at a house fire and put it out with her look. I expect her to burst into flames like Joan of Arc, to become wildfire, burn those woods around our homes. I haven't touched her, or even brushed a hand through her hair, which spills like an amorous cocktail on her shoulders. For all I know she thinks riding a mechanical bull is the same as sex. I'll have to renounce sleeping on a soft mattress and wear a cilice under my suit. Quit the ways of the world, its cupidities and pettifoggery, and crusade for some righteous cause I cannot possibly fathom the meaning of. I am more concerned with people than causes, she says. Your rocks and stones are just the artifacts of dead worlds and lost causes, like the Confederate monuments they're taking down in New Orleans.

—There's still time to turn around, first thing she's said in fifteen, twenty miles of fifth gear.

After the shotgun shacks of north Birmingham disappear, and the suburban exits of hyper-American cuisine are behind us, Clare and I rush forward to my past at eighty miles per hour, instead of letting it return to me when it's ready. This was her idea. The low estival sun is eclipsed by the shadow of Gardendale Baptist Church, proportioned like a pagan pantheon. The Baptists are a prosperous bunch with pockets deep as craters. Their big money donors — state senators, governors, game wardens, bankers, football coaches, state prosecutors, all of whom believe that Jesus ascended into heaven from the Mount of Olives — dip deep into the pork barrel for an extravagant, skyscraping cross the height of a space shuttle, as emphatic and Brummagem a statement as a billboard. You can see the Baptist's towering cross coming at you from miles away. Members of the local Southern Death Cult gather here around the solstice, waiting for the Gardendale Baptist cross to launch into low earth orbit.

Clare reads aloud from the reading material on the side of the road. Green highway department signs pocked with bullet holes. 35 MILES TO CULLMAN. AVE MARIA GROTTO. JESUS IS COMING signage nailed to a dead roadside pine. I think of the tree sap suppurating from the stigmata of the wounded bark, the mosquitoes crystallized forever there. NO CREDIT CHECK. WE BUY JUNK. DIVORCE $200. These prognostic signs of Second Coming and the culture of fuck yes, when read in her singsong voice, are like lullabies made from the cries for help of an endangered species.

Clare dials on the radio. On the local evangelical talk station, pundits hold forth on the affinities between humans and beavers with a Christian who recently got a face transplant to make himself look more like Jesus. The affinities linking humans and beavers finally exhausted, and there are more affinities than even a human would think, the show's caller invokes the fact that everyone's legs are exactly long enough to reach the ground as proof of intelligent design.

The programmers running this simulation from the outside are all laughing at us right now.

Clare changes the radio to NPR and we listen to Diane Rehm's shaky, gray voice fill the car with doomsday scenarios about the Gulf's Deepwater spill — what this could mean for Gulf shrimpers and the tourist industry — and the impending national debt ceiling crisis. That *I told you so* tone. The boys in Congress are really redefining the meaning of status quo. Diane Rehm debates a doyen from the National Economic Council while Clare picks at a nail and taps it on the window. The click of her nails on the glass is like some giant bird of prey with talons walking up the stair step vertebrae of my spine.

—I can't listen to her, Clare declares finally. —Rehm's voice is terrifying.

—And the moon will turn blood red.

—I'm serious.

—Why not?

—She takes forever to say anything.

—Think about her reading *Julius Caesar,* or *Principles of Geology.*

—The horror.

For some reason, I think Clare says *the whore.*

—How old do you think she is? Clare asks.

—We'd need radiometric dating for a fossil like her.

An emergency vehicle is klaxoning behind us in the fast lane. I do the Christian thing and yield, get the hell out of the way, as I would yield for Wilson's Raiders if they came anachronistically galloping across the interstate. JESUS SAVES. Two more miniature crosses marking the site where man and wife greeted eternity. DIVORCE $200.

We motor onto a county road and by green drills of soybean that aren't being harvested. Used to we could pay Mexicans to do all the work for us. Our baby-kissing lawmakers in Montgomery took care of that. Now we don't have currency to even pay ourselves. The Klan once ran Cullman, and a few of the old wizards cling to the hope of a Jim Crow Part II: an old, dirt-dumb relic is picketing the road with a hand-painted sign: WHITE AND PROUD OF IT.

Alright. How is that for a warm welcome to Cullman? The city ought to hire him to say hello to visitors. I hate it when I lose my only black friend in the dark. Cullman — a town settled by Germans with their Aryan tales of Siegfried, and their intellectual appurtenances, the explanatory myths of the Curse of Ham and the Great Chain of Being — is still a sundown town and I'll give you a hundred bucks for every black man you can find out after dark. Raccoon eyes glowing green in your headlights at the edge of the road. A howling at the back door. A shot in the dark.

Back home, my person occupies four-thousand square feet of house in an unfinished neighborhood at the end of a blank street, one of those zombie subdivisions that crept up after the housing crisis. The buckled pavement bottoms out in a tentative, rough-hewn dirt track cleared through tall pines. The community of weeds is reclaiming their demesne. I fight them back with gallons of warlike herbicide. I am glad to be away. I dwell there alone. The rooms annihilate themselves on the banquet of my four-thousand square foot person, an eremite in the belly of a sheetrock whale.

The barometric slipping under a booming sky, I've watched the stretch marks in the pavement grow like they were my own children, which I do not have. This logos of the earth and telluric calligraphy I interpret like a canonical text in contrition and concretion, the only two acts I know. Years ago, a simple and avid student of geology's amoral principles, I stood paralyzed in the basin of Barringer Crater, a giant acne scar on the face of the earth, and waited hours for another meteor to strike the same place twice. Astronauts trained in the crater for lunar missions back in the days of Apollo. We're becoming more like the moon every day. And I'm still knocking on the door of a stone.

Clare has never seen the inside of this sheetrock whale. A spec house that looks like all the others that haven't been built yet. The inside of my car — where we're making progress into Cullman — is the closest she has come to occupying my intimate space. We rendezvous at a neutral location. Did I say I've never touched her? Not with my body, at least. Is the earth six-thousand years old, as the "scientific" creationists at Gardendale Baptist would have us believe? I'll believe anything. Two contradictory beliefs held simultaneously. I can hold that antinomy in my head and not combust. We're becoming more like the moon every night. Perhaps it was in the Grotto, a boy who loved the impenetrable tangibility and empirical stoicism of rocks, that I discovered my calling and became a geologist for the state of Alabama.

Our little amour began with a transgression, when I wandered onto her property in search of rocks. I'd picked the land around my house clean. Two oppositely sexed individuals of our species finding each other in the woods, as our ancestors always had, coming together for comfort in one another from the omnivorous creatures that roamed on the perimeter of the campfire, the hostile elements, the whimsical gods. I watched her from afar, evaluating her like a brilliant gemstone. Clare was on her back porch, drinking coffee, still feeling the effects of the anesthetic after a bone marrow donation the day before. She later likened the needle drawing the liquid marrow from the sides of her pelvic bone to pulling an old shipwreck up from the ocean bottom through the eye of a needle.

I startled her from one of her full-body reveries that altogether abstracted her from her body and its milieu so that she almost ceased to exist; to interrupt one of these episodes was to disturb some legendary prehistoric animal, part dragon, part deer, from the *bestiarum vocabulum* that had been asleep for eons.

—What are you doing out here? I asked her, as if she were

trespassing on my piddling estate.

—I was waiting for the stars to come out, she said unconvincingly. From the height of her back porch, she looked down upon me like the Mount of Olives vetting its own shadow cast over Jerusalem.

—The stars are always out, even in the daytime. You just can't see them.

—Maybe they don't exist if I can't see them.

—That's the anthropocentric take on the matter, yes.

—Do you hear that blasting in the forest?

—I hardly notice it anymore.

—I can't stand it. I have to move, she said zeroing in on me now. —What's that in your hand?

I held the specimen up to the light, positioning it such that Clare appeared encased in the golden resin, locked in time with the insect inside.

—It's a piece of amber.

—What is in it?

—A spider, I think, millions of years old. Quiet. The spider is dreaming.

—What do you think it dreams about?

—A man meets a woman in the woods.

—I've heard this story before.

—Not like this, you haven't. The spot where we are standing was a shallow sea in the Late Cambrian. Marine transgressions created the Western Interior Seaway, the shoreline inundating Birmingham, your backyard would've been inhabited by leviathans like the plesiosaurs and *Squalicorax* sharks.

—What happened to them?

—They're all extinct.

—You live in that empty house on the dead street. The one without any other houses around it.

—There's a baroque chamber of amber panels embellished with gold leaf and mirrors, the Amber Room in the Catherine Palace of Saint Petersburg. An entire room built of amber. That's how I imagine my house, I said.

Clare seemed to be visualizing this room, placing herself inside the amber. Maybe she saw us, reflected in the chamber's mirrors, laughing and dancing to harpsichord music while armies from the West besieged the Palace.

—Sounds enchanting. We should go.

—The room vanished during World War II.

—I just had my bone marrow donated. I feel hollow and deadened inside, like a hollowed pumpkin with no face. Everyone I know has cancer. I hope you don't have cancer, do you? I couldn't bear to meet another person with cancer. Please say you don't have cancer.

Clare was hugging herself as she said this, her face contorted with pain.

—Hippocrates used amber as a healing agent.

—I don't believe in witchcraft and magic potions, she said looking up at the first stars surfacing in the blue black sky.

I left the amber spider by her bed, per Hippocrates' prescription, and for all I know it remains glowing there to this day.

Driving back to my hometown of Cullman, just enough speed to kill us, two more crosses on the roadside, I separate myself into mind and body like a good Catholic. This is the Cartesian exercise that has divided me against myself from the beginning. And the mental legerdemain whereby I can hoax myself saying I haven't touched Clare, which is untrue as far as she's concerned, but only in that trivially mundane sense of the corporeal, but is correct in all metaphysical and extra-mundane aspects. Who am I to disagree with St. Augustine of Hippo? The ethereal years at St. Bernard's taught me how to do this: become a discarnate mind, disembodied from the rocks and stones that cut our feet. As my body cuts through space like the prow of the Ark through the deluge, I'm thinking about the geese slaughter over at East Lake, because federal officials said the fowl posed a threat to aviation, thousands of geese euthanized to make the skies safe again for air travel, when I swerve my truck around a washing machine in my lane. I almost crash us into a big rig in the opposite lane. Two small crosses in the trees.

Up ahead is a brick mural in confederate gray of Colonel Cullman smoking a corncob pipe. Yeehaw and shit yeah. An upright and model citizen, no doubt. Cullman is hometown to a dry Oktoberfest every October. Apple cider and hayrides. Red-eyed dads flasking a contraband from the next county over. Excise tax just never caught on. Sobriety is the greatest punishment a petty elected official could inflict upon his town.

After an F-5 tornado redesigned the town I have to stop and

ask for directions to the Grotto, where I used to attend prep school at St. Bernard's. *Ora et labora.* You live the same day 365 times a year, thrown into a place with your pointless queer thoughts and the wind snarls around a cell the size of a box of condoms. St. Bernard's was a country club prison for children, ruled by nuns afraid of lightning. Anyone in Cullman will tell you these disasters — tornadoes, floods, house fires, mine collapses, earthquakes, car accidents — are God's way of getting your attention, but I stopped listening to that hocus-pocus long ago, and have never learned more from a cloud than could be guessed from the shadow thrown by a stone.

The streets of downtown Cullman are littered with dismembered buildings. Tornadoes are God's way of destroying ugly buildings. A Presbyterian steeple keeled over in the street. "For Sale" and "Redevelopment" signs popping up in wasted lots scraped clean of cinder block gas stations and thrift shops and payday loans. Growing up in Cullman instilled in me the abiding notion that the universe is an underfunded research experiment in a former Soviet client state. The nuns would say it was always the Protestant churches that were destroyed in tornadoes, never the Catholic, spinning this as a naturalistic vindication of the correct creed, and I accomplished nothing but proving to them that I was possessed by evil spirits and the Archfiend himself when I publicly relished the counter-spin that this was not because God favored Catholics, but because Protestants didn't believe in building codes, a perishable faith comfortable with *ad hoc* transience who worshiped in shoddy warehouses built of aluminum, little more than rafts for weathering the storm of the 21st century, which they prayed would be the last one, and Catholics would not consecrate anything that wasn't built to last as long as the Third Reich. I once saw a man collapse from cardiac arrest in the middle of the street. The coroner said the heart attack didn't kill him, but the tour bus that flattened him like an armadillo did. A tragedian's town.

The Baptists' great contribution to the public good of Christendom is the supply of superabundant free parking. For the world is theirs to flatten with negative space. I swing my door open and toe the ground experimentally — I have never trusted that it will be there when I need it — as Clare walks at me around the front end of the truck. The light is acid and the month is calescent, killing every warm-blooded thing. An equatorial boiling that will outlast all man has made. A descending poultry feather settles onto Clare's hair and I brush it away. That let's-get-a-room glint in her eye.

I hold the door for Clare into a flyblown convenience store that seems to sell nothing but pickled pig's feet and quail eggs, strips of beef jerky and brown bags of boiled peanuts. The Cullman diet. Still no booze around. The store smells like it did when I was a kid; then it smelled like what I imagined the 1860's to smell like.

There's a young hickish, dimwitted fellow who looks like a hammer behind the counter with some bad looking prison pussy sprouting on his chin. Why do grown men deface themselves in such a cowardly manner? He's picking fluffs of lint big as cotton bolls out of his bellybutton and watching a reality TV show called "Sweet Home Alabama," about a buxom, patrician-looking blond southern-belle with legs long as the Cenozoic era and who is nearly gang raped in every episode by upper middle-class frat boys who like to dress below their class in cowboy hats and gay-tight jeans, boots and overalls as if they'd ever put in a day's hard work in their cosseted, septic lives or knew which pedal was the gas on a tractor. Not all that different from life in Cullman. My greatest disappointment in life was never being cast for the TV show "Sweet Home Alabama."

The abbey nuns used to warn about the carnal pleasures and the way of all flesh, in highfalutin figurative language, but it didn't scare us from hell at all, just made us more hot and bothered, wickeder to discover the forbidden and eat as many knowledge apples as we could cram into our slavering mouths, even if they had worms wriggling out of a thousand holes rotten with damnation and brimstone. The poor abbey nuns were heartbroken that I did not care about my soul, just the rocks in the Grotto.

—Which way to the Grotto? I quiz the quadruped critter. The catechistic style is still with me.

The counterman spills some dialect all over himself, bastardized out of German and Cullman's patois that sounds like rocks rattling around in a box. I can see why, after two world wars, everyone here wants to downplay their German heritage. I expect to hear *Ride of the Valkyries* scratched out on an old phonograph in the streets while Hansel and Gretel dance a *Schuhplattler*.

—I only speak modern English. Do I need to get an interpreter here?

Clare says I'm often too quick to judge. If only men were more like rocks, steadfast, patient, cool in the shade, hot in the sun, transparently telling their history, and a little footnote of the physical universe, by the determination of their form and composition.

—What we want to know is, Clare's voice is dulcet as a waterfall, —Where can we find the nice nuns and the monks? You know, the ones with the cute miniature castles and churches? The pictures look quaint.

Our local yokel points easterly with a finger missing its nail.

How does Clare do it? Always bursting with that magical can-do go-getter attitude. Not a pore in her skin. She could tap dance on the head of a snake and then bake an apple pie.

—Where you all from? he's dying to know.

The counterman is afraid to be alone. His eyes are like two umlauts pressed into a melon. He coughs up some tobacco sputum and drips it on the floor behind the counter. Why are all Cullman males so abundantly sputative?

—Up from Birmingham. Just for the day, I say — already volunteering too much. A day is long enough.

Our tour guide looks at us as though we'd survived a very strenuous ordeal, a forced march or grapes of wrath. The word *city* in his mouth would be bookended with scare quotes. To the indigenous of Cullman, Birmingham is a place of depravity, gang-banging, municipal malversation, race riots, drugs, police dogs, fire hoses, and a mediocre college football team with a goofy dracontine mascot. What Cullman has in the way of a white-collar workforce commutes there and scrams out by five o'clock, sweating in their white collars for the mortal trepidity that every car driven by a black person might be a drive-by shooting. Next, he'll want to chew the fat about the hellacious weather. I can grunt and produce the appropriate social noises in response. I bend to Clare's ear and whisper, —Let's get out of here before he wants to talk about the weather.

—You two have a hoot in Christland, the counterman waves goodbye. —Watch out for the Flying Spaghetti Monster.

The abbey is coming back to me now. We prayed to the Flying Spaghetti Monster. I remember a fat and happy monk who held heretical views on the divinity of Jesus and prayed only to Saint Jude. Jesus was an iteration of Osiris or Horus. Instead of the falcon you get the Paraclete. Jesus was the end of religion, not its beginning, he whispered conspiratorially to us in the library.

Then I realize something. The counterman was John Abt, from the prep school. A respected family, the Abts were a fine horrible people with notions about everything that didn't concern them. John and I, possessed by malevolent spirits, emptied his father's goldfish on the floor and watched them slowly suffocate in the same medium that gave us breath. We performed this oblative sacrifice — his father never found out — till he stopped buying the goldfish. John's father once argued, refusing to relent, with St. Bernard's resident Biblical exegete that Siegfried, who slayed dragons, was a character in the Bible and not a pagan hero from some Middle High German epic poem called *Nibelungenlied* that he couldn't pronounce. John's father went to his grave believing Siegfried was a hero of the Old Testament like Moses and Samson. John stole communion wine and we got seven shades of shit drunk behind the horse stables. Even then, John's English was like those brightly colored magnetized plastic fridge letters that always need more vowels. His grandfather, who was old enough to remember the Weimar years, refused to learn English. The right thing would be to go back, swap stories with John like old buddies, ask about his family, but I can't. I don't mention a thing to Clare.

Clare opens the door of the truck for herself, signaling we are no longer at that phase of our courtship where I am expected to open the car door for her. The moon has set. Her left hand predominates in such tasks as opening a door or pointing to an interesting cloud above the deserted neighborhood, though it is oftentimes supplanted in my remembering by the plaster cast of her left hand I had made, and which — white and fragile as the breath of a ghost — sits on my desk among other strange and immortal artifacts. Tooling through downtown I recognize an alley where a man pressed a knife to my throat. It's all coming back and over me now. The foul high-heaven emanation of a restaurant dumpster. I should keep some things cloistered to myself.

I retract what I said about folks in Cullman downplaying their Teutonic past. There's a store advertising wieners, schnitzel, hooped wooden barrels of pretzels. Anything Germanic is for sale. *Lederhosen* and *Totenkopfs*. We cruise by houses obliterated by the tornado, folks picking through the trash in their front yards. A naked kid waves. After double-parking in the Grotto's lot, Clare and I stop to watch a service in the abbey cemetery.

—I hate cemeteries, she says.

—I was just going to suggest we join the mourners.

—We're not dressed right anyway.

I examine the registry of visitors inside the smoked glass doors, sign us in under the hieroglyphic scribbles that were supposed to be the names of eternal souls before us. Penmanship is in decline. Kids learn how to type a narcissistic Facebook status before they can hold a pencil. In the years to come our avatars will go to heaven for us. Clare is studying a map of the Grotto on the wall. I have seen her get lost for hours, raptured in the navigation of the maps of inexistent places I have hung on the walls of her house. Because the Grotto exists just through those doors, or so she's been told, the Grotto map does not hold her long.

We pass through the frankincense-smelling gift shop of votive candles and coffee grown on the abbey farm. No wine, since the county is teetotaling even in these modern times. Out the back doors of the chintzy gift shop — Marian trinkets, rosaries, prayer cards and bloody crucifixes — and down a ramp, Clare and I enter the phantasmagoria of Ave Maria Grotto.

Brother Zoettl worked out his own eccentric soteriology building the Grotto, beginning with the Tower of Babel. The Grotto was carved into a steep hillside of an abandoned quarry, which Zoettl populated with scores of architectural miniatures. UNESCO World Heritage Sites distant in space and time have been syncretized together right here in Cullman, Alabama, the most culturally advanced place on earth. The Great Wall of China sprawls like a stone caterpillar and a dragonfly alights on the dome of St. Peter's Basilica. The Pyramids of Egypt are but a few miles from McDonald's and about a half dozen Chinese buffets with a health rating that will kill you. The Mount of Olives with its necropolis of buried dead humps like a hazardous waste dump over a scale model of Jerusalem's walled Old City.

Zoettl's sculptural practice performed his theology: Christ born to the paupers not the aristocracy. No material was too base for Zoettl, who constructed the Grotto of stone concrete brick marble tile glass seashells plastic animals costume jewelry toilet bowl floats and cold cream jars. The locals will exult over the destruction of Zoettl's city, this visitation of wrath upon the City of the Sun, they feared it as they feared going into Birmingham. When he wasn't affixing seashells to the *Ecce Homo* miniature, the tower of Pilate, he was shoveling coal at the monastery's power plant. Zoettl didn't limit himself to only Biblical architecture. He sculpted secular monuments and pagan temples, allowing the miniature to evolve over decades of Zoettl-time. All the Grotto needed was a miniature of Gardendale Baptist Church and the Cracker Barrel.

In places, Zoettl's sense of scale is off just enough to be disorienting.

—The Parthenon looks smaller than the Alamo, Clare criticizes, then she pats the Statue of Liberty on the head like a good dog. The Statue of Liberty is gazed upon by the outsized faces of white men carved into the rock of Mount Rushmore. Zoettl seems to have the immigrant's fascination with Americana.

The work crews around my hermitic house have been blasting through limestone hillsides for a road cut and rattling the glass in my kitchen cabinets. Clare complains of the blasts rattling her dishware, pictures of the deceased falling from the wall. I wake to find a patina of ferric dust settled over the glass and wood surfaces of my friary. When the work crew packs home for the day I analyze their excavation, running my hands over the colored bands of tilted and folded sedimentary rock they have exposed to the eye of an ape. Oldest at the bottom, youngest on top, the pedosphere upon which we walk and rest, enter and exit. I am touching time, and I am touched by each stratum in return. I remember the Plutonists, who believed that all rocks resulted from volcanism, the deposition of lava from the underworld. On the other side of the fence were the Neptunists, countering that rocks settled out of an ocean whose water levels dropped. I am in the middle.

The blasters have disturbed much earth. I pick up a rock embedded with fossilized flora: crinoid columnals and holdfasts and bryozoa that cleaned the ancient winedark waters once covering the zombie subdivisions, and in dreams Clare and I cling to one another on a raft drifting aimlessly upon the Western Interior Seaway. I worry this rock of fossils in my hand and then toss it into the pines, in the direction of Clare's house, on the edge of an increasingly Martian landscape, red and bleak and low gray clouds. Tossing this rock into the forest is the greatest impact I will have on the geology of my environment, like some galactic giant heaving asteroids at earth.

Clare has gone on a tangent ahead of me in the Grotto. She stands before a monumental idol of the Virgin, a cat tonguing water from a pool in the stone. A tall iron gate defends the altar and the Virgin from approach by the muddy non-transcendent world, the one of long, silent eons fossilized in strata. Through evergreens I spot the sparkling pond where, as prep boys, we paddled shirt-less in canoes, collected insects and learned how to blaspheme like the public school boys who committed unspeakable acts such as pasting headshots of the principal's wife onto nudies of bunny girls and exhibiting them in the high school trophy case. At the beginning of each summer our wintry, spectral skins were like unleavened bread that baked and browned in the clear sun, and by September, when the nights were cooling, we were dark as we imagined Negroes and wild Indians we had never seen to be. The only blacks we saw played college football on TV, or endured in towns like Selma, Tuscaloosa or Birmingham where they live, so the sophisticated Cullmanite will tell you, on Section 8 under the Curse of Ham.

I once waited out a thunderstorm under the trees circling the lake and watched the fulgid flashes of quick lightning strike and spark the weather vane on the barn that laughed at a new coat of paint. Even after the lightning had pulled back up into the sky, ev-erywhere I blinked I could see the ghostly afterimage emblazoned onto my retinas, as if it was still there, influencing everything. In the lightning's afterimage, I saw all of Christendom encased in preserving, golden amber, the Amber Room restored. I am go-ing down the strata, deeper into my layers. I looked at the abbey church, the Grotto, afterimage lightning flashing across the gar-goyles and statuary — that lightning still flashes today, negatively illuminating Clare's face when I reach for her in the amber dark of her bedroom. The Third Reich of dreams recurs, and ends with an empty raft.

During that rainless lightning storm John Abt suffered a vi-olent seizure, superstitiously construed by the monks as a divine inhabitation of the corporeal complex. Like the Catholic torna-does that only raze Protestant churches, I knew better. I had read somewhere that Saul of Tarsus was epileptic, whence his conver-sion on the interstate to Damascus, which I first saw, years lat-er, in some city older than the Baptists, depicted by Caravaggio in a museum, a man whose name was not allowed to be spoken in the presence of the abbot or any of the nuns. Caravaggio was a heretic, his brush possessed by demons. You were better off reading John Milton than being caught with Caravaggio's name on your lips. John Abt bit his tongue so hard he lost the ability to speak for a week. The nurse wrapped his tongue in white gauze like a wounded appendage. He never got out of Cullman.

I never thought about the nuns as women, but as androgynous blocks of granite draped with rosaries and dressed like penguins. I have every respect for the Church. Where would I be without her? I never heard the nuns, unlike most women in my life, henpeck about the *de minimis* things. Buoyed by a water only they could walk upon, their criticism was light and sweet. Too solicitous of the state of my soul, or how much dirt was under my fingernails. Supervising the hygiene of a class of rowdy fellers with puckish Boy Scout faces and from good families was no facile task. It required nuns to grow eyes in the backs of their heads, to see around corners. They knew of your abominations before you committed them. They knew your disbelief too in the youth of the earth. They could examine your palm and know you'd been masturbating with an old-school Nintendo power glove.

The nuns enjoined us to pray for rebirth and remand ourselves to the Virgin, who was more their goddess than mother. We slept the aseptic sleep of saints in repose, the millennial, apocalyptic snore of Muscular Christianity. But I woke up and was ever the same little shitkicker. God, they said, wasn't diminished by our lack of faith. I took this to mean that God's size, like a rock, remained the same whether I prayed or not. The nuns would not allow us to have money because Judas' thirty pieces of silver are still in circulation, and you didn't want to get Judas' cursed blood money back as change for buying a Coke. The nuns peopled my dreams, clawing shrews with black hair on the skin of their arms and pale as boiled eggs. But there was a beautiful nun with an ugly, guttural name — Agnes. With a splash of golden hair under her black veil. She made the boys heartsick. She suffered terrible migraines and read a lot of Zane Grey novels from the Cullman Public Library, also wiped out by tornadoes, all those books strewn across the square. She seemed to survive on a dietary debit of communion wafers. Whatever happened to Agnes, and why was she convented in the first place? And why does Clare so much resemble her that I cannot but feel Agnes' migraines too in her presence?

Catholics emphasize the gory agony of the cross — we felt the maggots feeding in the gangrenous wounds of the godhead — where the sacred corpus has been nailed for two millennia and may never come down like the gruesome depictions of Christ in a Grünewald. His altarpieces made Christ look wan and green, more like a hungover, suffering plague victim than a resurrected godhead. I wouldn't want to die from crucifixion on the Gardendale Baptist's colossal cross by the interstate either. I remember a monk at the abbey, in my prep school days, who read a lot of Rilke's *Book of Hours* and wore an unloaded sidearm at all times. Christ was a man of the whip, he would say. Deep in the darkness is God. He described in infinite detail the outré creatures cataloged in the *bestiarum vocabulum* that he'd personally spotted in Cullman. My hometown was a bestiary and menagerie of outrageous creatures. I drank up his apostate kool-aid, viler in it, and he encouraged me in my preoccupation with earthly, soulless things like stones and rocks. He was the first to show me Zoettl's Grotto.

They never taught us anything worldly or useful like how to balance a checkbook, siphon gas, ask a girl out on a date, or even how or why to use contraceptives. The Protestant kids at public school graduated as pragmatic geniuses compared to us. If it wasn't for Clare's forwardness I would still be half a soul. Many over-draft fees and unwanted pregnancies might've been avoided among my graduating class. And we all did graduate, many going to hell on a scholarship at Notre Dame, Loyola or Tulane. I could read Latin, and knew my way around rocks pretty well, but the first time I was with a girl I'd have gotten her pregnant had she not been raised Methodist and was, therefore, not totally ignorant of contraception. A prep school girl might have her virginity violently seized more than once. Orgasm was a great crisis, a natural catastrophe that would rearrange the fundament, trumpets blaring, apocalyptic scrolls unfurling. Cullman was a place where country preachers make a pass at the bride even as she's tripping down the aisle. Where you pray for the day a good Catholic boy will be in the White House again. Blindness would be a blessing here.

The iron gate on the Grotto begins to rattle. Birds hush their hymns. A woeful commotion of wind blows early dead leaves like dry little kites. The boys splashing in the lake fall quiet. Somewhere a child crying. Not until the stalactites and dripstones begin falling from the ceiling of the Grotto do I realize what is happening. Clare. The Southern Appalachian Seismic Zone is faulting. And, by the way, there is a cloud shaped like a whale. Geologists are always looking at the ground

— anything above the horizon escapes us, the impact crater more tantalizing than predicting the trajectory of the asteroid.

Clare appears to be praying before the Grotto altar, as though she understood what was happening before I did, before the birds even. I feel the quixotic and rushing endorsement to tell her things, as though this might be our last chance. Then feel foolish in the aftermath. I want to eat in fancy restaurants with her every night of the week, and never come back to Cullman. I want to survive with her. I want a plaster cast of her right hand too, and the whole of her body.

The Grotto's altar has split in half. I would learn later that the abbey's granary was destroyed and the horses jumped fence and were found wandering downtown Cullman. The earthquake itself lasts perhaps a minute, but what is a minute to I am that I am? Are not His minutes reckoned in our lifetimes? A lifetime of quaking earth, and cowering under evergreens, clinging to makeshift rafts on an ancient sea.

The Leaning Tower of Pisa collapses and a tree dashes the Basilica. The Grotto is in ruins, an omnipotent punishment visited upon the miniature, presumptive city of Zoettl. The bronze statue of Brother Joseph Zoettl is toppled like a monument to an old Communist dictator in a public square. I'm old enough to remember the time before the fall of the Wall. Micro-earthquakes — just the smallest rumblings of the earth's bowels — happen all the time. We're floating on top of a hot roiling liquid. There's no point in running. It will end soon enough. Did they finish the funeral service at the abbey cemetery, get the unraptured corpus in the ground before it cracked open?

Brother David. That was the fat and happy monk's name, the armed one exiled for his heterodox interpretations. He had a copy of the Jefferson Bible. Jefferson excised verses from the Gospels with a razor, expurgating the inerrant word of God. You don't want to die in a Baptist hospital, Brother David advised me at age sixteen, but a Catholic hospital. The food is better, and the nurses look like those nubile Madonnas in the old paintings, which I guess was hot stuff if you were a monk. The poor monk had the diarrhea of a saint fed on grasses.

The quaking logos of the earth is speechless now. Have I interpreted it all correctly? The air is heavy and windless. Have I listened to the muted story of the stones? Has God been speaking to me through stones all these years, and yet I was deaf as the

Israelites of old? Did I water the houseplants that morning before leaving the only house in the neighborhood? I see John hiding under the counter as the sky fell in through the roof of his simple store.

Waterloo appears to have been wrought upon the Grotto. St. Scholastica — patron saint of nuns, epileptic children, invoked against storms — is crushed under falling stalactites and dripstone. A dragonfly darts on an aleatoric course through the Grotto's iron gate. Clare, beautiful Clare, approaches the altar now that the iron gate is broken open. I fear a stalactite might impale her. The Grotto — it's not a real cave, but it looks millions of years old. The stalactites and stalagmites are simulated like the undying roses the nuns left at the altar, like the blood and body of Christ in the transubstantiation of the Eucharist. St. Benedict has fallen like the Presbyterian steeple in town and shattered across the marble floor of the Grotto, the head still whole. Descartes' orthogonal, analytical empire overthrown. The fragments of a saint can be reassembled into a more exact likeness of who we are in the process of becoming.

I look back up the Grotto and the Tower of Babel is the sole structure standing, aspiring towards the bottom of the sky I expect to darken, as in the prophecies, but it's as sunny as a calm day at the beach, where Clare and I haven't been together. I should change that, but I hear the beaches are botched with oil this year; maybe the mountains, somewhere above the blasting and the zombie subdivision, far away from the seaway, closer to the belly of the empyrean. Maybe I'll ask her to move into the empty house in the unfinished neighborhood with me, after the blasting stops. It would be nice to have a woman's voice swell softly between those catacomb rooms. To thrive together, huddling in the dark against the yowls and screeches of the *bestiarum vocabulum* and the hostile elements, till some other hardier species finds us fixed in amber. But the blasting never stops, and now Clare is transfixed in one of her out-of-body reveries before the Grotto cave altar. I brush her hair out of her face, her eyes gothic deep as two craters. Whatever she envisions must eclipse what the dreaming spider saw before being encapsulated in the viscous resin of an extinct tree all those years ago. What are Clare and I doing here anyway, but waiting on the next meteor to strike twice in the same place? God, it is written, spoke through a burning bush because he wanted to speak through a burning bush. There was no other reason.

Ave Maria Grotto

THE SONG OF THE ABYSS EATER

Still and all, when I was packed off to prison, not only was I innocent of the wrongdoing and mortal outrage of which I was attainted, having clung to my virtue like a life raft, I was more than ignorant of how the Apostle Peter talked an angel into bailing him out. Ten years later I got out, and everything was different from itself, but somehow itself nevertheless, and I was the most convicted man in the State. And this is a State with a bad conscience hanging over its head like a tornadic wall cloud that won't be blown away. Sure, I was guilty before prison, but not for what that kangaroo jury convicted me.

—This is a man who by the words of the victim herself, words which the jury has heard in this very courtroom, repeatedly raped a little girl and the prosecution must therefore recommend the maximum sentence.

That prosecutor was slick as shit through a goose. He looked like Paul Ryan, a quarterback type in a sleazy suit, and a *summa cum laude* at Alabama.

—You got to drive a black Bronco and then you can get away with murder, I said to the Judge when he asked if I had anything to say to the courtroom before the manacles were applied like branding irons to my brown limbs. Sometimes, when the abyss fills the singing mouth like a fist, I feel the manacles cold against my skin.

My voice resounded like a silver light that grew wings and turned into a dove. When the dove perched somewhere, a dead tree downtown, they took a shot at it, and I fell silent. My bottomless gravelly baritone quieted, as in years past when punished for some contravention of the parliamentary rules of order set forth by some white man named Robert, I ate foul socks in the corner which I came to study and know quite scientifically, banished there by my mother who was dismayed that I would not stop singing, could not just plain talk what I had on my mind, but forced it out in song and finger-snapping and dance down the street. Now, with that prosecutor winking at the jury, the church choir would be sung without me into higher registers and the tenors and altos would have music space replying above the pews. All this attended by the angel Abaddon who I have arm-wrestled in jail.

The sorest part personally, is that I could've hitchhiked up to Nashville, singing *Mississippi Goddamn* or Erskine Hawkins, because they love a black man who can sing honky-tonk or classical folk and croon bayou blues in the music city. They clap for him and throw money at his feet. White girls like Dolly Partons hang on his arms. I must now be in a worse place to commit these thoughts to words. An Alabama prison is where men go to confront themselves, interrogate the terrible quiddities of self and other. Verses from Beecher's Bible recited in blood on the cell wall. Bring on the greasy spoon reality in your limousine hearses. I have no more song to sing than a dirge.

At about that hour when they say good Christ was crucified, the courtroom was bustling like a bus stop back when gas prices soared. These tailgaters lined the wall and filed disorderly down the hall and onto the plaza outside, like the aristocrats of old picnicking on the battlefield, watching the cannonball fly while stuffing themselves with caviar. They'd throw you out the front door of your own house, if there even was a door, so you can climb back in through the window and peekaboo, take a seat on the ratty couch and pretend nothing happened. I can't pass judgment upon creation by myself, can I? If I had a head for business, I might've made a killing selling tickets to my own trial, but they got laws against profiteering on your own suffering. Capitalize on your neighbor's suffering, they say.

Demeter didn't have the time to wait in line at City Hall before pawning the Wal-Mart wedding band that once sparkled goldenly on her finger. Two years of work flipping burgers and do you want fries with that cashed and collateralized for a shark loan in an instant. The gold flaking off the band. Demeter was gussied up for the show, my daughter Umbrosia nestling stoutly in her lap, bouncing on her knee.

I might as well say to you what was obvious to everyone then: the jury was white as a blank piece of paper on which you could write anything, whatever popped into your head. Not just folks who bubble in *white* on their income tax or the job application, in the box left for race, but a bloodless, pasty, deathlike specter modeled on anemic and doughy scarecrows I used for target practice long ago. This vampiric jury is shit-scared of the boll weevil like

The Song of the Abyss Eater

the bogeyman. They know how to set the dinner table, where the forks and spoons go. Women whose cunts are dry as a popcorn and wine fart. Men who are now on the Highway Patrol. And not one of whom would look me straight in the eye and give me a yes or no.

What would you sell those tickets for? The courtroom was about out of oxygen. I hooked a finger in my starched collar and loosened up the tie my lawyer put around my neck like a goddamn noose.

—You got to wear this if you want to impress the jury, he said. —Want you looking respectable like that choirboy you got inside you.

He looked me over like chattel at auction. He patted me on the shoulder like a high school gym teacher when he was satisfied that I would do and said, —Attaboy.

Attaboy is the do-gooding white man's name for *when I say jump you say how high.*

So I wore a suit for the first time that was not a funeral. Just on the off chance the jury had a sympathetic color blind soul after all or there was a nice looking lady in the audience you might want to ask out for coffee in ten years, holding your breath the whole way. Sing the end. The end. All of Christendom was around the corner and up the block.

Sure, I had priors. Third-degree trespassing and driving with no license, but even Saint Paul wasn't perfect. How's a man not supposed to trespass when they got the signs hung so high in a tree you can't even read it? The sign misspelled. Who can't use spell-check on a no trespassing sign? Sheriff comes out, points at the orange no trespass sign up in the tree, says see that sign up there, way up there? No, sir I didn't. Oughtn't it to be at eye level? What if a trespasser can't read? You going to book an illiterate for trespass can't even read no trespass sign? Oughtn't you to book the superintendent of schools who gave this boy a G.E.D. when he can't even read a no trespass sign? The Sheriff is a Ciceronian too.

When they cut me loose, I had some things: clothes folded and crisply laundered, smelling of primaverile soap, a letter from Judge Bahakel, some old keys that no longer unlocked any door, and a social worker's card that I tossed into the gutter among leaves and unswept trash. Above the entrance to Birmingham City

Jail, highfalutin words by some fool Cicero — *We are in bondage to the law in order that we might be free* — chiseled into the stone lintel above the courthouse door. Only a white man would write that on a courthouse for all the Jeffersonians and Ciceronians to see. Jim Crow was law, and I like my drinking fountains just fine, thank you. I saw that folkshit soapbox the hindmost day of my freedom, before the one long night of my incarceration began. A statue of a condemned man greets all courthouse visitors. It might be sculpted from bronze or placenta, I don't know. In the distraught night, when the downtown streets drag alone, I think the condemned man sheds his shackles and takes a royal crap heaven-sent with wings on the lawn in front of City Hall.

The sky was pinked and loud as the strike of the gavel. I picked up a paper from the newsstand and read about my own release. I rolled the paper and tucked it into my pants and loitered in the plaza watching cars run the red lights. I didn't know where to go or be. The highway behind the jail was taking people places in two directions. North of the highway was Norwood, and I didn't want to be there after dark. I could hitchhike, but you'll see later what happened to my thumbs.

Opposite the county jail, laughing wine-drunk white folks spilled out the front of the art museum and onto the sidewalk. Taking turns mooning over a waste of cinder blocks havocked into "art." I can peel the gum off my shoe and stick it on a tampon and call that art. Everybody clap for my song and dance.

I had some cash on me, enough for a bus transfer. I knocked around Scratch Ankle, the remnants of the 4th Avenue North District, where a great uncle once owned a drugstore on the ground floor of the Palm Leaf Hotel offering hot and cold running water in every room with fancy steam heat — the bulldozers got it the year Reagan was almost assassinated. Now it's the Eddie Kendricks Memorial Park, life-sized bronze effigies of Eddie Kendricks singing silent into a microphone. The Park is a quarantine for bums now, and I'd slept off many nights of Crown Royal there myself. Bronze is a type of incarceration.

I watched a man take a shave inside a barber shop whose ribbon pole was busted and wouldn't turn red and white. A barber's straightedge against his throat, I remembered that I was not alone. They give you cash, saying don't spend it all in one place and there maybe not one place to spend it. A legless man in a wheelchair grilling barbecue on an open pit in front of Green Acres Café. Birmingham is like that. Does anybody know or ask where amputated body parts go? Is an amputee reunited with his legs in heaven, or do they just rot for carrion in the dumpster behind the hospital?

I crossed 17th Street and bought a ticket at the Carver Theater and sat in the back next to a woman or girl I couldn't see too good. Just argent snatches when the movie light flashed over her comely silhouette. They were showing *The Defiant Ones*. I had a strong resemblance to Sydney Poitier I am told by women who would know. The movie reached that scene, after their chains have been smashed with a rock, where Sydney's character hops the train and extends a hand to lift Tony Curtis onto the rail car, but it's no use — they are both tumbled down onto the ground, black and white alike. I stood up in the dark and booed. Poitier should've saved himself! I want a do over! To hell with that white devil! I'd rather forfeit my legs than be chained for life to a white man! I got the heckle out of me, and resumed my seat.

But I had spoken the language of the girl next to me, for she leaned into me and poured honey in my ear, ran her long-nailed fingers up my thigh and over my crotch. Then the movie ended, and the Carver put on some low budget grindhouse porno — with just the audio it sounded more like a war movie, but I paid this harlot for a ten dollar hand job in the dark as others went at it on the screen that had a rip in it. How's that for not spending it all in one place? It's been ten years, cut a freeman some slack. The brochures at the Civil Rights Museum don't tell you what the Carver is used for now. Old black Leonardo and peanut butter man sure sore about the grinding carnal relations and womanhood up against manhood transacted in his namesake. When I was that misadventured age I was pulling pranks like changing the street signs on the cops. No use improving a fool bent upon being foolish, what you might call the protection of the criminally innocent. Cicero knows.

I turned south down 17th, night falling fast like a kidnapper pulled a black bag over the head of the city and dragged it off somewhere, behind a dumpster, down an alley, to be found cut into tiny pieces the next day. The evil air around the Leer Tower was cooler and my skin burnished brimstone in the neon atmosphere of the night clubs that bumped wub wub wub music chopped and screwed, makes your ears bleed and gives you heartburn and soul-burn. I love the gospel.

On First Avenue, I squeezed by the tight sequined girls in high-heeled cork wedges, booties like two honey baked hams and all that double-wide ass hanging out of miniskirts. In ten years, the skirts have gotten shorter and that is all I can report upon the nature of change while I was incarcerated. Though I had hoped for prog-ress in matters bearing directly upon the abyss-eater, shorter skirts shall do. Each cheek glared at me like two nefarious thoughts. I snaked through the demimondes and priapic shack dwellers who slumped in doorways catcalling the bordello cockteases, many of them mothers as well as daughters once bathed by goner fathers.

I fell in behind a girl who I thought might be Umbrosia.

—Umbrosia, I said, grabbing the girl by the wrist and jerking her around.

—Get your hands off me you old faggot, she said and clicked away.

Women on your backs, when you close them eyes think of Alabama. Do it for Alabama. There began to fall a simple rain — the first I'd felt in a decade. I unrolled my newspaper and shel-tered under it as torrents flooded my shoes. The photo of me on the front-page news bleeding ink in the downpour. I continued the lifelong exodus out of downtown, rainwater squishing in my shoes, and to the west precincts where even the churches locked their doors.

I walked over my shadow down the long row of ancient shot-guns into a part of town where shoes — Air Jordans and Converse — dangled on telephone wires by their own laces. Wife and child were on the porch just as they had been the night I was carted off in a police cruiser and they rolled my thumbs in ink and pressed them on white paper for my fingerprints. Umbrosia was no longer a child. She was with child herself. Looking about an ugly old fifteen or so. Prison yard lights in their eyes, they couldn't see me too good. Then I called out in that voice they knew from church years back, the angry baritone that exalted the deity, and then they saw me by hearing me.

Umbrosia stood from the wicker chair with Zeniqua her half-sister, older now, who testified before all I'd forced Sodom and Gomorrah with her. Rather would I force myself on the back of the devil himself.

—You might ought to get on somewhere else, Larson.

London's voice was like a creature scratching at the walls.

I stopped and the head of my shadow-self blackened the bottom step peeling white and flaky wood brown underneath.

—Just came to see my daughter. She ain't never visited me.

—She don't want to see you, Demeter said for Umbrosia.

—Never thought this day would come, did you?

—You fucked them babies. I don't care what no judge rule, she spat at me.

I stepped back. London came out of the summer darkness of the house and began loading red shells into the breach of a shotgun that used to belong to me. He looked bloated big as a tick. I'd pointed that very gun at him before.

—Shit, London. You can't shoot a man with his own gun. How many you had today already? You ought to put that away, if you can shoot straight. Why don't you step back inside and take another lick from the juice bottle?

—You still got that smart mouth, ain'tcha?

—Not smart enough not to spend ten years in jail, I said, extending in covenant my right hand for London to shake. I never got that hand back. Of course, London had been there that day in the courtroom to say before all that would listen, —If you don't convict this man of the awfulest crime that can be committed between members of their own family, I'll spill his guts myself. And y'all wonder why I said Sydney Poitier should save himself.

A child rapist is lower than a motherfucker in prison. Hardened criminals got a pecking order to inspire superior feeling. Even the lowest forms of life have hierarchy. I'd have been better off if I'd killed the girl after I was supposed to have raped her. As if the fact of her wandering alive still violated through the civil world was reminder that many had thought about heinousness but only a few were both righteous and wicked enough for the deed. As if the killing of the victim thereby also killed the deed.

I buckled down. I got my G.E.D. I heard the word *recidivism* used by a social worker and got down the dictionary and looked it up. I slept close to a copy of Malcolm X's autobiography given to me by the appellate lawyer who used a lot of fancy lawyerly mumbo-jumbo. Words like *reductio absurdum* and *audi alteram partem*. The sentence was read aloud by the judge in a flat and stony voice with a masterful straight face. Hauled away in handcuffs before the tearless eyes of Demeter and our daughter, I hollered and cussed the jurors using archaic jeremiads in a voice from which dulcet gospel had once begrudgingly praised all creation between heaven and its opposite.

Most nights after work I bathed Umbrosia first and then her half-sister Zeniqua and listened to the TV on in the back-room, commercials featuring happy, clean and successful white families selling things we could not afford. I washed lice out of Zeniqua's hair and washed carefully around bruises. Sometimes I sat on the toilet with the lid down reading the paper as they splashed in the bathtub. Stories about football and oil spills and white people problems. My daughter has never seen a beach. Waiting out in the back room for her half-sister to finish washing, Umbrosia clicked the volume on the TV up, an episode of *America's Most Wanted*. That TV show gave her and Zeniqua ideas. Their mother caroused home when she remembered where home was. That night, I'd promised to take care of the girls, little as I liked to promise anything. When I was younger I'd hustled through women. Now, I stayed at home, like I couldn't get a date to the dance.

I heard London barrel through the front door and into the living room. You always hear a man like that before you see him. —Where's your sister? he asked Umbrosia in his voice destroyed by smoking and screaming and drinking. London was half-white and he let it show. We'd once stood shoulder to shoulder together in the choir, an atheist who intoned songs of hope and afterlife. But he took to that godless outlook and he got hotter with spleen and became a late-night quarreler and more spavined in the head. He got mixed up with Demeter before I got mixed up with her, foresight being more survival than hindsight. The man can't keep his ears clean now without a woman around. I think he is barely employed and might not even be able to hold his own cock. Nor would I leave him in charge of a single houseplant on the kitchen table. See, after all those seasons of cropping another man's cotton we still as a people have no green thumb. Our thumbs got amputated in the machines of dicksquat. I took care of Zeniqua because she was half of Demeter, and I adored all of Demeter. The half belonging to London is not my problem. But I out-suffer, etc. I don't think he's ever suffered a hangover either, because he never bothers to sober up.

Though my clairaudience has been noted in the courts, where I heard the jury's whispers, I couldn't hear Umbrosia's answer — the cops on *America's Most Wanted* were yelling at some motherfucker to freeze motherfucker! — and London probably didn't hear her either. Umbrosia had the soul of her mother — anarchy. I'd met her mother sponging at the car wash, bending over the hood in blue jean cutoffs, her black Miss Alabama's ass peeking out like a scalding hot liquid poured onto your lap in the shape of a Venusian woman. Shit and goddamn, Demeter was a black mermaid and delectable Delilah of a woman. We had some good times together — I returned to them in prison. Happiness is always a recreated thing way back when, never the pot of food sitting before you on the table. The food might taste like nothing, but it always gets better.

I was toweling down his daughter Zeniqua when London weaved into the bathroom. I could smell the bar on him. I remember the towel, its downy texture. It was a white towel Demeter often used by the pool, and imbrued splotchily with here and there an oval stain from blood or coffee. I don't know what London thought he saw, or what he thinks he remembered, but I'll be goddamned if I wasn't more a father to Zeniqua than he was.

I worked the fryer at Burger King then moved up to McDonald's — a skill that served me as cook in the pen. A decade later and Leon was still working the drive-through window. I waited in line behind a Jaguar and when it was my turn walked up to the window.

—You ain't retired yet? I wheedled him.

—What's up, Larson? Heard you got a wrongful conviction.

—The little bitch revoked her testimony.

—Ain't that a blessing.

—After everything I done for her.

—That was a long time ago.

—Can you help a fellow out? I need my old job back.

—I don't know, man. You'll have to come back. Maybe the manager can find something for you on Monday.

—I can clean the windows, I said, pointing to a pink ice cream stain dripping down the face of the glass.

—Not sure we need any help right now.

—Remember that time you screwed that girl and found out later she was a he? What was her name? Donald?

—Come on, man. How was I supposed to know? She was hot.

—He was hot, you mean.

—Why you gotta go there? How can I forget when you won't let me?

—And then you find out, get this, its first name is Mac.

—That was a long time ago.

—He was one fine piece of ass though.

—There's a customer waiting behind you, Leon said leaning out the order window, a customer's irate voice squawking into his headset.

—Hold on a fucking minute, I said to the car inching its front bumper up to me.

—I'll have one of them hot McApple McPies, McPlease. Nothing more McAmerican than that.

Me and my McApple pie we McSorrowed over to Oak Hill Cemetery. A pretty picture of an ugly reality: the north side view of the big bad city, this Babylon dying slowly of buses and mayors and weeds. I saddled the ironwork fence that segregated the buried dead — governors, mayors and Confederate generals — from the living in their cars and office buildings. A water tower on the hill above threw a plumbeous shadow across the cemetery lawn. Each of the FBI building's dark windows an opportunity to confess.

The cemetery was trashed and disrespected. Among the living, reverence for the dead is basically at an all-time low. Old dentist chairs dumped by a crumbling mausoleum. Mattresses, tires and other household rubbish piled up against headstones. I took a seat in one of the vinyl dentist chairs and leaned back, opening my mouth so my carious molars got a peek at the sky for the first time. A passenger airline banked east overhead, ascending from Shuttlesworth International. The dental chair squeaked forward and from my throne I surveyed the headstones furred over with mosses and the lost names worn by rain. There were moments of green, freshly planted grass over the newest dead and white marble crosses christless and lichened and polished pink granite tombstones that reflected the living in their passing among the graves. A bird nest tucked away in the arm of one giant cross and the eggs fallen to the ground, broken and unhatched.

Mourners gathered under a black tent. I saw them first reflected in the gleam of a big hearse parked under a black oak: the crowd carrying candles across 11th Avenue North, singing of the resurrection of the body, then passing through the gate and dispersing among headstones. I was wondering whose grandmother had died for the second time, any excuse to get out of school, when I got a peek through the hunched shoulders of the mourners at the named carved into granite: Shuttlesworth. I couldn't believe they were putting Shuttlesworth in the same ground as Confederate Generals. Maybe everything but me has changed in these ten years.

Prison is where men go to face themselves in the company of other men's cell-block solitudes. You don't know who the fuck you are, do you?

I crossed under the interstate again and came up behind a black luxury car parked beneath the overpass. Windowless with the state license plate ripped off. It smelled like a barbecue gone bad. The upholstery was burnt up and the dashboard plastic curled and bubbled. I pulled my shirt up over my nose and peered in through the glassless window. A man and a woman still inside. Botched burning where here and there flesh clung cured but sure to the bone. I saw them speeding in a convertible, the radio on, her long hair trailing windblown behind as they drove into the wrong neighborhood. Ten years was long enough for the world to get worse; for a black presidency to be handed over to a billionaire baboon who mated with a supermodel.

The visitor's room had been clamorous with weeping and gnashing of teeth. Couples got into fights, Tasers were used. A hipshot out-fangled beldam was rolled up to the glass in a wheelchair, a brightly knitted afghan thrown over the sticks of her legs like one of those quilts from Gee's Bend down in the Black Belt. Mamma looked older, shrunken and aged since the trial, like Harriet Tubman if Harriet had lived to be two hundred years old. She'd been mourning my death already.

—You don't got to say nothing, Mamma, another I inside me said. Mamma was the toughest woman I knew and it broke me up to see her broke up. She reached her liver-spotted claw across the table and the fingers uncurled like the legs of a dead spider. Restrained by handcuffs, I couldn't take her hand. An ugly white guard kept an eye on us.

—My baby, she bawled.

The other inmates turned to stare quietly. First music. That's what I call that kind of grieving regret. It had to be the first music. I bet the first song was the word "no" over and over, sung by a mother.

—Everything alright here, mam? the guard asked.

—I'm fine. Fine. Excuse me.

When the guard returned to minding his own fucking prison business, I shifted attention away from myself. —How about Demeter? When she going to come see me? I been in here six months already and I ain't heard nothing from her. No perfumed letter, no panties in the mail.

—I think it best if she just forget about you. Her and Umbrosia. You can't be no father to that baby girl behind bars.

—Once a bitch always a bitch.

—She got some papers here she want you to sign, Larson.

Mamma pulled a square manila envelope out of her handbag and slid it across the table to me.

—I ain't sign shit. I got a lawyer says I don't have to sign nothing.

—I did my best to see you was raised up right. You had the best voice in the choir. What'd you go and break us hearts for, Larson? What for?

Back in my cell, I tore up the papers into an explosion of confetti like it was New Year's and turned over everything else inside of my nine by eight suicide watch. At night, I sang my fellow abyss eaters to sleep and perhaps to dream that the world is good, that it is on their side, that things as they stood outside that prison were not worsening.

My voice walked through the iron bars and reached like a hand into their hearts and crowned us brothers, heads bowed not in prayer but under the ponder of agonistic legal fictions evaporated into thin airs.

Man digs himself into a hole, meanwhile looking only at the sky. Woman points out that Man is in a hole. Man tries to dig himself out of the hole and the hole deepens. Man says thanks. Let's face it, some holes aren't holes at all. They're abysses. And all you can do is try to sing and eat the abyss at the same time. All that matters is your capacity for the out-suffering of others. Just give the abyss a hug, squeeze it like a child, and the abyss will hug you back.

I went back, way back to Beulah Baptist Church where I got churched in metaphysical bullshit, my soul brined in the pickle jar of the Gospel of John According to John. In my boyish irreverence, around the time my voice started cracking and hair budded in funny places, every Sunday morning it was the same worriment: my cock was unhappy in my left pant leg and how do I get it slung over to the right pant leg before we all stand up singing hallelujah and I with my Sunday best pants proud as a popped tent. I couldn't stand up in that condition. Adjusting oneself in the two hours of churching before the Lord and the community of the Lord is no facile task. Those wool dress pants were tight and hot, we couldn't afford more than the one pair and you had to wear them till the seat fell out and the knees were worn from so much kneeling prayer. The church shoes I wore were given to me by a friend of the family who lost his legs in an automobile accident in front of the Carver Theater.

The heavy wooden door of Beulah was open. From the profane street walked by the lessers of human nature to supernatural and sacrosanct twilight I passed into the dim vestibule, where I'd shook hands many times with the minister who, after a sermon on John 11, I once told Lazarus was only AWOL in the underworld for four days — big deal. Screams from the bully pulpit about the blab of life so as not to hear death pull up in the hearse.

The pews empty row after row. This very voice, in a purple choral robe, that is now loquacious in your head once solitudinized the sob story of the Christ child and the poor Jewish kids scared of Herod. Herod was one mean white guy. Outside, the tumult of jackhammers tearing up the street. I pulled a hymnal from the back of the pew in front of me and it creaked open to the Gospel of John According to John, the pages torn out by the devil. You see, if we ain't got no thumbs, we can't hitch nowhere, and I leave no thumb prints on the hymnal or Crown bottle. I tried to sing an old familiar song, but only an unmusical lament came out like the monody I heard sung at Shuttleworth's interment in Oak Hill with the Confederate Herods.

The door of the rental office chimed as I walked in and sank into a plush carpet about six feet deep. A brindled office man in a madras shirt was slowly dying behind a desk covered in papers.

A stuffed owl with bright yellow eyes watched us from the wall. I still felt that prison guard's eyes on me. The taxidermy of humans ought to be considered by all serious people.

—Can I help you? the office man said.

—Looking for a place.

—You come to the right place for a place. You'll just need to fill out an application, our office will run a background check. Then you put down a deposit.

—I can tell you right now what the background check's going to be.

—Maybe you come to the wrong place then, the office man said, returning to his papers.

—I didn't do it. I got a wrongful conviction.

—What'd you not do?

—Don't matter. I got cleared.

—Still, we'll need to a run a background on you.

—Cleared means I didn't do it. I'm in the church choir.

—I understand, but there are rules.

Ah, there goes that white devil Robert's rules again!

—Look here, I got a letter from Judge Bahakel hisself says I didn't do shit and I go to that Judge and say you won't rent he'll hand you your ass on a fucking silver platter like John the Baptist's head. Now fuck motherfucking Robert and his rules.

—That's some language for a choral man. I'll have to think about it. We got children in our buildings. What are mothers going to think they find out who's living next door?

The letter from Judge Bahakel under his nose put the heat on him.

—I got a vacant house on Cotton Avenue you can fix up.

—I'll pay you soon as I get a job. Be making McMinimum wage.

—Making McWhat?

I could see his face in a frying pan.

—Nothing.

—One slip up and your ass is on the street, you got that?

—The street ain't so bad. You and Robert should try it sometime.

I found the house unfurnished and unwatered on Cotton Avenue. The front porch held together with C-clamps and jerry-rigged four-by-four posts. Saplings sprouting out of the gutters chokedholded with leaf rot and dead birds. I fit the key into the door, which wasn't even locked, and the hollow board door swung open on whining hinges into an empty, pitchy room. Not much better than being on suicide watch. The room like a bird cage whose floor had been shat on by every pigeon in New York City and never cleaned. With my foot I swiped at dead cockroaches on their backs, skidding them huskily into a corner. I put my hand to a grey water stain bubbling the dry-wall ceiling, still damp and cool to the touch. Some animal had left fecal artifacts of its tenancy behind. I flipped a wall switch. Nothing works the way it's supposed to around here. In the kitchenette, the windows were without blinds if there was even glass and all the world let right on in, help yourself. A dark inkling of yellow streetlight trespassed into the room at nightfall. The only water in the dump was inside the back of the john.

I went out the next day to raccoon through street garbage. Back of an old furniture store I picked up a chair and a wall clock with no batteries. I hung the clock on the wall next to a hole someone had punched and then noticed the clock had no hands either. I placed the chair against a wall and watched my life turn smaller, a trapezoidal door of sunlight slide across the hardwoods and climb up the east wall like a creeping exit. Then the walls clanged and rattled as water coughed up the pipes.

I got up and went to the bathroom and sat on the roll rim of the cast iron claw foot. A thread of rusty cold water untangled out of the spigot and pooled in the basin before it swirled meaninglessly downward into the drain. I plugged the drain and took off my clothes like they make you do when processing you between worlds: out of Cicero's crowded wasteland and into the solitary wilderness with iron bars. The clothes I changed into upon my eviction back into the free world lay in a puddle on the tile floor.

Pure in my new naked blackness, I slid in up to my neck in steaming water. First time I'd even seen a tub like this since I'd washed my own daughter and her half-sister. Above the tub was a window grayed with soot and a little view of a true sparrow warbling to a white pigeon. What little leaves were hanging on were changing. It would be time to Fall Back soon. I'd never kept track of time in prison. No calendar to turn every month, with the days of perfectly black boxes to slash through. Ten years the same as one long day, the sun's rising light just good enough to bless the night before it comes.

I wiggled my toes underwater and drew in a breath. My mouth opened and a gospeler's verse unheard in a long time echoed throughout that empty apartment a thousand times stronger than the judge's walnut gavel banging on the bench when I was McThinking: I'll Sodom and Gomorrah all y'all's womenfolk, so when they come back for me, they'll have a real good reason this time and double jeopardy says you can't try me twice for the same crime. I cupped my hands and splashed water over my face. I thought of the ten-dollar woman in the Carver Theater, and that fool Poitier who let the white convict, whom we shall call Robert, pull him off that rail car. Goddamn if a sequined honey baked ham wouldn't be deluxe right now. My old voice came back and furnished the rooms with purple-robed people descanting the melodies of hymnists. They multiplied and crowded together singing until someone was beating on the door, begging me to shut up, like the cops had beat on the door the night I was bondaged. And because when I sing, my voice takes on a body that exists independently of me for as long as I sing, I am never alone.

I'll never stop with the melancholy hollering singing hosannas and misereres. For even in prison I had my singing voice, the only person that never left me. I call it the song of the abyss eater. I'll sing it for you, up to my neck in bathwater. Listen. It goes like this.

THE LAST SUPPERS OF VIOLENT MEN
EXECUTED BY THE STATE

As death row's cook, I take super-sized pride in my work —
a great sin, I know but the cook of *The Last Supper's* supper is
nowhere to be seen and its cookbook is written in dingbats and
wingdings — whipping up iota and glut of final grub and ultimate
victuals for the condemned without prejudice for the crimes, they
are electrocuted, hanged, beheaded, drawn and quartered, keel-
hauled, crushed by elephant, boiled alive, blown from a cannon,
necklaced, broken on the wheel, slow sliced, gassed, stoned, le-
thally injected or otherwise unceremoniously executed for by that
legal fiction known as the State of Alabama.

Ah yes, sweet home Alabama and its artificially sweetened
methods of executing conscious meat.

For some, death row is all they've known of life. Reagan or
Bush Senior were back-scratching, brown-nosing and boot-lick-
ing in the Oval Office when the crew on death row was locked
in. The prisoners can order whatever they want, a menu freedom
even those who idle in fast-food drive-throughs and blow smoke
in the great cosmopolitan cafés of the world have never known.
And when you can eat Popeye's at Abu Ghraib — why not? Eat
your vegetables, I admonish them. Drink that milk. As if it still
matters. The last supper's restrictions: no alcohol, tobacco or firearms and a limit of forty dollars. Mostly kind killers and mousy
murderers who seem incapable of committing the berserk crimes
— the Ten Commandments are a droll shaggy dog story — for
which they were sentenced. White folk on death row are in the
minority, for once. Maybe they were dealt a bad hand. The Zero
Tolerance State doesn't turn the other cheek. The Zero Tolerance
State does not practice Gandhism. The Zero Tolerance State believes in the gospel of classical and operant conditioning. The
Zero Tolerance State's motto is *Lex talionis*, and the anatomical
equivalences of Matthew 5:38 and Exodus 21:24. A foot for an
eye. A hand for a tooth. An eye for a foot. A tooth for a tongue. An
eye for a butt cheek.

Not every meal request is that lordly. Sometimes no more than

197

a trip to the local service station or convenience store is required. Escorted by armed prison guards, I slip down the candy aisle and charge to the Zero Tolerance State twelve candy bars, five gallons of chocolate, vanilla and strawberry ice cream and strips of beef jerky for myself.

—Shouldn't we be concerned about their diet? What kind of message are we sending here? the Warden worried, folding his hands in his lap. —You send them packing off to meet their Maker with junk food on their stomach, what kind of impression are we giving up there? I'll have to answer for that before God His Self. Not on my watch.

One box of a dozen Krispy Kreme original glazed doughnuts and a chocolate milkshake from Arby's.

—Your death row pals eat better than I do at home, my wife Angela crowed when I recite the ingredients of another toothsome last meal at our dinner table. I never cooked for her like I did for the triple and quadruple murderers. At home, in a non-prison kitchen with the cute anthropomorphic cow and chicken decor, I failed to be inspired without the melodramatics of the last supper.

Birthday cake and onion rings for an inmate who was executed on his thirty-third birthday. The Krispy Kreme doughnuts were shared with the prison physician, a pious thanatologist who believes Lazarus was literally raised from the dead, present at all executions and considers his job administering poison a Christian duty. The physician, a strict literalist, had bought himself and his wife cemetery plots with the Jews on the Mount of Olives where he was certain — more certain than I was the sun would rise tomorrow — the resurrection of the dead was to begin.

—You feed them boys any better and they going to be too fat to squeeze into the electric chair, the Warden ha-ha-ed.

—Won't be able to get them through the Pearly Gates neither.

A pack of Marlboros (denied).

The prisoners I feed are fat and happy, but their lives are the lyrics to the saddest blues song out of Lead Belly's Angola.

—When are you going to feed me candy bars and grapes straight from the vine and fan me with banana leaves? Angela croaked.

My favorite request: an everything pizza to be hand delivered by the Warden to a homeless person in Birmingham.

—Do some good for somebody, you cocksuckers, Johnny the

cop killer said.

I do miss old Johnny the cop killer.

—How could you possibly become attached to these cretins? Angela slimed.

Jumbo shrimp and lobster roll, egg rolls and egg drop soup. Pecan pie for dessert. Fresh drop fried chicken from Popeye's. Liver and onions. Gumbo and Skittles.

—I'll just have a glass of ice water, please, requested a man who had pushed his pregnant wife into oncoming traffic. —I could really use a glass of water. It's hot in here.

The Warden paid for the lobster out of pocket. He ate McDonald's every morning for breakfast, and filtered his coffee with a sock.

A boiled egg and shaker of pepper requested as the last meal for an abortion clinic bomber.

—What kind of eggs was they? Brown eggs? Grade A? Organic?

Three shots of a contraband whiskey (permitted) and a white onion sliced into a great circle so the inmate could rub it in his eyes and work up some crocodile tears to show the family of the deceased and the Warden how doggone remorseful he wasn't.

—Have you considered maybe working as a chef in a public school cafeteria? Angela asked. —Maybe making meals at the other end of the school-to-prison pipeline?

Once, a smart-alecky child murderer who, for a last meal, ordered Justice, Equality and World Peace and then ate none of it.

I sat down with Cornelius, and watched him ingurgitate his last regalement with a plastic spork. When he was done he slumped with his hands palm up like a Punchinello. He hadn't finished his supper, so as he passed through the heavy door and shadowed out of this life, I finished off his fried okra and fried chicken. His electrified screams were like the shriven wind rushing through the bloody holes of stigmata in Christ's body. All the witnesses are blind as Saul, I say. A few things are starting to make sense to me now. Like how back in the good old days, when the West was won and the Almighty still gave us salient bodements and writings on the wall, they prayed to God before slaughtering a sheep.

The first week of Lent I committed myself to solitary confinement. Just to see what it's like on the inside. I needed *me* time.

And I was giving up other people for Lent. No more society or companionship for forty days. Prison is a byzantine maze of corridors and barred doors, one-way mirrors and dead ends with many ways in and only one way out. The Warden held the door open for me a bit too eagerly.

—If I plead to be let out, don't listen to me.

—You don't got to do this.

—I've got to do this.

—Who is going to cook? he went right to the point.

—You don't have any executions scheduled until next week. Besides, the convenience store is less than a mile away.

I stepped into the *Götterdämmerung* of the cell. The moment my eyes fully adjusted to the dark, I was bored out of my mind. If character is who you are in the dark, then we should evolve our own source of bioluminescence like those ugly, fanged deep sea anglerfish with lanterns on their foreheads. And why not? When we were apes our hands were feet. A buddy once caught an anglerfish in Lake Guntersville and thereafter cited the catch as proof of the existence of Satan. We had mastered the light, wiring it into our homes and the electric chair, and could summon it at any hour like a luminous threat with the flick of a switch, everywhere except solitary confinement wherein the human tendency to whisper in the dark is confirmed. The voices of Death Row's executed whispered their last meals to me, an endless litany of junk food and fatty fetes. As a woman's voice will sound dearer, more sensual when spoken in darkness, I soothed them recalling the sweet nothings Angela had said the first time our power went out. I stuck my nose in all four corners of the cell, and tried out some yoga poses I'd seen Angela pretzeled in but none worked. I collapsed on the cell floor like a doughy push puppet. I bonged on the door. Footsteps clicked officially down the hall and stopped in front of the cell.

—I quit, Warden.

—Can't do it. Gave you my word. And it's only been five minutes.

—Let me out of here, goddamn it.

—If I let you out then I'm going to have to go back on my word. I gave you my word I would not let you out even if you begged. I hate going back on my word. You know that.

—What about my wife?

—She'll understand.

—What am I supposed to do in here? Beat off?

—You wouldn't be the first, partner. Maybe count as high as you can, or talk to yourself. That's what they usually do.

I tried talking to myself but ran out of things to say. The cell dark was so thick I could taste the dark and it tasted like shit. Unable to distinguish between wakefulness and the episodes of sleep dreamed between dreams, I listened to a gasbag describe some great place called Callipolis I've never heard of — white sand beaches, frozen cocktails, all-you-can-eat buffets, it sounded like the Redneck Riviera without the prisons. I later asked a travel agent friend where Callipolis was. He said it was closed to the public.

My sweat pooled on the concrete floor. I named these self-made bodies of water after old friends executed by the Zero Tolerance State. The Row is not blessed with the modern conveniences of air conditioning. In summertime, the cinder block walls bake and the tropical boiling air is like a miasmatic plasma passed through the intestinal tract of a demonic porcupine. Weather in the bastille is perfect with a slight chance of getting even better.

Plaster waste calcimine flaking off the ceiling and settling in my hair. I guess time passed, but there really is no time without light. Solitary confinement induces the apocalypse of the self, and the borders of my being expanded like a balloon, filling the cell to the maximum purlieus of solipsism. A self that when called does not come hobbling like a three-legged dog out of the doghouse. I imagined conjugal visits from gaudy succubi with painted faces who were not my wife. I refereed as androgynous archangels battled it out with transvestite cacodemons. I told the archangel and the cacodemon I didn't know them and they better pick a fight in another cell unless they wanted to be in solitary too. I wallowed in what I thought was my own blood, but turned out upon closer inspection to be mess, and the blood of the angels trounced by the cacodemons. I say it was like opening a refrigerator door in the middle of an especially dark night in Egypt, the Warden's silhouette outshone from behind by the luminous and glowering omnipresence of Angela. I crawled out on all fours like an emancipated roach. Unshaven and unclean, hircine in strange places, I looked up at my wife and saw how for years she had seen me.

—I had to let you out, the Warden explained.

—The inmates are bitching about the food. They won't eat anything unless you cook it.

I didn't blame them. The regular food was unfit for dogs.

—What the hell are you doing? Why are you in timeout? she asked.

She focused on the Warden. —What is this place? A kindergarten or a state prison?

My eyes then were scaled over; I couldn't see that the Warden and my wife were playing footsy. And if I could, would I have cared? I could stand on the damn street corner and flag down a beautiful woman like a taxi cab. I had just survived not one but several dark nights of the soul. Six of one and a half dozen of the other. A woman just wants to live with another woman, a man on death row said sagely. Only with a man's muscular thoughts and his pogo-stick to bounce through the nights on. I grant that we're all stuck in our own heads, but if I have to listen one more time about how awesome her gay coworker friend with the adorable broken boxer's nose is I'll commit a capital offense against the first person to cross my path. I've seen men who look like the Cyclops from *The Odyssey* with women who could make Jesus weep. Angela and her gay coworker belong together like milk and fucking cookies. Ten kids by eleven different fathers. This sissy who goes into medicine because he wants to do good. Well, the prison guards want to do good when they blackjack your skull. The prison physician is fulfilling his Christian duty when he finds that vein. Virgins want to do good. Angela wants to do good tossing her ponytail trying to make a gay man think straight. The last time we made whoopee we did not beget a child and I had a funny feeling I was emptying more than just my spermatozoa into her, emptying all the soul I could perk out of me, what was left after I fried my soul in the soul food I cooked for the fellas about to enter the Pearly Gates. I'd never speak that lickerish way about any woman who wasn't also shanghaied by a marriage certificate into sharing a tombstone with me. I already have our necropolitan plots picked out. I was a roach escaped from Alcatraz, a snail on the lam from Angola. My eyes adjusted painfully to the solitary corridor, and by the time I could see clearly again Angela was gone.

Cooking the last supper of violent men was taking its awful

toll on my marriage, which was by this time little more than the same argument seeking out new ways to ruin the bonhomie. Some of these hangdog fellows are on The Row so long you get to know them better than your own kind, and the revolving door — never have I heard death row's revolving door release a squeak — of inmates supplies me ceaselessly with new mouths to feed. More than the twelve apostles breaking bread in the Cenacle.

I tried a home cooked meal that tasted like boiled tennis shoe with a foot inside. Angela forbids me to cook now. She says I need a country mile between home and the office. Angela is a nurse at the university hospital, treating gunshot wounds and agricultural accidents, the tomfools blasted in the face trying to load a shotgun, run over by tractors and John Deere equipment; she comes home, her scrubs en-crimsoned with surgical cruor. She spends a long time alone in the bathroom washing off the day's hemic gore. Human teeth in the sink.

I'd run over a dog that evening driving home from the prison and I was feeling real glum about it. Thunder rattled the panes like dice in a cup.

As a courtesy, Angela asked about my day. I didn't return the favor of asking about hers — a courtesy as well.

—I think the Warden's watch is a high-end Rolex replica.

—That's interesting. How are the yard birds doing?

—I've been thinking about how to solve this problem where two prisoners don't agree even when it is in their best interests. The prisoner's dilemma.

—I'm all ears.

Angela did, god bless her, have elephantine ears. Everything on her body was big. She once bragged she has an hour glass figure — more like 90 minutes. Not that Death Row's cook has been dieting. I pray for a killer body. These portraits of a fat Jesus are more common in rural homes. The Cross structurally reinforced to support the weight of the Lord's rotund body. Obese Jesus cannot fit in the crowded cities in skinny jeans with the Millennials, with their Ubers and tiny houses. Whenever the prison despond got me down, I thought of corpulent Jesus — fried food at the Last Supper — and chortled in a way that is entirely indecorous in a prison. I'm mostly interested in targeted weight loss on my stomach. Most people say it cannot be done, but these naysayers of little faith do not own a box cutter and a pound of crystal meth.

—One of the prisoners, this felon Arthur on Death Row, asked me how I'd solve the dilemma. Asking for a friend, he said. Two crooks get themselves arrested and are detained in separate cells. The police offer both fellows the same deal. If one plays Judas and betrays his partner and the other guy keeps a lid on it, Judas gets out. If they both keep their mouths shut they get a slap on the wrist. If they squeal on each other they both get three months. They got to decide between betrayal and silence. What do you figure they ought to do?

—They ought to bet on the other guy ratting them out.

—Not much of an optimist are we?

—No, we are not. I don't suppose they would avocate his sentence?

—They're in prison so long they become innocent. They're not the same person who was convicted a decade ago. From the sanctity of our dining room the difference between their guilt, for whatever pettiness, and our unchallenged innocence is like the mucus trail of a snail that evaporates in the sun.

I'd prepared our whole night from a recipe I wanted to try: frozen dinner, then watching UFO videos, binging on each other's gentled gender, maybe knock a lamp off the table and start a house fire. But I couldn't get my mind off Arthur, who was scheduled to be executed the next day, though by this time, so long after his sentencing, he may've built up a mithridatic immunity to lethal injection, in his cell chanting *To Kill a Mockingbird* or *In Cold Blood.*

—You should open a restaurant.

Angela made no secret of the fact that she hated me most when I loved my job.

—What would be on the menu?

—You could call the restaurant *Last Supper* and serve everything on those ugly pink prison trays y'all use with plastic sporks.

I decanted red wine into two glasses. —Eichmann drank an Israeli wine before being executed.

—I'm not even going to ask why you know that. You should spend less time locking yourself in solitary confinement.

Angela's cell phone went off in her purse. She took the call in the next room and I continued talking to myself and the thunder that grunted in clapping responsorial, the dice in the windows rolling.

—Few weeks back, I said to the room, —This one fellow who ordered candy bars and ice cream for his last meal, he was sentenced to ride the lightning, but he just wouldn't die. No matter how much juice they pumped him with, he just wouldn't quit. Now there's talk about banning candy bars. Something about health regulations, obesity, diabetes, the American black plagues. It's impossible to electrocute a diabetic fat guy because he's insulated from the electricity.

Angela was excusing herself before she entered the room again. —I have to go in to work. I'm sorry.

I looked at the half-full wine glass and decided it was half empty. You take some molecule of happiness from the air, a particle of it from the dirt in the prison yard, the earth in the open mouths of the dead — wherever you can find it. A lifetime of emptiness and a moment of ecstasy both last for the same amount of time: all of eternity. Who has time for jury duty? I would hitch a ride to heaven on someone else's prayer if I could.

Angela vanished into the back bedroom. Drawers opening and bumping around. The rain rained and the lights flickered and powered down when a transformer on our street exploded bluely after being struck by a white bolt of hot lightning, a common enough electrical occurrence around here. I've caught lightning maybe two to three times in a lifetime of loitering outdoors during electrical storms. Being struck by lightning in Alabama is taken as a sign of God's blessing. As though the more the Almighty tries to fetch our attention by throwing us uninsured acts of God the more folks just don't seem to mind. Without the refrigerator humming, a strange silence thickened about the house, like gauze wrapped around my head, solitary confinement thickening like a dark roux in the kitchen.

I sat in my straight-backed chair, in the darkness of the dining room, thinking about what to make Arthur for his last meal, trying to fork cold food I couldn't see into my invisible mouth. With two glasses of wine to drink now. One is plenty; two is poison. At this point in the dilemma, the prisoners should keep a foot in their mouths so somebody gets out.

Let me explain in abridged biography the chapters that led to Arthur's incarceration. Arthur was a home-schooled creationist from Cherokee County convicted of patricide, matricide and fratricide. His freshman lawyer filed the insanity argument — everyone in Cherokee County is insane — which as any moron who's seen *A Time to Kill* knows is about as good as the Twinkie defense before a Dixie jury. But his counsel had the years of schooling, the exams and the crushing debt to think about while performing the legal eagle dance and purple oratory in the courtroom. Arthur's lawyer referred orotundly to recent history at Scottsboro and most of the state of Alabama throughout his speechifications. No one bought it. A few jurors asked where Scottsboro was and why it mattered.

Arthur was a stately black man who'd been adopted by a kind white family. His skin was so black it was blue. Distant consanguinity with Booker T. Washington did little to endear Arthur to the jury. The family babysitter, a prim pretty girl who had known Arthur since his diaper days, testified that from a young age Arthur was a rabid cusser.

—What do you mean by Arthur was a cusser? she was asked during Arthur's lawyer's cross-examination. —Tell the jury here more about what that means.

—Well, she said looking mortified that she was about to reproduce Arthur's wondrous expletives. —It started simple with one syllable words like shit, then it was damn. By sixth grade it was goddamn and then goddamn shit. He was really putting the words together. It was like he was playing jazz, but with cusswords. I recollect one Sunday in particular, after church, I heard Arthur alone in his room.

—And what did you hear Arthur saying alone in his room?

—Goddamn mother fucking bitch ass thundercunts, the babysitter said shamefacedly.

Half the courtroom laughed; the other half shrieked. Not long before the triple homicide, Arthur was heard improvising some scurrilous ragtime melody: gangbang fuckstain banana bitches necrophiliac asscracks jesus jizz nigger Nazis bag of dicks, and other courageous, indecent neologies which made the jury blush for shame and wring their hands. A few prudes left the courtroom, and an octogenarian had to be revived by paramedics. She later sued, claiming that the eyewitness' testimony — the recapitulation of Arthur's recreational, musical cussing — had so traumatized her that she lost her sense of hearing. It was true: Arthur was gifted with a golden tongue for salacious word salads, like a sordid boogie-woogie honked from a wicked saxophone.

Arthur's lawyer drove his point home, —I'm sorry your honor to repeat such things in your courtroom here. As you can see, the law-abiding public is horrified by such blasphemes. It should be apparent to all that the defendant is blessed with a facility of four-letter words that is without parallel in this State which has a long history of gentleman cussers. I refer you to George Wallace and Hank Aaron. I'd like to ask each of you a question that you may answer quietly within yourselves. How many of you have hit your thumb instead of the head of a nail? And those of you with poor hammer-aim, how many have cursed mightily at the pain thereon? I ask you, does a man's fluent ability to poetize with four-letter words make of him a murderer? The prosecution would suggest that such bawdy logorrhea is but the lingual gateway to the three murders for which Arthur today stands wrongfully accused. He speaks in tongues. He needs treatment for coprolalia, nothing more. Your psychosomatic evangelizing is nonsense. Acknowledge the innocence of a man whose only crime is jazz.

The day next I was summoned to the Warden's office. The Warden was seated behind his desk, which was blank as my mind had been in solitary confinement. —Have a seat, he said.

Have a seat is what Angela says when she wants to talk about bills or an unplanned pregnancy.

—There's no chair.

There wasn't a chair in front of his desk.

—Fine. Stand up. See if I care.

I looked at the Warden's wristwatch. Yup. Definitely bogus.

—What's up, Warden?

—I was just doing a Google search here for "German women." The image results come up with these buxom blonde supermodel types with baby blue eyes and mountainous breasts like the girl on the St. Pauli beer bottle next to scratchy old black and whites of Holocaust victims. What kind of world is out there? What are they on the outside hiding from us on the inside? I was appalled. Beautiful blonde women in the same image search results as these ghastly, emaciated Holocaust ghosts. It makes no sense.

—That's very interesting, Warden. You should consider a vacation.

—I'm on vacation right now. I didn't know where to go, so

I'm tooling around on Google to find out. You think he done it?

—Do I think who done what?

—You think Arthur killed them Christians?

—Warden, with all due respect, we both know that folks get murdered by the State just in that chamber over there for lesser offenses. Arson, maybe. Couple of rapes. Driving without a license. Stealing watermelons. Stealing horses. Whistling at a white woman. Thinking about whistling at a white woman. And it is common knowledge that a certain stripe of Christian has titillating fantasies about martyrdom.

—You think he done it.

—The kangaroo jury snores so well at night they could cut enough lumber to crucify him on.

—You have my blessing to make him one hell of a meal.

—I don't think he wants lethal injection.

—It don't matter what Arthur wants, does it? He prefers something more exotic, something media-worthy? He wants to go out in style like the Rosenbergs?

—I think he wanted a medieval execution. Like Scaphism, the boats.

—What's the boats?

—The boats is where you lash a prisoner to the mast of a small boat and force feed him with milk and honey. He gets some bad diarrhea. There's nothing venomous insects love more than honey diarrhea. Maybe they burrow in his skin. Birds of prey peck at his eyes and the prisoner is blessed with blindness. Maybe they feed him more honey and milk just to sustain his agony a while longer before perishing of exposure, gangrene, infection, malnutrition, diarrhea...

—Okay, okay, we get the picture.

—The longest survivor of the boats lasted seventeen days.

—I am not loving this. I am on vacation. This is worse than the German girls.

—I'll leave you to your, whatever you were doing before I came in here.

—Just wanted to ask you if you thought he'd done it.

—You know, Warden. Before I met Angela, there was a time in my life when I fancied myself a freeman. I could've picked up and moved anywhere. I wanted to pick the city where I would live based on the good looks of the professional football team's cheerleaders. That kind of freedom. I'd live in a hotel room, so I wouldn't be tied down, a DO NOT DISTURB sign hanging from the doorknob. And when the cheerleading squad looked better in another city, maybe after a bad season or shoddy coaching, I'd check out and move to the next city. That was my idea of freedom.

—That's a fine plan. Maybe you still can. They got prisons all over this country. Before long, the incarcerated will outnumber us. In the future there will be more perverts, creeps, rapists and murderers in prison than there are normal guys like you and me. Ain't that a thought to hang your hat on.

I stepped outside to smoke, which I hadn't done in a long time. Dulls your tongue so everything tastes gray. I let the smoke fill me, inhaling deeply, hoping the vaporous smoky exhalation might carry me away through the metal links of the prison fencing — so this is why the Warden did not want cigarettes to be a prisoner's last meal. Some big rigs smoked by on the shaded road bounding the prison. I felt the consideration of many eyes up in the Panopticon towers: armed guards sulked and paced in their glassy observation decks like the prisoners did in their cells, wearing down a path between walls. Miles of electrified razor wire fence scrolled around the prison.

On the inside, I sometimes forget that the guards are out there supervising the playground up on their pedestal. If I was governor, I would declare a moratorium on the manufacture of pedestals. Too long, the midget minds and tapeworm souls adored on pedestals. The normal guys outnumbered. The evening was cold and grey and greying colder as the sun slipped behind the crowns of tall pines, leaving the gloaming of its afterlight ebbing behind like a bright shadow and the guard towers growing longer against the prison yard.

Angela was at work, transplanting somebody's organs, stitching up a gunshot wound, doing good for somebody. I just wanted to help people was her answer when I asked her why she became a nurse. That's all I hear these days, other folks talking and throwing words through the air. She wept inconsolably when a baby bird tumbled from its nest, and tiny chest compressions on a featherless breast failed to resuscitate it. The foretokens of the Almighty silent as the prisoner who settles for a month in jail. In the prisoner's dilemma, it didn't matter whether the prisoners snitched or not; the panoptic fate of imprisonment in this yeehaw republic incarcerates us all in the prisoner's dilemma.

The kitchen is my sanctuary. Not even the Warden tells me what to do in there. Some men have woodshops or a garage. Man caves. I keep a kitchen on Death Row. Copper pots and iron pans flash in the cupreous overhead light. Caravaggio's postcard of Our Lord at His last supper hangs above the stove. I'm told by my travel agent friend that the original hangs in a refectory, which is where monks eat. The Lord is my shepherd in this work and I do not question why He has called upon me to perform such strange, awful work. Just yesterday night, I whipped up breakfast for dinner: eggs, pancakes, bacon, grits, hash browns, bowl of fruit, pot of coffee black as the solitary confinement cell with your eyes open. The man being executed that night ordered breakfast for dinner, he said, to trick his mind into thinking it was morning and he had another day ahead.

The boys on The Row are hanging in there. A hardy, scrappy bunch. A pharmacist accused of prescribing the wrong meds has been brewing julep hooch that lifts their spirits. A chunky concoction that tastes like prune juice, but gets the job done. A few doses of that hooch and I am ready for solitary confinement again.

—This is going to be our last meeting, I said to Arthur as we shared a Dixie cup of the julep hooch.

—You reckon correct, sir.

—Let me ask you something straight.

—Shoot.

—Did you do it?

—It's been so long now I don't even know. I'm starting to believe maybe I did. Who else could've done it if not me? It's a scarier proposition if I didn't do it, so I'll say I did and be done with it. Because if I didn't do it, then we are subject to the whims of extraordinary forces and there ain't jackshit we can do about it.

—You ought not to read too much of the *Book of Job*, Arthur. That stuff is bad for you.

I'd seen the prison chaplain hand a Bible through his cell's bars a few weeks earlier. I never thought Arthur would read it, but perhaps he'd arrived at this tragic sense of things on his own.

—How's things at home? Arthur asked, as if he knew something I didn't.

—Not good, Arthur.

—Your wife's seeing someone, bet you. See if she ain't.

—Why do you think that?

—That week you volunteered for the hotbox. How long did it take her before she noticed you were gone?

—I see your point.

—And who kept you in there so long?

Why would you believe a convicted murderer? Angela was already whispering in my ear, which were smaller than hers.

—It was something I had to do.

—What do you say? You think if I killed someone again they'd delay my execution another five years? Put me on trial again? I could live the rest of my life in death row if I just killed someone every few years or so.

—Maybe the governor will pardon you. There's still time.

—We both know they ain't going to commute nothing. Ain't pardon shit.

Alabama governors waged successful election campaigns solely on the commitment they wouldn't pardon anyone, especially not gang members. An Alabama governor would sooner kiss a Democrat than pardon a black man for killing Christians. No one gets out of Alabama alive with a gang tattoo. Whenever I want to know what Alabama is up to I peer into the malevolent, putrid blackness of my own soul. It was time to decide the menu of the last supper. Arthur was scrannel as a sheet that could be walked through; I wanted to make him a meal to talk about on the other side.

—Have you thought about your last meal?

—I'd sure like some pussy before I die. Is that on the menu? Can you cook some pussy for me buddy and serve it nice and hot?

—I'll see what I can do.

Arthur was moved to a death watch cell. They took his reading material away — Bible and the novels. The Zero Tolerance State forbids any reading material in the death watch cell. The chaplain from St. Paul's frisked by guards before he administered the last rite.

—Do you think unicorns and dragons exist, Father? Arthur cross-examined the poor priest.

—If God wanted them in His menagerie. Who are we to say what God cannot create? But probably no.

—But we got words for them.

—We have words for plenty of things that are man-made.

—Prison, Arthur said. —That's man-made.

—Arthur, if you have anything to confess, now is the time to repent. There is no sin that cannot be atoned through God's grace.

—I guess I got nothing to say.

—Let me tell you something, Arthur. The priest's vestments you see me in. They used to be prison stripes. The Lord walked with me across the abyss until I got out. You are going to walk into one of two worlds, both of which there is not a man alive who has seen what awaits in them.

—What'd you do, Father?

—God has forgiven me for what I did.

—Just tell the cook I'd like an olive, please. Just one olive will do.

The chaplain, I am told, anointed Arthur's forehead with olive oil as Arthur said his epilogue, —You know, before the day is out you won't even remember knowing me. Or what I ate. Shit, man. Maybe I didn't murder nobody, but I wish now I had. Even murderers get some respect on the Row. If I'm innocent, they'll resent me. And it ain't the first time a nigger's been juiced in this state for nothing more than being out after sundown, looking lewd at a white woman. I sure hope heaven and hell are fulled up with white women. You get that, Father? I say again: heaven and hell, overflowing with honey between the legs of white women and milk squeezed from the tits of white women. This in Jesus name I pray.

I haven't seen that particular prison chaplain come around for another execution since.

Arthur changed out in an orange shirt that resembled the blue scrubs Angela wore at the hospital. Arthur was generous with his organs — he donated every part of himself he could — and some dying animal already had his name on the waiting list for Arthur's insides. After the coroner ruled the cause of death as lethal injection, which was obvious to all, and the autopsy reports filed, Arthur's heart, liver and kidneys would be shipped to the university hospital, where Angela would transplant them into a body that had been dying on the waiting list. Do they use the eyes? I'll ask the Warden about that one. Even now Arthur's heart is beating inside another man's breast.

A rural calm simplified Arthur's dilemma, unlike those caitiffs who depart and quail like a hit dog hollering. For the Lord Jesus Christ, who is invisible and benevolent and risen, and a bunch of other adjectives, He puts in a lot of overtime on Death Row.

After Arthur, the next prisoner in the queue of executions was Beau — an assembly line of named meat. Alabama is trying to execute as many of them as possible before the Second Coming. Beau had the jaw from which you expect decisions to be handed down. The police blotter reported an effigy of the Virgin Mary engraved in the grip of his semi-automatic. I don't even want to know what damn fool speck he did. Could've been venery with a minor minor and killing the handicapped. Maybe he beat a blind guy in Paper/Rock/Scissors three hundred times in a row. I'll make him whatever sapid last meal he wants. My paperback interest in the prison's grotesquerie stops at my kitchen door.

Without Angela, who turned the gay nurse straight as a rainbow, the house is another cell in the panoptic system of solitary confinement: she left me nothing but a jar of olives in the fridge.

—But why don't you know what they're being executed for anymore? Angela would ask, —Don't you want to know? I'd want to know.

As for the Warden, he bought himself a cart then went looking for a horse to attach it to.

Now the heavy metal door — cruelly painted sky blue — of the death watch cell swung open, Arthur was escorted in shackles clanking from ankle and wrist. In the few minutes between the removal of the shackles and being strapped onto the gurney he would be jackass free for the first time in years.

I could hear the second hand of the clock face ticking on the wall above the execution gurney. In my life lifetime subscription to *Reader's Digest* — a gift from the Warden — I read that a woman died on the *It's a Small World* ride at Disney's Magic Kingdom. I want to go like that too — it's my favorite place in the world. Without me, Death has no body to die in. The Warden asked Arthur if he had any last words, some disfluent mutterings, a last licentious laugh, an electric howl into the abyss.

—See ya'll in the next world; I cain't wait to get a piece of justice in the next one. What? No stones? Y'all ain't got no stones to cast at me? I asked to be boated or stoned. Just knock down the prison if ya'll short on stones.

Arthur had requested no kickshaw, just a single black olive, the stone still in it, for his last meal, and I'd turned him down. Someone, somewhere, can say to themselves, in a transport of ecstasy and passion, I have the transplanted heart of a murderer beating inside me, but I am not the murderer, though he lives in me. Everything is coming to a quietus now.

Arthur was about to meet the Lord and his prisoner's dilemma would be resolved by habeas corpus exit from this deciduous life the way troubled sleepers enter a dream. Big-armed guards buckled and strapped him onto the cruciform gurney like he was going for a bumpy ride, arms outspread at nine and three. The Zero Tolerance State physician, a sickly and incompetent man who botched many executions, and believed in the resurrection of the dead, peered up at the wall clock above Arthur, waiting for the appointed hour, and medically nodding to the Warden and me, tapped the syringe hollowly with his Dracula finger. The prisoner, the Zero Tolerance State says, must be executed at the correct hour, not a moment sooner or later. I looked away when the needle pierced the black flesh of his arm. Still I wonder whether Arthur did it, killed them Christians, but that jazz tongue of his ought to be donated to that white jury.

I said I declined Arthur's request for a final meal. That is not strictly speaking true.

—Did that fellow got juiced before me ever get his olive? Beau asked while we discussed the menu for his last supper, which is to be served next Friday night at the appointed charnel hour.

—No, I said. Arthur can have the whole Mount of Olives.

WHEN CHRIST RETURNS TO A SLAVE STATE

Lest it be misunderstood that Gary cold-shouldered the Mormon missionaries' cordial cuff on the hollow core door, consider that his powers of auscultation, normally so acute, were dulled by the deafeningly high nasality of the vacuum plundering the green rug. A clean home is a happy home, Mama had beat into him, deploying a creative battery of implements: rakes, shovels, mixing spoons, belts, electric cords, the Bible, frying pans, cookie sheets, and even once a dead possum. After much procrasterbation Gary was getting around to the tedious, quotidian details of happiness, even if his cat was missing.

The Mormons, historied for their unphilosophical patience in the westward wagon train migrations out of the Second Great Awakening and through the soulless flatness of the Great Plains, waited outside Gary's door as if under strict orders from higher powers on their exoplanet Kolob to stay put.

Inside, they heard every genre of discord, mechanical failure and lamentation. A tumultuary struggle for life and death, between man and machine was being waged behind that apartment door. *Somebody* was home. The sound emanating from within was a multilayered orchestra: the vacuum purring along discordantly on top, and beneath it the Mormons detected a dull disintegrative bone-crushing like a broken washing machine immusically tumbling a large human head inside. One pictured the decapitated head of St. John the Baptist swirling circularly in detergent. A third dissonant layer, audible only at the limits of human hearing, but augmented by the Mormon's supernatural mission, consisted of a woman yelling.

Gary's rotary rock tumbler on the kitchen table was in its third week of polishing. The gemstones should be breaching any day now. Day and night, the tumbler tumbled with the ado and pother of a thousand teeth tiny chewing on the carved stones of civilization, finally dissolving into the background of Gary's aural consciousness. Gary fancied himself a lapidary sportsman. It hastened the time; the attrition and grinding of the product of eons quickened the blood. The tumbler wore the gaudy present down until it scintillated floridly in the palm of his hand or was necklaced about a woman's throat like a garrote about a tulip stem. The tumbler turned the rocks in abrasive silicone grit lubricated with filtered water like a mechanical mixer preparing a stew. Gary liked stew, but he wasn't hungry. These gemstones rattling in quantity about the tumbler were his friends. Confidantes. Onyx and amethyst, in particular.

Gary partook of reheated coffee and watched an attractive couple arguing on the television. The woman especially seemed to be getting off at this ruction with her jabberwocking asshole of a husband who she accused of having an extraterrestrial affair. She perspired and panted vigorously like a secretary in heat. But he grew bored with their little tiff and walked off. Gary consummated the coffee and returned to running the vacuum back and forth over the same green spot like a push mower until he got his mother's crabby voice out of his head while the woman on the television continued yelling.

Fearful that they might be interrupting a domestic situation, the Mormon missionaries knocked gingerly again, and shifted their weight. One of them yawned.

Observe the poster of Paul Bear Bryant left on the wall above the couch by the previous tenant evicted for non-payment of rent. Gary had always been fond of herringbone, and was terrified of blank walls, so he left the poster up. Blanks walls reminded him of the Army barracks.

The Bear's contribution to society was so staggering it left him feeling blah and otiose. The Bear was a hard-boiled stoic, and practically a philosopher. Like trying to perform a single good deed in the shadow of Mother Theresa, Bill Clinton, Gandhi, Lady Gaga — why even bother? The Bear's records remained unbeaten. Gary used the poster for target practice, which is not restricted to the legally defined limits of the imagination.

It was the winter of his twenty-eighth year and he had no wife. He'd always thought "Elizabeth" was a beautiful name. For a woman. Elizabeth was a woman who had stuffed her brassiere since age twelve with banknotes, to which any woman would aspire at the snap of the fingers. He'd gone so far to penetrate the high-water mark of white picket fence normalcy as to entertain an arranged marriage with one of the leftover girls from his bumble-fuck township. Fuck that shit, Gary was a winner all the way. He'd rather put on a black ski mask and crusade into Sunday school yelling at all the sheepish girls in their Sunday dresses and the boys in their suspenders that everybody, and Gary meant Everybody, was going to H-E double L and some folks were born without dicks and that's how things are so get over it.

Gary, who did not always discern the difference between word and deed, and being a man of his word, and therefore the deed, fulfilled the word — wearing the ski mask to Sunday school — exactly as it had been prophesied in the price bubble of razzmatazz. For this "trouble-breeding devilment," as it was styled in the church circular, mostly a marketing platform for congregants selling the strip center of shit in their garages like old lawn mowers and salt-and-pepper shaker golliwogs, he would be excommunicated from the church where he was baptized and ritually circumcised according to the law of the fathers. Gary has since bought several ski masks over the years, passing the time wearing the mask and nothing else, but hadn't yet worn them in the vicinity of a church again, nor has he ever really artistically topped that Mephistophelian culmination of his personality, the churchgoers checking their pockets for stones to hurl at the little satanic boy in the black mask.

But now, while the Mormons wait outside his door, and the rock tumbler grinds on, under a V-neck cashmere sweater Gary wore a bulletproof vest both around the apartment and to check the mail for his daily death threat. He could take a shot to the chest, a sniper-round from the pines or window of another apartment unit. Often, they were written in jaw-dropping, mangled English, letters written backwards like names carved in the bark of a tree. He'd experimented with an Israeli gas mask, but it was too sweltering, and he couldn't place an order at Domino's with it on. Ownership had been one value passed down the generations of Americans without interruption, and Gary amassed all the accouterments of a deviant shut-in. In the closet: guilt, a skeleton, rifle, red cape, handcuffs. In the sock drawer: pepper spray, flavored condoms, duct tape, ski masks, and a sock full of loose change.

He would soon be out of business if he didn't stop sandbagging himself. He could damn well pack the antechamber to his colon with whatever he damn well pleased, it was a free country, was it not?

After he graduated from the mirror stage of sexuation, goggled by his own specular likeness in the silver mirror peculiarly attached to the ceiling above his parent's bed, Gary wrote hopeful letters in crayon, encouraged by his mother, to Neil Armstrong requesting international citizenship in the first lunar settlement over which the American flag — by this time a *Don't Tread on Me* flag — was to be raised and the era of anthroparchy consummately enshrined. For his time, he got a boilerplate reply, thanking the letter writer for his interest in NASA, which was being defunded and sold for scrap to the Chinese, and asking him to pledge a donation to the manned mission to Mars. The return address was a private post office box. He remembered too when the Billy Idol song "Dancing With Myself" aired, the Religious Right marching on the White House lawn and the cockeyed "Silly Faggot Dicks Are For Chicks" campaign of the good old days, back when Napster was the only pirate in town. The aftereffect of all this was a volatile frisson of self-consciousness that could have put a man on the moon. On his resume: he could pass the mirror test in his sleep.

In the Dark Ages, he'd have volunteered for a monastic order, illuminating the Devil's Bible until his arm fell off and he went blessedly blind with cataracts, the calligraphy alone demanding a Faustian pact to complete, his hair tonsured in the style of the day, lewd visions of choral castrati afflicting his daydreams, athletic yearnings properly sublimated into surrealist landscapes where the laws of physics were unconstitutional. Instead, he bought his cashmere sweaters a size too big to fit over the bulletproof vest.

The missionary's knock was like a referee's whistle blown in the kerfuffle of battle, unheeded by the losing side which had the most to gain from a ceasefire. And so the Mormons waited. After his military discharge, Gary was host to no one, no guests of any size. He didn't even let his landlord in to spray for bugs or change the air filters. Leastwise, the old-fashioned dark came down quick now and Gary, when he finally admitted the Mormons entrance into the antechamber of his lair, would be glad to have the company in the fishbowl efficiency he rented merely for warming it from one draggy month to the next. He buckled before a dependency on day and night, their regularities, islanded as he was in this cheap date jerry-building set back from the highway on a pork chop of land haphazardly carved out of slash pine. Gary did use his extraordinary powers of imagination, his pittance of a birthright as an only son who never had a playmate, to overcome the suburban solipsism and brainwash himself that the world spun merrily on outside his mirrorless apartment. In the sobriety of The Bear's cold, analytical stare, he knew that it did not. A bottlenecking of expectations and gridlocked relativism were the natural issues of this; perhaps it rained on everyone else, but around Gary, protected by the antipluvial counterfactual, there was only a soft shower of clinquant confetti, party favors and throw beads.

He watched from his miniature balcony as deer herded through the parking lot of the apartment complex, flitting shadowily between parked cars hulking in their white stripes and disappearing through a dark wall of pines that conspired behind Gary's back. He never could shake the impression that his apartment complex was the recrement of a botched vasectomy retched forth by a paid-by-the-hour motel architect who worked from home in flannel pajamas. Gary thought how he could pull a condom off his dick after a one night stand with a man suffering hemorrhoids and throw it over his head off a ten-story abortion clinic and create something more fit for human habitation than this apartment with its dwarf balcony. At least the Army barrack had men. And men in uniform at that! A girl's wet dream, by gob!

One architectural detail, if it could be called that, that tilted him towards psychosis was the rough tongue of asphalt shingles where the roof snarled down between the blank windows to become the wall texture of 80 grit sandpaper. Every time Gary parked his car and looked up through the cracked windshield he couldn't afford to fix he had to endure the mnemonic associations, suggested to him by the asphalt roof doubling as a sandpaper wall that tortured him like a tapeworm in his brain. It was as though someone struck a match against the asphalt shingles, lit a cigar, and put it out in the center of his chest. He hyperventilated in the asphalt roof's presence. And so, wearing a bulletproof vest was insurance against the ghouls and bogeymen of that four-letter word: PTSD.

Gary's discomposure in the presence of his apartment's asphalt shingle can be contextualized by further study of his case history.

After practice, the high school football captain and his linebacker henchmen cornered him in the locker room shower and, pinning him down to a bench, his mouth gagged with a jockstrap, crudely tattooed the words GOD HATES FAGS on his chest. The tattoo wasn't even artful; if they were going to vandalize his chest with homophobic theology, they could at least make it look presentable. He wept in his parent's garage and with a roll of 240 grit sandpaper he stoically dermabraded the three words inked on the spot where he'd long felt a bullseye. The pain was so acute he blacked out and when he regained consciousness he lit off faster than Pickett's charge into the pinewoods behind the house, his white breath pluming into the cold dark, the trunks merging in menacing columns around him. He uncapped a bottle of peroxide, dousing it on his holocaust chest, the words GOD HATES FAGS whitely working up a froth as his screams rose like lead balloons in the treetops and a mephitic smoke of birds poured from the branches.

The antiseptic foamed and fizzed like Pop Rocks in his wound, runneling down his chest and spitting onto the ground where it committed genocide against soil bacteria. The pain was exquisite, worse than the tattooing or sandpapering, and he thought the peroxide would burn a hole straight through him like hydrofluoric acid. Gary fell angelically to the ground, as Lucifer and his horde were said to plummet through that interim between sky and earth, and he thrust tree bark and a pinecone into his mouth to stifle his mayday bawling like a pillow pressed into a victim's face.

His chest was slow to heal and he never took his shirt off in the locker room: he had a keloid scar like those in the history book photo of Peter the Slave from Baton Rouge whose back was a medical exhibit of the scarifications of the overseer's whip. He became interested in school when he discovered that the bombardier beetle could shoot corrosive, malodorous bubbles at its enemies and he daydreamed the class away dressed in a tutu and ballet shoes, blowing pink wrath upon his persecutors out of a bubble wand. How nature has armed its meek with abdominal glands of effervescent fatality. Why did those homophobic, pubic-brow jocks have to do this? He would've preferred tattooed lipstick, anything but those three words borne in secret on the infamy of his pale candy-ass chest; and GOD didn't hate fags particularly any more than he hated the dinosaurs, gypsies, the Jews, Negroes, the Kurds, midgets, three-legged dogs, et al.

He wasn't down in the mouth for long. He began a spartan workout regimen, call-boying anabolic steroids. He set his alarm for four in the morning to roll out of bed and do Wolverine abdominal workouts in the dark. He got cranked on injectable steroids that bruised his ass. His chest ballooned into the size of a blacksmith anvil. He'd rabbit punch anybody who called him a three-letter word. Gary was nearly expelled from school when he wrote a book report on homosexuality in the Continental Army, with a hagiography of Frederick Gotthold Enselin, boulevardier sodomite and Lieutenant who rakishly wore his coat inside out and was drummed out of General George Washington's heterosexual army.

Before the Mormon's unheard cuff at the door, Gary had depressed the parking brake and quickened from his car, bounding the three flights to his apartment three stairs at a time without looking at the asphalt shingle roof-wall, thinking later within the asylum of his living room that the beetle's defense mechanism was a corroboration of intelligent design, as the scar pulsed on his chest like a throbbing star in stygian abyss. The rock tumbler's crunching hellmouth prevented him from returning to an otherwise eerily quiet apartment. It was plain: he was living from one bowel movement to the next. With his iPhone camera he photographed the plasterboard ceiling's water stains like Rorschach tests he'd been given by an Army psychiatrist. He had them printed and framed like family studio portraits.

The building in which he lived hermetically sealed from the highway feeder was invisible through the tall cathedral of pines. Hundreds of renters like himself, each in identical floor plans differing only in their inconsequentiality: latex paint instead of acrylic, beveled door frame instead of chamfered. A window overlooking a concrete culvert instead of the parking lot. There was no one within two-hundred miles he could even borrow a cup of sugar from. A face perhaps, yet nameless in his mind, or a faceless name he'd seen on a utility bill or greeting card delivered to the wrong address. He realized that the sole interaction he had with those most propinquitous members of his species was when their mutually divergent paths briefly intersected in the laundry room, where Gary sometimes loitered atop the dryer, like the waiting room of an auto body shop. Vacuuming at least gave him a sense of making his mother proud, and he liked to honor The Bear by cutting a herringbone pattern in the carpet.

The pulsing of his chest scar subsided with melancholy, as it was a faithful companion, and Gary felt something pounding now, inside and outside his cranium. Keep on knocking and some Matthew will open it for you in a towel wrapped about the waist. Layered over that was the murderous electronic beat of Dubstep. The soap opera couple was still arguing and the blonde looked fit to be tied. Then taking his bearings like a bat closing in on a mosquito in the dark, he located the pounding in a distinct point not only outside his cranium, but outside the walls of this apartment. The vacuuming surceased. Gary yanked the electrical cord out of the wall socket and the rock tumbler wound down. Yes, it was certain now, someone dared knock on his castle door. In Gary's mind, a scene in a suburban horror movie began. His bulletproof vest fit him snugly, and he checked the kitchen drawers for knives.

The Mormon missionaries pressed right and left ear to the door so that they faced each other.

He ran over the virtuously short list of potential knockers. He didn't remember ordering a pizza, but neither did he discredit Domino's contract with the occult to read his thoughts. There was a car fag who lingered in the parking lot, engine idling below Gary's balcony; he thought how if he had longer hair he might Rapunzel it over the balcony experimentally and let the carrier of the torch pull himself up if he had the strength in his arms. A carrot top from hustler's row of the Castro District; frequenter of hucklebuck truck stops and ill-lit parks. *That* guy who leers over the urinal partition while you whip it out. The haveable queens of Miami Beach who sit out sunning by the pool like teenyboppers on Spring Break, picking the best man's nose and sighing over Louis L'Amour paperbacks. Truly, heaven is a torment on earth.

Gary appeared at the door in battle dress camouflage. There was no peephole viewer through which to preview his assailant, rapist or pizza delivery man. He opened the door on good faith and was helloed by two young babette-faced, daisy missionaries; Rhodes Scholars or Ivy League business majors in dark trousers and suit coats over a pressed and starched white dress shirt. In that necktie they looked sharp enough to sell snow to Eskimos.

—Don't want any. Have a good day, Gary said closing the door.

—We're not selling anything, the oldest tried, inserting his foot between door and jamb. —What are you all dressed up like that for?

Gary looked at himself. —The camo?

—We're not disturbing anything, are we?

—Sorry, couldn't hear you knocking over the vacuum.

The boys wore name tags identifying them as Elder Romney and Elder Call, but they didn't look old enough to be on Medicare or Social Security, what's left of it. Elder Free, White and Twenty-One. Raised on Homeric amounts of fried chicken, cornbread and yams. The name tags reminded Gary of the name tapes stitched into Army uniforms. Maybe they were here to tell him the Spice Girls had died. Here it was, both name and face, and two of them, barely beyond the age of consent. What about cheese please did they not understand?

They introduced themselves as Elijah and Joel. Elijah had a momma's boy's evangelistic haircut — cousin of the militaristic crewcut — and a classic Colgate smile sparkling like Prosecco that would've made a dental hygienist proud to be an American. Sylphic faces plagiarized from an Attic vase. They reeked of flowery soap and early-rising do-goodness. Too much volunteering. Reading to the blind. Buying groceries for the elderly. Still they could feel the laying on of hands blessing them before the mission, the divine touch once believed to cure scrofula in the most mirific moment of their Mormon-est lives. They could also feel the soft, platonic pat on the ass as the mission coach said, Go get'em champs. Belying the pneumatological soapy wholesomeness was an underlying animalistic spice. Gary had read *The Screwtape Letters*, goddamn it, and played hanky-panky by the monkey bars. And he knew that Jesus' trick of *Get thee behind me Satan* didn't work on Mormons. Joel and Elijah were so pure they wouldn't drink out of the same bottle. Gary saw that plain as the angelic nose on Elijah's face.

Just so they knew who they were dealing with, Gary recited chapter and verse from the second epistle of John: If there come any unto you, and bring not this doctrine, receive him not into your house, neither bid him Godspeed. For he that biddeth him Godspeed is partaker of his evil deeds.

He was not going to make this easy for them. They had to earn their mineral rights.

—I musn't partake. Sorry, gentlemen.

Despite John's exhortation against Southern hospitality, Gary couldn't close the door in their buttery faces. Why did they seem so familiar? They could've been the twin sons of his drill Sergeant. Had he met these hand-me-downs at The Quest, Birmingham's only gay dance club, where grown men dance on tabletops and virgins were known to contract leprous corruptions of the flesh? Where not even the agony and the ecstasy of Aaron's Rod could work its enchanting wizardry against unnatural rodism?

Even in the contrivance of his discharge from the Army he was a plagiarist. Kim, the only guy in the Army who knew about Gary's tattoo scar, was the brain behind the break: they would be faggots together to get booted from the Army. If the Army wanted to hide behind Don't Ask Don't Tell, then very well; they were neither going to ask, nor tell, but *do* it. In such circles, it was a truism that gays in the military were a sort of fifth column of *Arschficker* hellbent upon corroding the Department of Defense and handing it over to the highest bidder, all the while eating the taxpayer's lunch.

The official military report, which there is no reason to doubt as anything but the whole truth and nothing but the truth, said they went AWOL at the Riverchase Galleria, where they knew the drill Sergeant Poteat moonlighted as a mall cop. Saving money for his child's college education: straight people problems.

Kim and Gary strolled happily hand in hand through the food court, walking with a lisp. Be certain that two GI's wanking about the mall was destined to produce mass hysteria. The food court cleared out, chairs scraping the floor like fingernails against a chalkboard. Epithets were heard. Mothers covered the eyes of their children. An old WWII vet, survivor of the Battle of the Bulge, donning a veteran's ball cap that sat high on his head, brownly spat quid on the floor and grunted, —My, times've changed. I ain't fight the Nazis and the So-vee-yets so gays could lark around in uniform. Their drill Sergeant approached like a bomb squad surprising a suspicious package. —What's this all about, men?

Did Sarge have baby paste in his ear? Before explaining himself, and since he'd earned the Bugling Merit Badge as a Boy Scout, Gary dexterously trumpeted out a not inexpert interpretation of Reveille with his mouth. Then, with the equivalent of 21-

gun salute, —Sir, we're lovers, sir!

Gary thus signed his court martial in super-dupery pink ink.

Kim and Gary embraced, per the plan to get kicked out of the military, and billie-coo kissed in the marshal presence of the Sergeant's crewcut. Gary felt a tingling tumescence and hot humectation located somewhere south of his bellybutton. That was wrong. Bad! Bad boy!

To the Big Cheese Sergeant, who looked like the Marlboro man, and whose panties were a size too small and an inch too tight, Gary expatiated on the services rendered to country by homos throughout the centuries; the best Greek warriors were queer as a three-dollar bill. But they were no queeny androgynes. Hadn't he heard of the Sacred Band of Thebes, hoplites handpicked by Gorgidas himself, in his military history class at West Point? Was it not obvious to any enlightened military theorist since Sun Tzu that amorous male couples would fight more ardently than bondless strangers? Wasn't as much put forth in *The Symposium?* Plato, who had a dick like a tall boy beer can, even that ethereal brainiac kept catamites. Gary was prepared to die a thousand deaths, Sir, for The Republic For Which It Stands, for Reaganomics, for the Bush Doctrine, for the Black Budget, for Trumpism, for the Indian and the buffalo on the nickel, for the lesbian mayor of the city of Houston, for family planning and lead balloons, for gobble gobble gobble, for the grim heat of Chicago lightning and the stranglehold of the Chinese squeeze, for bailouts and the sweet lady on the Mercury dime, for…

The Sergeant interrupted him with an imperial wave of the hand.

Gary contained multitudes.

What he did not tell the Sergeant was that the entire Sacred Band of Thebes — an elite force of 150 male lovers — had been annihilated by Philip II of Macedon in a single engagement and then buried in a mass grave so their corpses would not become carrion for dogs and buzzards.

Sergeant Poteat, who did not care about the Sacred Band of Thebes, put the bracelets on them and said he had a mind to line them up against a wall before a firing squad. Gary thought: cream pies, tomatoes from the balconies, various handpicked fruits and vegetables descending in a volley. Even if he cried wolf, the Big Cheese would declare him the wolf. It was no use.

Sure, he probably could've filed a class action suit with the 13,000 other gays who had been harassed out of uniform, but he didn't care about gay rights or same-sex marriage. He wanted out of the Army. During those fugitive moments when his lips were parted for Kim's tongue, Gary learned something about himself: he wasn't pretending to be gay, he *was* actually, truly, quintessentially very gay. Soon as he was in civvies again he went straight to a tattoo parlor and inked up his arm in anti-sodomy legislation, beginning with Leviticus.

He simplified his demands on life, wanting merely to camouflage himself in the apartment with his rock tumbler, bulletproofed against assault by standpatter cave dwellers and anti-gay skinheads who came out from under their rock only by torchlight. This was Alabama, after all. Even a straight man had to watch his back. And defense and offense were indifferently distinguished. He preferred the canaille status of a Genet. Twas Bear Bryant who said that defense might win championships, but the offense sells tickets, so who cares if you win the Iron Bowl in an empty stadium? Gary required no audience, and so went on the defense. There was logic in there somewhere, Gary was sure of it.

The Mormons blinked at him. Who were these…these…these Mormons, and what did they want with Gary? The problem, as Gary framed it in the only terms he knew how, was that nobody in this town worked without a retainer, and therefore a settlement of payments was in order. Traveling salesmen? Had he ordered Boy Scout cookies? Boy Scouts didn't wear suits back when he was working on his Bugling Merit Badge.

—What can I do you for?

—Glass of water, please.

Ah yes, the old glass of water ambush. Sir, glass of water, sir!

—I'll buy you drinks, but I won't give you any money.

Did the Boy Scouts even sell cookies?

—Water is fine, thanks, they said in unison, one voice pitched an octave above the other.

—Water would be copacetic, the younger one chimed in on his own in some flaccid assertion of independence from his elder.

The two missionaries snooted on it behind Gary, standing sentinel just inside the door.

Gary closed the glass sliding door onto the third story balcony. No jumpers — he couldn't risk himself or one of these proselytizers flinging himself melodramatically from the balcony and onto the parking lot below. He contemplated two red bicycles leaning against a tree and guarded by the Holy Ghost from thieving by local, motherless child gangsters who roamed the parking lots with runny noses and violence in their eyes, then he crawfished slowly away from the tempting provocation of the balcony.

Two, three steps max away from the front door — it was a small apartment, like his barracks in the Army — and they were in the kitchenette. The missionaries never beheld so much media. The livid television on mute now. A solid case of secular books. Even the temperature was weird. Elijah and Joel had been hatched in an information black hole. No books, no music (except religious, and even the missionaries knew that Christian rock music was some of the most god-awful noisome drivel ever composed), no movies, and especially no books. Literature of any kind was expressly verboten by the Mormon's Comstockery. Satan lived in the literary products of deranged, unsaved, writerly self-expression.

Soon as Joel shook Gary's hand, his gaydar went haywire and he knew Gary was queer as a football bat. It wasn't an effete or limp handshake, to the contrary. But Gary's handshake had over-refinement of grip, a recherché grasp that smacked roundly of the wrong kind of decadence and genetic disorder.

Joel pulled a book called *A Clockwork Orange* down from the shelf. —What's this about?

—Don't be rude, Elijah upbraided his companion.

Gary was uncertain whether Elijah and Joel were brothers or more like Batman and Robin.

—You're too young for books like that, Gary said turning to a conspicuous copy of *Psychopathia Sexualis* which he deftly pulled from the shelf and reinserted spine first between two lesser offending books.

Gary decided to test them. He fetched some ruinous looking ice cubes from the freezer and fixed one glass of ice water and handed it to Elder Call. At the moment the glass was received into Elijah's hand, Gary remembered a guy in his Army unit who had a freakish amputation fetish, a junkie of the grotesque nub, he was hard for the paraplegic women, and the girls with no chests, requiring only a mouth at best to work with. A sort of amatory minimalist. Gary felt the collywobbles churning his stomach. —I only have the one glass, was Gary's ballad.

—Quite alright, Mister, he said quaffing enough water to put out a small fire.

Gary wondered if water was an aphrodisiac. Probably it just made you pee a lot. And was the lagoon between their ages so great that he should be called Mister?

Elijah handed the glass of water to his missionary partner who refused it.

—Are we okay to drink after each other? the boy said, staring at the rim of the contaminated glass.

—Shut up, Joel.

They gazed raptly on his bookshelf, as if the characters in each shelved book might spring alive from the texts and attack them. Gary wished to displace their attention from his books, — Have you ever seen Wall-E?

—We don't watch movies, Elijah said.

—It's Disney, so I thought maybe y'all had seen it.

—Especially not Disney.

—Why not Disney?

—Walt Disney had inappropriate ties to Henry Ford. Wall-E depicts robots with free will and an earth rigorously trashed by humans in a distant future, which could be the day after tomorrow, which is problematic from a theological perspective. Not that I've seen it, of course.

Gary gazed at the boy's perfectly spherical head. He imagined the boy coiffing himself before the mirror. Prancing. Strutting. Peacocking. He applied camo face paint from Party City in a woodland pattern and vanished in crypsis, dissolved shadowily into a tree until you wanted to picnic in its shade and the boy pressed a bowie knife at your throat and placed a cold hand over your mouth. If Gary had stayed in the Army, what would've become of him?

—Who's the guy in the hat? Joel asked, pointing to the football coach on the wall.

—That is Paul Bryant, known locally as The Bear. He was a genius of the wishbone formation.

—Sounds important. So, what did he do?

—He won six national championships, thirteen conference championships and upon his retirement held the record for most wins noted among collegiate football historians. It's a big deal in

Alabama. It's all we have to live for.

Gary was going to run as a food stamp president one day and really do something with himself; *really* do something with himself, Scout's honor. Meanwhile, football trivia would serve him well in his future bids to run for public office in Alabama.

—How long were you waiting outside?

—We heard shouting and crying. We thought there might be a situation.

Gary laughed wickedly. —That was the television.

Elijah and Joel looked at the noiseless box and were seen to snarl. Elijah said they were just getting over their hump, or the midpoint of their mission adventure; Joel was getting trunky, ready to head back home so Mama could tie his shoes for him. And he was growing a faint wispy mustache that sickened Elijah.

Gary's second gaffe was admitting them into the apartment; the first was answering the door to be proselytized. He knew they hadn't been bitten by the neighborhood dog, because the Church of Latter Day Saints compelled all missionary candidates to test for HIV.

So, putting faith in his aim in the hands of insensible forces, Gary took a shot in the dark. —Let me ask you something.

—Sure, Elijah consented, passing the half-empty glass of ice water to Joel who finally relented and accepted the glass. So they would drink from the same glass! Science! Eureka! The cubes rattled like dice in a tin cup. He should go gambling in Mississippi sometime, let loose, support education.

—What is the official Mormon stance on the practice of circumcision? Blind as a boiled turnip?

Would the missionaries report him to the blue boys for perversion, being an acolyte of Onan? The missionaries mumbled in reply about health and aesthetic concerns, trying to changing the subject; so Gary told a stupid story about a possum in the dumpster that didn't actually happen to him. —Why do they call it an opossum? fetching for something, anything to say. —Makes it sound Irish. Do they even have possums in Ireland?

Elijah made a note to investigate at a later time whether Ireland had possums.

The two missionaries took the couch facing the television. They had unimpeachable posture and laced their fingers over their knees. Gary felt like he was on a job interview; one for which he was woefully underprepared. His hair was unwashed and wind-blown, though he couldn't remember how long since the wind had vouchsafed the small kindness of even blowing away his farts, dissipating them upon unsmellable, montane altitudes high above the terrene.

—Where you boys from?

—Illinois, said the older. —Utah, said the younger.

—The Lincoln state, that's a fine state.

Gary wowed himself with his fumbling ineloquence. A different couple was on the television now, silent mouths flapping.

—Did you know the missionaries over in Texas? The ones who were murdered and the authorities never found the bodies? Or at least they didn't find all the pieces.

Elder Romney looked at Elder Call who looked at the door.

—No, we didn't. But we pray for their souls and their family, and the devil who committed such a terrible iniquity.

Gary reported on a missionary who was savagely mauled by lions in Guatemala. The missionary's remains unidentifiable. Elijah interpreted this as an omen from the Lord, as the first Christian martyrs had been thrown to the lions of the empire by pagan emperors thirsting for bloodsport, and the fulfillment of Joseph Smith's auguries in which persecution was an expression of God's love. To be devoured by wild animals meant that God loved you more than those who died a prosaic and laic death ensconced comfortably in hospital beds, surrounded by loved ones, the sting of death softened by morphine and flowers.

Elijah abruptly stopped talking and looked at Gary's center.

Gary's borborygmus was getting out of hand. He felt like his throat had been slashed and sustenance wasn't communicating its way from his mouth to his stomach, Cheerios and cold pizza dribbling out of his slashed throat. He excused himself to the kitchen, and pulled what Elijah and Joel expected to be a body part, but was not, from the freezer.

He coerced black frozen bananas into a blender and punched the frappe button, chopping off the end of one of Elijah's sentences and mixing it furiously with the banana smoothie. He'd even forgotten to peel the bananas.

Gary needed a program to either get these boys out of his apartment, or else he was not to be held responsible for what he might do. This was queer baiting was what it was and Gary wasn't biting. The younger one, with the face of a crazy ferret, he especially didn't trust the brown-noser. Somehow, he thought he could feel the inside curvature of his own skull, and he thought about the rind of a watermelon after you've eaten the red meat and spat out the black seeds all over the place. These boys needed to wear burkas. Somehow, that was hot, in a cosmopolitan post-modern globalized way. Ooga booga!

—Tell us about your relationship with God, one of the two asked sweetly.

Oh boy, here's where it starts — they ask about your relationship with an imaginary whangdoodle being, and then they want to know where you keep the furry costumes. He wasn't sure which missionary had asked; they blended into one person like his banana smoothie.

—I was raised religious, Gary said noncommittally.

—We are all raised religious, the oldest said. —Nothing is secular, if you think about it.

Gary thought about it and saw a prevision of himself banging his fists on the doors of the Mormon's spirit prison. Gary had been a foxhole Christian ever since he had "come out," though what he'd come out of he did not exactly know, and the purgatory outside the closet into which he'd been delivered and then discharged down the fire escape was even more *terra incognita*. The Army seemed like a good idea at the time, and maybe it kept him from worse troubles. Yet he persisted in the belief, perhaps an evolutionary holdover necessary to survival, that he was exiting one closet with a foot safely planted without contradiction in another. At least Gary could still pick up the phone and call his mom when he wanted, without having to wait until Mother's Day, whenever that was. In a weekly letter, To Helen.

The older Elder nickered down a short hall to the bathroom and left Gary and the younger missionary alone in the living room snacking on banana smoothie. Gary knew this was against protocol to leave a missionary in the altar room without someone standing guard outside the door. The missionaries were under strict orders to remain within earshot of his companion's voice at all times, lest he spontaneously burst into chocolate brimstone, or commit some beastly deed like watching television or reading a book or — Joseph Smith forbid — get his paws on Kay Burningham's *An American Fraud: One Lawyer's Case Against Mormonism.*

—What are those pictures above the bookcase? Joel asked.
—They look like birthmarks.

—Those are…water stains. I think of them as family.

Joel blinked.

Elijah was back, but they hadn't heard the toilet flush.

Gary left Joel blinking at the framed familial water stains on the wall, and went to the bathroom after Elijah to stand over what appeared to be a deflated jellyfish in the water, but was on closer inspection a condom floating on the surface: a latex spoor Gary was intended to track. The missionary — cabareting in the bathroom? — hadn't bothered to flush and his urea fizzled and popped like cheap champagne. Gary wasn't going to be the first to flush either. Was he being buffaloed into some paraesthesia? Was he coming down with chicken pox? He wanted to slap himself sober. Desire is no great respecter of persons or taboos. Was it advisable, this leaving Joel and Elijah alone in his living room? Books were in there! The television was on! His framed water stains on the wall!

Now it was Joel's turn, leaving Gary and Elijah alone. Touchdown! Should he give Elijah a little sibling peck on the cheek?

—What are you waiting for? Gary asked without knowing what he meant.

—For when Christ returns to restore the kingdom of peace and grace and low taxes. What do you wait for?

—I'm waiting for an older man on the brink of mortality with a Swiss bank account and no heirs.

—Christ will liberate you from the shackles of mortal sin, Elijah rejoined as if reciting a memorandum.

Where did these kids learn such precocious and ponderous King James language? Shouldn't they be playing Grand Theft Auto and stealing cigarettes like normal suburban kids? These missionaries and their mindless sanctimonious cant!

Gary, by now a perfectionist of auto-sadism, stood up and wrestled his camo shirt over his head, a striptease revealing the cicatrice that blemished his chest. It looked like a hickey imparted by a giant sucking mouth. Legible through the scar tissue were the ineffaceable words GOD HATES FAGS. Joel skipped into the living room, and tried to tiptoe back into the bathroom when he saw Gary shirtless. Elijah coughed and looked about with boredom.

—Can Christ liberate me from this? Gary shrilled. —Can your

fucking Joseph Smith liberate me from this shit? Gary demanded pointing at his scarified chest. So far, Elijah was unflappable before Gary's outburst and exhibitionism.

Well, they couldn't exactly promise a money back guarantee, but...

Nor was Gary finished. —Smith was a conman, polygamist, a debtor and a murderer who perished in a jailbreak gunfight.

This was the best Gary could come up with.

—Moses was a dyslexic half-wit, and the Lord chose him to deliver the Commandments, Elijah said calmly. —He could've chosen a doctoral student in quantum physics, if he wanted, but he humbly chose an illiterate dolt as messenger of his Word.

—Thou shalt not stutter.

The remaining stuffy light was rotting in the room; dark flashed and coiled like a plug of hair dragged out of a shower drain with a clothes hanger. His apartment's electricity did spooky, erratic things. Fluorescent bulbs usually buzzed overhead, but Gary hadn't replaced them, and the living room bedimmed like a floodwater rising up from the floor around them. He watched Elijah and Joel for some tacit signal, a meaningful wink or nod. Nothing. Pokerfaced schoolboys. Gary wondered whether Elijah or Joel had developed the mental powers to control electrical current.

It was almost checkout time. The Mormon boys would have to bike home in the dark, weighted down with lugubrious and heavy thoughts and the pressure of duty performed by the book. The image of Gary's scar bedazzled in Elijah's mind. Joel volunteered to lead them in closing prayer before dusting out. The three of them joined hands in a lopsided circle around a pile of cat vomit on the carpet. Geometry wasn't Gary's best subject, but it would have to do. Gary's palms sweated ickily in Elijah's and he was getting an anteater. He couldn't allow these little Mormon peter-eaters to backstage him so easily. Elijah led them in prayer, something platitudinous about Christ overcoming the scandalous fictions and base enslavement of the abject body, something that did not sound pleasant at all, then about the time his palms stopped sweating Gary was alone in the room, eyes closed, his arms outspread, hands empty where Elijah's and Joel's hands had been.

When the missionaries were gone ("Go ye therefore...") Gary stared at the door for a long time until he could see through it and to the lemon world beyond. The rock tumbler would need tending. He fished up a plastic baggie that might've been used for coke and poured finer 500 grit into the barrel for the next polishing finish and plugged the rock tumbler back into the bottom wall socket. Sweet, blessed attrition of stone, the grinding was strangely comforting. He locked the door behind them and picked up a leather-bound copy of *The Book of Mormon* the missionaries left him on the coffee table. He thumbed the lightweight offset pages, fanning them like a time-lapse of the ages, like he'd seen old timers at the health clinic search a large-print paperback for a health insurance card tucked in the pages, and stopped at *The Book of Abraham*, where he read about a planet or star (even the professionals didn't know which) named Kolob that in the incomparable prose style of Joseph Smith sounded like a mongrelization of Disney Land and *Battlestar Galactica,* ghostwritten by L. Ron Hubbard. He must ask the Mormons about this Kolob. Maybe he could go there.

That night, from the balcony, he watched a larcenous midnighter crook between cars parked in the lot below, smashing windows delicately with a ball-peen hammer, grabbing smartphones and GPS units and the forlorn spare change in ashtrays. Gary did not intervene. Instead, he rearranged the order of the water stain family photos, according to the last shall be first. He dodged between rooms thinking up names for the stains. Turned on and off the lights in each dark room until the bulb burned an afterimage glowing on the surface of his retina, incrementally increasing the speed of flipping the switch till he was blinded and on the verge of a seizure. The living room light stayed dark as Gary flipped the switch up and down maniacally. He grew tired of waiting for a lion to rip him apart, some sign that God loved him more than other average mortals.

He plumped down on the couch to veg out before Japanese pornographic films. He patted the spot where Elijah's bottom had rested, now cold. Gary ogled, still a little prudish, at the grotesque body, analingus in a nunnery, intercrural friction in a prison camp, then clips from Ron Athey and Vito Acconci's *Seedbed,* the art gallery masturbation. He watched these films with the same detached, scientific method he viewed black and white footage of nuclear tests in the desert, high-altitude explosions like Starfish Prime over the Hawaiian Islands. The old scar burned over his chest. How did one get to Kolob? What was the cost of living there? Did they enjoy the low-hanging, market-priced fruits of democracy and much, much more? All these questionings were accompanied by Gary's sinistral auto-eroticism; he survived the Army, and on Kolob he could raise his own army, then attack earth. The films flashed on, briefly illuminating the water stain portraits. Amputees in a prison camp somehow engaged in *coitus more ferarum.* Several times Gary closed his eyes and counted to ten.

When the kinky-haired slave boy in leg irons got peed on, accompanied by the raucous grinding of the rock tumbler, he couldn't take anymore. But wait! There was more! A Sapphic interlude, overdubbed with *The Sound of Music,* women writhing atop one another like worms lit on fire in a bucket. Some sick creep in need of immediate evaluation by the American Psychological Association thought such a juxtaposition of audio and visual was a *good idea,* like zippers and Tupperware and anti-lock brakes were good ideas; the good idea reduced him to a biopolitics of such total abjection that — the rock tumbler reminding him by associations of circular motion that his laundry was still in the washing machine — he cut the experimental art house porn off and hastened to the apartment building's swampy laundry room where he sometimes mumbled without making eye contact to his fellow apartment dwellers. Eye contact could be misconstrued.

The laundry room was empty. The scrubbed atmosphere drizzled on him; condensation grayed the dewy windows and wept down the panes. Goddamn it if his waterlogged clothes from this morning weren't in a heap on the floor. Assholes can't even move them into the dryer for you. What manner of unconscionable knave removes the wet, clean clothes of another suffering renter and throws them, flings them maliciously, like a body out of a trunk, on the laundry room floor? He did a shakedown of the laundry room for the culprit — probably some straight homophobe who recognized his clothes — but came up only with the titillating mechanical moans of a spin cycle reminiscent of his rock tumbler. Gary was a vigilante; under the stout influence of his state's motto, we dare defend our rights, and ask questions later, and that be all you can be crap that was drilled into him, he took reprisal upon his fellow renters, interrupted the spin cycle and in a balletic whirl of machine and clothes wholly unbefitting a grown man cast the soggy, lukewarm garments out upon the floor and left them there, defeated and his own laundry's pride avenged, to mildew. Ba-gock!

Sheriff Elijah and Deputy Joel returned with backup a few days later. They had literature this time. Lots of it. Gary hadn't left his apartment. The knock came while he was seated on the couch contemplating the cat vomit and wondering where his cat was. Gary seemed to drag his right leg behind him, like an Ahab with his peg-leg. The missionaries thumped into his bachelor pad, the dewy-eyed Joel with his genetically modified cornstarch face and the lilt in his step like a bonny cabin boy, the smarmy little fucker. They were reinforced with books, pamphlets, brochures, screeds, broadsides, bulletins, leaflets, tractates, leaflets, circulars, handbills and instruction manuals, a paper army to squelch his peasant uprising. He'd never seen so much printed willing suspension of disbelief, the gist of which could be gotten from an afternoon in any downtown public library in the country.

He'd tangled with Mormons who didn't know who Brigham Young was, the American Moses, but these boys knew their shit. They knew their Hussites, Landmarkism and spread-eagled Anabaptists from their Zoroasterians, Talibans, Islamic States and Mooninites. Did the Mormon missionaries compete with one another for the most souls — not saved, per se, but converted to the correct doctrinal flat-earth-ism? Gary conjured elaborate betting systems and prizes, racetrack touts, esoteric filing systems in underground card catalogs: *Visited fag with scarred chest again. Fag highly resistant to traditional methods. Returning with backup.*

The overall effect of these Mormon missionaries visiting him again was wholly environmental in the fullest sense of that word. He felt surrounded, as the Mormon settlers in their wagons must've felt, Indians in full headdress regalia and war paint yahooing around them. Gary searched for self-defense and came up with an obscure state law in North Dakota providing all lawful citizens with majority shares in the Second Amendment the right to shoot an Indian; but there was a catch: he had to be in a covered wagon, and the Indian had to be horseback. The Indian on horseback part he could finagle, but where was he to find a serviceable covered wagon?

He had a small speech prepared. Will they find the whipped cream in my sock drawer, Gary wondered. That morning, he'd been watching a workman on a ladder painting the apartment building next door. The paint made it look more ghastly, a loathsome and cantankerous shelter unfit even for a dog's funeral. The asphalt shingle roof with the sandpaper texture of a cat's tongue licked the painful memory of a wound on his chest. It occurred to him in the presence of his visitors that people spent most of their time living in rubbish.

—The more the merrier, Gary welcomed the missionaries like a hosting hausfrau.

Joel sliced his eyes at Gary, thinking: what does this erectile dysfunction see?

There were definite vapors circulating like dopamine between Gary and Elijah. He needed to excuse himself and go bash the bishop.

Gary poured a whiskey and water for himself, dispatched it and topped off a second. It was not yet noon. Time to get stewed and man up, to make decisions for himself. He didn't want to spend a lifetime bumping uglies. While the missionaries fussed over the arrangement of their proselytic literature, he put his hands on his head for an interim and pressed his tongue against the back of his teeth, thinking disconnectedly about the difference between a tenderloin and a sirloin.

He wanted these missionaries — this banty gang of boys — to decamp. What did they think his apartment was — a Roman bath house? But then thoughts in direct opposition to this line of argument were shouted at him from the pulpit — every action Gary had ever undertaken, whether it was joining the high school football team or the Army, was questioned and undermined by this vicious, bigoted little voice shouted from a pulpit installed in the sanctum of his mind — and was there no place on earth where conditions were suitable to founding a utopian society instead of a leper colony? Even the more libertine among the gay rights activists had gone public with the knowledge that Gary would force himself upon the Thanksgiving turkey if no one was looking. Even if that was true, one did not come out and publish it in print for every literate common jack to blog about; as if every gay man was an out-of-body-experience for whose indiscretions he was not to be held responsible, a sort of sexual retard neither God nor science could retrieve from the bowels of perdition. What had all those boys died for in the French Revolution then? In the Huguenot Wars? In the Mexican-American War? And so on and so forth.

Stop global warming! Scalp a child with a butter knife! Huh?

If his missionary interrogators must know, he had shot off inside a woman, but if you closed your eyes it felt exactly like boom-boom with a Hollywood uterus. He nostalgically remembered dry humping in his parent's basement. Those were the good old days. You still get your rocks offs; no blue balls, no risk of reproducing the species in an already redundant and overpopulated public house whose puppet strings were being snip-snipped by a homintern in the deep-pocketed payola of the contraception racket. The worst-case scenario was maybe you got an Indian rope burn from denim abrading your crotch.

There was a little white church in his steepled hometown. Hometown also to a cranky dotard famous for his celibacy and taking to heart Paul's admonishment that if a man was strong not to take a wife. For all Gary knew, he went to his grave as virginal as a Hilda. Sheltered within this god-fearing congregation slinked a man who choked his wife to death during intercourse. This congregant, this fellow Baptist with whom Gary had shared a pew, and even read off the same hymnal standing in the aisles, this cretin had reduced the channel through which air might pass to her lungs by millimeters until it was the diameter of a drinking straw and then a needle. The Baptist wife lost consciousness in their kitchen, and her body was found by cadaver dogs shallowly encased in concrete. To Gary, this was the logical culmination of every heterosexual relationship — the man killed the woman in some odious, tabloidal fashion even a caveman would be morally outraged by. The congregation feigned outrage, but Gary couldn't say he hadn't seen it coming, the way the man sang deliberately out of key and Gary could smell the booze on his breath. His father did not believe passionately enough in anything to choke a woman out — only that you weren't confrères with your neighbor unless you'd seen his wife in the same state in which Eve found herself upon waking in the first of the Harry Potter books, a series Gary read with the same zeal Joseph Smith must have devoted to those Egyptian papyri counterfeited in a Latter Day Saints board room from the future — but he did kind of believe if you were going to open your mouth in church you should sing on key and brush your teeth. When the blue boy authorities came for the wife killer, in the middle of a Sunday sermon, they found him cowering in the church basement.

In his hometown where the most damnable thing a man could be was a carpetbagger or scalawag, and the preacher man spoke on good authority that the country was so overrun with faggotry that anyone who discharged a firearm within the region was liable to hit a Sodomite or at least a man who had rolled in filth before the age of sixteen, where the organist was a closet case sodomite, up to his blowhole in pieties, cursing the skunks who lift Gideon Bibles from hotel rooms, who practiced the clavier and would've lubricated and fucked the organ pipes were such an abomination possible; yes, in this hometown Gary was the missing link, the lost cousin of Cro-Magnon just before the forehead got bigger and *homo sapiens* entered the scene to sapiently fill out the entire tuba section himself.

It is not good for man to be alone; but neither was man created for woman. Man was created to crush the woman's windpipe and then pee himself when caught. I wish that all were as I am. Hometowns such as his would be eradicated on Kolob.

A disembodied voice whispered in Gary's ear, —Ask them about Kolob.

And so he did.

—I'm interested in buying property on Kolob. I am willing to pay the pearl of great price.

Was Gary pulling their legs?

Elijah coughed into his fist. He looked at the ceiling so that Gary could see the whites of his eyes and said, —I've interpreted Kolob as a metaphor. And even so, the property values would be astronomical.

—Before we talk money, what's the weather like on Kolob? Humid continental? Tropical wet? Marine west coast? Subarctic? Highlands would be nice too.

—The climate is celestial, I think. One day on Kolob is equal to a thousand years on earth.

—So, it's probably a huge planet that rotates very slowly. Not the best seasons for crop rotation. The cotton concerns won't like it. Any geopolitical data?

—Kolob is beautiful and the people are happy.

He wanted also to ask if the left testicle would hang lower than the right in Kolob's atmosphere, or vice versa. Gary struggled with a lot of things, but most of all he struggled to be human.

I am as all wish I were not. But Elijah assured Gary, they stood steadfast on a ball of rock tumbling through the pitch dark which approximated the earth they were all familiar with from secular tales. Heliocentrists who looked heavenward and said the eyes play tricks upon the credulous mind. If he believed that, then Gary would stand on his head until such time as the Good Lord Jesus Christ chose Alabama, a slave state, instead of, as the Mormons held, Missouri — somewhere around Mark Twain's hometown — for his imminent return. Gary struggled to be human, like trying to climb a greased telephone pole.

The younger elder look bored out of his wits by this symposium on extramundane miscreations. His intelligent, glassy eyes dulled as two colorless Skittles set in a tombstone. He yawned and his mouth opened obscenely like a canyon into which Gary plummeted without a parachute. —Isn't Elijah something? the young missionary spoke up finally.

—Tell the man what you mean, Joel. Speak clearly, the third missionary enjoined him.

—I mean that...that...

And Joel lost it.

Elijah and Gary looked away, Elijah at Gary's midriff; Gary at the pile of cat vomit, adjusting the Kevlar vest under his sweater, until Joel recovered himself from his rident conniption.

—Christ does not countenance laughter, Elijah reprimanded him. —Laughter is of the Devil. Only weeping is Christlike.

For the sake of peace and amity, all those abstractions for which real and true friends once more unto the breach, there was always switching pulpits, a sort of spectrum theory bisexualism of religion: a Mormon preaching in a Baptist mosque; an ultramontane selling market-priced indulgences in the parking lot of the Church of God; placenta eaters (they preferred to be called "placentophagists") and state's rights boyfriends, the most wall-to-wall cosmopolitanism and encyclopedic syncretism since the Thirty Years' War. All must be screened by metal detectors and lie detector tests. But Gary knew his efforts to please everyone only added a little color to *Les Grandes Misères de la guerre.*

Recovered from his satanic laughter, Joel led them this time in closing prayer, something along the lines of rub-a-dub-dub, three pigs in a tub. Who, then, was the candlestick-maker?

When he was sure the missionaries were gone, and not lingering in whispers outside his door, Gary picked up his iPhone from the slew of Mormon literature and held the home button. A monotone female voice greeted him — Siri.

—Where will Christ return? Gary asked the lady in the phone. He envisioned her as the sweet, silver lady on the Mercury dime.

—Missouri, she answered emphatically.

—When will Christ return?

—No one knows the appointed hour.

—Why not return to Alabama, which has low corporate income taxes and cheap labor?

—I hadn't thought of that, Gary.

—Who is the greatest college football coach of all time?

—Paul Bear Bryant.

—How do I get to Kolob?

—You'll have to ask Joseph Smith, Gary.

Siri, like the gemstones rolling in his tumbler, was also Gary's friend and confidante, even though it was female. She was a good listener. She advised him: appointments to be kept, deadlines, bills to be paid, reminders for basic hygiene. She was the best friend of the opposite sex he'd ever had. Today, she reminded him to polish his gemstones.

Gary dashed some tin oxide into the tumbler to heighten the final polish and watched the barrel slowly revolve, a thousand years of geological process squeezed into one day.

It was clear to Gary the he was on a collision course with Elijah, unguided as a rogue missile, that was bound to end, not in explosive releases of pent up libidinal worlds, but a flaccid anticlimax, a right-as-rain alleyway cat fight intersecting on tangential planes of immanence, exchanging feminine fluids under the regime of masculine rigid mechanics. Gary was a blue-pink gemstone being ground down by heteronormative forces to his essentialist glassy haecceity, then polished and exhibited under glass. He didn't trust himself. He went around pouring salt in every wound he could scare up. He considered having his cat placed in protective custody. Where was that cat lately? The vomit continued to appear in chunky dribs and drabs, but still the cat was scarce.

He scooped gemstones from the tumbler, approving of the lustrously smooth and creamy surface sleeked as a seal's coat. His face reflected back to him in the glazy finish of a fragment of obsidian tumbled down to the shape of a kidney and the dimensions of an exit wound. This shiny black mass cold in his hand, this was the exoplanet Kolob. He spent the rest of the night navel-gazing and fell asleep in his clothes, in his camo fatigues, on the floor, arms folded over his chest, beneath the omniscient wink of The Bear.

In a dream, horrid as all dreams are, the only restoration of oneness he'd glimpsed between bowel movements, Gary zoomed away from his hometown on a red bicycle and when he stopped pedaling the world stopped. He was at a rally of some sort. From every quarter came black stones of judgment thrown, maledictions handed down the ranks, and at the end of a black rainbow, under the guise of freedom of assembly, a skinhead Christian was making a sign in an anti-gay parade: GOD HATES FAGS. Gary was the artist's assistant, mixing his paints, gessoing the canvas, pre-chewing his food for him, cleaning the brush, which he then turned over to the hateful creator to do his dirty work upon the sign; at last, Gary asked the skinhead artist to pretty please flex his biceps with the swastika tattoo. The pagan symbol of the bent crucifix rippled across the artist's bulging arm and Gary offered the skinhead an apostolic hand job and called it a day. He woke up when he heard the booing of a baseball game when the umpire makes a bad call against the home team.

In the velvety quiet of a Baptist Sunday morning Gary put on his bullet-proof vest and stepped out onto his balcony like a Pope about to address the masses. A blessing of *Urbi et Orbi*. Perhaps he even waved his hand through the air beneficently in a queer performance of the sign of the cross. He took in the air, fresh and piney in his nostrils, feeling a compunctious pang about throwing his neighbor's wet clothes all over the laundry room floor, the pang subsiding when he thought about Frederick Gotthold Enselin being expelled from Washington's army. The parking lot below the balcony was on an incline and he watched a boy set marbles at the crest of the lot and roll them down the blacktop and gutter down into the darkness of a storm drain. The boy did this, again and again, expecting a different outcome, though his marbles never returned to him, never rolled back up the slope of the parking lot and into his empty hand. Gary scoffed at this witless child he'd run off before for pelting his cat with marbles.

He feared, not without reason, since their founding prophet had a history of crawling through windows to escape capture, the Missionaries might steal through the window or the airshafts on perfumed winds of frankincense and myrrh, and for once Gary's fears were justified: on the third visit the missionaries let themselves in without knocking, as if Gary had knocked on their door. The back door to the hometown church was always unlocked — you never knew who, at what hour, might want to bend a knee and say a prayer for our troops in their defense of your freedom from Sharia Law.

Gary had prepared for this Third Coming. The vacuum was away in the closet next to the rifle and the carpets sparkled. The gemstones shone like newborns. Siri nagged him about this and that. He prepared a breakfast luau of pancakes and dark roast coffee and Cezanne oranges. He flushed the toilet for the first time in days, and made sure the framed pictures of the Rorschach test water stains were all dusted. And so what if the abject object began to speak? What would it say? He read the morning headlines: *chocolate penis ejaculates money-flavored semen.* In the future, Gary must remember: do not make eye contact with the abject object.

Gary had four oval golden plates set out on the table and on each an actual black crow for the Mission's arrival. He could hear his hometown church's organist piping away now in cathedrals of blue shadow. Bear Bryant, who'd spent his career optimizing the schemes whereby men in spandex smash each other, did not blanch at any of this. Sergeant Poteat barking orders at a row of saluting crewcut sissies. The tattooing footballers chasing him through the locker room. The Sacred Band of Thebes perishing in a pointless, unwinnable internecion but loving every minute of it. But it was Elijah who came frisky hitching as the lone missionary, a rose in his mouth, his mother's two-piece bathing suit under a letterman jacket; to tell Gary: your curtains don't match your carpet, honey; to emancipate Gary's ransomed soul that was floating away, rising into Kolob's alien atmosphere like a lead balloon.

DOWN THE BLACK WARRIOR
I SAILED TO BYZANTIUM

The sky totalized my landless vision as I floated on my back against the buoyant membrane of the Black Warrior River's watery body, my lungs filled with balsam inhalations of heaven. A passing plane would've seen a cruciform body tracking downriver. A third baptism was superfluous. I'd done treacherous things to the river. A blue heron swept over the sun like a mercurial eclipse, pulling the autopsy of the dream of a dying animal and the architecture of the dying animal's holy city behind it on black ropes, and when it was gone the sun shone bright as a hole in the head of a seraph.

Upriver, Indian summer kids swung from a tire roped and dangling on a dead tree. They were pushed by someone unseen onshore and after gathering swinging momentum they cannon-balled laughing into a splash made for them in the Black Warrior, which was effloresced algal green and snaked and gatored. Their wavelets rolled over me like all the other trash bobbing on the water and rubbing against the riverbank: a tampon, plastic coke bottles, aluminum cans, entire mobile homes floating downriver, the plastic red hulls of spent shotgun shells, fish lures snagged on branches, Styrofoam coolers. All the refuse of Western civilization's moral high ground with its commanding view of the terrene, like surveying El Dorado from the vantage of a landfill. I used to fish on this river with my old man who was old as long as I could remember and who meant nothing more than a statement of the facts when he told me I was the side effect of a shotgun wedding. We swam in dappled summer water fresher than anything that came from the baptismal fonts. He had grandiose theories about things Southern. Why plantations were painted white. Why the South lost the war. Why Lee resigned from the U.S. Army — something about family and state before nation. I never listened.

He was fond of the yarn about churlish and unscrupulous weather, the cyclonic, otherworldly whirls that fished antebellum boats from the river bottom, an ancient steamer he'd come across upside down in a cotton field, miles from any water deep enough to hold it. But he was absent from my first christening in the font at the Basilica of the Immaculate Conception. I was baptized under the ciborium by a priest who read Spinoza and did not believe in the letter of all the sacraments. Below the Basilica was a crypt where the bones of bishops were interred and I could not kneel at the altar without their bones rattling in the dark, silent space between the words of my flatfooted prayers. Dad was barnstorming around Walker County, cursed Carbon Hill and its plague of churches. He might as well've been selling coal to Newcastle. He wrote a meshuggener editorial to the paper itemizing all the things he'd found in the Black Warrior River, and recommending to the mayor that deer crossings on heavily used county roads should be moved to less trafficked regions — he was sick of putting down half-dead deer by the roadside. I never had to ask the old fisherman why I was named Sipsey, after a coal mine, which was named for a river.

I knew the soul of every fish and tree by name: phylum, genus, species. Even the river's molecules of water that flowed like liquid glass and parted around me. It is only the way of anthroparchy to see wild nature and creature at the end of a chainsaw or a hunting rifle, running away from us, trailing its bleeding life behind it like a man tied to the back of a pickup and rough-shodded across the earth. For this reason, we name random groupings of stars after hunters and killers like Orion and Hercules, but the stars could just as easily be re-constellated.

An invisible, prevenient hand submerged me into the Black Warrior, an emergency baptism, and I held my breath without counting. I've spent as much time on water as land, piloting Drummond's private touring yachts out of the Port of Mobile, through the Yucatan Channel and on to Santa Marta, a postcard town of sparkling white beaches set against the crumpled Santa Marta Mountains. Somewhere south of Key West you crossed the North-South Divide and the poor just got poorer, and the colors brighter.

The yellow-brown fetor of banana plantations torpid and syrupy on the breeze. You'd think after the Banana Massacre they'd never eat another banana again. Gangs of youth played soccer in the water until the ball floated out to sea. They can spot an American before he even steps off the boat. You come upon their handmade soccer balls miles at sea. For some reason, they thought I was a Texan and they wanted to hear all about John Wayne and the Alamo and the cowboys and Indians. At times like this it was useful to pretend I couldn't speak Spanish. But they knew: even *No hablo español* will betray you.

You walk by tatty haciendas at eventide and see light constellated through the bullet holes in the walls. An entire village gathered around an airplane that had skidded off the runway and nosed into the Caribbean Sea, its translucent blue marred by the linear conveyor belts for loading coal onto barges bound for Mobile and the Black Warrior. Besides coal and bikini lines there really isn't much more to say about Santa Marta, except that it was a place through which I traversed many times in the dour company of corporate chieftains and suzerains of coal. Patrician businessmen with Christ-like faces who wear bulletproof vests under white linen suits. Whose glowing supermodel wives couldn't hold their liquor and were so factitiously fine they looked like extraterrestrials.

I was assigned to bodyguard Carolina, a lingerie model with skin the color of Colombian coffee mixed with milk, like she was some sort of invaluable investment. You felt slapped just looking at her. Somehow, she got mixed up with César, an avuncular Colombian whose bald head he claimed made him a better a swimmer. César spoke of no family — they were all dead or lost, turned into informants. He liked Bob Marley and Charles Bradley. He adored the Virgin Mary — because his linen shirt was always open at the neck, one addressed not just him but his chest tattoo of the Mother of God — and his fist was studded with gold rings — a skull on each hand. She may look like gold, but her smegma tastes like fish, César said. I told him not to worry; I was a eunuch. In Colombia, a eunuch bodyguard is entirely plausible. He cross-examined me, asked why my voice was not a castrati's soprano. I gave up my balls for Our Lord. Keep that to yourself, César exhorted. Alabama and Colombia are made-to-order business partners. Contempt can be a special case of admiration.

I strolled around the station plaza while the two paramours, moneyed geezer and his dazzling concubine, took their sweet time blubbering some valedictions. I've never had patience for long goodbyes. I watched a man leaning against a column unfold a newspaper and peel a banana like the flayed skin of a dying animal. How could they eat those things here in the enchanted land of Marquez? The mountains upraised to give us breathtaking pause and a few paltry, altiloquent words, perhaps in *ottava rima* verse, for the belittlement of our earthly enterprises: pushing boulders skyward, like poor Sisyphus, but each boulder makes the mountain a little taller. You can count on men like César to look at a mountain and think, "I'd love to take the top of that thing off," as if he were talking about a woman's bikini top and not the product of eons of natural history, a process commenced before we were arrhythmically bashing turtle shells with the bones of our tribal ancestors and calling the noise music. I looked on as medics carried a man on a stretcher with a dog's chew toy in his mouth so he wouldn't bite off his tongue. The two valentines were still going at it. Carolina pecked him almost platonically on the cheek and turned away, with what I thought was gratitude, toward the train. So, that's how it was. I danced on the table of my desperation for her.

César rolled his pretty Latin eyes — great white enchanting orbs circling a dark center plugged into a face of sandwich meat — across the station to indicate that we should speak privately. We conferred in Spanish and then he produced a pistol, grip aimed at my chest, and I was too polite then to refuse it. Coming from the South, whose Christian Soldiers and KKK roamed the outskirts of every jerkwater hometown like paramilitary carnivals, I was used to men in tailored suits who carried handguns. That's not what rankled. But what did was that I couldn't answer who was I protecting — Carolina or myself? César was unafraid to hand a loaded gun to a stranger, muzzle aimed at his own chest, because the vest he wore under his Italian suit protected him from all the bullets in Colombia in search of a corpse.

On the train ride through the Colombian countryside, we vectored towards the coal mines in La Loma. It was none of my business really why César was sending this assy investment of his out to the boondocks to swat at mosquitoes and be gawked and eye-raped by a company of coalminers. The train was enjungled, and the ferocity of the forest reminded one of how rapidly and totally nature will flourish when man steps out of the picture and there is no gas for his chainsaws.

Carolina was taciturn and avoided eye contact, so I went about woolgathering, my gaze directed out the window at peasants and cattle blurring by, a bucolic scene not altogether different from those around the state back home. The passing scene was like watching the news with the sound off, and you could fabulate the storyline yourself. Something along the lines of paradise in a Garth Brooks song.

Perhaps at the behest of César, or to quell his ireful jealousy, Carolina conservatively dressed herself, and I wondered if she had children. She looked dressed for a business meeting. The architectural eyebrows, the Cleopatra eyeliner around her shrapnel eyes. I also knew that under her clothes, she wore the best Aubade underwear coal money could buy. Information about the finery of estrus is not actionable. We sat across from each other, and I kept my paws to myself.

—I bet you taste like the episode of the madeleine, I tried.

—I speak English, you know.

—I'm not some gun for hire, if that's what you think.

—Yes, your Spanish is excellent.

Carolina spoke to the window, through her own reflection. After a while, —Aren't you going to ask me for my number? she said in a smoky voice.

—Never occurred to me.

—Good, because I don't have a phone.

Then later, while rendering unto Caesar on the queen bed of the villa's mosquito-netted bedroom, my face in Carolina's lap and her legs vise-gripped around my neck, I would read the tattoo above her womb in Gothic blackletter: "Abandon All Hope, Ye Who Enter Here."

I opened my eyes, but saw only subaqueous blackness. The sun does not plumb beneath the Black Warrior, where it's always the end of the world and you could set your watch on the punctuality of its dismal arrival. I resurfaced and my lungs took in air like a ship taking on water. The carapace of a turtle humped through the water like a floating island and the warm river water undulated in stratified streams like serpents beneath me. The down-going sun seemed to converge with the ascending moon on the silver mirror of the river. I cupped water in my hands from the long dark shadow of twinned riverboat smokestacks cast upon the rippling river.

What I wouldn't have done for a fucking margarita.

The tire swing was empty but swaying still, abandoned just before I surfaced. I breast-stroked back to the pier and drew myself dripping out of the water that slid off my body in sheets onto the lichened wood of the rickety, crudely constructed old pier. I toweled off with linen that had once covered Carolina and wrapped it around my waist, but then reconsidered and threw it into the river like a bad catch being returned to its element.

I pressed up the gangway into the double-decker inland riverboat Drummond used as a party boat for entertaining out of town guests. The riverboat, gingerbreaded with white and red and gold trim, sails by the name of *Carolina* now. I looked back to shore, my eyes scabbing over with salt, to the view similar to that seen for the last time by a gang-pressed sailor, the view of the village descried by slaves kidnapped in the cargo hold of ships like the *Brookes* and *Clotilde.* The lesson of Lot was whooped into me: never look back unless your position is so far ahead of your point of origin that it no longer threatens improvement by the fact of your absence.

I climbed into the pilothouse, and performed the sign of the Cross, a superstition of the Colombian miners. I pressed the control throttle forward and as the screw-driven, twin diesel engines muscled up we debouched at twenty knots of fugue into the plotless downflowing profluence of the Black Warrior, the pier slipping away into the riverine dark below the bald cypresses that fingered the oncoming gloaming choked with gray bats rising.

A muscular and malefic fog curled cruelly and opaque above the river like smoke off recently fired cannon. I pulled back on the throttle to the pace a blind man taps with cane crossing a cemetery. Not too long a time passed and I hit Mulberry and Locusts Forks, some twenty miles west of Birmingham. Howton's riverside camp and a nondescript church, a missionary outpost to convert the river pagans. At this crossroads, a decision must be made. You must choose a fork. The Black Warrior snakes south, bending towards Tuscaloosa, my alma mater, and a holy city for Alabamans, where I intended to port among Tuscaloosa's football zealots, triple-option sages and neurotic literary types hyperconscious of their Southernness.

I harked to the whispered innuendoes and susurrations of the riparian forest illumined yellow as if by torchlight. Drummond's kingdom is out there, somewhere, dragging more darkness out of the equal darkness of the earth, and burning it for the domiciliary light by which you persist in the controlled weather of phantasmal peace and safety of your homes. Perhaps in the very darksome carbon light by which you read this.

The river stood up on its haunches like a beast and coiled and corkscrewed in the frying pan that flashed before me. The harrowed and reprobate writhed and cursed in the fiery river, among them children and conquistadors, colonial Colombians and Americans who shouted in a tintamarre of lost languages. I even saw our State governor, who pats himself cheerfully on the back for not drawing a salary. He was dancing with Andrew Jackson and César, and Carolina danced with everybody in the frying pan. The river spun round like a vortex, spraying my face with water, and coalesced into a polycephalic serpent. I counted seven heads in all, baleful names carved in blood across the forehead of each and announcing itself with a multi-story horned diadem and papal tiara like a chimera off the floor of a tenebrist's diarrheal imaginings.

From seven slavering mouths came seven forked tongues that hissed and licked the night air, but they did not entwine me, nor did the snake's fangs find my flesh, for there is some alexipharmic clemency meted out from the cosmological surplus — some inscrutable general fund to which men like César helped themselves — to those of us who have work left to do before the hourglass of sands sifts down and the demons call upon their hominids to come home. Then the ophidian river becalmed itself and metamorphosed, returning to the familiar Black Warrior that carried the riverboat along until its end.

I'd done perfidies and many nights of *mea culpa* to the river, and now the river was in a retributive mood and had gone and found a guardian against me. I pulled down a bottle of bourbon and poured a double over ice and downed it and then another. I had chosen the wrong fork. Was it the Greek sage who said you can't step twice in the same river?

Fine by me. I wouldn't want to step in it once.

Before Drummond there had been a woman, an engineer also, pale and leggiadro as winter light. Referred to as Hurricane Theresa, we spent most of our time fighting on street corners downtown and locking each other out. She worked in the materials science division of Drummond, researching more efficient, futuristic methods to process Colombia's coal. She came carpetbagging down here from somewhere up North — the exact place never the same, shifting like the river bottom — and every time we agreed to a ceasefire and peaced ourselves in coition it was like the Civil War all over again, the North fucking the South. Yeah, that's how I remember it.

Drummond had been offshoring Alabama jobs since Fob James was governor. So, I boarded the gravy train and never got off. I knew the serpentine switchbacks and temperamental kinks, the odd oxbows of the Black Warrior better than I knew anyone else in my life. I preferred the particular curvature of the river to the oceanic generalization of the Gulf and the Atlantic. I can't endure the ocean's nihilistic expanse, its pelagic zoology, the deep sea eyeless creatures, the way it effaces and one-dimensionalizes everything above and below it. The horizon line to infinity so straight and liminal, receding from you with every nautical mile logged, it curves back upon you like a boomerang. The way, like the women in your life, it asks for everything and doesn't take no for an answer.

Some say the nearest approximation to hell man has ever made is the cargo hold of a slave ship, but they have misunderstood the open-pit mine. An infernal gash in the surface of the earth, carcinogenic dust blotting out the sun, but the lights in Alabama must be kept on. Football stadiums and castellated homes demand illumination. A grey sore suppurating in a lunar crater, earthmovers rounding the earthen benches up to the surface. The train expressed through the flashing green countryside like a gale, lurching towards the open-pit mines, and then Carolina and I arrived in La Loma and the train stopped just as suddenly. The tall grasses along the rails swayed to and fro and then righted along the windless coal air. Carolina had fallen asleep on the train, her chin bobbing onto her chest, such rural beauty in so vulnerable a spot. When she woke up I was standing over her and she failed to recognize me or her surroundings.

—Welcome to the Pribbenow Mine, I said.

—Enchanted.

As soon as we disembarked from the train, Carolina began coughing. Oh, to be the air sucked and suffocated into her lungs and then exhaled as climate change. The air was heavy-sounded with industrial activity over a child squalling. Masked private armies in digitalized camouflage barking angry Spanish into walkie-talkies and carrying side arms on which the safety has been permanently disabled. Spanish is supposed to be a romantic, mellifluous language, the language of Neruda and Lorca, but then you hear it macheted by the tongues of warlords trained in torture at our very own School of the Americas just next door in Georgia. And then it sounds like truculent shouting into the barrel of a gun. There are languages in this world that have no word for the color green. And if we can talk in a greenless language, a language with no word for the green of paradise, as Wittgenstein has said that the limits of my language are the limits of my world, that is because we can imagine a world in which there is none.

After years of producing feasibility studies for new mines, including the Pribbenow, I'd been backwatered and demoted to body-guarding Carolina, who disappeared the first day in a villa with dark, bulletproof windows and fortified by a long adobe wall. I was happy to be alone.

The miners survived the week in cheap hotels or the worker's camp off the main street. I was almost run down by a short native behind a rickshaw. I crossed through a shaded courtyard where desecrated statuary stood unvenerated and headless. An abandoned child sat cross-legged in the dirt, picking at a scab on his knee. A collision up the main street diverted my attention. A two-headed calf zigzagged dizzily through the main street, both its brains quarreling like an unhappy couple. It dithered in the street, uncertain where to go, and then slumped against a wall. The two-headed beast didn't resist the wall, in the process of perpetually dying, calling forth a lonely plangorous bawling as no mother could console. No one noticed.

Some of the Alabama boys had been with the local women to produce a special breed of idiot. Drummond was creating a Global South, and had been in Colombia long enough for many of them to be college aged. Two miners were handcuffed to each other at the wrist. A lot of good Plan Colombia had done for these people.

I bought some plantains from a fruit stand and dithered on the threshold of all the doors left open or else no door at all. For Jesus, they said. For the Lord when He returns to walk right in the house and announce His triumphal return. A closed door is not welcoming to the Lord. But this open door policy sometimes welcomed the wrong guests. Highwaymen and the godless. The bicephalic beast sometimes wandered in through the doors left open for the Lord.

I fled to a cantina taking shots of tequila cruda and sucking on quartered limes and licking salt from the back of my hand like a wound.

—Did you see the two-headed calf? I asked the bartender.

—Si, senor. The freak belong to César.

—Why doesn't he put it out of its misery?

—César, he like to show it off to tourists. Big attraction. They like to see freaks of nature.

The counter was laden with tropical fruits soaked in pure grain alcohols. A crucifix glowered above the bar. Every peasant and drunk is a Mariologist. I understood why everyone in Latin America made such terrible decisions under the influence of this pernicious rotgut that went down like a dog's tears. "I was drunk" might be a plea for help or an excuse for any folly whatsoever. Mary, Patron Saint of Drunks, forgave all indiscretions.

Two children — brother and sister, perhaps — wriggled into the bar. The older brother pulled a box of colorful condoms out and began filling them with water from a tap.

—¿Quieres uno? he asked, as the condom distended.

—No, gracias.

—¿El americano no quiere coño?

—Watch your mouth.

He had no inkling of what I said, but he knew by the dark tone it was something adults said when they were wet on te-quila. This sort of macaronic code-switching between languag-es was making the tequila hit hard. The boy tied the condoms off at the top and handed the ballooned rubbers to his sister. As the boy did this with a dexterity that indicated it wasn't the first time, I saw that he was missing a thumb on his left hand. Cristian, the bartender, was talking out of his face. —Lost my brother in the mines. Never find the body. I have no place to grieve him. He wanders the mines till we bury him. One cannot get over the death if we never find the body.

Cristian's shoulders shuddered with sobs. I rested a condoling hand on his shoulder. Everyone has lost someone to the mines. Drummond will pave the main street as a gesture, to ease the passage of the funeral cortege through town and to the camp's bustling cemetery.

—You want I should tell you prayer to Mother Mary?

—Just pour me another drink.

—You work for César, no?

—I work for Drummond. César works for Drummond. Colombia works for Drummond.

—You want the coitus with Carolina?

Where the hell had he learned a word like coitus? Drummond ran out the Catholic missionaries, but not before their lexicon of guilt and sin had been disseminated among the locals like blankets infected with smallpox. I needed to work on my poker face.

—Women run this country. Look around you. All these sad, blue Virgins, I said.

I picked up my tumbler and headed to the window that faced the main street. Mostly other dives and bordellos where the miners had their coition with child prostitutes under the auspices of the weeping Virgin nailed to the wall above the lousy bed that creaked with busted springs, a mattress bloody with bed bugs.

I knocked back the tumbler with grim pleasure and detachment. Thinking about the mountain above Santa Marta, and how its height increased with each boulder pushed up by a Colombian. I looked down into the bottom of my drink and remembered — a thought that belonged to another man — that Eichmann's last meal had been an Israeli wine.

Carolina cut across the square where another street ran perpendicular to the main street and knelt in the dirt before the little girl holding her brother's water-filled condoms. Anyone else viewing this tender tableau might have mistaken them for mother and daughter. Carolina gave something to the little girl and wrapped her long, beautiful arms around her in a durative embrace, the little girl seeming to wilt beneath more affection than she'd received in her short lifetime.

I couldn't hear their conversation, but like the passing scenery through the train window I could narrate their story for them. Something about a new life in America.

—You supposed to be guarding her, Señor? the bartender spoke to my back.

—Something tells me she can take care of herself.

— César will be very unhappy about this.

— César beware the ides.

—What are these ides, Señor?

The girl departed holding hands with Carolina, leaving her brother with his water balloon condoms alone among roosters, which by nightfall would be headless and boiling over a charcoal fire, but till then were pecking at invisible seed in the coal dirt.

I evaded, as much as I could, the orbit of the mine itself. Those great mounds of blackness excerpted from the earth like anthracite quotations of darker things to come — they were like granular nightmares sieved into hills on the surface of some life-less exoplanet. The boy with the condoms found me outside the bar watching the two-headed calf drooling and stumbling around the square. It would muddle a few feet, then feebly collapse again in exhaustion; it recovered enough energy to struggle a few more feet before collapsing again. The animal, though crippled and dumb, appeared capable of this minor struggle for thousands of years.

—No condoms, please.

—¿Has visto a mi hermana?

—No, lo siento.

The boy spat on me and sprinted down the main street. I knew his sister had been disappeared, and was probably on a train to Santa Marta.

I was thinking that the only grave at which Cristian could be-reave himself over his brother's death was at the mine itself when I was pierced by the pathetic, bovine keening of the two-head-ed freak on its back. The two heads had been unable to agree on which fork to take, and attacked each other viciously.

I withdrew César's gun from a shoulder holster concealed under a linen blazer woven from cotton grown along the Nile. I looked at myself mirrored four times in the calves' dark, watery eyes. I was pointing the gun at myself, those quadrupled reflected doppelgängers, when I fired off two rounds, one for each head, and then the calves' saturnine eyes closed, the beast's four legs crumpling beneath its dead weight, and my four brothers in that other, silent world inside the creature's eyes were disappeared.

Our state's urinous waterways are fiercely deregulated. You can't get a toothbrush on an airplane these days without some

TSA official suspecting bombs planted inside one of the bristles, but you could traffic a boatload of human chattel through the old French colonial capitol and Port Authority would look the other way. Mobile was an easy town, more Catholic than Southern, more Mardi Gras than Christmas. I'd seen the police commit crimes on Dauphin Street, the bars serving all night. Two cops, one black, one white, who beat up on a defenseless "dirty fucking nigger." The black cops stab their own kind in the back to show their white colleagues on the force what they're made of.

Cocaine is small ball compared to the profit that can be made in human trafficking. If you'd ever wondered what a college graduate of the University of Alabama did with his degree, now you know.

I knew what languished in the claustrophobic contraband of the dark cargo holds, but I never questioned anything more than where to dock the boat. Many of the women — they were girls, but a bad conscience called them women — trafficked back to the States in this way were beautiful and dolorous, a painter's model for the sorrowing Virgin. The Middle Passage today is made by dark-eyed, dusky village girls purloined from the green jungles, promised a life like the Olsen Twins. Arriving in ports like Miami, Tampa, Mobile, New Orleans and Houston, they are indoctrinated into Stockholm Syndrome, living in windowless basements on your street. It wasn't just Carolina that César wanted out of Santa Marta. He wanted me missing as well. I saw the two gold skulls twinkling on his fists. Carolina was hiding more than just her panties from me.

Cristian set some blue agave spirits and lime in front of me without having to be asked. —Lick. Shoot. Suck.

—You come in search of Carolina. I see it writing in your face.

—You must be blessed with powers of divination, Cristian.

—She is one hot bitch, no?

—Pardon?

The bartender emitted a golden laugh. His mouth tooth-blacked where dark squares of teeth had been punched out like lights.

—No, Señor. You think of Carolina. I mean our Madre, he said pointing to an amateur portrait of the Virgin behind the bar.

The Virgin looked ill and fastidiously disgusted, and not at all virginal. —She protects us from the mines. But every miner wants to fuck her. This is our Cross.

More tequila arrived. Blue agave is grown in volcanic ash and it kicks like cool lava when it goes down. You carry that firewater rotgut in you until the volcano explodes and you're hugging a toilet bowl and staring at a first trimester fetus. Enough tequila that I felt prepared to leave the bar.

I was the only figure in the cobble square cut with astringent light like a de Chirico. Doves settled on the villa's terra-cotta roof, framed by billboards with Drummonds' environmental propaganda. Officials referenced them for the journalists who would find their cameras mysteriously destroyed, reels of film wiped out by magnets.

I scaled the villa's roseless trellis attached to the adobe wall: Carolina was naked, waist-deep in a swimming pool of limpid aquamarine water, probably the cleanest in all of La Loma. I lost myself in watching her for a long time and then she felt a strange pair of eyes on her — like the bicephalic beast's eyes on me — and ascended the low mosaic-tiled stairs out of the pool and wrapped a towel around herself, but not before I got a good look at her.

I was waiting for her at the front door.

—I'm so glad someone finally put that poor creature out of its misery.

—Tequila Regulatory Council here to lick shoot and suck you, I slurred.

—What took you so long? she said without looking at me, her face the model for the appalled Virgin in the bar, though Carolina waited on no one.

Carolina pulled me into the dark of the villa by the belt and closed the door behind me: the Lord, if he returned at the appointed hour, could not come in.

I woke in the pilot house of the *Carolina* with the sun burning in my eyes, a senseless surfeit of light, like a hole in the ozone layer. A red-cockaded woodpecker was drilling away at a dead pine somewhere. I could feel the woodpecker's beak drilling my brain. I couldn't tell if it was tide of evening or morning.

A violent coughing seized me. Fine coal dust blackened everything. In the water, green with runoff oozing from catchments like a phlebotomized vein, dead fish turned in a slow current silver belly up. Cahaba Shiner and watercress darter, all endangered species that inhabited no other swatch of earth. A river once crowded with mackerel. Once vociferous with birdsong, the birds' throats torn out and slashed. Not even the scavenger birds followed me. I watched the sun slide into the cabin.

Drummond impended by the hour.

The cookroom was outfitted like a five-star French Quarter restaurant for the feting of Drummond's executives who liked to eat like gourmands and then puke it all starboard into the river. I fried green tomatoes and okra and potatoes with eggs for breakfast and sat alone at a table set for six in the riverboat's banquet hall. The chandeliers swayed and tinkled above as the riverboat rocked. I wandered the empty estate rooms appointed *de rigueur* with fleur-de-lis patterned wallpapers and rococo furniture from a sepia-toned century found now only in museums and perhaps the memories of a few old fishermen on the river from genteel families who had auctioned off everything in the New South.

I must've murdered a lot of time on that riverboat. How nature's art will trivialize even our most enduring monuments. The shoreline exploded in carnal bouquets and civil wars of color: russet on apricot, bittersweet against burgundy, titian beneath canary yellow and all of it sanguine such that I had to remind myself that these were trees with Bibles verses nailed to the bark. Most traffic on the Black Warrior is recreational these days: a girl braced up on water skis or tubing lazily behind a cruiser. Drunk boating the cause of a few fatalities every summer, most of them avoidable but inevitable.

I sailed the riverboat south and the water darkened from green to Mississippi dishwater, a slow brown roiling like turbid river water poured from the mouth of a recovered drowned corpse.

On deck, I talked to myself in the best King's English and narrated the river's history over the loudspeaker — my voice booming over the river — for the edification of birds and trees.

—This is your captain speaking from the deck of the *Carolina*. On our right we're cruising by the scene of a massacre of the Creeks by General Andrew Jackson. Indian tribes once roamed these waters with canoes forty feet long. Their average life expectancy was about the age of Our Lord, but the Creeks lived an idyllic and animistic existence in the prehistory of phantasmal peace, subsisting like our Lord on sustainable fishing and hunting practices. Then Desoto galloped in with horses and gunpowder, crucifixes and European diseases, primarily syphilis and other debaucheries, with his Spanish language and its god-awful romance. The Spanish killed the natives by reading *Don Quixote* to them. The Enlightenment arrived in the New World with its monuments of unageing intellect.

My calendrical sense was off, but it must've been the Lord's day, for I spotted a nuclear family all spruced up in the holy gaud of its Sunday best going at a picnic on the shoreline choked with watercress. The family was mortified and slightly embarrassed by this hungover riverboat captain's importunate narration over the loudspeaker of atrocities committed by their ancestors. Who wants to hear that their ancestors slaughtered Indians while munching on a pimento and cheese sandwich? I fired my vitriol over the loudspeaker at the starchy father. —That's right, you like your wife and kids, Señor?

The little girl pointed at the riverboat and her mother turned her daughter away and together they disappeared under sheltering boughs. The father crossed his arms over his chest and listened. His little boy, who had been throwing saltines to the fish, was mesmerized by the paddle wheel whipping the water behind the boat. The fish never bit, and the soggy crackers turned on the current and washed against the banks.

Downriver, I piloted the riverboat by two damsels, one sunbathing topless on a towel spread across the shore and her friend skinny-dipping. I thought I heard a bird's melodious lullaby, but it might have been nothing. The sunbather's breasts were full and brindled and it was the sunbather who waved and blew a kiss at me that might've been sent as message across the threshold separating our world from Carolina.

Carolina and I had a train back to Santa Marta to catch, but we spent the rest of our time together in the villa like a normal couple vacationing equatorially, walking hand in hand through citrus groves and avoiding the main street and the two-headed cow's corpse crawling with flies. The first thing she took off me, before removing a single article of clothing, was my watch. We drank all the wine in the villa, and swam in the pool's blue moonlit glow, and we forgot about the strange confluence of economic momentums that had brought us together. Few periods of my life have been more felicitous. I fed her mangos in bed, and drank the liquor cabinet's supply of tequila out of the cup of her hand. I kept César's gun on me while she slept in nothing; at times her shallow breathing stopped, and I told myself this is not Byzantium. I have been sick with desire all my life, and Carolina would be mine only when she is a ship sunk at the bottom of the Black Warrior. When our time was up, without changing the sheets or signing the guest book, we went separately to the station plaza and took a train, watching the tangled pastoral movie of the Colombian countryside, a jungle labyrinth replay in reverse. The lush poverty of this country mirrored how I felt — shacks and hovels set in the richest green — but God how I loathed the pathetic fallacy, which seemed less risible here than sitting in traffic on the Red Mountain Expressway. No more than my double in the two-headed beast's eyes mirrored Sipsey. The villa containing no more trace of us than a Grecian urn, and the wind teased and danced with a resplendent nasturtium from Carolina's hair floating on the pool.

Without access to Cristian's blue agave liquor I needed a nurse or a minister for my hangover. Tequila, you can stay drunk on it for days and never feel the vise on your forehead until you come down from it. My head throbbed with the train's wobbling motion. We sat facing each other, with my back towards the train's direction of travel, and I listened as she told me about her life. Carolina was in an expansive, tell-all mood, as women often are in the after-blush of new sex. —César is not a bad man.

—That doesn't make him a good man either.

—In Colombia a good man is one who isn't bad.

—That's an interesting moral algebra.

—Does the American want a condom for the two-headed beast? Carolina quipped, laughing loudly through her beautiful mouth. She could banter about contraception, because we hadn't used one, and they were impossible to find here. —You never told me what your name means, Carolina said.

—My father named me after a coal mine in Alabama.

—I'd like to see it.

—What happened to that little girl? I pressed her. —The one with the boy and the water balloons.

—She'll have a better life in your country than she ever would here.

She had a point.

—What about you, Carolina?

—It's too late for me, she said unsentimentally, and I could tell she meant it.

Why was her worldly fatalism so attractive to me? The Anthropocene had come and gone, and we were still here, so who gives a shit? When our own species starts growing two heads to one body, I just ask that the successor species is merciful and humanitarian enough to put us out of our misery.

The train slowed just outside of Santa Marta, before it should've, and I was pressed by an invisible hand against the back of my seat. I followed Carolina's eyes around the train car.

Bored gangs of insolent youth sometimes played a daredevil's game of chicken with the train, ducking between the rails as the train passed over them, if they're lucky. The same adrenalin shit I'd pulled with my frat brothers in college, robbing a convenience store in downtown Tuscaloosa not because we were stupid and poor, but just for the hi-jinks and because we knew the cameras didn't work. I connected how the boy with the balloon condoms had lost his thumb.

We turned at orders barked in Spanish. Bandas criminales. Bolivarianism hasn't quite lost its rustic charm here. They use assassination the way some states back home use a referendum. If only a bus gets hijacked it's been a good day. Generations of paramilitary guerrillas such as the Black Eagles had been aberrating through the countryside with chainsaws and machetes. Decapitated bodies found rotting in mass graves in the jungle. Fly fodder. The general atmosphere of Colombia sometimes reminded me a lot of New Orleans after Katrina. You never knew if you were in the middle of an intergenerational civil war or the party of the century. I bet they won't be naming any little girls Katrina for a long time to come. Troops boarded the train and their Commandante picked out the one person who didn't seem to belong on the train — me.

—¿Dónde está César? he asked at the other end of a gun, ordering me off the train. The stench of putrescence hit me like a sucker punch.

—César no está en el peatón.

—¿Ves estos cadáveres?

Yes, I saw the corpses lined up in a ditch like meats in a butcher shop window.

—El ejército privado de César hizo esto. Commandante tossed me a shovel. —The American can start digging first.

I hadn't dug one pit deep enough to hide the body of a newborn before I was feeling woozy from the torrid tequila and sweltering heat, and that two-headed beasts' moaning was still echoing in my brain and I had to shoot it between the eyes again to end its misery. Carolina watched to see what I what I would do. I tried to quell thoughts of her from that morning, her eyes rolled beatifically back in her head. The bodies of women and children, their unblinking eyes focused on me, seemed to beg to be put out of their misery, but I still could not say whether they were better off in my country, where the Bronze Age was being computerized. In their repose, they might have been playing possum, or a hecatomb of human sacrifice to propitiate the warlords. I'd seen bodies pulled from the river before, foul play and accidental drownings — men, women, and children — but not an entire village caught up in a feud between guerrillas and a multinational corporation. A bored soldier kicked one of the corpses, aggravating the habitat of worms and flies that swarmed around us in a vexed black cloud. I staked the shovel in the ground and the soldier's trained their automatic rifles on my chest.

—Te diré que César es, I said to the Commandante while looking Carolina not in the eye, but at the space between the eyes, her forehead. Carolina stormed off and reboarded the train. I had a sudden and desperate zeal for watermelon. I tasted the terror of tequila again and vomited on the Commandante's black polished boots. Lo siento.

The riverboat slowed before the eremite of the river: a crapulous fisherman passed out in his fishing boat, his face smudged with a hoary beard. He was sprawled across the bottom of the boat, an arm hanging across the gunwale. I honked the riverboat's horn and he riled himself from a logy dream and looked around and cursed. There is nothing more endearing than the sentimentalizing self-pity of an alcoholic who is low on fumes.

—You got a drink, captain? he hollered.

—It's not yet noon.

—It's always midnight on this river, friend. This is the cloaca of the devil's anus. I know what the river did to that man came for you. You got any tequila on board?

—Tequila is the best terrible idea.

I didn't want to get entangled with people on this downriver trip, but I could see that was impossible in a vessel like this. I retrieved some expensive liquor stowed in the galley and tossed it overboard. The fisherman fumbled the bottle and we both watched helplessly as it slipped below the Black Warrior. He collapsed into his boat and wept into his hands.

All manner of crimes — larcenies, sodomies, molestations, lynchings and general shittinesses against the spirit of things — had been committed in Tuscaloosa that would never make it to the local sheriff's office, much less the county court docket. There was this one fellow, Fidel, a hard worker who kept his nose clean, he was an old union man from a village that no longer exists in Colombia. His collar was bluer than the blood of the aristocratic families who wiped their asses with money back in Santa Marta. He joined the ranks of the unskilled laborers, the shitty-faced crackers in coveralls coking and welding, but it was better than the pineapple plantations back home. Fidel fancied himself a vaquero and despite his politics he was one of Drummond's best, trusted among the executives as well as the unskilled laborers. For that reason, I didn't trust him.

I was scrubbing down the deck with a wash of vinegar a few months ago when Fidel appeared through the gangway. I leaned on the mop and asked what I could do for him. He gestured towards a table and pulled out a purple Crown Royal chalk bag and pulled on the drawstrings. He upended the bag and a dozen or more gleaming white human teeth scattered across the table with the sound of dice rolled in a tavern. Even without a mouth the teeth seemed to smile. I knew that smile. Those skull-less teeth had smiled at me in the humid mango dark of the villa.

We passed a bottle of Islay back and forth and I homed in on the silence above the river, where once the lamentations of bullfrogs and the din of insects would've deafened the approach of Hannibal's elephants. The peat and smoke of the scotch burned like a vanilla bonfire going down, the peaty butterscotch aroma suggesting the cloying stench of women and children decomposing in that railroad ditch. I'd sensed that if I dug deep enough, I would find Carolina at the bottom of the pile, even as she watched me from the train.

—So the remains couldn't be identified, Fidel explained.

When I didn't say anything Fidel added, —She had beautiful teeth, didn't she?

In that moment, I could've murdered him and gibbeted his body on exhibit from the side of the riverboat steamer for anyone on shore to see.

I remembered coming upon her in that swimming pool that seemed filled with the Caribbean. That was too bad: Carolina wasn't the type of prima donna who'd expect me to fix everything around the house or squash bugs. I had a happy life for us all planned out, a life without César and mines and two-headed mutant beasts that had to be euthanized in the streets before the eyes of children who disappeared in the night, and now there would be billboards in Santa Marta with her lonely image modeling lingerie without the veridical and originary double for whom riverboats are named.

I noticed that Fidel had the face of a bloodhound.

—You ratted out César to the guerrillas, Señor.

—I was digging graves for women and children. That wasn't in my job description.

—Ah, but who will dig César's grave?

—I frankly don't give a shit if you feed him to parrots.

—You are not simpatico this evening, he said taking another draught of Islay. Fidel's flinty eyes burned blacker now.

—Why are you here, Fidel?

Fidel's answer was a suitcase of cash he deposited on the table. I wondered how much Drummond thought my silence was worth. —I'm not in the slave trade anymore, I said.

Perhaps I can be exonerated because I did not see the fanged creature that struck Fidel on the ankle and then snaked over the side of the riverboat and slipped sibilantly back into the Black Warrior. But even if I had, what would I have done about it? The river still had unfinished business with me and my hourglass was not yet up.

I put Fidel down in the estate room and stayed with him until the end, flipping through pages of Fanon and avoiding the Crown

Royal bag. The envenomation was bad, real bad. The riverine serpent got him in the heel, right where Genesis 3:15 said it would. His skin paled cold and tacky and he slipped into a calenture and never returned. Necrosis set in and his eyes bagged and bruised, blood trickling from mouth and nose. Even an old wound on his abdomen reopened and suppurated and hemorrhaged blood that would not be stanched. I wrangled Fidel's rigor mortised body in a sheet torn from the bed and dragged him up the companionway. He is now aliment for alligators and crawdads and bottom feeders without even a cenotaph. The Black Water protects its own.

I resumed my downriver hegira, leaving the drunken eremite floating in the wake of my paddle wheel, thinking that only fools who intend shipwreck name their boat after a disappeared woman whose prize teeth you still treasure in a Crown Royal bag. Further, Mexican hombres were casting lines off a concrete overpass that connected opposing shores of the Black Warrior. I eased back on the throttle and went on deck.

—Pescar más?

—El hombre blanco habla español.

—Sí.

The two amigos laughed. No matter how broke or sad a Mexican is he can always find it in himself to laugh. You can move mountains with tequila.

—¿A dónde vas?

—Estoy navegando a Drummond y luego a Tuscaloosa.

The Mexican fishermen reeled in their lines.

—Dios. Mierda.

I could speak technical engineering Spanish, and I often spoke behind the backs of upper management. Sometimes mierda was all there was. The Latinos and resident aliens at Drummond's plants counted on me more than my own countrymen. The State's new immigration law had them all scared shitless. Trump's Wall was a joke to them; the gringo, they said, had yet to build a wall they couldn't climb or pass through like border ghosts, they appreciated the challenge, but the gringo law was a ubiquitous and omniscient eye that never blinked in the face of a Lady Justice blindfolded by rags torn from the backs of children miners and little girls in the dark holds of ships.

Carolina and I cut south through brown, coagulated river and around the hairpin turns of the sandy shoals where a backhoe had been derelicted in the water. The riverboat passed without hindrance through the Holt lock and dam. Landings of hunting shacks and crumbling, kudzued plantations looming whitely over the river choked thicker and grumous now with waterweeds and other hydrophilic species that flourished on trash and bile. I read the hand-painted sign tacked to trees. Save the Black Warrior. What were we saving it from, but ourselves? Why did these Luddite folks think it was alright to use a tree as a billboard? I caught a sulfurous whiff of Drummond coal on the rankling wind, the nepheligenous stacks looming over the trees. The next tree sign informed me that Jesus saves.

The riverboat's wake rubbed up against the coal barges parked on the river, the great semi-trucks of the water. Not far now the vespertine lights of Tuscaloosa winked under the roiling clouds of an umbrageous empyrean and rain pricked the river like bubbles formed in a sheet of lead glass. South of Old Patton Ferry Road I moored the riverboat and chased after a tavern where heretofore white men sat against one wall nursing beers and stuffing themselves with burger while the river blacks were given the other wall and drank and ate in grim silence like monks satisfying themselves in the rectory. Many nights the workers entertained themselves shitting in the can, declaring that you could flush and then run to the river and see your shit bobbing on the waters.

This was the first time I'd set foot on land in a week. The bipedal, landlubber life has not been easy. I toed the ground like a soldier at the vanguard of a march wary of land mines. I moved athwart the bottomlands, tripping over cypress roots. I fell after a cynosure of misty light that flickered between trunks of pine and sumac wild with autumnal color wherein a few late fireflies incandesced in underbrush of bracken and nasturtiums. I dipped into a swale and smacked into a familiar tree in the bark of which I'd once found musket balls embedded from conflicts long over but unsettled. A fidicinal strumming and pale voices harmonized in a canticle, clapping to soul music. The voices stopped when a twig snapped beneath my feet. I was surrounded by a cleared emptiness in the forest and the rain hissed in the campfire.

Four figures stiffly seated on old tractor tires and milk crates. One among them at an acoustic guitar strummed a tuneless ballad that was still dulcet to the ear. They pulled tall beers from a cooler and stared crazily into the burning heart of the campfire. I'd once been told in the mining town that if a pilgrim could but locate the wood of the cross on which God's other third had been crucified he might light a fire that would burn perpetually until it was the only light left in the world.

—Evenin'.

I stepped onto the outer ring of the circumferential light cast by the fire — the first circle of the inferno.

—We thought you was black, the guitarist spoke up.

—Is that so?

—We never seen a white man on a boat like that. It's just getting on to be dark, can't see you too good. Come, gather round our table.

In the firelight I recognized the two girls as those water nymphs I'd seen sunbathing and skinny-dipping obliviously up-river. I wouldn't mention it.

—Where'd you get that boat? the prettier of the two asked.

I picked up a stick and began scratching at the dirt with it. In the distance the fall of a cataract swelled beneath whippoorwills.

—I don't remember, but I'm glad to be off it.

—You look like shit.

—I haven't seen myself in a while, but I reckon that you're not wrong. Just imagine what's on the inside.

—No, thanks.

The other spoke up. —You ever get to Birmingham?

—I try not to.

—That ain't no kind of place for an old man.

—I guess so. You ever make it to Bryce, the crazy house in Tuscaloosa? That's a place will turn your soul black.

—Nah, but we got a couple a friends broke in.

—They broke *in* to the lunatic yard?

—It was an initiation thing for Rush Week.

—That is the goddamn dumbest thing I've ever heard. Broke *in* to the state nuthouse. Are things that bad out there that you young folks are desperate to break in the nuthouse? Maybe I should get back on that boat.

—Ain't no worse inside neither.

—Maybe that's so.

From afar the cheers of a football game reached us like the bellicose clattering of a coliseum. Someone must have scored a touchdown. The Crimson Tide would be playing homecoming tonight, destroying another sacrificial opponent in a cupcake game.

—I used to play football at Tuscaloosa, I confessed.

—Bullshit.

—This was back in the Dark Ages. When women would've aborted a little shit like yourself. If I say I played football at Tuscaloosa, then I mean that I goddamn played the sport of foot-fucking-ball. Is that clear?

The underclassman shifted nervously on his crate.

—You been on that floating casino too long, mister.

—Your lady friend there's got a nice set of tits.

—Thank you, she said.

—Excuse me? her man said.

—You want to watch us screw? the other kid said.

—I'm just busting your balls.

—Shit.

I snapped the stick in two and condemned the shorter end into the campfire. —You ever heard of Jesus Christ?

—Hell, you ain't some kind of holy roller are you?

—What do you think his last thoughts were on the Cross?

I could tell he'd spent much of his life softening behind the safe walls of a church, but had never given much thought to this question in particular.

—I don't know.

The other fellow left the campfire and swerved by a canvas tent and vanished in the sylvan darkness. We passed around more Natty Ice and listened to his yellow stream hit the side of a tree and foam on the ground as he made water. A favonian wind thrashed the trees above us all and suspired against the campfire which dimmed nearly to nothingness.

—What are you college kids doing out here in the woods? Why aren't you at the game?

—We want to get away from it all. Just waiting on eternity to hurry up and get here.

—Well, look here. I found myself among lords. Every dying generation after mine has been full of shit.

—What's your story, old timer?

—There's a place up in Pennsylvania coal country called Centralia. Little old town. Nobody there anymore. The coal seams beneath the town have been burning nearly thirty years now, smoked the whole town out. The earth so hot you can't hardly stand to walk on it. Melt the soles of your shoes right off. Now if that isn't hell's unholy fire bubbling up from beneath I don't know what is. And we made it.

—What's in the Crown Royal bag? The sunbather asked, huddling up to her beau.

I hefted the purple bag in my palm, heavier now than when I got it from Fidel. How long would it take for teeth to disappear in a fire? How hot would the fire have to burn?

—I'll show you mine if you show me yours, I suggested.

The temperature had dropped and snowflakes descended darkly like the spirits of dying animals through the forest canopy, flashing ephemeral and white above the wood smoke — the flakes swooning like perne in a gyre — and then disappearing entirely in the campfire. Our breath plumed before us like puffs of river fog, and I warmed my hands by the campfire's dimming embers, the Anthropocene's last balefire.

—You running from something, the smart girl said.

—Used to work for Drummond. I'm sure you've heard of 'em if they teach you anything.

—I heard what they done, basically took a big old crap in this here river. I wouldn't eat nothing come out of that sewer.

—You're right about that. But Drummond keeps those stadium lights on.

—Who is Drummond, anyhow?

—Drummond is all this, I said, sweeping my hand grandly across the landscape to indicate its extent and scopelessness. — Shush. You hear that?

—No, don't hear nothing.

—Exactly, friend. That is the birdless silence that Drummond created. This place used to be paradise when the Indians had it. But then your ancestors came pilfering for the gold to hammer their death masks. No birdsong in golden boughs, no fish splashing. No golden bird keeps the dozing, somnolent Emperor from his lethargic oblivion. Me and Drummond got unfinished business to take care of. You'll see, I said tightening my grip on the purple Crown Royal bag. I had a happy life for us all planned out.

Though I shouldn't have, I took another deep sip on the Natty Ice, enkindling the raconteur in me and, while untying the golden drawstring on the Crown Royal bag, told those utopians of what is past and passing, and what is not yet come, and the afterword about the supermodel and her blackletter tattoo — Abandon All Hope, Ye Who Enter Here — which I have told many times foregoing to those who have listened and those who have not, in various voices, even foreign languages, a little different with each retelling, but I've never told it like this before.

LAST OF THE OLD GUARDSMEN

The opening pitch at the Birmingham Baron's new baseball stadium was this spring on a soft night that felt like summer. Tony condos modeled on the rat maze from Third Reich, Florida now where there used to be a juke joint, a greasy spoon, a fried chicken shack, and some African hair braiding studios. I see Christian Crossfit types running around the block garroted with truck tires slung around their necks — who does that for fun? White Millennials training for the Apocalypse. After dancing with dynamite, I realized you cannot change this city — this city changes you. I watch the prices on the gas station marquee change from $3.35 to $3.42 to $3.53. The condos give the bums more walls to pee on. We got two Waffle Houses; inside, seated at the bar, pushing a large hash browns in a circle around the plate, my waitress asks if everything is alright. In what sense do you mean that? The explosions now are not bombings — demolitions. My teaspoon rattles against the coffee cup. Can't even properly gentrify the place.

The first pitch was a fastball, 95 mph. The breeze off that fastball felt in general admission. Knocked me out of my seat. The National Anthem heard far afield as the hobo train depot and the police headquarters where I've smiled for the camera. That police sergeant snapped the photo the way a bored serial killer photographs the crime scene of another of his gruesome murders. Everyone this side of 1963 knows the Birmingham police have killed more blacks than what the CDC calls murder and "diseases of the heart," which sounds like some kind of romantic hemorrhaging, as if we died of an epidemic of brokenhearted plague. But I am carrying on.

A new tribe arrived in town. The snickering, smug hipsters have brought their strange facial hair and tight denim and expensive craft beers to the city, turning Birmingham into a hipster douche version of the Australian penal colony. One of their boutique beers costs more than a six pack of Coors Light, the one with the mountains on it. I flex my tattoo of the Grim Reaper on my forearm. The hops-smelling hipsters love it and coo for more. I've never been to prison, but I've done a little jail time. Robbed the Regions in Five Points for a dollar to get treated for blindness. I slipped the teller a note that said, "Give me a dollar." She gave me the dollar. I stole a car once, but it was a stick shift and I dumped it three blocks away. Took me three days and a Sunday to write that note, too.

I got dinged for saying *y'all* at a board meeting. But y'all solves all manner of problems. What am I supposed to say? You guyses?

Hell in a hand basket.

I've been pepper-sprayed in the face by a woman I was trying to ask for the time. I've yielded to some side effects. The crimson Christophanous visions of the temporarily blinded. Self-defense against dogs and bears. Riot control, crowd control. Am I alone a crowd? Was I a bear or dog to this woman who thought nothing of reaching into her fake designer purse for her spray can and letting me have it full on in the face? Been unable to cry since. Could've been worse — I could've woken up in Selma or Tijuana with a collapsed lung. After taking that mace to the face, I walked around in football pads and a helmet and didn't ask anybody for the time. I tried to tackle a telephone pole, but I woke up on the sidewalk.

I was asking the time. The ballgame started at sundown when the batter would not have to stare into the dying day's ultraviolet afterglow, though sometimes the nights here last for days at a time.

I said *y'all* at a board meeting convened to discuss the merits and excellences of relocating Bull Connor's armored tank to the Civil Rights Museum. The tank that once terrorized protesters and small children — Momma said to stay out of the tank's way but I say that which stands in the way becomes the way — was rusting in a police junkyard somewhere and there was a notion that the tank's display would get the white folks in. They would want to see ole Bull's tank, and the Civil Rights Museum could use the coin. All in favor said Aye. I said Aye, but didn't mean it. As I never do when I agree with a crowd. Honorary board member.

I have a grandson pitches for the Barons. Minor league baseball is a major sport here. I bought him his first baseball and his first glove, a beefy leather catcher's mitt even though he never played that position. The family had, between twenty people, one baseball thrown back and forth at Rickwood Field until we lost it in a thunderstorm — the family baseball sailed skyward and never came back down.

My peppery vision — I was not born with sight — returned

sometime around the bottom of the seventh, just in time to see him strike out the Montgomery Biscuits' first baseman. A man crammed two hot dogs into his mouth simultaneously. If a man had two mouths, I have no doubt he would eat four hot dogs. Four mouths and eight hot dogs and so on. Between innings, a circus car piloted by a demented clown circles the infield shooting t-shirts into the crowd from the mouth of a miniature cannon. Swallows and bats dip and ascend the sky-colored firmament above the stadium, surrounded by an expensive skyline of empty buildings. The bald children with all the incurable, petrochemical cancers behind the glass wall of Children's Hospital had the best view of the diamond in the city. I get up from my seat, squeezing down the aisle, rubbing my ass in everybody's faces, and am hit in the back of the head by a balled up t-shirt.

I follow other men to the gender correct restroom. I know North Carolina has issues with their bathrooms — that botheration hasn't hit Alabama yet. I scrutinize myself in the mirror. What did that frightened woman see as she reached into her purse for pepper spray? Did I resemble a riotous crowd, a predatory animal, a race riot from May of 1963? Do I look like O.J. Simpson to her? Do I look like a long hot summer? The stitches were still in my head from the last attack, a mugging in Railroad Park where men and dogs chase brightly-colored, artificially flavored Frisbees. The man at the adjacent sink left the water running, and was telling the man washing his hands at the next sink that the government should send in the Crimson Tide to fix Syria, Nick Saban as field commander. The Syrians, he said, would be so confused they would surrender. I asked him if it was okay to bean the batter. He said he didn't know anything about baseball, he was here for the specials on beer and hot dogs. I tore a rectangular brown sheet of towel, dried my hands and crumpled it into a ball and as I cast it into the garbage can outside the men's room I saw the woman who pepper-sprayed me in the face. She was talking to a cop, clutching her purse as though it contained her genitalia.

Zilch is what I felt.

I played ball for the Bear's first black team, recruited after Bama lost to Southern California, a stinging loss that got the white folks' attention. And for some fans in Peckerwood a loss that stings still. When their beloved lily-white Bama got beat by West Coast Negroes that got the attention of the Alabama-Football Industrial

Complex. I tackled everybody — black and white. Didn't matter. I tackled cheerleaders and sidelined players. I tackled sportswriters and fans of both teams. I tackled sports analysts and the ministers who prayed over the team before a game. Cameramen and newsboys — tackled. I tackled Bear Bryant, but only once. I tackled the other team's head coach every game. Baseball was too philosophical for me, all that waiting, hanging on, the tobacco spitting, the center fielder bored out of his mind, the illegality of the tackle. The quarterback was always a white boy from a good family. The kicker was a cracker farm boy who didn't know he had black blood in him since before the one-drop rule. I always smiled for the cameraman as I tackled him.

Y'all called it white flight, but what it was, was really the blackening of the city. When white people come back to Birmingham, I heard a preacher say as he looked up and through the church's raftered ceiling, the joists nested by dirt daubers, when the whitening falls on the city like a rare snow then you start blowing bubbles and flipping houses. For example, the Belgians evacuated and left Hutu, Tutsi and Twa to slaughter each other. The bus stops started changing, and old white churches were taken over by black congregations. I've never been to the Botanical Gardens, not even in bloomless winter, even though it's merely on the yonder side of Red Mountain, where that Holloway girl is from. Flowers pink as a white woman's nipple. You can't exactly run for the hills when the hills are running away from you. Like Atlanta is so much better. What do they got? Coca-Cola, Chick-Fil-A, the Atlanta Braves, Delta Airlines, satanic traffic, cancers of the mouth? We don't need more frontier at this point — there's plenty to go around.

After Katrina I went down to Gulfport to visit that side of the family. Whenever I need a reminder that Alabama isn't so bad I visit the Mississippi side of the family, which did not have even one baseball. Alabama ranks among the most windless states. So many deprived childhoods, we couldn't even fly kites, but still it was not Mississippi after Katrina. My Gulfport relatives begged me to take them back to Birmingham with me, so I spooked them with tornado stories — at least you get some warning with hurricanes. My Mississippi family's plight on the coast makes me hanker for comfort food. I wanted a chicken biscuit, hash browns, and a vanilla Coke. The Waffle House was blown away by storm surge but the bar stools were still bolted into the cement pad. I took a seat at the far right bar stool, and watched cars pass on the road. I'm just trying to live a good life in a bad world. I've been wearing a black suit most of my life, waiting for the noble savage to die. Y'all call me Colonel Stone Johnston. I've worn a ski mask, but never led an army that God would countenance. If I tried to find every stray bullet that ever missed its mark in this city I would be looking a long time. I do wonder, from time to time, where the bullets that missed my body went — are they still speeding somewhere in the world searching for a target? The X-ray machine at the Jefferson County courthouse has been turned off. I never did go back to Gulfport, and may you finish this life without having to.

I was still young the year Birmingham outlawed Communism. Seemed like a good idea at the time. Communists were rumored to be cannibals — they ate babies. Each other. They ate Capitalists, and they ate Mercantilists and Agrarians too. I'd never met a Communist before, but I knew a cannibal when I saw one. If they outlawed Baptists or utopians and you'd never met a Baptist or Utopian would you get heartburn over it?

The Tutwiler Hotel had the grandest men's restroom in Dixieland. That was in the 60's, the Hotel's waning days, and the men's room retained that distinction right up to the bitter end. The expense lavished upon a hotel's shitter when a simple outhouse would do just as well. Follow the wire in the dark. Listening to white men's shits. The olfactory and auditory senses utterly assaulted. I harkened to the eliminations of Birmingham's business elite like a scatological symphony. How water can be used like a percussion instrument. I heard things their wives never heard. I think maybe this was before the invention of pepper spray. Confessions, explosions. Every conceivable consistency. The constipated, the loose-boweled. Prayers and business secrets. They regarded me like a cigar store Indian, deaf and blind, not even there enough not to be there.

And what was I doing there in the Tutwiler's men's room? This was not the métier I had in mind — hotel ice maker isn't a job — when I was tackling everything that moved for Bear Bryant: towel man, shoe shiner, necktie knotter, lighter and cigarettes, yes sir. Never any black men, this was during Jim Crow's last act. The stall doors reflected in the opposite wall's long mirror.

Suit's trousers puddled at their shaggy, hirsute ankles. A man who hummed Elvis as he voided a business lunch. I've read that objects in mirror are closer than they appear. I replayed the national anthem in my head...*and the rockets red glare*...as explosions of flatus echoed off the walls' hard white tiles...*the bombs bursting in air*...the toilets' simultaneous flushing like two cataracts. Those who left toilets unflushed, those who entered a stall and seemed to do nothing, neither peeing nor shitting for hours. Those who masturbated and then wept. Those who peed like their bladders were on fire. Those who ran out of toilet paper. Picture it. An account executive — a man with a direct line to the Governor — hollering for more toilet paper. Right away, sir. Overheard two men's conversation between the stalls' walls. A joke or a business conference that ended with Jesus saying to Paul I'm not healing your fucking hangover. Both men laughing, one puking lunch and drinks. The creamy splash of vomit on the white porcelain bowl. Despite these confidences and presumptions I was the most resented black man they encountered in their day, and yet they were powerless to let me know it.

The Tutwiler's women's restroom was a free-for-all. Blood smears on the walls. Monkeys in there throwing feces at the wall. Ooga booga. The mirror busted monthly. Once a fetus in the toilet. Stiletto points tipped in blood. I've been studying how to pass a polygraph instead of learning to tell the truth's side of things. Names and curses finger-written in menstrual gore on the mirrors. But *The Shining* is about one white man slowly succumbing to his demons. It doesn't work when your lead starts off the film looking one glass of spilled milk away from murdering a daycare. Jack Torrance is what I imagined these business executives to be like in the nethermost of when no one is looking. We're going to shoot all the white men to the moon, but keep the white women right here on earth because we can work with them.

Then a spooky thing happened, which you are not behooved to believe, but I shall tell the Vulgate version of what happened anyway. This was years before the wicked tank was put to rest in the police junkyard. Bull Connor himself came into the Tutwiler's men's room. He handed me his coat. He looked like a grotesque pale crab that had crawled out of a bucket, dressed for Elton John's funeral. Bull had a governor's handshake, and a small town mayor's swagger. He seemed in a pother over which stall to choose. In any given business day this is one of the most important decisions a man might make. They were all empty. He teetered on the cusp of a limitless possibility. I've peed against more empty buildings than I have in stalls. A towel man and shoe shiner could learn much in the course of a day about the nature of his fellow man by the stalls they chose and which they rejected. Me, I would've rejected all of them. He had his bull horn with him, I don't know why. I thought he would hand the bull horn to me as well, but he closed the door on the stall and took the bull horn with him. If you've been paying attention, then you know that Bull Connor's bull horn was used to recite his favorite scenes from *Birth of a Nation*.

Never a word good or ill had passed between us, and even some white folks, the Jesus Christers wouldn't sit next to the man in a church service — but working the men's room at the Hotel is the ultimate college in democracy and scatology. It was here, at the Tutwiler, that Connor brought his mistress, his secretary, it was public knowledge, even to his wife. I'd heard Connor's was an itty-bitty thing, a shrimp, really, and I who am hung like a bowsprit wanted to get a look-see for myself. Between the stall's door and the stall's frame is a small crack, just wide enough to pass a note or a letter through. Oh, it was a teeny, bitsy thing, a pee-wee midget yea big. Pocket-sized. Limp as a faggot's handshake. A boiled bantam baby turnip. A hand over my mouth to squelch laughing. I'd never deserted my post at the bathroom wall before. I never told a soul what I saw, not even King. I heard Connor's shit hit water. Sounded like any man's shit hitting any body of water on earth. Ploosh and a splash, king and peasant.

Then the bull horn. Connor's bark through the bull horn was indelible, a bawling howl that keened into a rancid fascist blathering like trying to read *Mein Kampf* with too many marshmallows jammed in the mouth. I'd heard his voice before, an obscene lament in the streets. He needed help. He was out of toilet paper. Very few men asked. Most would rather walk out with soiled breaches and inoperable delinquent dingle berries than ask me for a roll. The roll handed to him under the stall's door. A white hand reaching for the roll delivered by my black hand. What would these white businessmen do without me here when the toilet paper ran out? I saw my own hand reach the toilet paper to Connor's hand as if from a long distance off.

At a time in my life when I was beginning to fickly question the existence of minorities — confined for the workday to the hotel men's room one begins to feel outnumbered — with the dogged sincerity of a Southern Ivy League scholar, but without the scholar's sobriety, a team of blacks, what y'all would now call hoods or gang bangers in the contemporary Urban Dictionary parlance, decided to integrate the men's room at the Tutwiler. I was the only black man to ever enter the Tutwiler's men's restroom, and I wore mostly white. Connor's tank was parked in front of the hotel; the integrationists came looking for him. It must be hard to be anonymous when you drive a blue tank. Four blacks waiting outside the Commissioner of Public Safety's bathroom stall door in the men's room of the Tutwiler Hotel is not a situation I ever imagined myself in as the Tutwiler's towel man and shoe shiner.

The quartet of integrationists — what were they doing? They'd lined up, pants around their ankles, and when Connor at last came out of his stall he was greeted by four heroic, triumphant black asses. The superior nausea on Connor's face has not since been equaled. Connor departed the men's room without a word, leaving me with his coat, and his bull horn, a white flag of toilet paper trailing from his left shoe. He hadn't flushed. If I'd known then that he would spend the rest of his days in a wheelchair, I might have fetched one from the hotel's lobby, offered to roll him out to his tank waiting at the curb of the Tutwiler Hotel.

Martin had a dream. Did you dream last night in your bed in Peckerwood? Did you masturbate to tiny Asians getting pounded by black guys? Makes you feel powerful every time, right? Martin's dream was Bull's nightmare. Unsuccessfully as anything I've ever done, I dream-dabbled in blocking Bull's tank's way when it was rolling down 4th Avenue, I was going to tackle that tank but was pushed out of the way before the tank could crush my running legs. Tank Man got his idea from me. Connor's tank patrolling the neighborhood made me want to be the last rifleman defending the Alamo, an irrecoverably lost cause but you keep on shooting anyway because what the hell.

Sinkholes have been opening up around the new ballpark. The darkness beneath the world gathers in sinkholes and spills upwards. Fans exit to find their precious SUV named Phylicia at the bottom of a thirty-foot pit. A few pints at Good People Brewing, the bros in pink and yellow Oxford shirts, tasseled loafers, pressed khakis with their bro-science and bro-degrees, passionate as hell about the S.E.C. and cleavage. The lynx-eyed, leggy blondes, girls who have been to the Botanical Gardens, and not for the flowers. The sozzled hipsters, they fall inside these sinkholes, never seen again. No one misses them. More take their place, they are like soldiers in a cavalry charge — shoot one down and there's another behind him. Y'all slap my back as if I were choking and ask me about the bombs. Ask me about the dynamite.

I was among the last of the old Guardsmen who held sticks of lit dynamite in his hand. Carried like a summer sparkler, extinguish the dynamite in a bucket of water. Hear that angry snake hissing. Handling a Klansman's stick of dynamite is the closest to madness I have ever come. Every week I got me that mummified mothball ole time religion. The preacher inside Bethel Baptist is reading from Chronicles. The uptick of bombings around Christmas time. Technically illiterate, he reads aloud a passage from Kings that he's memorized, recited to him by a lisping fifth grader who spoke like she had peanut butter in her mouth. The congregation's coughing was like flu season. The preacher looked up from his memorized Kings, dynamite smoke groaned and swelled into the sanctuary, palling the church beneath dark clouds like in Psalms, the sunlit stained glass as if behind a blitzkrieg of locusts.

I vaulted from the pew, almost a saltation, as if pulled by the ghost of shackles on my ankles out the church's front double doors which open for baptisms, weddings and funerals. Smoke inhalation may have addled my brains. I launched the dynamite into the street. Nothing exhilarates and brings you closer to the quick than holding bundled Klan dynamite, the fuse sparking like the Fourth of July. The bomb detonated and destroyed the attached parish house. Mangled a few evergreens. The blast left me stone deaf for days, too short a time, it could've been permanent if I had my druthers, spared listening to all the carrying on, but at least I didn't have to hear any more Kings. Bethel Baptist Church was still standing, ready to receive the sinners, the meek, the handicapped, the idiots, the homeless, the illiterate, the lisping, et al. The preacher wanted to know why didn't I throw the dynamite at City Hall or the police headquarters. Come on down to the brewery on 14th Street, across from the new Barons' ballpark, and ask me about the bombings.

Today the bombings have slackened off, quieted down, the

Klan veterans gone underground or too geriatric and enfeebled in mind and body to light a stick of dynamite, but the nonviolent hit and runs are weekly funerals. There's a statue of Martin in Kelly Ingram Park. Pigeons shit on his bronze head and shoulders, bums leave offerings of tall boys wrapped in brown paper bags at the plinth. A man urinating against the same plinth, steadying himself with a hand on the King's kneecap.

I had a buddy, Gordon Parks, who took photographs. He came in one day to the Tutwiler's men's rooms and took my picture, a grim and thwarted smile. In Parks' photo, I am standing there against the white tile wall, my white-gloved hands clasped before me, a quasi-military pose, as if precariously balanced on a golf tee. He got his camera broken many times. A cop would grab it and smash it against the ground or against the wall. Stomp on the broken camera pieces as if stamping out a fire. But he kept taking pictures. Particularly a color photo of a pretty woman outside a department store in Mobile. Her bra's strap fallen below the dress' cuff, which is green or teal or turquoise. Too many colors in this world. The color of the Gulf at dawn, after ruffling by a storm's cleansing winds. A child in Sunday clothes at her side. I hear Patsy Cline's "Walkin' After Midnight" or Ella Fitzgerald's scatting in the photo's background over the cursing of traffic. I try to make a move on the girl in the teal dress, ask her the time, but hers is a slap that dislocates my jaw. The neon sign above woman and child glows COLORED ENTRANCE. I wanted to put my arms around her, whisper in her ear it would be okay.

Mobile is still a shit town, even if they named the BayBears' stadium after Hank Aaron.

Today everybody's having Rocky Horror Show sex changes or twerking it to death, and liposuction and making calls on burner phones to buy positive pregnancy tests off Craigslist. Ladies, we know your racket. My eyes are still on fire with pepper spray! What a below-average, milquetoast, obnoxious cunt. Go drink another Cosmopolitan and deprive your boyfriend of a sex life you little zilch of a shrew. The wisest man I ever met drove a taxi off the Edmund Pettus Bridge into the Alabama River.

It was after seeing Parks' photo that I got the idea to switch the Hotel's men's sign with the women's sign and for twenty minutes before I got found out and fired I had women coming in in twos and threes in the men's room, utterly confused, lost, some upset, horrified, and they stormed out when they saw the long wall of open men's urinals, an obscenity. Some had never seen the inside of a men's room in their lives.

I bought a cowboy hat and a seersucker and when white America was blowing bubbles for a living, I got work when he was in town as King's bodyguard, and I don't mean Elvis. My forehead got bigger. I protected myself and my neighbor with a nonviolent .38 police special. I stopped attending church because of the bombings. Church on Sundays was the most dangerous place you could pray. When he came to town King stayed at the A.G Gaston Hotel. We had some good romps and frisks. The wee hours' rollicks. Women came and went, come and go. I asked them all the time. They loved a man who danced with dynamite. Women didn't carry pepper-spray in those days, this was before the 70's porn star bush; their purses had conceal and carry. I'm an old geezer now, but I can still get it up hey-hey. Room 30 at the Gaston Motel was the target of a cowardly bomb thrown from a moving car, and we employed the rubble of the Gaston to build the letters of a SOS message in the middle of 5th Avenue, so that if there is any God up there, if he is literate in Southern American English, he can look down and read our plea for help.

When I discovered dynamite beneath the wrong car — an unmarked police car — I let it blow up. Don't get me wrong — I love this country for its push-up bras and suicide rate, but we cannot save a country which from the beginning had no quality control. I love this country and its first-person shooter games and its blue lives matter police, where a man can die from a fish hook infected with flesh-eating bacteria. I love this country and its sinkholes and oil spills. I love this country and its Dixie Deathmen. I love the country's Southern Death Cult and its Trojan horses. I love this country whose tawdry skies ate the family baseball.

Aye. Bull Connor's sky-colored tank is being sent to the Civil Rights Museum, which will restore the tank's blue luster to its original racist polish and visitors will pay the equivalent of two hours at an Alabama minimum wage rate to see it and pray over it. The white folks in Peckerwood will come see the tank and their children grub it with their sticky hands. Those who gone on to the Lord before me have pressured me into this. The tank will be parked right behind Room 30 of the Gaston, unless I stop it.

An early spring day like the murmur of summer, a great day

for baseball. The Barons — an integrated ball club now — are hosting a farm team from Third Reich, Florida with a mean, unsportsmanlike pitcher who beans black batters with his alligator curveball. Expect a brawl by the 3rd inning, the catcher throwing off his mask and rushing the pitcher's mound.

Protected in nonviolent football pads and helmet. My jersey number is 44. I tackle a few crape myrtles, hit a telephone pole and a utility box for practice. Nothing — and brothers and sisters I mean *zilch* — can stop me from stopping that blue tank. The sidewalk peopled with a rubbernecking crowd, as if for a parade or second line funeral. Half the crowd cheers on the tank, and the other half cheers for me.

I step off the curb and into the street, as if walking the plank off the side of the *Clotilde*. The tank is trundling through the intersection of 14th Street and 4th Avenue. Who can it be steering the tank again through the streets of Birmingham, or is the tank on autopilot, policing the streets it must have memorized? A pack of wild curs follows curiously sniffing behind the tank. The tank's tracks' clanking smothers the ballpark's National Anthem. My grandson is about to throw his signature fastball. The beers spilled, the free t-shirts shot from a pneumatic cannon, the total absence of cheerleaders. Last of the old Guardsmen, I stand over the street's white centerline, the unstoppable force meets the immovable object, to ask the tank driver for the time. A couple of hipsters take my and the tank's pictures with smartphone cameras. The bull horn projects my voice onto the tank's armored cladding like stray bullets. I'm down in a three-point stance. Keep one eye on the approaching tank and another on the women's purses, because you never know what they got in there. I have the home-field advantage now. I've waited long enough I could polish an apple by holding it up in the wind. The malodor of white men's shit stifling my life was never deodorized. The tank and I play my favorite game: chicken. Do not fear. The Trojan horse is empty. I'm trying to live a good life, not *the* good life. I will not die in this city. No one with pepper spray will stand over my grave.

LONG HOT SUMMER OF 2018

In 1930, J. Thomas Shipp and Abram Smith, two African-Americans, were hanged outside a courthouse. A third young man, James Cameron, was saved from the mob by a woman. Lawrence Beitler took a photograph of the lynching, which he sold copies of for days Cameron later opened a Holocaust Museum to record American racism.

The long hot summer of 2018 is the crapehanger of American antiquity. Just look at the harum-scarum decorating of the Oval Office. The touch of a Martha Stewart intern. They got air-conditioning in there. Cool as the shade under banana trees. Chairs covered in human skin. The Thomas Kinkade portrait of Old Hickory dusted off. Makes you wonder how they scrubbed shadow out of that trim white paint.

It's as though — from the consensual inertia with which the birthday cake flavored wall came down, the wall's willingness to be crumbled — jailhouses were once designed and constructed to be penetrable by outraged mobs of pale rat-catchers inbred of the synthetic gene pool on the *Mayflower*. Three sledgehammers — one each with our names on them — awaited six hands, as a bride awaits her groom, three middle-aged, married (to a mouth, a voice, a pair of crossed legs, a scream, a rose), white fathers of three named Matthew, Mark and Luke, or was it rather this: Matthew, Mark and Luke awaited the sledgehammers to find them. The hammer always finds you, like a heat-seeking missile. A sledgehammer is the assegai of God: see what it can do to a man's fleshy face, which is not a concrete wall, even though it looks like one.

When they struck with sledgehammers at the jailhouse, they struck at the chips on their shoulders. The chips went flying. Rumors of rape did little to lighten the load of the chips upon their shoulders. The walls crumbled like wet birthday cake. Matthew, Mark and Luke hauled out Shipp first, Smith second-last but one, and then me, last as usual, but I never minded, being last you get the convenience of seeing what's coming down the line, in order of age, oldest to youngest, so there was some logic to it. As done in Hamelin. Logic flourishes amidst the hurry-scurry and the farrago, such as Thornton Dial was fond. We would skip the courthouse, straight to the trees. The courthouse was ugly and grisly as ever, and even today a Martha Stewart intern might gag its soul, squeeze it dry a little deader. Such crucifixions of the *polis* cannot be gay. Judges in Lexonic periwigs huddled over the portentous flumadiddle of their law books. Shouting flatulent judgments in high-sounding Latin. That was on a good day. Nonesuch good day when the shoulder chips flew. Shipp, Smith and myself, after some colloquy, in which we debated the merits of meliorism, the possibility and desirability of extropianism, at last agreed that it was prudent to go in order of age, oldest to youngest, and to go screaming. That our voices in this crab bucket might be heard. Out to the corner of Third and Adams, where the judge's groundskeepers tidied and nursed the maple trees just for the occasion. The rat-catching mob foregathered about the hanging trees, united in their purpose as a single waspish, sullen person.

Shipp took a lick. Another lick. So far so good. What started simply as a lick from a hick became a licking. Another lick. A kick. The licking became a kicking, and that kicking a beating, and Shipp's right eye distorted like a deluxe red apple fattening on his face. And we didn't have to wait long before the beating became a suggillation. Shipp gave as good as he got. Got better than he gave, too. Die on your feet! Come at me, bro! he shouted at the rat-catchers, to no avail. For they came at him. They came at Smith. They came at me. They came at us all. As done in Rwanda. I was Hutu, Smith was Tutsi, Shipp was Twa. The red apple bulged bigger than the red dot on the face of Jupiter. Smith, I believe, though I am no coroner, no county medical examiner, not by a long shot, Smith was already without the generally accepted medical and spiritual signs of life — heartbeat, pulse, cares — when they hanged him in the square. I tried to call for a timeout, but Polyphemus is blind and cannot see my hand-signaling. Hanging a corpse in the courthouse square for the vultures, rubberneckers and postcard makers, a lesson to the sons of Shipp and Smith.

Because this was a moment in local history to be fondly remembered, Lawrence Beitler was called upon to take our picture. This was before the religion of Instagram. The selfish iconography of the selfie. A man hanging unconscious from the courthouse maple cannot exactly take his own picture. Beitler's equipment shot us with light. We smiled big and white. I have good teeth. Correction: had good teeth. Now my teeth are catawampus, carious tombstones. Smith's teeth on the other hand. Smith's teeth were bad before the beating, before Jupiter broke out on his face.

The rope is on hand. As if there is an assistant waiting stage right, or stage left, who tosses Matthew, Mark or Luke a rope on cue. Every lynching has its anonymous assistants without whom the chips could not fly. Let us acknowledge the service — to community, to the *Mayflower*, to the public good — of the many unsung assistants who frequent the country's many courthouse squares with rope in their pockets. Hanging a corpse is, at its most literary acme, a symbol, like the moon, like the roses are symbols of lunacy and love, respectively. The town would hang an elephant, if it could. And circus workers in Duluth. The town's love affair with symbols. I have seen townfolk fistfight, go to blows, over the body of a dead relative. This town is renowned for fistfighting. Gladly, would I skip my own funeral for a good fistfight. Matthew, Mark and Luke versus Shipp, Smith and me. *Mano y mano*. Progress happens one funeral at a time.

The rope cinched around my neck — I thought of a goose neck, a swan neck hanging from an olive tree in Bethlehem. Smith and Shipp are the heart and soul of the maple tree. Smith survived a lightning strike, a single mother, and an encounter with the Devil. Shipp survived all — till now — that would've put Smith under. I thought the sun was shining; no, it was Beitler's light in our faces. Say cheese. I said cheese, but tasted birthday cake, vanilla on vanilla. It was after midnight, and Beitler's light blinded us, three black Sauls on the road to Waco, and I am still in uninsured convalescence from the effulgence of that flashbulb, I see it in the moon flashing on passing cars each midnight. Whole towns blinded by Beitler's flash, their sight never returned to them.

Beitler's portraits of hetero weddings and church groups hung on the walls of happy homes and crappy churches. Beitler didn't want to take pictures that were not weddings, smiling schoolchildren, churchgoers, postcard panoramas; Smith, Shipp and myself were not getting married, never finished no school, and our church burned down once every other year, so asking Beitler to photograph us, in the shape we were in, was like asking Gordon Parks to photograph weddings, church groups, and circus performers. But to enjoy the patronage of the rat-catchers, Beitler took our picture, then left in a huff, and never took another picture with that camera again. The camera was cursed. I said goodbye to Shipp, goodbye to Smith — parting is such sweet sorrow, the sentimentalists will say! Smith and Shipp said good riddance to the rat-catchers, the mob foaming for me next. The rose tightened about the goose's neck. A woman's voice, like a flute playing in a house fire, sang my name, and her green eyes comforted me with a promise of paradise. I'd never heard my name on a woman's voice that was not harping me. I followed the flute's notes out of the house fire, like a rat charmed by the Piper of Hamelin. The one rat who did not drown in the Weser River.

I swung to and fro, and swinging I keep the meter of the miserable wind. From the bottom of my feet, a mob rises to the top of my head. I may have swung like this, in the fashion of a circumbendibus, for some years; I may even be swinging still, how would I know? The rat-catchers grew bored with my interminable to-ing and fro-ing and dispersed back to their lairs, never bothering to cut me down — no one in all that crowd had on their person a pocketknife, an unlikely story. For years, I never heard any high-sounding Latin from the courthouse. I hung exposed to the eyes of the rat-catchers like some black Aris Kindt. The *Mayflower* and the *Santa Maria* ferried these rats over. I saw wrought on their masks an awful exuberance, how death is an exhibit for the living; the dead don't take selfies and send postcards of other dead. The sensation of dying, after all, is little more, considered as Smith and Shipp would consider the *acer floridanum*, than a heathen of living. The woman's flute voice charmed me and I was yanked back into the living's realm. I'm still not dead enough to bury. Flies get off me. Coroner get your paws off this black body!

No insurance for loss of consciousness. Sun and moon in opacus. Clouds form and aim for the sun. Such is my observation over a murder of years from an elevated position. I saw the moon but once and never again. Why I was spared, if spared I was, when Shipp and Smith were strangely fruited — but it is fruitless to interrogate fate's controversy. Consciousness returned like a slap in the face, and everyone I knew and loved was dead. The taste of birthday cake a distant delectation. Shipp and Smith — gone, both long gone. To the destinations of Matthew, Mark and Luke, the very same. Beitler's postcards sold for fifty-cents a postcard. The rubberneckers took home — if home is the exclusion of offense (their hearths heated by fires lit from Moses' burning bush) — with them macabre souvenirs and memorabilia: shreds of Smith's or Shipp's rags, tree bark, segments of the one true lynching rope. I refused autographs.

The well-off walk by, feel sorry for me, and give me handouts. They leave cash tips in jars, metal cans, and hats. I don't want your money, keep your money. Not that I couldn't use it. But there are causes — good and bad — better and worse than mine, causes which could use a new roof, or a new Executive Director. By now there must be millions of dollars at my feet. The GDP of oil-rich nations. Let the wind have it. If someone sticks his hand in my hat, and makes off with a thousand dollars, I think nothing of it. The wind is running a deficit. I'm not charging admission, this is not a museum. No paintings of the tristesse tropics hang on the wall, no callipygian nudes, no sculptures needlessly taking up space, and no security guard squeaking into a walkie-talkie. Museums are where the artsy-fartsy rat-catchers put you after they appropriate the fragments and vestiges of your culture. They hang it on the wall, which is not sledgehammered, with a name tag and stare at it very seriously and thoughtfully, then after a few bombs have been dropped somewhere on the Global South, they walk off, confused or disgusted. Blue and orange and brown paintings hang on the walls of the well-off. The walls of the well-off are tossed up by the less well-off. I have watched the homes come and go, ghetto and posh purlieu exchange places.

I have wished for requiescence, but Matthew, Mark and Luke's descendants are constructing indefatigable cities and tony townships around me, heavily defended, improbably fortified, highways and roads snuggling up to me, the great black fields of blacktop and asphalt struggle to annihilate the color green from the enjoyment of all eyes. I feast on the perennial green of her eyes. The orchard of strange fruits cut down for the rodeo of William V. Sullivan, United States Senator from Mississippi. As done in Waco. Mine is the penultimate tree standing. The second-hand stores, Dollar General, Family Dollar (somehow, without any provocation, people still form families), the beauty shops and barbershops, all that culture vanished. Police tape around the whole town. Miles and miles of yellow crime scene ribbon. The wind raised its voice between the fingers of the trees. Dogs in packs of three or more, and once a dog solo, brave and curious thing, a student of the art of war, approached and sniffed me, nipping at my heel, yelping into the blue and orange and brown evening. Dogs in twos also but I do not call this a pack, dogs in twos are no more than a couple. I gave up kicking at them long ago, around the time of the Trump presidency, the cinnamon Hitler. That seems so long ago now. The town crestfallen and morose the day Bill O'Reilly was fired from Fox News. Blessed *Schadenfreude*. Joy in the sufferings of others the only feeling left to me. The base, salacious demises of their talking heads bring me the ravishment and transport the sledgehammer must feel upon bashing the jailhouse wall. Long white streamers of toilet paper waving in the branches after my tree was rolled. Cats roam the square yowling for a human hand. My swinging from the tree branch stopped, and in this stopping began the era of the rope's creaking. Time kept by the rope's angle between branch and ground. A bug flew in my mouth in 1973. Momentous, memorable meal. The requiescence came but it was not a total requiescence. I am sharp of hearing still. The rope's creaking kept me up at night when I cursed the stars and wished them gone, no more than distant, failed sparks in this galactic crematorium.

I saw reluctant improvements. Enhancements of the waste. Citadels of commerce encroach the town square. A retailer of sledgehammers. Another store sells only rope and soap. Snail mucus for ladies' facials. The sale of rope in length stimulates the local economy. The mayor of Milledgeville decided by mayoral decree to Cuba the town square, flooding it with faster and faster food, and midget-wrestling pizza. A Bed Bath and Beyond intercepted my view of Mars. The "Beyond" of that retail store's name has rankled. Beyond what? Beyond this ash heap of odds and ends? Beyond the lees and leavings, the dross and dregs of the rat-catchers? It implies too much. It winks. Pretends to know more than it does.

How lynching can coexist in the same town as brunch is a mystery for Arthur C. Clarke. The annual Brunch Fest consumes all the orange juice in the county. Brunchers walking sausage dogs and ballerina poodles. They cosset these odious creatures, dressing them in scarves and bandannas and sweaters. I counted, when my eyes were open, fewer children; closed, I count the faces of the mob. When I was a person, this was many Augusts and long hot summers ago, I formed a family. Together, one Sunday, we added three shadows to the town square. Be you still, be you still, trembling heart. But to be outnumbered by sausage dogs! Owners more and more resemble their creatures. I was the unwilling recipient of a hug from a woman who bragged she ate Atlanta. The softest touch of another excruciates. Grown men behind strollers. People form families, and families form people. At times, I cannot resist the rat-catcher's ultracrepidarianism, but from my elevated position in the umbrage of the courthouse maple the family seems an anachronistic institution. Oh, the view is spectacular. And to come down would be to enter their world, to touch the same ground as the others. And the ground of others is a minefield. The legless shamble by in ones and twos. Once a one-armed man pumping the pedals of a bloody bicycle built for two.

If my brain could talk to my foot, I'd kick their little ratty curs, but kill not the albatross. Signal lost. The thought alone will have to do. The thought is supreme freed from the gross importunities of the body. Descartes was a rat-catcher. My wants are fewer than my haves, but all I must do is want, and instantly I have. I possess by wanting, and my needs are lesser still than my wants. I need only a little of something that is less than the pith of nothing. At all less than more than the lee of nothing, the heel of nobody. To have more by needing little, less than Hamelin needs me. And having most by lesser still. Wanting is the only thing I have never not had, and for this reason I have never had, for having is for the haunters of Bed Bath and Beyond and the Pottery Barn.

Improvement steadfast encroaches. The celestial crematoria lights, once strong when Smith and Shipp were alive, they too are blotted out by the Bed Bath and Beyonds of Hamelin. Jesse Washington was once the brightest light in Waco. So, the celestial lights darkened by the spunky, gallant lights of the Enlightenment oozing across the hemisphere, and men ceased to raise their stony eyes skyward, as their ancestors once raised their eyes, as there was nothing to see but the bright black night they created for themselves and their offspring. Is this the species you want colonizing the stars with McMansions and Section 8? A bunch of cognitive washouts, Huck Finns with a Titanic of hamartia, and xenophobes. Mars is a ghetto for parking lots and strip malls. The universe is methane and manure. We had one nice planet with a few decent water slides and we poisoned the water.

Were it not for the extreme differences in temperature, Independence Day and New Year's would be indistinguishable: both celebrate their respective inanities with the detonation of fireworks, vain attempts to dazzle the stars with uncouth explosions. The stars are not impressed. Jupiter, look at what we can do! Alpha Centauri A, look upon our combustion and despair! The town square sparkles green and red for the holidays. Here and there the county has sequined the streets in silver — a tinseled flag of the county commissioner's eutaxy. These gingerbreaded holidays are vexingly Christian. The blood and the piety. The fandangles and curlicues of the holiday are all garbage by the New Year. The Department of Corrections has the inmates out New Year's Day to sweep up the parade's trash.

By such tinsel and garniture, a wreath on the undertaker's door, I know another year of hanging has passed in the darkening umbrage of this hanging tree. The jailhouse is gone now, long gone like Shipp and Smith, and the town square is a jail for the wind and the de-institutionalized, the paroled, the insane. Asphalt four leaf clovers connect the town square to other towns, but it was not enough a dream of asphalt — measured in funerals — to goad the town into metropolitanism. I opened my eyes — how little time has passed since their last opening, I hope for more time to have passed than has — to see a bronze plaque commemorating the day Smith and Shipp and me hung beneath the maple like Christ flanked on either side by Gestas and Dismas. The mayor cut a red ribbon with scissors — the blades twinkled in the angular lemon light. Civic applause. It was reported in the local paper — read aloud by my assistant — the mayor was struck by lightning the day following the historic plaque's ribbon cutting.

The plaque is goosebumped with lines of raised dots caressed by the fingertips of the sightless. As done in Damascus. The sightless are grouped into the cane and the caneless, some escorted by dogs, these generally without the accompanying cane, seeing the story of Smith and Shipp and yours truly through the eyes of their fingertips, like Geordi la Forge. Canes that were more clubs than canes, canes that were more staff for striking than aids to sauntering, staffs carved wickedly into snakes and other vile hideous creatures. We can wrangle over who was winner and who loser in the Chomsky-Foucault debate, but I do not cotton well to the blind man of any color brandishing a serpentine staff; too many times the staffs of the sightless knocked on my noggin. Before we get too far, let it be hereby recorded that nobody is forgiven anything, not even the heel of nobody, my dying wish is a regrettable life upon them and their descendants, and may they be remembered by no one, and swiftly forgotten by everyone. As done in the Republic of New Afrika.

Here comes somebody! It is rare now to receive a visitor. This somebody could be anybody. This somebody briefly stops to read the plaque, extinguish a cigarette against the maple, and continue on his way. Oh, for a cigarette, somebody! Oh, for that burning butt to conflagrate this tree! This town could use a good burning, as Atlanta benefited from Sherman. The same man in a Geo Metro has driven by day after day, always with his lights on, searching for something in the gross inutility of the daylight hours. The sun too is an anachronism. Searching for Sir Thomas Browne's missing skull, they say. He waves, but my hand will not lift. Not even an itch can I scratch. I am covered in unscratched itches. My hand does not respond to the signal sent it by the brain. The hand is a cold spider; the mind — free of that atrophied, bloated institution of the body — no longer embodied in a bag of bones hanging beneath this dying maple tree. I am a false positive in the masquerade put on by the regime of presence. My charcoal body is too precarious a patchwork for the de-institutionalized mind to recognize myself any longer. Hunger has not entirely left me. Yes, I once caught a leaf in my mouth. For months I masticated it, savoring every motion of the jaw. Such leaf pickings are a meal lasting years. Locusts and the various nocturnal species of flies too. Inadequate circulation of ideas, goods, and services between town and metropolis has resulted in the rustication of Hamelin and Waco, the town as unresponsive to external stimulus as my hand is to the brain's signaling. The signal intercepted by the sledgehammer. As done in sinkhole.

Every morning a black boy reads me the paper. I don't know who taught him to read, and I give him a lynching postcard to mail. I send lynching postcards in the mail to all my correspondents, many famous persons and non-persons, Tom Cruise and Morgan Freeman. I gave the black boy a name I can never remember. He looks familiar, like a woman I once knew. My personal assistant — he could've been a eunuch in the Forbidden City — synopsizes *The New York Times'* coverage, complete with infographics, of Henry Smith's demise. Albeit, here I refer to a difference not in kind but in degree of Smith by the same surname. Smith and Shipp were unrecognizable once Matthew, Mark and Luke had Matthewed, Marked, and Luked them. The face of my friends disfigured, unrecognizable, as an apple is disfigured rotting in the sun. As done in Milledgeville.

My assistant collects the day's mail and delivers it to the post office — in the same brick building on the same block of the town square from which Beitler's postcards were mailed. I keep up the old traditions — I too send lynching postcards in the mail — old friends, family and admirers. Black and whites by hack photographers like Bleitler. A crotchety old rat-catcher himself, he was on hand to photograph the ribbon cutting and the plaque unveiling. Tourists — all races — wanted their picture taken with me, posing with me like a celebrity. Harry Haywood posed with me, and I congratulated him on the good work. I am on a thousand Instagrams. I thought of a cigar store Indian I once knew, and frowned a smile for another selfie. As done in Dealey Plaza.

A long hot summer because August and September are the long-suffering months. Hot because the corn was sweating, temperature of a bullet as it leaves the chamber, hot like the internal temperature of Jesse's viscera. The White House's air-conditioning bill must be exorbitant, those chairs covered with human skin sweating. Even in the shade, shaped like the crack of a whip, the heat outnumbers you. The equator runs through the Congo of my skull. The closer to the equator, the further you get from the middle-class, and the higher the bullet's temperature. Copenhagen and Stockholm — pale cities chockful of pale people, rat-catchers, inadequate circulation of the hemic globules — are so far from the equator the crack of the shade's whip is felt as a cool, benign breeze. Copenhagen and Stockholm should be relocated to the Gulf Coast, and then see how they like it: the flesh-eating water, the Jimmy Buffet themed hotels, the fried food buffets, the hurricanes named for ex-wives. The water eats flesh. The water grows a mouth and teeth and eats a leg, an arm, a torso. The ravenous water eats Copenhagen and Stockholm. The water in its eternal insatiety eats Kierkegaard and the Nobel Prize Committee.

For privacy, as I am exposed to public view day and night, I draw a room about myself, a room in that house on fire from the flaming rooms of which I was summoned, saved by the green-eyed woman's silver voice. Three shadows live in that tumbledown house. Daisy Miller standing at a kitchen sink. The room gains in light, or loses darkness, according to this planet's pathetic attempts to eke out another year. A maple tree grows in the center of this room. It was Daily Miller called my name, the voice that spoke to me but not Smith and Shipp. The room gains in darkness, or loses light, as the Bed Bath and Beyond's parking lot's sodium lights burn. Looking at me with the greenest of green eyes, Daisy took my hand on the settee, adjusting the rope for me, and the room rustles in the dry breeze. She dusts the bronze plaque, vacuums the grass. Daisy Miller is so good to me, her smile bright as Beitler's flash.

A body suspended in space for years from a tree branch frees the body's mind to live a life the body never could even if it would. The unhanged, they could if they would, yet they won't. And because they were unhanged, they are enslaved to their bodies, walking where the institution of the body orders them, squeaking up and down the aisles of Bed Bath and Beyond. Bodiless, my mind is freest. Not a corpse will I leave hanging.

The elements — all the same to me, rain, snow, sleet, hail, sunshine — no need to make distinctions nature has already sarcastically made. It costs me nothing but irony to make distinctions. The empty space between the bottoms of my feet and the top of the ground has further expanded; the tree grows — my personal assistant or last surviving local member of the United Daughters of the Confederacy waters it — and the branch, from which I dangle, rope-bound, grows higher above the ground, the tree branch and the earth in a tug-of-war over me. In spring, pollen paints me a loud shade of yellow.

What else? How various are the means of locomotion! Horse-drawn buggies became minivans. A howdah passed. I thought nothing of it. What was I to think of it? I ceased to entertain thoughts when the thought alone of kicking a yuppie's dog no longer excited me. A cop policed the square silently on a Segway, sometimes clubbing me in the gut. I refrain from complaint, I perdure.

The first aircraft in the sky was a blue bodement: the sightless pointed their fingertips skyward, and the next Saturday the town flooded; it took on water like the *Henrietta Marie*. There was nothing to be done about it. Crying for help had never helped anybody except plutocracy. The rope's swinging gave me the vertiginous sensation of being at sea, I am a slave ship listing on the floodwater. The notion followed the sensation. I was up to my neck in water. So be it. The water rose up indifferently, starting at my toes, no differently than if I were a house, a tree, a thing in the water's way to be worn down and away by the water's will.

I might have been a stone; the water grew a mouth: it became flesh-eating, hungry, cannibalistic.

The water overtook my nose. I saw the Sphinx in a bathtub. My personal assistant — I cannot go so far as to say he was a friend, though not unfriendly, for we did not do friend things, but he assisted me in personal ways — devised an ingenious craft, attaching an outboard motor on a casket, *Smith Shipp* painted in Victorian picture alphabet on the craft's starboard. He stuck a squiggly Krazy Straw in my nose. The water put a hand over my mouth, and by the ingeniousness of this respiratory contrivance I switched mouth for nose. I breathed through the straw. Glorious oxygen, gas of Waco's lights. For comfort, as I'd been living like Belacqua, my personal assistant kindly adjusted the rope about my neck. Profuse, hearty thanks. I hadn't been submerged in water since as a child — I will not refer to the organism I then was as a boy, for I never did boyish things, even the Christ child had a boyhood, I am told, in his tripartite transformation from baby Jesus to teenage Jesus and then grownup Jesus — I was washed in dirty water by a woman who was not my mother. She may have tried to drown me. And because she failed, the town tried to hang me, and on account of the town's failure to complete even that simple task — men of an I.Q. less than Stockholm's temperature on a summer day have successfully hanged men with greater I.Q.'s — Mother Nature wastes her water on this tree to drown me. Not her screams did I hear as I entered this un-plu-perfect sound byte of a world, nor her blood on my flesh as I slipped out the way I came in, son of a uniparous origin, making me the first and the last of my line, at that teat I drank from the Devil's Punchbowl. The names on the ship manifest of the *May-flower*: Matthews, Marks and Lukes born at sea. Even Andrew Jackson and Genghis Kahn had boyhoods; little Jeffrey Dahmer, the poster boy white boy, enjoyed the companionship in his youth of God's creatures.

The floodwaters backed down, there were cars in the trees, dead animals rotting on rooftops. Rat-catchers had chopped through their attics with hand-axes. Milledgeville is not quite so far below sea level that it will be inundated by the warm future's new seas. Ah, too bad. Neither is Hamelin at all safe from flood-water. It would make a peachy suburban Atlantis for the noble animal. Now the Krazy Straw is stranded below me, beached out of reach. The seasons blend into one long hot summer. Green gave way to gold for briefer spells, till summer green grew in perpetuity. The equator got diabetes, pole to pole. Copenhagen and Stockholm get the corn sweats like Haitis and Angolas. Palms on Drottninggatan, mangroves on Strøget. As done in Chernobyl.

The 20th century was a terrible time to be alive. I lead with that when meeting new people — the townsfolk who will never get out of this town, and so presume to speak to me from out of their mouths, as if we were equals. Hi, I'm James Cameron. Personally, the 20th century was a disaster for me. Halloween costumes aren't what they used to be. The Internet has pictures of the century's highs and lows: rapes, lynchings, murders, arsons, famines, porn stars, mudslides, crashes, and cats.

The disasters came at me without cease. My tree was struck by lightning; maples burn like Rome. The conflagration spread from my maple to the town hall, and from the town hall to the Bed Bath and Beyond. My personal assistant borrowed a fire extinguisher — a bright red cylinder that releases pressurized smoke from Rome — from Bed Bath and Beyond, and sprayed the tree with dry chemicals like smoke from a haunted house. The maple's nightingales flew away to sing in another tree. The requiescence's mouth's tongue was cut out. Bed Bath and Beyond and the town hall were rebuilt with thirty pieces of silver before the Geo Metro driver's body was claimed by family in the Republic of New Afrika.

The *genius loci* is mad, mad, mad. Another *Casement Report* could be written on this town, proving the null hypothesis false since it was accidentally founded. In addition to Rome, a few other burned cities deserve honorable mentions. The first chapter of such a *Casement Report* ought to tell how a policeman, a sergeant or lieutenant, maybe even a high-ranking somebody like a colonel or general — known throughout the town for his charm, brutality, Christianity, and mercilessmost soul self-styled after Terminator and John Wayne, made a routine traffic stop in front of the square. Finally, some action! Months pass with only dry leaves for friends, another false positive. Earthworms mock me. I feel their hungry pity emanating from the ground. Only Smith and Shipp know, and they're dead, why it was my personal misfortune — for some, misfortune is a bad marriage, a bad hair day, or a stock portfolio depreciating in value — not to be hung somewhere with a better view, a beach, a mountaintop, a strip club, anything but this dull blue-blood town square. But a traffic stop by a high-ranking, crewcut rat-catcher could spice things up. The blue and red lights strobed the maple tree, the town square convulsing like an epileptic no less than it convulsed when Beitler's camera flashed in our bruised faces. The driver emerged from the Geo Metro, hands up, as if he were going to dive upwards into the town's flat sky. But the driver's hands up in the air — no more useful than telling a Nazi that the swastika belonged to the Southern Death Cult. The nightingalic requiescence was rent by four pops from the cop's gun.

I have suffered misaffection at the hands and feet of Matthew, Mark and Luke's descendants — my contemporaries, though not coterminous with what humans are searching for in the long hot summer of 2018 — who my personal assistant relates are involved 2018's evil clown sightings: pelted with pellets from a pellet gun, egged by the midnight eggers, as any scarecrow has, pointed at by the accusatory fingers of pre-teens like the bones of a dinosaur in a natural history museum, clubbed with bats like a piñata that won't give up its prizes, and on my birthday, beneath the maple tree in plain view of this hanging false positive, they eat birthday cake like it was Atlanta. But nothing like I saw that day of the traffic stop.

The Geo Metro's driver fell, as I have never been able to, to the ground, like a marionette collapsing when the strings are cut, and then the triple report of — I counted them off like paces in a duel — one, two, three more shots — Smith, Shipp and me, exactly what humans are searching for — at the immobile silhouette. The Geo Metro's driver-side door remained open, and I had the thought, because the thought must suffice, of closing it, as a courtesy. Between the firing of the penultimate, or third shot and the final fourth shot — an eternity if you're the Arab — I sauntered hand in hand with Daisy Miller on the beach (we watched a statue of the Emancipator drowning) of Provincetown Harbor, where Meursault shot the Arab four times, even though the first shot fired is fatal. Because we are a species splendid in ashes. I never hope for violence unless it's of the giant robot versus Godzilla variety. The street was still bloody — the rain around here has been seen before in flagrant failure to uphold its end of the bargain, as originally agreed upon in Ezekiel 38:22 — when the protesters assembled disturbed the peace, which is less peace than the cutting out of war's tongue, and nailing it to the door of Howard Finster's *Paradise Gardens*. God couldn't human-proof a single fucking garden. Is that any fault of the worm, the tree, or the apple on Shipp's face? No one comes outside anymore unless the sky is falling. Apocalypse is a New Age way to get to know your neighbors.

This disturbance of the peace — shouting slogans, hoisting signs, throwing rocks — was other than the cop's disquieting of the requiescence. Those who could marched, bearing aloft signs, banners, and placards with rhyming messages in need of spell check. One sign encouraged its readers, *y'all come back now.* Then things got really interesting. Whoever said protests are boring should put on a Crimson Tide away jersey, get a box of a dozen glazed Krispy Kreme donuts, a card table and folding chair, and go down to the protest and attack the donuts, one by one, with knife and fork. Behold. The Bed Bath and Beyond's windows came crashing down; cars burned like Jesse Washington. Tear gas smoking in the town hall. And we did it all by ourselves, without the help of Antifa! The Geo Metro — Oh, imperishable product of the Orient! — untouched by the carnage! The protests nearly annihilated quiet, sleepy little Hamelin whose inhabitants — direct descendants of Matthew, Mark, and Luke — as the long, hot summer shows not the slightest sign of abating, revel in the WASP fallacy, a Christian fantasy as old as Matthew 5:38-40, that Smith, Shipp and Similar will not, when presented with the opportunity, turn the big white house's garden hose or the fire hose upon those who once doused them with the municipal water supply, a resource better used for watering the Tree of the Knowledge of Good and Evil, or unleash equally vicious police dogs on them when their backs are turned. Any more than Gyges' ring won't turn a man into a crook. For if he did cease to revel in this fantasy, the poor thing, bloated and dyspeptic, would have to concede, like Smith, Shipp and Similar, that Hamelin dwells perpetually, soullessly and by his own making in a daymare.

A hospital darkens one side of the square. No one I knew died there, but the Geo Metro driver did. Hospital death is rich white people death, as coded into the architecture. I say, catch them when they fall. Townfolk don't die on the streets unless it's from choking to death outside the Outback Steakhouse. The mayor — no Mandate of Heaven here — dresses in a sad clown suit and walks the town square late at night. He stops in the lamplight of a darkened street. He rhymes his jokes with noose and goose, rope and pope, lynch and summer. The hospital doors open and close.

Death is a standardized procedure. In the hospitals, they talk about a good death: calm, quiet, cost effective. A clean corporate death. I told a man, *en route* to a wedding ceremony, that when I finally die, the great wolf will swallow the sun. And it will. Beitler's light will flash no more. More enter the hospital than come out. Births at the hospital are underperforming the number of deaths. It's not natural childbirth unless you're in a leaking mobile home surrounded by state troopers. Birth was like that scene in *Alien*. The Huck Finns and Daisy Millers force feed their offspring every. single. bite. Nothing like shoving food down a mammal. As done in this maple tree: a mother nightingale shoves the worm down the throat of the next generation.

The hospital lies by a church with an ATM inside for big-time cash-on-hand tithing. The Lord knows who tithes big and small, according to his/her means. Stranger than the formation of families is the *wytai* of Sunday morning in a small town: the unangelic fracas of voices wailing in the choir. There they pray for Meursault, but not the Arab. But the Arab has his own bag of arabesque wiles that their church and its choir of petulant, middle-class voices be silenced in Provincetown Harbor. As done in Dunwich. Sundays they gather like crabs in a bucket, like bedbugs to warm blood to heal the Gerasense demoniac. They were laying hands on him and praying. This maple tree allows even a sciolist to calmly, competently form an opinion of goings-on. It occurred to me that those were adults saying a magic spell to protect someone from demons. Twenty-first century humans do that. They check their email or the weather on their smartphone, activate their internal combustion engine, and drive to a central location to practice magic against threats from the spirit realm. This may be a strange world, but this is not a battleground state. Following the kerchiefed sausage dogs, there passed herds of possessed swine in search of a cliff. I directed each to the nearest cliff. The heirs of Matthew, Mark and Luke sleep in the tombs, cutting themselves with stones. As done in Legion.

I want my name on my jersey, and I ask in pitch perfect Anglo-Saxon, that the name on the jersey be spelled: *Hell is my minimum*. And another thing: on behalf of the participants in the melodrama of hell, we want some iced water down here. Sweet tea would be a luxury to parched mouths. Even poor Job got his name on his jersey, and could at least, though encumbered by a termagant wife, wander unroped the shade of the maple trees planted on his suburban estate, freely cursing. Human suffering has no penultimate, limit or maximum, matters are always subject to worsening, aggravation, extravagance, elaboration, exacerbation, laceration, evisceration, retrogression, corrosion, and immoderation. I should know.

A reporter asked me for a quote. If you've been lynched, then you know what it's like, and if you haven't been lynched then shame on you. They don't know what it's like to decorate a tree. Humans have decorated the trees of this world like so many black baubles. A journalist asked me what was my favorite food. Birthday cake. A journalist asked me what was my favorite memory. A circle around my neck sometimes burned on cold nights. The colder the night, the hotter the rope. I have studied the stars for some clue, some sign of my fate, what to expect next, any lodestar or key — nothing. Less than the flea of nothing. Windward and leeward I searched, clueless, keyless, not a notion out there. The flea of nothing bites at my ankles, and the dog of nothing yaps in my starboard ear. A journalist asked me about my friends, he wanted to know their fates. Smith and Shipp were thrown off the *Zong*. If I saw them — Smith and Shipp — today I would be slow to recognize them; then I would fail to recognize them altogether. A journalist asked me if I knew the whereabouts of Meursault. Try the beach. A lynching no more an event to remark than the rampaging wind harrying a blade of grass. A reporter asked me for a final quote. Humility is no virtue, it is looking at the world with the codeine eyes of common sense.

The rope is thinning, though. Like my hair. I may drop at any time. Oh, the ground — to feel the ground again! Have you ever experienced joy? I'll tell you what joy is. Every morning I tell myself not to commit suicide, to finish the noose's handiwork — that is the very apotheosis of joy. Such joy is less good and less bad. Years without feeling the ground. The ground has not missed me. For we are not yet at that phase of the organism's development where we no longer need not to lynch our fellow organism. Because what would be the point of not doing what the organism cannot help?

I have chewed through the rope like a rat, the rope tastes like the host, a long thinning intestinal of holy wafers. Dangling by a few threads, I dream of escape, dreaming the tree which hangs me: the rope follows me about like an umbilical cord. The noose is more intelligent than the executioner. Even if I came down from the tree, where would I go? To Bed Bath and Beyond? The Dollar General? A place where the broken body goes aroaming in searching of its panacea soul. I should avoid the papers. No more is the newspaper read to me. The news should not be read, it should be wept. As done in Ferguson. As done in Baton Rouge. As done in Milwaukee. Every town built from pieces of the Berlin Wall, pieces of the levees, pieces of 6221 Osage Avenue, West Philadelphia. The rope's creaking ceased and then the requiescence, at long last. The silence mobbed me. I did not wish the creaking to cease, but the rope did not ask for my opinion. The rope's ceasing to swing as all things exhibit this tendency towards stasis and changelessness, a hanging equilibrium, Smith and Shipp stopped swinging before the palinopsia of Beitler's flash vanished.

What is the expected lifespan of this tree? It cannot die soon enough. The tree could die before me. Alabama's football fans poison trees. I invite the fan base of the Crimson Tide to poison this hanging tree. All of nature could perish before me. I watch the weather happen, with glee and sprinkles of *Schadenfreude* I name the clouds that blot out their sun. One cloud is Matthew, another Shipp. I have seen skies flavescent, vermilion, lavender, indigo, cerulean, alabaster, canary, emerald, violet, royal blue carnation, scarlet, tangerine, Windsor green and royal black, skies the color of Skittles vomited up by a rat-catcher's baby. Skies above this town with no more color than the pale mob.

You are born with your mother straddling your grave, her two feet on either side of the pit, and she pinches you out and down into the pit after a nine-month gestative period screaming and praying — the drop, before you hit bottom, is called by some life, and for some it is short, and for others it is long. A few manage a laugh on the way down. Those for whom it is long will say it was not short enough, and those who got the raw deal, too short, will say it was not long enough, as their mouths fill up with dirt. How the mother got to be astraddle the pit no one really knows, but neither does she ask why the father did to her what he did. The laugh managed on the way down — that's known as style and personality. I carve my style out of this tree like a sneer in a pumpkin; I'm still working on my personality, as Huck Finn and Daisy Miller are perfecting blackfaces for their roles as Laura and L.D. Nelson.

My drop down has been long, the longest of all, and I fall —

please, do not waste your efforts to catch me — into that winking Beyond that is beyond Bed Bath and Beyond, at the same rate of fall as any other mundanity — a dead dog, a baseball, a bowling ball, a child's skull — as demonstrated in that Italian's Leaning Tower of Pizza experiment. There must be something beyond it, when I get down from this maple tree — I will find it, behind the wheel of a Geo Metro. I think of Smith and Shipp, their faces disfigured like battered *cucurbita*, but at least — and at least *at least* is not *at the minimum* or *y'all come back now* — they were not charred like Jesse Washington. Enough was left of Smith and Shipp to bury in the Negro cemetery. Oh, the rat-catchers mis-imagined that flesh-consuming fire was of their own indignation, but to mistake the fire which consumes another for your own is a fallacy, the rat-catcher's fallacy, the fire that consumed his flesh was Jesse's, the pure flame of the star twinkling dead radiation each night just above the Bed Bath and Beyond.

Every year the town bakes a cake and brings me birthday cake on my birthday. Plus one candle each year.

There are enough candles to burn Milledgeville in 2018. The miserable wind — which filled the sails of the *Henrietta Marie* with its misery and decided the outcome of naval battles — blows the candles out before I can inhale a breath to exhale on the flames. Yes, the cheapskate wind would deprive me even of that satisfaction, blowing a wish on my birthday cake. The wind laughs at me in the leaves of the maple. The last time the town turned out for my birthday, I took the cake, and threw it at the historic plaque, exhausting years of energy saved for the purpose. The cake sailed and smashed beautifully, the townsfolk agog and aghast at my cake profligacy.

But this year I did something different — applaud me for that; slow clap if you're that guy — when the mayor in clown costume presented my birthday cake. A second-line marching band blew from brass instruments "The House of the Rising Sun." I reached for the knife, and cut the birthday cake into wedges with the exacting, humane eye of a murderer who personally knows his victim. The birthday cake was Julius Caesar. That cake was Beitler, and everyone who bought his postcards. That cake was Matthew, Mark and Luke. That cake was Old Hickory. That birthday cake was the maple tree, and it was the blue and red strobes in the blue and orange and brown leaves. That cake was all the pompous judges reading law in the courthouse. Then I handed the birthday cake knife to my assistant; it was for him to cut the rope. He took the knife, looking about for a Meursault to lunge at; when he cuts the rope, and the rat-catcher's umbilical is sliced at last, I will see if I can manage a laugh on the way down. I may have a laugh or two in me. I never wanted to see a maple or a southern Live Oak tree again. The tree — my darling maple tree! — is brown and dead, and the rope is an impoverished thread now. A thread — or is it a strand? — no thicker than an old man's skin. The unhanged — here comes the mayor with his scissors and ribbon again — got it wrong: not I who hangs from a maple branch dangling in space; it is this hanging tree which hangs from me. As done in 2018.

Amos Jasper Wright IV is native to the dirt of Birmingham, Alabama, but has called Alabama, Massachusetts and Louisiana home. He holds a master's degree in English and creative writing from the University of Alabama, Birmingham, and a master's degree in urban planning from Tufts University. His fiction and poems have appeared in *Arcadia, Birmingham Arts Journal, Clarion, The Fieldstone review, Folio, Grain Magazine, Gravel, The Hollins Critic, Interim, New Ohio Review, New Orleans Review, Off the Coast, Pale Horse Review, Roanoke Review, Salamander, Tacenda Literary Magazine, Union Station Magazine, Yes, Poetry* and *Zouch.* He is currently at work on several novels titled *Petrochemical Nocturne, King Cockfight, The Dead Mule Rides Again, In the Basement of the Anthropocene,* and *When A Good Thing Lasts Too Long.* For now he lives and works in New Orleans. His author website is available at www.amosjasperwright.com